Praise for Lucy Dillon's previous book,
Unexpected Lessons in Love:

'Real, heartbreaking – I loved it.'
Katie Fforde

'My heart is smashed and repaired for reading this
wonderfully romantic and strong piece of fiction.'
Milly Johnson

'A heartwarming romantic comedy that tells us to
be brave and to listen to our hearts. Suffused with Lucy's
trademark warmth and gentle humour (with a
splendid canine supporting cast), it's sure to win
your heart. Irresistible!'
Veronica Henry

'Such a great "what would you do?" book about love,
truth, friendship and of course dogs. Kept me
guessing all the way.'
Laura Kemp

'Brilliantly written and believable, this book
is a real class act.'
Fabulous

By Lucy Dillon

Unexpected Lessons In Love
Where the Light Gets In
All I Ever Wanted
One Small Act of Kindness
A Hundred Pieces of Me
The Secret of Happy Ever After
Walking Back to Happiness
Lost Dogs and Lonely Hearts
The Ballroom Class

For more information on Lucy Dillon and her books, please visit her website at www.lucydillon.co.uk

 www.facebook.com/pages/LucyDillonBooks

 @lucy_dillon

 @lucydillonbooks

After the Rain

Lucy Dillon

PENGUIN BOOKS

TRANSWORLD PUBLISHERS
Penguin Random House, One Embassy Gardens,
8 Viaduct Gardens, London SW11 7BW
www.penguin.co.uk

Transworld is part of the Penguin Random House group of companies
whose addresses can be found at global.penguinrandomhouse.com

Penguin
Random House
UK

First published in Great Britain in 2022 by Penguin
an imprint of Transworld Publishers

A CIP catalogue record for this book
is available from the British Library.

ISBN
9781529176209

Typeset in 11.75/14.1 pt Adobe Garamond by Jouve (UK), Milton Keynes.
Printed and bound in Great Britain by Clays Ltd, Elcograf S.p.A.

The authorized representative in the EEA is Penguin Random House Ireland,
Morrison Chambers, 32 Nassau Street, Dublin D02 YH68.

Penguin Random House is committed to a sustainable future
for our business, our readers and our planet. This book is made
from Forest Stewardship Council® certified paper.

For TAR, my anchor, and Barney,
my little pal. Gone, but never very far away.

Prologue

Branston was not the most convincing lion Tara had ever seen but she wasn't going to tell him that.

'You look terrifying, Branston,' she said, and adjusted his mane: her old yellow ballet tutu with plastic spiders stapled at strategic intervals for added Hallowe'en effect. To be honest, he looked more like a sunflower than a lion but he was sitting there patiently, letting her finish off his outfit with bits of tissue cobweb.

'And you are the most beautiful Labrador in the world,' she added, to be kind.

Branston gazed at her with his patient, melted-chocolate eyes, and trod on her foot with his big golden paw. Tara thought, not for the first time, *You are the one person in this house who actually listens to me.*

'I wish you could tell me what you're thinking,' she said. Then added, 'Actually don't,' because she didn't want to hear how bored he was with the whole dressing-up routine. Branston had let her put bunny ears on him for Easter and angel wings last Christmas, but this was going to be a public premiere – if anyone ever appeared to take her, Toby and Branston out trick-or-treating.

Even if he could speak, Tara sensed that Branston

1

wouldn't have said a lot, but even so, it would feel more like a conversation than anything she was getting from her parents or her brother this evening. Toby was being particularly irritating. First of all he'd told her he didn't want to go trick-or-treating because he had 'better things to do', then he'd changed his mind but refused to go along with her theme, and now he was making his own costume with a school shirt, red ink and Mum's dressmaking scissors, which even Tara thought was a dangerous idea.

She didn't know why Mum was letting him.

Mum was in one of her funny, glassy moods where she closed her eyes deliberately before she said anything. Her friend Diane had 'let her down' about taking them out tonight – 'Not my problem, your father can do it for once!' – and Toby had answered back *so many* times, and now Dad had come in an hour later than normal from his office, and Mum had shoved him into the kitchen and turned up the television. All of which was a very good reason to hurry Toby along.

'Toby?' Tara yelled up the stairs. 'Toby, are you ready?' No answer.

She glanced at the clock above the kitchen door – which was still shut – and chewed the loose skin around her thumbnail. Mum and Dad had been in there since ten past six and it was now nearly seven. The local news was nearly over; the weather forecaster was bellowing about rain. Tara didn't care who was taking them out, but if they didn't leave soon, it would be too late. And too wet.

What was she supposed to do? She sat on the stairs and put her arm round Branston.

'I wish people would just *talk* to me,' she whispered into his solid head.

Suddenly, the kitchen door was flung and Tara's dad – Keith – flew out, followed by an apple. He ducked, and it crashed against the frame of the front door, knocking a family photo off the wall. The photo dropped on to the floor but amazingly, the glass didn't smash.

'Jesus Christ, you crazy—' Dad started, then swivelled to see Tara standing by the door with the dog. 'Tara. Hello, pickle.'

'Are we going trick-or-treating?' she asked hopefully.

'Trick-or-treating?'

'Mum said you'd take us. Diane's sick,' she added. She didn't know what with, but Mum's expression had made it clear she wasn't supposed to ask.

Dad wiped his hand over his face. Tara caught a glimpse of something she didn't recognize in the brief second it was uncovered, and a shadow went across her heart.

'So can you take us?' She smiled up at him, not wanting to push but at the same time wishing *someone* would just say how magnificent Branston looked. 'Please?'

He glanced over at the kitchen but the door was shut. 'The thing is . . .'

'Do you like Branston's outfit?' Tara prompted him.

'He looks terrific! And you're . . . Alanis Morissette?'

Tara opened her coat to show him her blue gingham summer uniform. 'Dorothy. From *The Wizard of Oz*.'

'Of course you are. Well done, sweetie.'

Dad winked, and Tara's anxious heart jumped with relief. Her dad's smile always made *her* smile; it was the twinkle in his eye that hinted that some treat might be in the offing, as he would say: chocolate from the stash in his office drawer, or a tenner from his back pocket to

3

splash out at Claire's Accessories, a palace of glittery delights that Mum frequently muttered should be burned to the ground.

Tonight the smile was as warm as usual but it didn't make Dad's eyes crinkle up. His eyes were the same, but different. Sad, almost. Tara felt panicky without knowing why. A thick lump bulged in her throat, as if she'd swallowed bread without chewing.

'I, er, need to nip out somewhere first,' he said.

'To get sweets for the treats?'

'Yes. Well, something like that. Here, this is for you . . .' He was grabbing his heavy wool jacket from the coat stand by the door, fishing in his pocket at the same time.

'Toby?' she called up the stairs, willing her brother with their special twin radar to get down here, to help her understand. Adults tended to prefer Tara to Toby, but he always seemed to know what was going on with them. 'Toby, hurry up!'

The reply from upstairs was muffled. 'Don't rush me!'

'Now!' she yelled, sending silent shrieks of panic.

'Here.' Dad was offering her something from his clip of banknotes, and she took it mechanically without looking because she didn't dare let Dad's face out of her sight. 'I love you, Taransay.'

Taransay. He was the only one who ever used her full name. *But only on special occasions.*

'I love you too, Dad . . .' she said, but he'd crouched down and had her head in his hands and he was kissing her along her sharp centre parting, where her dark hair split into two neat plaits.

'Dad . . .' This was so weird. He never kissed her on the head like this either. He bear-hugged her, or tickled

4

her, or planted loud raspberries on her tummy, although he hadn't done that for a long time.

'Right then,' he said cheerfully, and ruffled Branston's ears. 'You hang on there, I'll see you in a minute.'

'Toby!' Tara turned for one second to yell up the stairs and when she turned back, the front door was shutting, and Dad had gone. 'Toby!'

Branston whimpered, and went to follow him, but Tara said, 'Branny, please!' and he sat back down again, confused.

Tara flattened her palm over her heart. She could feel it hammering and hammering. What was happening? Dad said to hang on, he'd be back in a minute, and that was absolutely normal, but somehow it wasn't.

She looked down to see what it was he'd given her. It was a note she hadn't seen before. A red one. Fifty pounds. Why had Dad given her *fifty pounds*?

This wasn't right. She stared at the apple-bobbing apple, which had rolled over to the coat stand. It looked fine, but it would be bruised inside under the skin, spoiled brown and spongy when they cut into it later.

Feet thundered behind her, Toby clattering down the stairs.

'Where's Dad gone?' He was wearing one of her old school shirts, now splattered with red ink and slashed like a jellyfish with the dressmaking shears.

'Out.' She showed him the note. 'He gave me this.'

'For you, or to share?'

'To share,' said Tara automatically, because she and Toby always had to share things. 'I think,' she added, more uncertainly.

'Great. Why's he going out with Ashley?' he asked.

'What?'

Toby's gaze flicked towards the door. 'Ashley was outside. In her Corsa. Dad got in and they just drove off.'

Ashley was their babysitter, their cleaner Jen's daughter. She was at Reading University and she had long blonde hair, and let them stay up very late on the nights when Mum and Dad went to 'functions' – usually parties, sometimes awards. Dad got invited to a lot of parties because his business was doing well. He often had to travel as far away as London, which Tara thought should have made Mum happy but it didn't.

Tara was about to say, *That doesn't make sense*, but Toby's dark expression said it for her. She could almost hear his mind working, putting the pieces in order.

She pressed her lips together. She had a sickly feeling that speaking now would confirm that something was wrong and Tara didn't want that.

Branston groaned, and flopped down with his head on her foot.

Outside, it started to rain. Hard.

Chapter One

'So tell me what happened. Start wherever you like, doesn't have to be the beginning,' said Tara, and when Grace Jordan didn't reply immediately, she pushed the box of tissues across the table and waited.

The words would come. Tara had spent enough hours with clients struggling to make sense of Longhampton's freak floods to know that the experience loomed over its victims like an iceberg: too big to see all at once, too unexpected to explain away as 'just one of those things'. They'd been the worst floods in local memory – the most destructive, the most disruptive – and had to be broken down into small, easily comprehensible chunks of shock. A bloated sofa floating in water spangled with red and blue emergency lights. A policeman in waders on the doorstep, insisting the family evacuate *now*. A carpet, newly laid for Christmas, filthy with slime and human waste and God knew what from the swollen river that had risen and risen, and then covered half of the county in a muddy blanket.

Eventually, Grace spoke. 'I didn't realize until the water was already coming up the stairs.' She stared ahead, at Tara's peace lily. 'My little boy, Harrison, he went downstairs to get a drink and he come running straight back up. "Mummy, Mummy, there's water in the house." And when I looked over the banisters, the cushions from the sofa

7

were in the hall. I thought, why are they there? Then I realized – they were floating.' She pulled a tissue from the box and started plucking it. 'I didn't know what to do. All I could think of was the guinea pigs. Harrison's guinea pigs in their cage by the washing machine. Fluff and Peppa.' Her hand covered her mouth, suppressing a sob. Above it, her eyes blurred, as the scene played back in her mind. 'Sorry. Sorry . . .'

Tara made a soothing noise. 'It's OK, Grace. Take your time.'

'I think it was worse that it happened in the night? The electricity had gone off and I didn't know – there were lights downstairs but it was the fire brigade on the river, getting Mrs Brody from next door out. She's in a wheelchair. They had to lift her on to the wall, you know where I mean? By the bridge?'

Tara nodded. She knew exactly where Grace's house was: it was on a pretty terrace near the town centre. Whitewashed frontages with red roses climbing around shiny black doors – and about a metre above the normal level of the River Martle. But the River Martle hadn't been at a normal level recently. For three days, it had been on a level with the fan extractor on Grace Jordan's kitchen hob.

'But they got you and Harrison out safely?'

Grace blew her nose. 'The firemen in the dinghy came and Harrison jumped in, but I couldn't move. I kept thinking, what do I save? Dad's ashes were in the lounge, and I wanted to go back for them, but the fireman grabbed me. He said the river was still rising and there was gas . . .'

Tara made some discreet notes – *Harrison, six, guinea pigs, Swan Terrace* – giving Grace time to gather herself.

Everyone she'd counselled in the last three weeks had tried to go back for something: wedding photos, a handbag, phone chargers. Baby books, family jewellery. Quite a few urns. Tara wondered what she'd save, if her house – well, her mother's house, now hers – had been half a mile closer to the town centre, within reach of the creeping water.

Her mum's ashes would probably have been safe enough, on the top shelf in the pantry. Nine months on, Tara and her twin brother Toby were no closer to confirming a place and a time to scatter Ruth Hunter's remains. If the River Martle had intervened and swept Ruth into the Severn, then back out into the Bristol Channel and on to the Atlantic, it would actually have been a solution to the problem. Also usefully equidistant between her in Longhampton and Toby in America.

Other than that . . . Tara decided she'd probably have grabbed her handbag. It was a good one, Mulberry, an unusually generous but sensible thirtieth-birthday present from her ex, Justin. For most people, she mused, since Grace was still blowing her nose, a family home contained a paralysing dilemma-load of stuff to rescue from floodwater. But she wouldn't have had that problem. There was nothing irreplaceable in Wye Villa. Ruth had saved her (and Toby, not that he'd involved himself too deeply) that bother by ditching most of their childhood memories with an efficiency that even Marie Kondo would find somewhat ruthless.

The family photo album, Tara thought, with a pang. She'd have grabbed that – if she could only find it in the house. It contained precious evidence of the Happy Years, pre-divorce, photographs of summers in France with Mum and Dad; her and Toby's awkward boy–girl twin birthdays, cakes split between dinosaurs and ponies; 5 p.m. Christmas-dinner tables messy with wine glasses and discarded Quality Street wrappers, long-suffering family dog Branston in a variety of paper hats. Tara had searched without success for the album. *Surely* Mum hadn't chucked it out? Maybe she had, along with every trace of Dad.

Well, every trace of Dad apart from her and Toby. And Toby had removed himself thoroughly as soon as he'd left school. Tara still missed Toby, even though he'd been living away for nearly fifteen years. Like the album, he was the only surviving evidence of their childhood.

'Sorry.' Grace sniffed. 'I know it's only stuff. Apart from Fluff and Peppa.'

'Did the firemen . . . ?' Tara left a discreet pause.

She nodded. 'Nice policewoman waded in and got them out. She got an earful from her boss but she could see Harrison was in a right state. I was too, to be honest.'

'And they're OK? The guinea pigs?'

'More or less.' Grace blew her nose again. 'Peppa's not quite right.' She managed a weak smile. 'Guess I can always replace her with another one. Harrison's only six, not sure he'd notice the difference!'

'No, don't!' Tara hadn't meant to speak but a memory pushed its way out with unexpected force. When Grace looked up, startled, she felt obliged to explain. 'My dad ran over my brother's rabbit, Simon, then replaced him with another one without telling us.'

'Did you notice?'

Tara hesitated. This was the first time she'd told anyone about Simon's demise and suspicious resurrection. Not her supervisor, not her therapist – not even her brother. She wasn't totally sure why she was telling Grace now. 'I saw him run Simon over.'

'No way.' Grace was temporarily distracted from the flooding. 'Did you tell anyone?'

'Well . . . no. Mum and Dad acted like nothing had happened and I was only eight so I . . . went along with it.' Gaslighting, they'd call it now. Mum and Dad had instantly ceased their sniping for as long as it took to gloss over Simon's premature end and source his stunt double. Tara supposed she should give them credit for that. Bronze parenting stars all round, Ruth and Keith.

Tara checked herself. She'd always been an expert compartmentalizer but over the past few months, the oddest memories had started tumbling out of her mental cupboards, often at inopportune moments like this, and it was getting harder to shove them back in and carry on. She frequently agonized about the further qualifications she'd put off starting, usually when facing the Centre's tougher clients, but lately she found herself wishing she had some better strategies to use on herself. The problem was, further training would mean opening up *all* the mental cupboards, and . . .

Tara leaned forward, focusing her attention on her client. 'So, to go back to your earlier question – how can you help Harrison's nightmares? I'd say, be honest. He's only little – he doesn't need lots of detail but he does need to make sense of what's just happened in his world. Let him draw pictures if it's easier than talking. But don't hide fear away. Yes, it was scary, and it's very sad you've lost some things, but you're both safe. Walk him through what you'd do if the river ever floods again.'

'And if Peppa . . . doesn't make it?'

'Be honest about that too. You don't want him demanding someone calls the *Guinness Book of Records* when the new Peppa magically reaches her nineteenth birthday.' Toby's insistence on his 'miracle rabbit'. Her guilty silence.

Grace was looking at her curiously now. Tara wondered if her face was betraying the churning in her chest.

'It's amazing what people will believe if they want to.' She smiled bleakly. 'Especially when it comes to families.'

At the end of the session, once Tara was on safer ground talking Grace through practicalities – did she need help dealing with insurance? Was she in contact with the flood support team? She showed her out of the consulting room and into the long corridor.

Down the hall, the Centre's new counsellor, Dr David Dalloway, was also saying goodbye, to an emotional middle-aged couple with a tubby Labrador. The dog was soft and golden, as if he'd been moulded out of short-bread dough, and he turned towards Tara while his owners carried on talking over his head.

Tara blinked: not just because there was a dog in the Centre (Jacqueline, the Centre's director, was vigilant about airborne allergens) but because it was the spitting image of Branston, her childhood confidante. The Labrador gazed straight back at her. Was it her imagination, or was he trying not to roll his chocolatey eyes? As if he despaired of his humans' madness but loved them anyway?

That was probably too subtle a communication for a Labrador. Branston had had two expressions: 'Give me toast' and 'I'm sad that you're sad'. Both resulted in a cuddle, his heavy head leaning carefully against her small neck, his warm, biscuit breath in her ear. He always smelled of biscuits. Usually because he'd just stolen a packet of digestives.

The Labrador wagged his tail, and just as poor Simon had popped up out of nowhere in her mind, Tara suddenly had an almost physical memory of Branston nosing open the bedroom door to lie by her side, loyal and comforting, when her parents were arguing in the kitchen below. Her throat tightened.

It had been a really, really strange few weeks, coming right on top of a miserable few months.

This was Tara's first full day back, after a sabbatical spent talking constantly about the floods and the emotional wreckage they'd caused, and she couldn't concentrate at all. Usually her emotions were laid in careful, protective strata like a well-packed suitcase, but the floodwater seemed to have forced its way through them too, pushing up memories she'd packed away years ago.

'. . . really helped us, David, thank you so much.' The lady was grabbing David's arm as if he were a vicar, not a relationship counsellor. 'I don't think I've ever said this before to a marriage guidance therapist, but I'm almost looking forward to our next session!'

'I'm delighted to hear it,' said David. 'But that's just a reflection of your hard work, Gillian.'

'Yup.' Tara watched the husband scratch his stubbly chin. He seemed stunned. 'You've got us bang to rights, I've got to say.'

David Dalloway raised a modest hand. 'Think about what we discussed and we'll pick it up again next week. Thank you, both.'

The dog wagged its tail and he bent to give it a friendly pat on the flanks.

'And thank you, Fudge.'

The couple turned and Tara leaned back into her doorway so they wouldn't see her. As they walked down the hall, the wife hissed, 'Ray! Don't say bang to rights, like we're in court!' and the husband replied, 'Well, it feels like that! It's like he knows what I'm going to say before I say it!'

'What do you expect?' she hissed back. 'He spends his whole day listening to people lying their heads off.'

The dog swung his tail from side to side as he trailed out between the pair of them, towards the wide stairs that led down to the foyer and the street outside.

David watched them leave, tapping his fingers thoughtfully on the door frame, and as he turned back into his room, caught Tara staring at him.

'Hello there!' She tried to style it out with an awkward wave.

'Hello.' He flashed a quick, not unfriendly smile in return, then stepped back inside his room before she could say, 'I'm Tara.'

'Oh,' said Tara aloud, surprised, as his door clicked shut.

David had been at the Centre nearly a month, but she still hadn't found a good moment to introduce herself. He'd arrived while Tara was on annual leave, moving into her mother's house; she'd just recycled the final box when the first fat drops of the record-breaking rain began blotting the patio tiles. After that, Tara had been out of the office organizing the town's volunteer effort, offering emergency counselling while fitting in her own clients as best she could; David's welcome drinks had clashed with an Environment Agency meeting. But she'd heard a lot about him from Jacqueline. A lot.

'He's tremendously *experienced*, and comes with quite

exceptional references, and he's been published in journals!'
Jacqueline swooned in one of her long email updates.
Bryan, another senior CBT therapist, had been a bit more
specific in the kitchen that morning. 'Seems like a solid
bloke, proper psychologist, none of your angels-and-auras
bilgewater. Bit aloof, maybe, but can you blame him with
half the claptrap that goes on round here?'

And yet there was Dr David, letting clients bring their
dog into session. How'd he got that past Jacqueline?

Unless, Tara conceded, the couple had insisted on bringing their dog as part of the family unit. People round here
were a bit like that.

Longhampton Wellness Centre was located opposite the
town hall in a grand Georgian building that had once
accommodated the Farmers' Union. The county's farmers and landowners would gather on market days in the
oak-panelled bar of Pomona House to sink ale and peel
notes off fist-sized rolls of cash, while their wives – if
invited – sat in the upstairs ladies' parlour with their
handbags on their knees, safely out of earshot. Although
the building had been sold several times since its heyday,
once to a wine merchant, more than once to short-lived
restaurants, an agricultural atmosphere lingered in the
decor. Carved sheaves of wheat ran up the staircases and
a life-sized plaster bull's head presided over the reception
desk with a glassy-eyed gaze. Tara had asked to swap to
her current consulting room, ostensibly because it had an
original sash window and a view of the cathedral spire,
but really because she found the moulded bunches of
apples on the ceiling significantly more soothing than
the anxious lambs peering down at her clients in the first.

The spacious upstairs kitchen – where grand Farmers' Union feasts were once prepared – was now the therapists' hang-out between appointments, where they'd make coffee and offer each other advice on container gardening, aura cleansing and the like. Tara had hidden a kettle in her desk so she wouldn't have to hear quite so much about aura cleansing, but washing the cups was an unavoidable part of the day and she tended to leave it until the very last moment, or lunchtime, when the holistic therapists went to the park to do tai chi and affirm each other.

Tara had been scheduling evening appointments in an attempt to get through her backlog, but tonight she'd made sure her last appointment finished on the dot of five. She was running on the last fumes from the emergency chocolate in her drawer, and the mental picture of a long bath and her pyjamas had been keeping her going since lunch.

As she dragged herself round her consulting room, gathering up used crockery, there was a brisk knock on her door and Jacqueline's head appeared. 'Are you off?'

Tara raised her mugs. 'Just got to wash these up then I'm heading home. Been a long day!'

She hoped Jacqueline wasn't going to choose this moment for one of her in-person catch-ups. Tara was Jacqueline's unofficial deputy, and nice as it was to be trusted with her dilemmas, Jacqueline prided herself on her '360-degree consideration' of issues and right now, after weeks of homeless children and drowned guinea pigs, Tara didn't have much bandwidth left for ethical handwash policies.

'Good-o!' Jacqueline seemed too smiley. 'I'll pop along with you.'

'OK,' said Tara dubiously.

But as they turned the corner and she saw the crowd in the kitchen, the penny dropped.

'Surprise!' trilled Jacqueline, and a muted cheer rose from the assembled Wellness Centre staff, including a couple of people she knew didn't normally have appointments on a Monday.

Jacqueline held out her hands to Tara with a warm smile, directing her to pride of place in front of the pre-war tea urn that had managed to survive all four previous ownerships, mainly because no one knew how to unplumb it without destroying the hand-painted tiling.

'Tara,' she said, in her motherly, prize-giving voice. 'I know you hate blowing your own trumpet but we wanted to let you know how very proud we are of you, and the hard, hard work you've been doing to help rebuild our community after the terrible events of these last few weeks.'

'Honestly, it was just . . .' Tara spotted a bouquet of flowers on the table behind Kemi the massage therapist.

'We know what a terrific counsellor you are, Tara,' Jacqueline went on, 'but to give so much of your *time* and *energy* when you've had your own challenges to overcome this year . . . well. It must have taken a huge amount of courage, as well as strength, to step forward to help others like this.'

Murmurs of agreement rippled around the kitchen. It was a unanimous reaction – from Hero the crystal therapist and Anji the heart-field healer at the unicorn fringes of the Centre's therapy list, to Freudian Judith, and Steven, the tough-love life coach at the 'get a grip' end. And everyone else in between. David – so far unplaced on Tara's private scale of credibility – nodded approvingly. Their eyes met, and she wished she'd made the effort to knock

17

on his door and say hello. What did he know about her? Jacqueline was making her sound like a cross between Wonder Woman and Mother Teresa.

'So! Now the worst's over and you've been released from your duties at the crisis unit, we're *delighted* to have you back! And we wanted to give you this small gesture of our admiration, for representing the Wellness Centre and everything we believe in. We're *so* proud of you.' Jacqueline gestured at Kemi, who stepped forward with the bouquet like a nervous child shoved to the front of a royal visit.

There was a round of applause and Tara accepted the flowers with an uncomfortable smile. The truth was, she wasn't at all sure she deserved them.

Tara had volunteered at the crisis centre because being stressed to the gills fixing other people's problems was infinitely preferable to sitting in her childhood home that now held no traces of her childhood, while she checked her phone for offers of help from her brother that didn't come, and mentally compiled lists of questions she wished she'd asked her mother when she'd had the chance. Obviously she'd been glad to help people struggling with every kind of loss, but Tara knew herself pretty well: she'd also been shamefully grateful for the distraction.

She wasn't Mother Teresa *or* Wonder Woman. She wasn't even the Tara Hunter Jacqueline seemed to think she was.

Kemi coughed, self-consciously.

Everyone was waiting, expecting her usual cheerful reaction, but Tara was unexpectedly gripped with panic that if she opened her mouth she'd blurt out an apology, not thanks.

She was saved by the sound of a chair scraping on the

tiles, and the crowd parted to reveal Hero standing up with a chiffon bag in her hand.

'Actually, Jacqueline, I've got something for Tara too?' she said, making a namaste gesture in her direction.

'Oh, how lovely,' said Jacqueline uncertainly.

Hero handed Tara the chiffon bag and she juggled the bouquet to undo its golden drawstring. She already had a suspicion about what it might be as she tipped out the contents. And yes, it was. A jagged bracelet slid on to Tara's palm.

Crystals. She closed her eyes, in order to roll them privately.

'It's for comfort as you progress your healing journey,' Hero explained. 'Rose quartz, which is, as I'm sure you know, an exceptionally effective heart healer. Apache tears to absorb sadness and protect the hollow spaces inside you until you're ready to fill them with positivity. And, of course, amethyst, to connect your intuition with those soul spirits who want to help you. If you reach out to them.'

Tara bit her lip. Irritation rattled inside her, completely out of proportion to what she knew was a gesture of kindness from a well-meaning but completely loopy woman.

Which crystal, she wanted to demand, was supposed to undo the shock of your mother dying without any warning of a heart condition she'd hidden from everyone? Was there a crystal to combat emotional exhaustion? One that helped you make better decisions? Which crystal made you feel *normal* again?

Hero gently closed Tara's hand over the bracelet, cupping it with both her hands in a blessing. The sharp edges cut into Tara's palm. 'I've charged the crystals with loving energy but any time you feel you need them boosted, just let me know, OK? I'm always here.'

'Thank you, Hero,' said Tara.

'Yes, thank you, Hero, for that heartfelt gesture.' Jacqueline clapped appreciatively. 'And it goes without saying, Tara, we're all here for you. Any time.'

They clapped, and the smiles were warm and sincere, but Tara knew that the very last people she'd be sharing her current state of crisis with was her colleagues. For one thing, she had her professional reputation to think of. For another, she didn't think angel healing was going to cut it.

Chapter Two

Tara tried to phone her brother again as she was getting ready for work the following morning. Ironically, despite Toby's visibility on all major platforms in his capacity as a freelance lifestyle columnist/Influencer-with-a-capital-I/blogger/fringe social media personality, he was hard to get hold of in person. Maybe that was the point.

She scrolled through the Instagram photos of the restaurant opening that had alerted her to Toby's presence online, and thus the consequent possibility that he had his phone in his hand. Tara needed to talk to him. Actual talking, not texts or likes. The brief period of renewed communication that had followed their mother's sudden death had begun to peter out after a few weeks, but she was doing her best to maintain the momentum, even if it meant she was mainly chatting to herself.

Tara still felt Toby's absence, even now. When she thought about their childhood, the world seemed several shades more colourful, and that wasn't just nostalgia. It was Toby: his outlook and his outrageous humour and his wordless understanding of her. She knew why Toby had left – Longhampton was never going to be big enough for him – but it hurt that he'd left her behind too. It hurt so much that she'd never found the right words to tell him.

Tara sighed, listening to the long American rings at the other end. Toby, of course, would counter that there was nothing stopping her coming out to spend time with him. And he was right.

It was ten in Seattle, if he was at home. Not that late. Was he ignoring her? Tara buttered some toast and flicked on the coffee machine. Maybe he was posting from his laptop. Maybe his phone was in his bag.

There were at least two tricky conversations Tara needed to have with her brother, both related to Ruth's will, neither of which she was looking forward to, but wouldn't be able to avoid much longer. Ideally, they were face-to-face, in-person conversations, but Tara knew the chances of luring Toby back to Longhampton any time soon were low, unless she invented a new form of underwater yoga or launched a carbon-neutral noodle bar.

The call went to voicemail, and Tara hung up, feeling snubbed. Then she frowned and dialled again, using the time until the message kicked in to fork cat food into a porcelain bowl with Princess Paws written on it.

'Hey, Toby, just me calling for a chat – I saw your restaurant post on Instagram. Looks amazing! Guess you're too busy editing to pick up.' Tara poured hot coffee into her travel mug. Anji at work was spearheading a 'Ditch the Drive!' campaign for June, so Tara had to park two streets away and pretend she'd brought coffee for the bus. She tucked the phone under her ear, and put the bowl of cat food down on the floor for Sybil.

There was no sign of the cat. Typical. Sybil had only been living with Tara for a matter of weeks, but she'd realized early on that she was a cat who liked to make an entrance.

'Hope all's good with you,' she went on. 'Still a bit damp here in Longhampton, but we're getting back to normal. Listen, I'm calling because you and I need to talk about . . . hang on.'

Tara put the phone against her chest and shouted, 'Sybil? Breakfast!' towards the stairs. There was a worming tablet concealed in the pâté that she wanted to make sure was eaten before she left for work.

'Sybil's not my flatmate, by the way, she's my boyfriend's cat,' she explained, as if Toby had asked. Tara liked referring to Phil as her boyfriend; she'd noticed he started fidgeting if she used it in his earshot, which was not a good sign. But asking her to look after his cat was definitely a step towards something more official than 'man I see three/four times a month for fun times'. 'I'm pet-sitting! Not sure how long for. Anyway . . .'

Tara turned back to the open kitchen and allowed herself a moment to admire the clear morning sunlight streaming on to the slate floor. The brass taps, the deep Belfast sink, the reclaimed French cupboards: it was perfect. She reminded herself that she probably shouldn't get used to living in such a magazine dream of a house. Which was the whole point of the call to Toby.

'So, yes, we need to talk about the house. The estate agent's chasing me about putting it on the market. The thing is, Mum . . .' Tara stopped just short, right on the edge of the cliff, unable to speak the awful words. If she could guess Toby's reaction to Ruth's bombshell then it'd be easier, but she no longer knew what was in her brother's head. That in itself felt like an open wound.

I need to see his face, she thought. *I need to see what he's thinking.*

'To be honest, it's a bit weird,' she confessed instead. 'When I walk around the house, I keep remembering things from when we were little, but none of it's there. Nothing. I mean, I always knew Mum loved a makeover but this is *forensic*.' Her eye fell on the spot by the kitchen door where their pencil-marked heights had level-pegged until their teens. Toby had cheated, levering his heels up the skirting board to edge ahead. Tara had let him. All now obliterated by Elephant's Breath.

It had been there, hadn't it?

Along with the scuffs where Toby dropped his bike in the hall. The back door that used to swell in wet weather, so you had to kick, then pull. The sticky clatter of the letterbox offering the daily hope of a letter. The house was the same, but every memory had been wiped away by Mum's determined improvements.

Tara closed her eyes. 'It'd be nice to . . . I don't know, just remind myself that we did actually live here?'

She could hear the forced laughter in her own voice, and grimaced. Time to end the call before she said something embarrassing.

'OK. Right, I'm off to work now but ring any time. If I'm in a session, just leave me a message, let me know when's good to have a chat.' She paused, fighting the urge to say, *I deserve more than your Instagram followers.* 'Bye!'

She hung up.

On cue, Sybil slunk in from the tiled hallway, a black streak of disdain against Ruth's neutral woodwork.

'Morning!' said Tara brightly, but got no response other than a dismissive flick of the tail as the cat sniffed the breakfast offering with suspicion. They both knew she would eat around the worming tablet.

Tara sighed, no longer up for that fight, and went back to her cold toast. There was, of course, one other person who could corroborate her childhood memories, but he was even more disconnected from Tara's life than Toby. She wasn't even sure how she'd get hold of him to ask.

Tara slid the photo out of her diary and stared at it, trying to superimpose the chaotic scene on the immaculate house around her.

It was a party sometime in the early nineties. She'd found the photograph in the pages of *Delia Smith's Christmas*, one of the many cookery books she'd carted down to the charity shop. Mum was deep in her Liza Minnelli period (raven pixie-cut, sooty eyeliner and a 'bold red lip' working hard against a spangly blazer, rolled up to the elbows). Toby and Tara were centred, with matching bowl-cuts and non-matching T-shirts (The Clash for Toby, a ladybird for her), and between them, his hands on their small shoulders, was Dad. He was holding court in his velvet jacket, black hair smoothed in a slight quiff, smiling at the camera with a bonhomie that Tara remembered so clearly she could almost smell it: smoky Lagavulin and Eau d'Hadrian, and cedar balls from the wardrobe where the jacket hung in between parties.

That party had definitely happened. It had happened here, in the newly finished kitchen-diner – to celebrate the final work being completed. Keith's first major renovation had transformed a standard post-war four-bed into a mid-century masterpiece of bold lines, Scandinavian wood, skilfully harnessed light and a seamless extension that led the eye out from the marble counters into the deep green of the garden, at the bottom of which rose Keith's airy home studio, a pale ark of pine and glass amidst the trees. Two storeys: the upper floor flooded with light, perfect for inspiration; downstairs, perfect for escaping. It had been the start of an architecture career that had taken him away from Longhampton – and from them.

On the back, in her mum's writing, was the date: 18 August 1992. Early in the evening, thought Tara, noting the untouched plate of salmon blinis and the relative absence of empty glasses on the table in front of them. She took a photo of it on her phone and sent it to Toby, hoping it might prompt a response.

Keith Hunter was now sixty-four, not the ambitious thirtysomething in the velvet jacket. The last time Tara had seen her dad in the flesh had been at her graduation, twelve years ago. The hair was still dark, the bold Elvis Costello glasses had been toned down to tortoiseshell frames, the confidence mellowed into assurance. She'd noticed then how her mum had watched him, eagle-eyed, and wondered if she was checking for signs of change the same way Tara was. She'd wondered if Mum still cared. He hadn't brought a plus one, although Toby's internet sleuthing unearthed an opera singer called Helen, and Mum had gone alone, and talked constantly about the joys of independence.

Dad put on a good show that day, Tara had to concede. Champagne, flowers, a certain energetic charisma that impressed her friends and tutors.

But after that, nearly nothing. Contact had faded into sporadic birthday and Christmas cards, and she'd been too proud, and too conscious of Ruth's still touchy reaction to Dad's name, to chase him. Occasionally, out of late-night curiosity, she'd search online to see what his architecture practice had built most recently. The tortoiseshell frames mutated into expensive rimless glasses, and slowly the flesh-and-blood man vanished behind press releases about hotels and urban developments. Eventually, Tara realized she didn't actually want to know what sort of life her dad had created without her and Toby, and she stopped looking.

One strange phone call summed up everything Tara felt about her dad. Several years ago – after graduation, before Justin – Tara was on the train home from a weekend in Cornwall with a new boyfriend: their first weekend away which, she realized belatedly, contained every red flag that he wasn't the Ideal Man she was trying to convince herself he was. She'd answered the withheld number, mainly because Hugh had been explaining cricket's Duckworth–Lewis method for over twenty minutes, and when she'd heard her dad say, *Hello, Taransay*, the world had abruptly narrowed around her ear and his voice, as if they'd gone into a tunnel. He was 'in Cyprus' and didn't seem to have phoned her for any reason in particular. He sounded a bit tipsy, but jolly, and then tearful. He'd said something about the sea, and asked her how she was doing without listening to her answer, and then they'd gone into a real tunnel and lost reception. No way to call back. She'd unpicked the conversation over and over afterwards – was the sea a metaphor? When he said he was well, did he really mean he had terminal cancer? – until it fell to pieces in her hands. Later, it had occurred to Tara that maybe her name was next to someone else's in his contacts and he'd phoned her by accident, then decided to chat anyway.

Tara stared at the Hunters in the photograph as if it

might contain clues as to why this little unit would only last a few more years. What did her dad look like now? Where did he live? Who did he love? What did he sound like? Who had he turned into – and would she, one day, see those changes creep over herself?

More than once, in the middle of the night, lying in her old room, Tara had wondered if she should make more effort to track her father down, now Mum wasn't here to be hurt. But even as she was thinking it, Tara could hear Ruth's voice in her head, reminding her gently not to rely on her dad, hinting at the efforts he could have made for her, but hadn't. Mum's own lifelong singleness was an unspoken reminder of how badly he'd broken her trust with his infidelities, his selfish ambitions. In terms of solid things to tether yourself to, Keith Hunter was about as useful as a marshmallow bollard.

Tara gave Toby another five minutes to respond to the photograph, but when he didn't, she shouldered her bag, gave an unwilling Sybil a kiss goodbye, and left for work.

Tara power-walked into the Wellness Centre in her trainers, after parking her car in a discreet spot in nearby Coleridge Street, to find Jacqueline energetically plumping the rainbow cushions on the foyer chairs. It was the receptionist's job but Jacqueline was obsessive about first impressions. Deflated cushions, in Jacqueline's opinion, gave the wrong message to clients. Ditto wilting flowers.

She stopped as soon as Tara came in. 'Tara! I was hoping to catch you – have you got a moment? In my office?'

'Of course,' said Tara, because it wasn't really a question.

Jacqueline's was the biggest office upstairs, the one with the three-window panoramic view of the high street and cathedral, as befitted her status as Centre Director. She was the first to admit her skills were more organizational than therapeutic; Jacqueline had retrained as a marriage guidance counsellor after taking early retirement as a primary school headteacher, and was the first point of contact for new clients. She had a habit of referring clients 'sideways' if her own brand of therapy (nodding, shortbread, ballroom dancing classes) wasn't making headway, and 'sideways' normally meant 'to Tara'. But for all her counselling shortcomings, Jacqueline was a very capable manager, always launching initiatives and awareness-raising efforts that kept them in the local paper. Most importantly, no one had her ability to prevent the various factions in the Centre passive-aggressively diagnosing each other to death in the office kitchen.

'Tara, first things first,' Jacqueline began, pulling out a purple biro and opening her to-do book, 'we need to talk about the Summer Party. Can I pop you down for that lovely trifle of yours?'

Tara made a vague noise. The Centre held four seasonal get-togethers, normally good-natured affairs – apart from the Summer Party, which for some reason had a history of getting badly out of hand. Hero and her gang attributed it to the summer solstice.

'Incidentally, we've decided – no party games.' Jacqueline looked over her spectacles. 'Not after what happened with the Mr and Mrs quiz last year.'

'No,' Tara agreed. 'Poor Judith.'

'Poor Roger, more like. And her a Freudian expert.' Jacqueline made a face. 'Anyway, Kemi's suggested some gong therapy instead!'

'Do I want to know what that entails?'

'Apparently she's got this gong, and it . . . vibrates while we, sort of . . . Anyway, she went on a course on the Isle of Wight at Easter and said it was very uplifting. Very spiritual. She says she can give us a gong bath after the buffet.'

'That sounds . . . good for the digestion,' was the best Tara could manage.

'Well, quite. Now, our new colleague – lovely Dr David. He's having some trouble arranging an external supervisor so I wondered if you could step in? Just until he finds a new one.'

Every counsellor in the Centre had regular meetings with another therapist to discuss their work and address any problems they were experiencing with their clients. Until the start of the year, Tara had supervised Kathleen, the therapist David had replaced; Kath was an experienced NLP therapist who never had any real problems to unpick, and their sessions had been a good excuse for some extended lunchtime shopping.

'He's terribly nice – you'll get on like a house on fire. Oh, and you can start by giving him this.' She handed Tara a card. 'It's a thank-you card, from Mrs Richardson.'

Tara blinked. '*The* Mrs Richardson?'

Mrs Richardson – no one was permitted to use her first name – had seen everyone in the Centre and tried every available therapy in the hope of curing her insomnia. Tara's CBT approach hadn't worked. Neither had Hero's amethyst pillow crystal, Darren's acupuncture, Lionel's homeopathic sleep drops, or any of the others' attempts to get her off to sleep.

'She slept through the recycling lorry last week!' Jacqueline was visibly impressed. 'Says she's a new woman.'

'Wow,' said Tara, with a twinge of envy. For both David's success and also Mrs Richardson's deep slumber. 'I'll drop it in.'

'She actually called David a miracle worker.' Jacqueline looked almost starstruck. 'The last review she did of her treatment here was "unlikely to cause permanent damage".'

Tara seized the moment. 'One thing I meant to ask about . . . I noticed David with some clients who'd brought a dog with them?'

Jacqueline nodded, as if this was completely normal.

'And . . . since when did we allow that?' Jacqueline had made a *huge* fuss about Tara's electric diffuser.

'Oh, it's a key element of his methodology. Animal-assisted therapy. I said we'd give it a month's trial, with provisos, but so far the results seem to be speaking for themselves. Anyway,' Jacqueline indicated her ringing phone with an apologetic shrug, before Tara could probe further, 'here I am, holding you back!'

It was Tara's cue to leave, and she took it.

David was scribbling furiously with a proper fountain pen when Tara knocked on his door and put her head round later that morning. He shouted, 'Come in!' but carried on scrawling notes, his brown hair falling into his face as his pen flew across the paper.

'Sorry, forgive me. Have a seat. Just . . . one . . . second . . .'

Tara sat down on the chair next to the desk – not the couch; no therapist ever sat on the couch – and let her gaze roam around the room. A spider plant on a bookshelf filled with proper psychology textbooks, not *He's Just Not That Into You* and *It's Called a Break-Up Because It's Broken*. A red oriental rug between the chairs, a brass lamp. Framed diplomas on the wall. The room looked as if it had belched out the previous therapist's IKEA vibe and sided squarely with the original Victorian farmers. It even smelled more serious.

No, she corrected herself, her eye falling on the source of the leathery, library smell: it smelled of an expensive candle. Which she assumed, in turn, was to mask the aroma of the Border terrier that had just left, along with its owners.

'Sorry about that.' David clicked the lid on his pen with a snap, and looked up. The smile was mild and guarded at the same time. 'How can I help?'

Something about the way he said it put her on the back foot. Wasn't she meant to be helping him? 'I thought I'd pop in and introduce myself. I'm Tara Hunter, relationship counselling and life coaching . . .'

'I know!' said David. 'I've heard a lot about you. In your absence. All very complimentary!'

'Great! Well. Jacqueline mentioned you were between supervisors, so if there's anything I can help with, until you get sorted out . . .'

'That's very kind of you. Thank you.' He smiled. Tara hesitated and smiled back. There was something offputtingly familiar about David Dalloway. Had she met him somewhere? At a conference? But then he had the sort of face that felt familiar from period dramas: the chestnut fringe flopping into shrewd brown eyes, the fine-boned, slightly academic features. The crumpled linen jacket, hanging on the hat stand. Maybe not the lead detective, but certainly the honourable young sidekick who might have Seen Terrible Things in the war, and always had a clean handkerchief.

'Good. Good. Oh, and Jacqueline asked me to give you this.' She passed him the card, and pretended not to know who it was from as he opened it.

'Ah! It's from Bernadette.' He propped the card up on the desk: it featured a snoozy Dachshund.

'Bernadette?'

'Bernadette Richardson?'

'She was always very much Mrs Richardson to me,' said Tara.

'To be specific, it's also from Frank. Her Dachshund.' David raised his gaze to hers with a glance that might have been faux-serious or just serious. 'Short for Frankfurter.'

'Because he's a sausage dog?'

'Exactly.'

'I didn't even know she had a dog.' The mysterious world of Mrs Richardson – Bernadette – was opening up in front of Tara. 'Did she bring Frank to her sessions?'

'He was the breakthrough.'

'Really?' Tara seized the chance. 'So how does that work? Dogs in consultations? It's not something I've come across before.'

David swung on his chair. 'I've found that encouraging

clients to bring their pets along can be useful. Breaks tension, encourages empathetic projection, promotes honesty, lowers cortisol . . . lots of recognized benefits. I can send you some links, if you like?'

'Please do.' It came out more accusatory than she'd intended.

He stopped swinging on his chair, and looked at her. 'Do you have a pet, Tara?'

'No. Well, yes. Sort of. A cat.'

David tilted his head, as if she'd said something intriguing, and Tara managed to stop any of the thoughts stumbling through her brain from escaping. Never say anything intriguing in front of a counsellor, unless you're paying them. She didn't want to get on to the messy topic of Phil with a trained professional.

When nothing was forthcoming, he went on. 'Jacqueline and I agreed on extra cleaning and sessions in the meeting room if other clients had allergy concerns. To avoid triggering anyone with a phobia, pets enter through the side entrance, and there's a marker on the appointment calendar to make everyone else aware there's an animal in the building.'

Oh. The red dots on some of David's appointments. Tara had assumed they meant . . . actually, she'd noticed they were there, assumed they were for something and then forgotten to ask what.

'Sorry.' This wasn't making her look very on top of things. 'I'm still working my way through my inbox.'

'Of course, I hear you've been very busy. It's unorthodox, I know. But it works for me. And I'm always happy to discuss it.' He smiled, and Tara felt like a school sneak who'd been put in her place.

'Of course! Great! So, about those supervisions. I don't know if you want to put a date in the diary now,' she said, in an effort to match David's effortless professionalism. 'Obviously you can cancel it if you find someone else, but . . .'

'Your time is precious, I know.' David had already got his diary out. It was a little leather one, with a tiny pencil slotted down the spine.

'I didn't mean . . .' Tara started, then stopped herself. Her time *was* precious. 'How about Wednesday?'

Chapter Three

Although the waters – rain, river, run-off, drains, puddles – had dropped back to their normal levels, the after-effects of the flood's rampage through the countryside were taking longer to disappear. The flood crisis centre in Much Larton village hall still opened its doors at nine in the morning so residents could access help with insurance claims, or register with the volunteer clean-up squad, or just sit with a warm drink and a sympathetic ear. When Tara dropped in on her way to work at half past eight, there were already several people waiting outside. They looked exhausted, in mismatched, borrowed clothes.

Tara had brought another selection of Ruth's wardrobe for the emergency clothing bank. She hadn't even hauled the bags out of the car boot when an older lady hurried over and started bombarding her with questions.

'Tara, love, I need to talk to you about Muffin. I'm so worried about her. Her fur's falling out with stress.'

'Mrs Williams, I'm only trained to deal with human stress. And I'm not staying, I'm just dropping some clothes off.' Tara started walking; she had her first appointment in half an hour back in town. 'Have you seen the vet? He's got a box of pheromone diffusers – that might help?'

'Oh, I hope so. Poor Muffin's having nightmares, keeps hiding whenever it rains.' Helen Williams had lost the entire contents of her cellar and ground floor – family photos, furniture, a Steinway piano that had been in her family for generations – but the only thing she cared about was her three-legged cat. 'And have you heard? Joan Cartwright's Bobby *still* hasn't come home . . .'

Tara shouldered the big door to the hall. 'Let me see what I can do.'

Inside, school exam tables and chairs were set out in discreet clumps, with food boxes stacked up along the stage. Tara's counselling area – with softer chairs, privacy screens and tissues donated by the local chemist – was in the far corner, away from the representatives from the council, Citizens Advice, the police, animal rescue, GP surgeries, and a hastily assembled squad of volunteer tradesmen who were trying to make houses safe until proper renovation work could start. Until a few days ago, there had been a soldier from the Royal Engineers, who'd been coordinating temporary structural repairs. He didn't have much advice to offer but the solid presence of nice Jonny in his army uniform seemed to raise spirits, particularly among the ladies running the soup kitchen.

As she walked in, Tara caught sight of a familiar figure sorting tins into plastic bags: a broad fabric collage of scarves and drapery, topped off with a gold headwrap from which a few silver-red-blonde corkscrew curls were escaping.

'Diane! I've got something for you!'

Diane turned round, a family pack of loo rolls in her hand, and peered over her half-moon glasses in the direction of the voice. When she realized who was calling her, the warrior-queen resting expression softened into something more welcoming. 'Oh hello, Tara, love!' she said.

Diane Sefton was her mother's best friend and lodger – or she had been, until a few months ago. She'd moved into Keith's studio at the bottom of the garden just after Tara left for university, when Ruth needed money and Diane's own philandering husband, Ivor, had been caught in flagrante with one teaching assistant too many. Diane and her collection of screen-printed scarves and dog-eared political handbooks had turned Keith's minimalist creative space into what Toby dismissively referred to as 'an Oxfam shop with a bed in it', and she lived there until Ruth sold her interiors business and decided the studio was the ideal Airbnb project for her retirement income. Then Diane took over Toby's old attic domain and they carried on as before: arguing about the news, nagging the other about their drinking, and quietly supporting each other through the big and small pains of middle age. Despite being diametrically opposed on almost every political standpoint, from nuclear power to oat milk, Diane and Ruth were good friends.

Diane had only just moved out of Wye Villa. When Ruth died, Tara had had several months left on her own tenancy, so she'd been happy for Diane to stay until she found somewhere else. It also gave Tara time to get her head around the empty space in her life where her mother had been. It wasn't that they'd lived in each other's pockets – far from it, really – more that Mum had . . . always been there.

'These are for the clothes bank,' she said quickly, as the cold wave of loss swept over her again. Not the tidal wave it had been at first, but still a wash of sorrow that froze time for a second. 'Some of it's a bit smarter than what we've been giving out, but I kept thinking about that poor woman last week who needed to go to job interviews and had nothing to wear, and I thought, *Mum would want me to do this.*'

'She absolutely would,' said Diane.

They both paused.

'Well, no,' Diane conceded. 'She'd put up a fight first, just to be contrary, and probably have something to say about people who didn't get insurance.' She blinked hard, her eyes glassy. 'And then I'd find two bags of skirts and jumpers by the front door in the morning.'

Tara blinked too. Her mum had always been kind. 'Yes, you're right.'

Diane wriggled her half-moon glasses back up her nose. 'Oh, I miss her, Tara. Even our daft arguments.'

'I know.' Tara pushed the bag into her arms before they both got any more emotional. 'It's mainly black and white, obviously . . .' Ruth's wardrobe was curated – long before the word became fashionable – into core components, accents and accessories. She and Keith had met at art college, where Ruth had studied Textile Design, and her clothes were beautiful: expensive dark trousers and perfect white blouses splashed with colour in the form of statement jewellery and elegant shoes. In the spare room, Tara had found unworn T-shirts and brand-new trousers, with a note attached for her tailor regarding 'the usual' alterations. Something about it pierced Tara's heart.

A thought occurred belatedly to her, and she looked up at Diane. 'Diane, I'm sorry – was there anything *you* wanted from Mum's wardrobe?'

Diane's sombre expression dissolved into a throaty laugh. 'Me? In your mum's clothes? I don't think so, love. What do you reckon would fit? There's maybe a *scarf* or something I could squeeze into . . .' She stopped, then said, 'You know what I'd like? That crazy rainbow necklace she wore. We had some great conversations about how hideous I thought that necklace was. Only Ruth could carry that off.'

'I'll bring it next time I'm here. You know, you could have taken whatever you wanted before you moved out.'

'And *you* know I wouldn't have done that. It was kind enough you letting me stay.' Diane made it sound like a favour, but she'd cleaned the place from top to bottom, and been there with the kettle on the first few times Tara had had to go back to the house without Ruth in it. 'Your mum would laugh if she could see where I moved to – my new flat is three doors down from her shop on the high street. Her happy place! I could have looked right into that famous window of hers.'

Tara smiled. 'She'd be glad you were near the shops. Toby suggested we scattered her ashes down the high street, if Liberty wouldn't let us.'

Diane blinked hard, then gave herself a little shake that would have been discreet if it hadn't made three necklaces jingle and two scarves shimmer. 'So have you got the Sindys sent off?'

'Not yet,' said Tara evasively.

Ruth had collected, amongst other things, vintage Sindy dolls. In her will, which Tara now suspected her mother had written after two bottles of white wine and a *Poirot* boxset, Ruth had bequeathed her sizeable collection to the Museum of Childhood in London. Tara was supposed to be in charge of arranging the donation but hadn't done anything with them yet, aside from discovering they were quite valuable. It was tempting, given her own variable freelance income (and the fact that she technically now owned them), to stick them on eBay.

There was a cough. 'Hello? I need to talk to someone about the food bank?'

The hall had been filling up with people while they'd been talking and there was now a queue by Diane's desk.

'I'll give you a ring.' Diane popped the bag of clothes behind a table. 'Is that old dear waiting for you? She keeps looking over here.'

Mrs Williams, now accompanied by another old lady, was perched on Tara's counselling chairs and staring in her direction. She seemed crumpled with grief, clutching her handbag like a comfort blanket. From the way she kept glancing in their direction, Mrs Williams seemed confident that Tara could sort out the missing Bobby issue.

'How are you with cats?' Tara asked Diane. 'I need an expert.'

Diane peered over her glasses and sighed. 'When you're a single woman in your fifties, you tend to avoid them,' she said. 'They're quite . . . ageing.'

Wednesday was Lunch and Learn Day at the Wellness Centre, the monthly chance for the team to gather over a selection of sandwiches, and for one therapist to hold forth about a topic of their choice – almost without exception, their own brand of therapy and the benefits thereof. There were a few notable exceptions: Harry the sports masseur liked to practise his stand-up routine on a captive audience, and Darren the acupuncturist was passionate about hedgehog conservation.

The format was familiar: Jacqueline ran through the agenda as everyone grazed the buffet, starting with major upcoming events, followed by reminders about the state of the staff kitchen and pleas for website content, and, as a grand finale, any thank-you notes sent to the Centre from clients. Most of the therapists visibly snapped back to life when the thank-you cards emerged from Jacqueline's manila file: under the smiles and applause there was a certain amount of professional rivalry about who got the most.

'Now, this is a lovely message I wanted to share with you.' Jacqueline waved a postcard; Tara couldn't make out more than a sunny beach from her position at the back of the room, nearest the door. 'It's from a couple who, I'm sure they wouldn't mind me saying, came in last week in a bit of a state for some make-or-break counselling. Anyway, they write: *Dear Jacqueline – just wanted to drop you a line to let you know that the wedding is back on! And it's all thanks to . . .*' She allowed a minute *X Factor* suspense-pause, then said, '*David. He was amazing. We're back on track and we're eloping next month! With best wishes, Jodie and Jack. Kiss kiss. And a paw from Monkey.* A happy ever after! Well done, David.'

David was sitting on his own near the front, with three sandwiches in a neat stack. He waved away the ripple of acknowledgement as if he hadn't done anything particularly special. For some reason, Tara found that annoying. He could at least pretend to look modest. Two thank-you cards, in the space of two days? What was he, some kind of magician? Was he hypnotizing clients?

To compound Tara's annoyance, Hero gazed at David, tilting her head in a sort of benign yoga blessing, while he maintained an awkward semi-eye contact, as if he wasn't sure if she was performing some official kind of religious benediction. Tara had never imagined there could be a hand gesture more annoying than air-hook inverted commas, but Hero's humble namaste bowing – which everyone seemed to be taking up now – took the gluten-free biscuit.

Jacqueline cleared her throat to continue. Tara wondered if there would be a note from Amy and Don Bishop, a couple she'd 'signed off' before the floods, after nearly a year of working through Amy's affair with their financial advisor. It had been a gruelling process that had turned up a *lot* of old grievances, and Amy and Don's combined obstinacy had stretched her professional ingenuity to its limits. Tara had been surprised but pleased when Amy had announced she felt they were at a point where they could carry on the rebuilding process on their own, and stopped rebooking appointments. She had a folder in her top drawer with every personal note she'd received from clients over the eight years she'd been qualified, and it would be nice to add the Bishops to it.

But instead Jacqueline swept on with one of her familiar meeting-punctuating phrases; this one was the phrase that signalled the end of the beginning, and the beginning of the lecture. 'Of course, we're a team here at the Centre so let's take a moment to applaud *everyone* for their positive contribution.' She started clapping, file clamped under her arm, and everyone joined in, albeit in a less enthusiastic way than before. Tara managed three claps and across the room her CBT colleague Emily raised her forefingers in a discreet 'one nil' gesture. Emily kept a beady-eyed tally on the thank-you cards, and the split between what she called 'the docs and the quacks'.

'Now then!' Jacqueline beamed round the room. 'I'm

delighted to say that Kasia will be talking to us today about a vital element of everyone's practice – self-care. Over to you, Kasia!'

She stepped back, and a tall blonde stood up in front of the carved oak frieze depicting a bountiful if geographically suspect harvest scene resplendent with hops, grapes, pomegranates and sheep. Kasia was holding two teddy bears and an orange, which looked ominously like props.

Tara sighed and slipped her hand into her bag for her emergency Chelsea bun. She didn't need a lecture about self-care. The last thing she wanted to listen to over this precious time out was someone with a degree in Feelings telling her the exact things she spent all day telling other people. Meditate. Sleep. No social media after teatime. Eat kefir for your gut brain. Declutter.

As Kasia got going with her self-care spiel, Tara's thoughts drifted towards the spare rooms at home. Seeing Diane had reminded her that she'd barely started sorting Ruth's personal effects. If she was honest, Tara was squeamish about what she might find in her mother's drawers. Now Ruth was gone, Tara could admit an awkward truth of adulthood: that she didn't really know the non-Mum human her mother had been, despite living no further than twenty miles away from her childhood home for her entire life. She'd been a good parent; a tiger mom before they were invented, ambitious yet endlessly supportive, always first in line on parents' evenings. But Tara had thought for some time that their cordial mother–daughter relationship depended a lot on not actually transitioning to an adult–adult one, with all that would have entailed.

What would have happened if I'd taken that job in

Glasgow? Tara mused, as Kasia droned on about boundaries. It had been a turning point: the chance to join two friends-of-friends in setting up a community counselling practice/charity. Three years later, it had won an EU award for its mental-health projects. *I mean,* she thought, *what did Mum even know about Glasgow to be so against me going? Why didn't I just . . . go?*

She knew why not. She was trapped by her own paranoia of 'turning out like your dad': i.e. a runner-away. A tunnel-visioned abandoner. Combined, of course, with her saviour complex about protecting her mother and a rejected child's fear of failure and need for familiarity. Tara had got all that information free with her counselling qualifications; other therapists dismantling her psyche had not been a fun listen.

'. . . serious consequences for the quality of support we offer, and on our own lives outside work. I want to outline a few effective techniques to protect ourselves from burn-out . . .' Kasia wasn't a hypnotherapist, as far as Tara knew, but she certainly had the sort of soothing tones that could put you into a very relaxed state.

Tara subtly scanned the room to see if she was the only one zoning out. A few heads were nodding – some in agreement, some because it was hard not to succumb to the gentle ebb and flow. David was wearing the rapt 'engaged' face of a Channel 4 news anchor, mid-interview. It was impossible to tell if he was listening or not.

David's familiarity niggled at Tara. Had he been in her year at university? One of those never-left-his-room types, seen only at the occasional party, blinking in the light? Was he one of Justin's insufferable village pub mates? Tara studied David's angular face, probing her memory, then jumped when he unexpectedly turned in her direction and – *again* – caught her looking.

God. He was going to think she had a crush on him. Tara smiled, distantly, as if she'd been thinking, not looking at him at all, then pretended to focus intently on Kasia's mellifluous nonsense talk.

'. . . imagine you're surrounded by a calm pink light, the colour of care, and then project that light away from you until it's like a beautiful bubble of protection . . .'

Pink light, lovely. Tara settled back and thought about the calm pink places she could go on holiday. Was it too late for her to do her Grand Tour at last? She'd planned to travel round Europe with her housemates after graduation; Tara's Rough Guides were fluttery with sticky notes, local delicacies highlighted in yellow, her modest budget carefully spreadsheeted. She'd experienced such exhilaration planning it, balancing on the edge of a different life, the smallness of her childhood behind her, the future full of everything. Toby, of course, was already out there exploring the extremes, sending her updates from the big wide world of work and adventure. Unlike her, he didn't care whether Mum thought he was selfish. By the time Toby left for university, he and Mum were barely talking. Which, Tara supposed, was the real definition of being like Dad.

'. . . crucial to acknowledge when we need help, and to learn that reaching out to colleagues for advice and support isn't a sign of weakness, it's a sign of *strength* . . .'

A cloud moved across the sun and the warmth dipped away. In the end, Tara hadn't sipped her Aperol spritzes in Rome or hot chocolate in Prague. She had drunk a lot of instant coffee in Longhampton hospital, when her mum slipped over outside Boots the week before the Eurostar departed, with Kate, Nadia and Meg aboard. Too easy to blame the temporary job she'd taken in the local Citizens Advice while Mum's shattered vertebrae healed, instead of the legal-practice course she had planned that would have converted her into a fully functioning solicitor. Toby hadn't stopped: he'd carried on freelancing, six months here, six months there. Each job a step higher, further into his future. Whereas Tara had stayed put, fixing problems and finding she enjoyed it. Eventually she'd taken her counselling diplomas, got her psychotherapy qualifications. And here she was.

She stared out of the window, right into the old CAB office where she'd helped lonely people dispute traffic fines while her mates were deliriously consuming God knew what in Amsterdam.

Was it too late to pack it in and travel now? There was nothing keeping her in Longhampton, other than her clients. They'd cope. Emily and Bryan could do everything she did.

Well, there was Sybil. The cat. But that would mean a call to Phil to discuss what to do with her. Tara had made a solemn promise with herself that this time she would *not* crack first and ring Phil. It had never been as long as this before. But a promise was a promise.

Phil Shawcross swaggered into her mind's eye in his black jeans, his blue eyes twinkling as if he was thinking of something very bad, his confident, slightly retro attitude thoroughly inappropriate for a meeting about calming pink light.

Tara shoved the distracting mental image of Phil to one side. *Fresh starts are the silver lining of disaster*, she reminded herself. She'd said this, gently, over and over, to people crushed with despair at the prospect of spring-cleaning their homes with shovels and a skip. *Take this opportunity to work out what truly matters to you, let go of what doesn't.*

But what *did* she want? Really? If no one was watching her, what did she want?

Imaginary Phil winked at her, as if he knew *exactly* what she wanted, and Tara squeezed her eyes shut and crossed her legs. At no point in their five years together, had Justin made her feel flustered in a Lunch and Learn.

'Any questions?'

She snapped to attention with an embarrassingly obvious jerk. Kasia was smiling at the front, and a few people were angling their heads to see if Chloe had remembered to order pudding for the buffet.

Tara wondered who would ask a question. If no one did – and usually someone managed a question, even for personal-agenda-driven reasons – Jacqueline always came up with an enquiry about something or other, to show willing.

David raised his hand. 'Would you say that functioning self-care is an ethical imperative that we, as a cohort, should take a lead on? My previous practice had a seasonal team sport initiative, for example.'

Across the room, someone muttered, 'In English?'

'That's a *very good* point, David!' Jacqueline jumped in before Kasia could respond. 'I've actually been planning a group sporting challenge, to help us get to know one another a little better. Details to follow!' She tapped her nose and beamed at him.

'Oh . . . great,' said Bryan heavily, summing up the

mood of the assembled therapists – apart from Lionel, who had found the slab of brownies Chloe had ordered and was busy helping himself to the middle bits.

Tara started with a headache after lunch, not entirely brought on by 'all the processed sugar in the brownies' as Anji disapprovingly informed everyone.

It persisted through a long afternoon of client appointments and was still pinching her head when she got home. A strong gin and tonic didn't fix it, because Tara knew deep down what the cause of it was: she still hadn't talked to Toby about the house.

Sybil was nowhere to be seen, even when Tara produced her bowl of cat pâté, and eventually, worried, Tara went to look for her.

She found the cat on the low wall that separated the patio from the long expanse of back garden: Sybil's spine was arched and her mouth wide and pink with outrage. She was hissing at something, and the tension in her rigid body gave Tara the creeps.

'What are you looking at?' The cat was furious, almost dog-like in her guarding.

Tara followed the direction of her furious stare and jumped: Sybil was hissing because there was someone in the garden.

A man. A man in a dark jacket was walking around the studio, taking pictures on his phone.

Tara's heart thudded with panic, then she remembered the message from the estate agent. Bryn Thomas of Thomas Bliss Thomas had provided the probate valuation before the floods, but she'd managed to deflect his questions about when she planned to put the house on the market. He'd phoned again, earlier in the week, 'offering' to 'pop back' – this was probably him now.

She marched down the garden, past the beds of roses and the big outdoor table Mum had used for al fresco dining, towards the studio.

And I don't want them to manage the Airbnb either, if that's what he's after, she thought.

Then the man turned and saw her coming down the lawn towards him, and Tara's stomach flipped. He smiled. He smiled at her . . . and waved.

Tara stopped walking.

He waved again.

Her dry lips moved, but it took an effort to push out her voice.

'Dad?' she croaked, and the word sounded strange in the air.

'Hello, Taransay!' said Keith Hunter.

Chapter Four

No one called Tara Taransay, just as no one called Toby Tobermory. Not many people even knew it was her real name. Dad was the only one who ever did, because, according to Mum, he was the one who'd insisted on their ridiculous names in the first place.

Tara stared in shock at the man standing in front of her. He looked exactly like her dad, but with the colour turned down. The hair swept up in a quiff like Superman's was silver, not jet black. The velvet jacket and black T-shirt that had been his uniform had faded into a grey linen jacket and paler grey trousers. His handsome face was shaded with a silvery beard that tortoiseshelled from dark grey to pewter to white, and he seemed smaller than she remembered. In Tara's memories, Dad was tall: he towered over Mum, he filled a room with his laughter. This man wasn't much bigger than she was.

If it hadn't been for his eyes . . . Dad's eyes hadn't changed. Still North Sea blue, sharp under the beetly eyebrows, looking straight at her and still making her want to smile, even though the adult Tara couldn't think of a single reason to smile right now.

Instead, she felt a weird sense of panicky betrayal, that her mum might appear out of nowhere and find them talking.

'Dad?' she said. 'What are you doing here?'

'Couple of reasons.' He nodded towards the house. 'Can I come in?'

Say no, yelled her mother's voice, somewhere in the back of Tara's head. *Do not let that bloody man into my house!*

Tara's brain spun frantically, the cogs disengaged. She stared at the semi-familiar man standing about four feet from the spot where she and Mum had buried Branston, and a thought popped randomly into her head: Dad was always so *rude* about men with beards. Uncle Peter. The vicar. And now he had one.

'Oh, wait.' Keith mistook her shock, and lifted an eyebrow. 'Is there still a password to get back inside?'

Tara blinked, momentarily thrown off-balance. The password game was their end-of-day game: her and Toby guarding the back door at five o'clock when Dad left his garden studio office to come in for tea. Toby's password changed daily, and he made Dad work for it; it would be based on his current hobby or schoolwork or a television programme. Tara's was always just 'Let me in'. She didn't want to waste time, when Dad could be back in the house with them: it was when the fun started.

That was a lifetime ago. Resentment flamed inside her. Dad hadn't earned the right to lead off with happy childhood memories, when so many painful ones sprang to mind first.

Her voice snapped out of her, cold and high. 'Sorry, perhaps?'

Keith rubbed his face as if she'd slapped him.

'I *am* sorry,' he said. 'That was clumsy. It just brought everything back, standing here. Seeing you, with the house in the background. The roses.' He paused. 'You haven't changed at all.'

'Since I was ten? I've changed a lot,' said Tara bluntly. 'And so have you.'

That made him wince, but he took it on the chin. 'Ouch.'

'How did you get in?' she demanded. *Calm down. It won't help. Stick with the facts.*

'The gate in the hedge.' He pointed towards the far end of the garden, where it backed on to a footpath.

'There's a gate there?' Tara had never seen one.

'It's nearly overgrown now. Didn't you know? I put it in when I built the studio so I could nip in and out without trailing mud through the house.'

So he could nip in and out to the pub, more like. Or other people could nip in and out to the studio. Ugh. The things that dawned on you as an adult.

Tara ran her hand through her black curls, trying to anchor herself in the moment. It was too much to process: reality and memories sliding over one another like an almost lucid afternoon-nap dream. And Dad, somewhere in the middle of both.

'Can I come in, though?' he went on. 'I'm dying for a . . .' His eyes darted meaningfully.

There followed a long pause in which Tara struggled hard with herself and finally said, 'Fine,' because what else could she say? *Pee in the begonias?*

She turned to walk up the path, ignoring her own voice of common sense, which had now joined in with her mother yelling at her inside her head, and Sybil watched them from the wall. She did not seem impressed.

*

53

Inside, Keith went straight to the downstairs loo and Tara grabbed her phone to call Toby, mentally calculating what time it would be with him, then realizing she didn't care. He could drop whatever spa review he was writing for this.

To her surprise, he picked up.

'Dad's here!' she hissed before he could speak.

'What?'

'Dad's here. He was in the garden. He got in through some secret gate – I don't even know where to start with that!'

There was a long pause on the end of the line. A suspicious one.

'Toby, did you know about this?'

'Not exactly. Dad rang out of the blue, last night.' He sounded evasive. 'Listen, I tried to get hold of you earlier but your phone was off, then I was in meetings . . .'

'I was working! And why did he ring you and not me?' Even now, there was a nip of something childish about her dad talking to Toby first.

'Don't ask me. We got talking about . . . Mum, that sort of thing, you know, and I said you were in Longhampton, sorting out the house. He suggested he could give you a steer about what was worth selling. I said why not, because he does know what's what, Tara.'

Tara struggled. He'd rung Toby *out of the blue*? How had he even got his number? From his agent, maybe. It wasn't as if Toby was hard to get hold of, unless you were his sister. She squeezed the bridge of her nose with her free hand. 'Dad is the *last* person Mum would want going through the house.'

'I know that. But you said you needed some help.'

From YOU, she wanted to say. *I wanted YOU to come back and help me deal with the emotional furniture in this place, not the actual sofas and beds.* 'Why didn't you ask me first? Why didn't you *warn* me?'

'Well, naturally, I assumed he'd ring you beforehand, not pitch up on the doorstep.'

Tara glanced towards the downstairs bathroom, and saw Sybil staring witheringly at her in the hallway. She turned back, jangling with panic. She felt small again, when Toby had been by her side, muttering his mysteriously accurate commentary on adult behaviour into her baffled ear. 'Why is he *here*, Toby? Really?'

'Maybe he's seen God and wants to make amends for walking out on us?' Toby's tone was annoyingly reasonable. 'Maybe Mum dying's triggered a mid-life crisis. Maybe he left a buried treasure map in the airing cupboard.'

The toilet flushed. She didn't have much time.

'Look, I've got to go – he's coming out of the loo.'

'Say hi from me,' said Toby. 'Actually, no. Don't do that. But call me back, let me know what's going on.'

'I will, because there's something important we still need to talk about . . .' said Tara, but he'd gone. She shoved the phone into her back pocket as Keith emerged into the hall.

'I see your mother decided to remodel the wet room.' Keith gesticulated behind him. They'd had the first walk-in wet room in the area, years ahead of everyone else; Tara had always assumed it was a bathroom for the dog. 'Very Moroccan now.'

'Er, yes.' Tara hadn't been there when Mum had done that. She'd had a builder called Lorcan who she relied on for her regular renovations, working her way around the house season by season. 'She went on holiday, got into tiles.'

'And . . . oh.' He stopped short of the marble kitchen counter and gazed about the place like someone in an art gallery, stumbling across a Picasso. 'Oh, wow.' Tara's hands clenched and unclenched by her sides. Was he seeing the glass-chinking, laughter-buzzy parties? The family dinners at the breakfast bar? Was he seeing her memories, or just his own handiwork?

'Still an incredible space,' he said, gazing up at the glass extension, angling his hand against the fading light to see how it fell. 'And the colours work so well. Your mother always had a great eye for design. She could have been a world-class interior designer.'

'She was very successful. More work than she could take on.'

Keith nodded. 'It's held up well, hasn't it? Hard to remember what a poky little place this was when your mother and I first bought it.'

Tara couldn't stand it any longer. 'Have you just come here to congratulate yourself on your own DIY?'

'No. Of course not.' The middle-aged stranger posing in exactly the same way her father had, elbow on the breakfast bar, gazed at her as if he were taking in every tiny detail of her face. 'I was in the area for work, so I thought I'd pop by and see how you were.'

Tara stared back at him.

'What do you mean, how am I? In general, in myself? My health? Professionally? Or how am I coping with my mother dropping dead of a heart condition I didn't even know she had? What do you mean, *how I am*?' Her voice had risen, despite her efforts to keep it level.

Keith didn't react to her anger. Infuriatingly, he was as calm as Tara wished she could be. 'All of the above. Where do you want to start?' He smiled apologetically, and the crinkling of his eyes stirred up memories inside Tara's heart, fluttering like eager moths against a darkened window: the bedtime stories, the birthday cakes, sitting on Dad's knee in his parked car, pretending to drive it. Memories from Before, when being happy with Dad was allowed.

At no point since Tara had moved into Wye Villa had the ghosts of her own past stepped out of the shadows so vividly as now. She'd forgotten about the dog shower (Mum yelling in horror as she and Toby lathered Branston in her Molton Brown shampoo). She'd forgotten about the passwords (Dad laughing, carrying her, upside down, across the garden for sweet tea). And after the years and years and years of listening to her mother retelling tales so eloquently, often hilariously, about a total shit whose genes were, after all, Tara's own responsibility to overcome, she'd forgotten her dad's voice, his smile, his laugh.

Tara stared furiously at her father, who was still smiling at her as if they'd bumped into each other in a restaurant. This man. The cause of so much pain and yet still the man she'd yearned to come back for her. He was here, and she didn't know what to say.

She dug her nails into her palms and tried to summon up the calm voice she used at work with difficult clients. 'Normally, when it's been this long since two people have seen each other, there's a phone call first. They don't just *crash in* on each other because they're in the area for work.'

Keith – Dad – rubbed his face with his hand. 'Darling, when Ruth, *Mum*, died, I . . . I started a lot of emails that I didn't send. I've always been a pick-up-the-phone sort of bloke. I thought it was better to, you know, speak to you in person but then . . .' He shrugged, and smiled. 'You know what would make all this easier?'

Years of therapy? A gun? Subtitles?

'What's that?'

'A nice cup of tea.'

'Seriously?' She'd expected him to say whisky.

He nodded. 'Go on,' he said. 'Let's have a nice cup of tea.'

Tara couldn't speak. Again, tea. Tea had always been their thing, their in-joke. He'd poured her her very first milky cup, aged three, to her granny's horror: 'He'll be giving her alcohol next! Teaching her to smoke!' (That wasn't an actual memory; it was a memory of what Ruth said her mother had said. But it had been repeated often enough to stand in its own right.)

I would advise a client to ask him to leave, she thought. *No, not ask, tell. It's outrageous.*

Yet she couldn't. Even with this fury simmering in her, Tara couldn't bring herself to tell him to leave. What if that was it? What if she never saw him again? It would definitely be her fault he'd left this time.

'You look like you could do with one,' he added. 'Why don't I make it? I bet I can guess where.'

'No! No. Sit down.'

Tara moved around the kitchen on autopilot – the tea bags, the kettle, the teapot which was in the same place it had always been. Keith didn't seem remotely on edge. He was too busy charming Sybil, the traitor, who was curling around the doorway, eyeing him up while snaking her tail in a flirty manner Tara hadn't seen before.

'Have you inherited him along with this house?' he asked. 'Very Ruth, a black cat. Chic!'

'I'm looking after her for a friend,' she said, shortly.

'What's she called?'

'Sybil.'

'She's a very elegant cat, aren't you? Yes, you are.'

Tara played for time, hoping her brain would snap into gear and make sense of this situation, but she couldn't get hold of any sensible thoughts: they kept slipping away, overwhelmed by a curdling fear that she was handling this badly.

Eventually, she turned to face her father across the marble counter. 'I don't know how to say this without sounding rude, so I'm just going to say it: what are you doing here?'

'I was looking at a property in Perryfield for an old friend who's thinking of buying it. Turville Court – do you know it? Lovely old pile, two hundred acres, woodland. He asked me to have a look around, see what I thought.'

As it happened, Tara did know Turville Court. It had been the property section's front page in the *Gazette*; an ivy-covered Brideshead, up for sale now the semi-aristocratic family had fizzled out in a disappointed splutter of elderly sisters. The kettle boiled and Tara poured the hot water into the pot. She let the silence brew along with the tea bags.

'So, as I was literally a few miles from Longhampton I thought I'd drop by to see you,' he went on. 'Worth a knock, on the off-chance, surely?'

Tara turned to examine his face. No mention of the phone call to Toby. No mention of the house. No mention of her mother, or condolences. What did he want?

59

'Why didn't you come to the front door, like a normal person would? What were you doing in the garden?'

'Well,' he said, a touch self-deprecatingly, 'this is going to sound silly, but I wanted to check that silver birch in the garden hadn't come down in the storms. So many trees down in Perryfield. Lots of damage. That silver birch always bothered me. We should have taken it out years ago, it's not safe.'

'Really.'

'Yes, really, if you don't get it lopped back it could easily come down in a bad storm, right on top of the studio.' Keith read her expression and changed tack. 'And when I was so near, it felt wrong to be in the area and not try to see you. Especially after what's happened. I wanted to say how sorry I was about—'

'Don't!' It snapped out of her. 'I don't want to talk about Mum. And there's nothing you can do, before you ask. Everything's under control.'

It wasn't. She didn't know why she'd said that.

Keith raised his hands. 'OK. I'm sorry.'

Silence spread between them, and Tara's shoulders dropped. Mum had been acknowledged, and she'd managed to put up a boundary. Her brain hadn't left the building yet, but her heartbeat was still skittering anxiously.

'Bloody awful mess in the town, where the river went over,' he went on. 'Cheering to see how people have been pulling together, though. The land agent was telling me about the community response. I had a look at the Flood Relief website – you've been a real pillar of the community, I hear!'

Tara pretended she didn't feel pleased he'd seen it. 'Why were you looking at that?'

He sipped his tea. 'Due diligence for the client. Turville Court's on the edge of the flood-risk area – you need to factor these things in. Where was the worst hit? Much Larton? Yarrold?'

Tara was surprised he could remember – and he was right. 'Yarrold was cut off for a few days. They had to rescue people in boats. Human chains for pets and valuables.'

'Oh, dear. It's always been like that – Yarrold flooded one Christmas when you and Toby were tiny. Well, *everywhere* flooded – it caught us all on the hop. Your mother was coming back from something with you two when they closed the roads and she was stuck down a lane. We had to get you home on a tractor.' He smiled over the edge of his mug, something of the old twinkle in his eyes. 'Luckily I was working on a site that had a big digger, so we rescued you on that.'

'I don't have any memory of it.'

'Well, you were just tiny, you and Toby in your froggie wellies.'

'I don't even remember the floods.' Had it been a traumatic forgetting? Or was she just too young? Toby had never mentioned it. Mum had never mentioned it. But then if it involved Dad riding to the rescue in some capacity, it probably wouldn't have gone into the anecdote rotation. Tara had plenty of childhood memories – Dad drunkenly bidding two months' wages on a child-size JCB in a charity auction, Dad driving to Bristol to get them McDonald's when Toby broke his ankle – but as she got older, she realized they were all seen through the Mum prism. Sharp and funny, yet delivered with a weariness that made you feel a bit guilty for smiling.

Her throat dried, and she had a weird sensation of

Ruth standing behind her in the kitchen, arms crossed. What would *her* memory of this story be? Even thinking about Ruth's face – and the smile she'd be wearing, the too-bright one that hid her real feelings – sent a cold gust of loss across Tara's heart.

I can't call Mum to check this out, she thought. I can't ask her about my first words or her first love – there are moments of my own life that have vanished now she's not here to tell me about them. I can never ask her how she felt, what she remembers; we'll never have that adult relationship I assumed would just . . . evolve.

Tara straightened her shoulders, falling back on the rote things she'd tell a client to say.

'This is very unfair.' She looked her father – this man – square in the eye. 'I don't know what you want, a reconciliation, or closure, but this . . . it's not the way to go about it.'

'Is that your professional advice? Or are you telling me that as my daughter?'

'Both.' Tara didn't do much work with estranged families but she knew the basics – long preambles, short meetings in neutral spaces. Not ambushes in the family home. 'You should have phoned first.'

He sighed, then said with a heartbreaking honesty, 'I thought if I phoned, you wouldn't see me.'

Tara was torn: she wanted to say, *You're right, I would have told you to get lost*, but Dad had finally come home. And underneath the frostiness, the fury, a small voice whispered, *He wanted to check you were OK.*

Keith looked as if he might try to reach out a hand, but decided against it. 'I've wanted to see you for such a long time, Tara. There was never going to be a "right moment". But we've got to start somewhere. And look — we have.' He smiled, again hopefully. 'Haven't we?'

'Dad.' The word felt artificial in her mouth: this middle-aged man wasn't her dad. Dad was younger, darker, funnier — someone who'd maybe even stopped existing the moment he left in the babysitter's car. Unhappiness swooped in Tara's chest, suffocating her thoughts. She shook her head, miserably. 'I don't know that this is going to work out the way you want it to. I'm an adult. I can choose how I conduct my personal relationships.'

Keith looked at her for a long few seconds, then let out a breath. 'I'm sorry. I misjudged it. But I thought I should try. Was that such a bad thing?'

She hesitated, then shook her head. She could tell, now she was grown up, that he was a charming man, probably used to getting his own way, to talking around any hiccups or resistance. But she hadn't let him do that. That was something.

He pushed himself off the stool and picked up his satchel; a battered leather one, the same kind he'd always had. Were there still toffees in the side pockets? 'I should make a move.'

'Where do you live now?' Tara put the mugs in the sink, to make it clear there would be no refills. She didn't want to know *who* he lived with.

'London – Highbury. I just drove up for a night to check out this property for Steven. It's mainly what I do now, consultancy, one-off projects that I like the sound of. One of the benefits of age — there are younger, keener architects to do the grunt work for us old goats!'

Tara didn't push for details; she could tell he was being deliberately over-modest, itself a sign of vanity in her opinion, and she wasn't going to feed his ego by letting him know she'd Googled him. He'd sold the practice he'd built up, staying on as a director. She smiled, her lips tight.

'Thanks for the tea,' he said. 'It's good to see the old place is still standing. And that you're . . . doing so marvellously well.'

Tara stood up, and followed him to the door. At the step Keith turned and gazed down the black-and-white hallway, as if the years were scrolling back in a fast rewind through every iteration of Ruth's redecorations to that last time he'd seen it. Hallowe'en. The cobwebs on the banister, Branston in his tutu mane. Tara on the stairs, bewildered by the fifty-pound note in his hand.

Are you remembering? she wanted to ask. *Are you sorry?*

Then he shook himself. 'It was good to see you, Tara. I wish we could do this again, but I . . . understand if you don't want to.' Keith kept his eyes fixed on hers. 'I needed to say goodbye to your mum. And this house. We had some happy times here. I'm sorry, Tara, I know you didn't want me to mention her but it's true. And I wanted to see you.'

A thick lump swelled in Tara's throat.

She'd planned this conversation since she was about fourteen, when she still thought Dad might crawl back to her and Mum and Toby. As the reality gradually dawned on Tara that Keith wasn't coming back, ever, her 'Fuck you, Dad' speech had mutated; sometimes glacially angry, sometimes passionate, sometimes indulgently lyrical and forgiving, depending on where she was in her own life and how forgiving she could afford to be.

Now her father was here in front of her, ready for that piece of her mind and apparently willing to hear it. Instead,

Tara felt hollow: looking at herself from the outside, as if the angry Tara were as much of a stranger as this man was. Her mother was gone. And any happy times Mum had in the house had happened long after Dad had left.

Keith waited on the step, braced for her words.

'Goodbye, Dad,' she said mechanically, and closed the door.

Chapter Five

Tara didn't sleep well that night, as the old voices in her head started up a familiar argument. If it hadn't been for the sleep app playing fruitlessly on her mobile phone, she could have been transported back to any given evening between the ages of ten and eighteen, when she frequently lay awake agonizing over the impossible micro-balancing of family loyalty.

One voice dominated proceedings. And it was furious. Who the hell did Dad think he was, waltzing back in like that, expecting everything to be forgotten in a lovely Hollywood ending? How dare he 'need to say goodbye' to her poor mother, when he'd left them without a backwards glance – if he'd cared about his family, he'd have kept in touch. It wasn't that hard.

But a smaller voice kept butting in. Seeing him had been surprisingly easy, hadn't it? Maybe he'd changed. Maybe it was time to stop defending Mum's feelings, now she was no longer here.

But Ruth's feelings were almost all Tara had left of her mother. It felt wrong to let go of an anger she'd shared with her, through those years when it had just been them.

She turned her phone over to see if Toby had responded to her texts, or her phone messages. He hadn't.

Oh God. Tara stared at the ceiling. The email from the estate agent had now been joined by another letter from the solicitor, chasing her about probate.

Maybe I should just fly to Toby, she thought recklessly. *Tell him in person.*

Ruth had, for reasons best known to herself, left the house and its entire contents to Tara. Just Tara. There was a lump sum for Diane, donations to various charities, and that was it. Tara had no idea why her mother had done something so blatantly divisive; Ruth and Toby had argued a lot before he left – she remembered the tension too well – but it was totally out of character for her mum. She was a kind person. Tara only discovered how many charities she gave money to when she closed Ruth's bank accounts and found the direct debits.

Tara turned, then turned again, restless. She was going to give Toby his half, no question about that. The problem was how? She didn't have anywhere near enough savings to buy him out, and she couldn't get a mortgage with her freelance income. Even covertly selling everything in the house (starting with the Sindys) wouldn't add up to half. The only possibility was putting it on the market, and the thought of another family moving in made Tara want to bar the front door with her whole body.

It wasn't just about leaving her mother behind. Once she handed over the keys to Wye Villa, that would be it: she'd have to walk away with a head full of questions about her own story that would never be answered. And those doubts and half-explanations would gang up on the happy memories, smothering them out of existence. The truth, Tara sensed, was still there, in the house. Why Dad left, why Toby abandoned her, his twin soul, in his determination to get away. Mum had decorated over the past, again and again, but the fresh paint didn't change the sensation of secrets lingering like ghosts in the hall, behind doors, slipping just out of sight.

Tara didn't want to sell Wye Villa. But what choice did she have?

A deeper spot of darkness stirred in the corner of the room, disturbed by the yellow screen-light. Sybil blinked at her, as if to say, *Go to sleep.*

Tara groaned, and pulled the duvet over her head to blanket out the world. Somehow, all these years on, the darkness under her covers was still exactly the same.

Toby responded eventually, by text, and his advice was short, to the point, and exactly as Tara expected: **You need to talk this through with someone who doesn't know any of us.**

The trouble was, Tara didn't want to.

She should, in principle, have taken this work-affecting crisis to her own supervisor, Eric – a softly spoken truth machine who enquired remorselessly about her self-care and asked the type of probing questions that Tara didn't feel up to answering right now. Starting with, was she up to date with her own therapy? So she opted for the less stressful approach of lunch with her best work friend, Emily. Emily was the Centre's family specialist, although Tara had spotted not one but two of Emily's clients sidling into David's room, Cockapoo in tow.

'Em, can I get your take on something professionally?' she floated casually, after they'd discussed the likely fall-out of the upcoming Summer Party over their soup, and skirted around the issue of exactly what David was doing to get everyone eating out of his hand so soon and with so little contribution to the cake rota.

'Sure!' said Emily, scanning the menu in the cafe for a pudding. 'Don't tell me – you want to start bringing a horse into sessions? Or making everyone sing their presenting issue as if they're in a musical?'

'No, it's a family thing, not really my area of expertise. What's the best way to handle contact from an estranged parent?'

Emily looked up. 'Adult or child? How long an estrangement?'

'An adult, parent walked out when they were ten. Messy divorce.'

'Uh-huh. And no contact in that time?'

'Sporadic up to university, since then a few phone calls. Nothing significant. It's someone I've been helping down at the crisis centre,' she added quickly. 'Her dad heard about the floods on the news; now he's got in touch. She's not sure what to do.'

Which was accurate enough.

Why don't you just tell Emily the truth? Tara asked herself, but the embarrassment scorching through her was enough of an answer. She maintained strict work/home boundaries for this very reason. Work Tara was a friendly professional, with an out-of-focus home life that had only come into focus when her mum died. It wouldn't make her look particularly good as a counsellor, Tara felt, if it emerged she hadn't spoken to her dad in years and had never questioned her mum's obsessive collecting of Sindy dolls. Not to mention her own broken engagement and the Phil Shawcross situation. When it came to rocky relationships, the Centre team were *all* marriage guidance counsellors, even Harry the sports masseur. It had been worth swapping her engagement ring to the other finger each morning and sacrificing the whip-round toaster not to have suffered the collective sympathy when she and Justin split up.

Emily ordered a slice of carrot cake ('The big bit on the end, please, not that slice with no icing') and turned back to Tara. 'And does this client *want* to re-establish contact?'

'Not sure. I mean, she's got a lot on her plate as it is, with the flooding.'

'You don't feel this might be an opportunity for reconciliation?' Emily was looking at her intently and Tara wondered if her cheeks were as red as they felt. 'Something positive coming out of a bad situation?'

'No, I mean, I don't know. He's quite a . . . The father sounds quite a chaotic personality. Emotionally.'

'OK. Well, I usually suggest a letter as a starting point, more for the client than for whoever they're writing to. Sometimes it's the first time they're seeing what they feel set down in black and white. It clarifies the situation, and also defuses some initial emotion.' Emily's cake arrived and after a brief check of the icing level, she nodded at the waitress. 'Whether they then decide to *send* the letter is another discussion.'

'Uh-huh.' Tara had written a fair few letters to her father over the years, most of them during the compulsory therapy during her own training. All of them remained unsent – and only sometimes because she didn't have a forwarding address.

'Having said that,' Emily resumed, in a warning tone, 'I strongly encourage clients to explore what exactly they want from renewed contact before taking it further. What they want *realistically* – not what their inner ten-year-old is hoping will happen. It's hard for children of any age to stop idolizing an absent parent, even when they can see as adults what damage they've caused. Or indeed, holding them responsible for the resident parent's version of events.'

'Mmm.'

'It's funny, isn't it?' She waved her fork at Tara. 'The problems *I* see over and over with family therapy end up being ones *you* have to fix.'

'How do you mean?' asked Tara warily.

'Women sabotaging their lives with feckless commitment-phobes exactly like their dads. Furious men-children who want revenge on womankind because Mummy left.' Emily dug enthusiastically into her cake. 'Why don't you suggest she books in for some separate family therapy? I'll give her fifty per cent off her first session.'

'Thanks,' said Tara. 'That's very helpful.'

It took Tara several hours to write her email to Keith.

Deliberating over how to address him took half an hour. The rest of the message looked wrong with *Dear Dad* at the beginning, to the point where no other words would come, and *Dear Keith* was even worse, so in the end she took it out altogether and started off with a non-committal *Hello*.

> *I've been thinking a lot about your visit – why you came, what you said, what you didn't say. I take your point about having to start somewhere, but is there any point in starting?*
>
> *I don't know what we can offer each other – two virtual strangers – at this stage in our lives. I'm not interested in reminiscing about a past we probably remember very*

differently. I've spent years working through the issues you created, and my focus is on the future which I can control, not the past, which I can't. And I don't need a father figure. Mum did a great job on her own.

This probably isn't the email you were hoping for, and I'm sorry. One thing I've learned through my work is that you have to be clear about expectations, with other people but most importantly with yourself. My life is already pretty stressful, and I don't need the additional stress of you dropping in and out of contact once or twice a year, purely to satisfy the idea of 'being in touch' with a daughter you don't really know. I'm not the little girl you left. I'm much better and much worse than her.

But thanks for the nice words about Mum. We did have some happy times in the house, you're right.

Love from Tara

Tara looked at the words on the screen – too formal, not really her – and pressed send. She didn't even know if she'd get a reply, but at least it made her feelings plain to herself, if no one else.

Once she'd sent it, she turned her attention to the other painful task of the evening (why spoil two nights?): forwarding Justin's post.

Tara and Justin had lived at 16 Otterburn Lane for three years and six months, and had entwined their lives to the point where mail addressed jointly still turned up in her redirection service.

Seeing Justin's post mixed up with hers didn't make Tara sad. The calling-off of their engagement seemed to upset Ruth more than Tara – 'Can't you give it another go? Justin's perfect for you!' – but as Tara had muttered many, many times to herself, Ruth wasn't the one who had to stand there listening to Justin opine self-righteously about how he simply didn't see colour or gender at work, while she did the washing-up.

Their relationship had been petering out when Justin was offered a golden promotion opportunity at a hospital trust in the north-east. He'd dropped this bombshell at his sister's wedding, at which Tara's mind had been made up anyway when the bride threw the bouquet directly at her and she'd accidentally elbowed a junior bridesmaid in the face, trying to avoid it. After that, their engagement was over in the time it had taken for Justin to calculate how much she owed him for the washing machine he was graciously leaving in their rented house.

Tara stuffed a brown envelope with charity circulars, a Save the Date from one of Justin's friends (clearly not a close friend) and his alumni magazine from Edinburgh University.

Edinburgh was David's old university too; he had his degree framed on the wall. Tara stared at the cover – fresh-faced students engaged in some sort of performance art – and a thought occurred to her out of nowhere.

Was David one of The Four Ceps?

Ironically – for someone who now displayed minimal sense of humour as a badge of honour – Justin had been in a med-school comedy group at university: 'Footlights but for real people,' as he put it. The Four Ceps (there were twelve of them, ha ha) had done two Edinburgh Festivals, and garnered zero reviews, but the way Justin talked about his 'comedy background', you'd think he'd turned down his own BBC Two sitcom in favour of a career in hospital trust management.

Tara opened up her laptop again. She'd never actually met any of The Four Ceps but Justin had talked about them *a lot* in the early days of their relationship, before some of their 'routines' became socially unacceptable. Ben, Ryan, Tom, Dave, the other ones . . .

Justin had blocked her on Facebook – or she'd blocked him, it happened very quickly – so she couldn't check whether he was still friends with David, but Google Images threw up a handful of images of 'The Four Ceps Edinburgh' and she peered at the screen.

Baby-faced men in white lab coats, posing with a kooky selection of props. Justin was in the middle, his blond hair backcombed into Einstein-like craziness. There was so little of it left now that Tara felt almost nostalgic on its behalf.

Then – wow. Tara peered closer. Yes! That was definitely him, David Dalloway, back row, far left. There were no details on the web page other than that they were medical students from Edinburgh University, but it *was* him: a bit more brown fringe falling into his eyes, a bit less multi-diploma confidence, but yes. Dr David.

Oh no, thought Tara, as half-forgotten snippets of Justin's witterings gathered together like iron filings to form some actual facts. *If that's him, then Dr David must be HYPNO Dave.*

Hypno Dave's party trick, which Justin had thought hilarious at the beginning of their relationship and then backed away from very sharply as he got promoted, was to hypnotize people. Hence the name. And he was very good at it: according to Justin, he'd once put two prop forwards 'under' and convinced them that they were on *Strictly Come Dancing*, leading to some 'potentially career-ending photos, ha ha!' Rumour (Justin) had it, he had also hypnotized his way into the rooms of several of the more attractive female medics.

'He is an absolute legend,' Justin had insisted, misreading Tara's stunned expression for approval, rather than horror. 'An absolute banter-meister.'

'Well, now it makes sense,' she said aloud, and was surprised how disappointed she felt. She'd thought he was better than that, with his qualifications and nice office furniture. David wasn't just the kind of smug knob who made other people look stupid for fun, but if his success rate was down to some sort of hypnotherapy, why wasn't he being honest about it? And what were the pets about – a distraction?

She looked at Sybil, stretched across the back of the chair. 'Maybe he's grown out of it,' she said, and Sybil swished her tail.

Tara pushed the rest of Justin's post into the envelope, then sealed it with a sigh. Experience had led her to believe that no one really grew out of anything. They just found better excuses for it.

This new knowledge put a different spin on their scheduled 'chat' about David's first month on the Wellness Centre team.

Tara was already on edge. That morning, David's reputation as a miracle worker had taken another leap when Eric Fitzpatrick, one half of world-class marital argument tag team the Fitzpatricks, had suddenly burst into tears and admitted something to his stunned wife Sheila that had caused her to hug him for the first time in seven years.

'I can't say what, obviously, but I feel Eric's had a break-through,' David had explained later in the kitchen, under pressure from everyone who'd seen the Fitzpatricks leaving arm in arm. Tara stared at him with new suspicion – had he hypnotized perpetually fuming Eric into an apology? – but everyone else had been impressed. Particularly their old counsellor Jacqueline, who had sent them to ballroom dancing classes so many times the local teacher had had to beg her to stop as the stamping was ruining her dance floor.

'I was totally wrong about David,' mused Kasia, as he excused himself to go to his next appointment, 'he really does seem to *get* people. Like, really get them.'

'I thought that too!' Hero widened her eyes. 'Normally people with that many degrees can't . . . feel.' She extended her upturned palms in illustration of what feeling might feel like.

'And he smells lovely,' added Emily, almost to herself.

Tara boggled at her. Emily was the hardest to impress out of anyone: she'd nearly reduced Bryan to tears, unpicking his understanding of free will.

'They've been coming here for ages – there had to be a breakthrough eventually,' she pointed out. 'They've probably spent more on therapy than they did on their wedding.'

Emily rolled her eyes. 'Where's the romance in your soul? Come on.'

'Yeah!' said Hero, possibly the first time she and Emily had agreed about anything ever.

Bloody hell, thought Tara, irritably. *Maybe they're all on the crystals now.*

'So, as I'm sure I don't need to tell someone as experienced as you,' Tara began, self-consciously shuffling her pen and notebook on the cafe table, 'this is an opportunity for you to discuss any issues you might be having with your current clients. Or even with the Centre itself. It's confidential so—'

'Sorry, Tara? Can I stop you there? I did tell Jacqueline – I've got an external supervisor lined up,' said David. 'An old colleague from my last clinic. He confirmed yesterday.'

'Oh.' Jacqueline could have said something. 'Oh, well, I guess that's better.'

'I really appreciate your offering, though.' David smiled, holding her gaze in an affable manner. 'At least let me get you lunch to say thanks. I mean, I do *have* questions. Like, that positivity tree in the foyer. Does anyone check it?' He leaned forward. 'And what are you supposed to write?'

Tara tried not to see David in a lab coat surrounded by gurning medical students. Was he trying to hypnotize her? She blinked hard, then looked away. She'd been hypnotized once before, many years ago, and she definitely hadn't enjoyed it.

'It depends,' she said. 'Buy me a coffee and I'll tell you everything you need to know.'

The coffees arrived, and they discussed the cake rota, the impact of the floods on appointments, and topics to avoid in the kitchen during the full moon. David ordered another round. The question Tara was itching to ask, though, was which side of the credibility canyon did he fall on? David's expression wasn't giving much away.

'So how do we compare with your last practice?' she asked. 'Was it a similar sort of set-up?'

'Oh, totally. Totally different. Not that it isn't . . . um . . .' David hunted for the right word. '. . . interesting, to see traditional therapy sitting next to more holistic approaches.'

'Interesting.' What did that mean? That he took crystal healing seriously or not?

'The practice dealt mainly with clinical referrals,' he explained. 'A lot more psychiatric evaluation, working alongside the hospital, the court system, police. Quite tough going, sometimes. But that's the same for everyone, isn't it? Nothing's easy.'

Tara found her guard rising, despite herself. She knew deep down – well, not very deep down, quite close to the surface, actually – that David's impressive qualifications poked her right on her Achilles heel: her professional development.

Tara knew she could have done further training. No, not could, *should* have. She'd had the time. She'd definitely had the ability. But she'd always found reasons not to. There'd been her workload, and Justin, and Mum . . . She knew herself well enough to identify the true reason, though. More qualifications meant more therapy, more probing around the darker corners of her psyche. And Tara had done all the talking she wanted to do about Keith Hunter.

Jacqueline and the other therapists thought Tara was hugely capable but she knew that was down to her practical solution-led approach. You didn't have to have a psychology masters for that – everyone loved a to-do list. But more and more, during the floods, Tara wished she had something more to fall back on to help her clients. And more and more she worried that someone would catch her out. Someone who *had* done the exams.

David was still talking. 'I like to think that every approach to understanding has its own particular . . .' He stopped, then squeezed the bridge of his nose.

'Sorry, is the sun in your eyes?' Tara looked round. Only two other tables were occupied: one couple sharing a slice of chocolate cake, and a woman with a Basset Hound that was gazing straight at David. The sun had come out and was streaming through the big windows, although not into David's face, as such.

If anything, David seemed to be staring at the dog.

'No. Just hay fever.' He blinked hard. 'Lost my thread. Where were we?'

'Do you know Justin Biggins?' The words spilled over from Tara's brain into her mouth. She frowned. Maybe he *had* hypnotized her.

'Justin . . . ?'

'You were at university together? At Edinburgh?'

David's expression cleared. 'Oh, Justin! Yes. With the . . . hair.' He mimed a sort of wild bush around his head. 'Nice chap.'

'He's a friend,' she said, then corrected herself. Better to be honest. 'Ex-boyfriend, actually. But still a friend,' Tara elaborated, and immediately wondered why. Why was she telling him this? She clamped her lips together, but not before 'Nothing bad happened' slipped out.

'Ah,' said David, because what else could he say?

'He told me a lot about you,' she said, then added, 'and what you all got up to.' It was only fair that he knew *she* knew about his party trick.

But David just shrugged amiably, as if she'd discovered he was christened Sextus or liked taxidermy. 'If you mean that comedy troupe we were in, it wasn't exactly Monty Python,' he said. 'It was barely the Chuckle Brothers. Things you do when you're young, eh?' He paused, then looked at her sideways. 'Since we're on the topic . . . Do you mind if I ask *you* a personal question?'

Tara braced herself. What had Justin told him? 'Um, yes?'

'Taransay? Very unusual name – do you have a connection with the island?'

She stirred her coffee. That meant David must have researched her; she never used her full name at work. 'My parents were on holiday in Scotland when, um . . .' She tapped her spoon on the edge of the cup. She'd tried to train herself out of the embarrassment but it never quite went. 'My twin brother's called Tobermory. My parents were quite . . . creative types.'

Narcissistic, more like. I mean, what kind of parent gives their children names that literally conjure up mental images of holiday sex every time they introduce themselves? Muscling in on every introduction for the rest of her life, looming up behind her like the hippie couple from *The Joy of Sex*.

'And how does that make you feel?' David asked, one eyebrow raised.

No one, outside a therapist's office, had ever asked her that.

Their eyes met, and Tara felt a funny sliding sensation inside, as if half of her wanted to pull up the drawbridge, while the other half wanted to tell David everything.

'We're Tara and Toby,' she said. 'What was it you wanted to know about Jacqueline's positivity tree?'

Back in the office kitchen, the noticeboard had been overhauled with stars and cut-out trainers, and there was a new hand-drawn chart in the middle.

Jacqueline bustled in behind them before Tara could comment. 'Just the pair I was looking for. After Kasia's *inspiring* talk I thought I'd implement one of her ideas, and boost our community harmony at the same time. Here you go, one each.' She pressed a plastic gadget into their hands.

'Is this a pedometer?' David examined it.

'Exactly!' Jacqueline nodded. 'We're going to have a Wellness Centre Step Challenge. To make things fairer, everyone's in teams of two, and it's your combined step score that gets counted at the end of the week. Whoever has the highest total at the end of six weeks will win a magnificent prize.'

'How magnificent?' asked Tara.

Jacqueline's smile didn't falter. 'I haven't decided yet. But I want us to try to walk the length of the M6! I paired everyone up over lunch, and since you two were out, we popped you into a team in your absence. If that's all right?'

Tara stole a sideways glance at David. He had long, rangy legs: he seemed like the type to walk everywhere. In fact, compared with most people in the office (Hero: mostly sitting in lotus position; Bryan: retired from sports, except armchair rugby; Chloe: 'allergic' to fruit and vegetables, etc.), he wasn't a bad pick.

'Fine with me,' said David. 'You walk into work already, don't you?' he added, turning to Tara.

'Er, yes.' Something about the way he said it caught her off balance. How did he know that?

'Yes, Tara's setting a *wonderful* example with our Ditch the Drive initiative.' Jacqueline beamed.

'I like to incorporate a walk into my morning routine, yes,' she said carefully. 'I find it helps me run through my schedule in my mind.'

'Absolutely. It must help you *park* some of your stress for the day.' David's face was completely straight but there was a glimmer in his brown eyes.

'Good-o,' said Jacqueline, oblivious to Tara's sudden coughing fit. 'I'll pop you on the chart as Davara, if that's all right? Just a bit of fun! Chloe suggested doing celebrity combo names, and we thought Tarvid sounded a bit . . . icky.'

David nodded in agreement as Tara struggled to think how she could pull this back, but before she could come up with anything, he was clipping the pedometer on to his trouser pocket and pumping his arms as he strolled out of the kitchen towards the reception area, where a man and a Weimaraner were waiting for him.

Chapter Six

One June morning, summer arrived with unusual energy, as if to make up for the miserable weeks before. Under the cloudless blue skies and glorious sunshine, the famous rose beds in the town's municipal gardens burst into spectacular life, which Tara thought was some compensation for the lunchtimes now spent pounding round the park with David, listening to him deliver fascinating local-history nuggets like an off-duty tour guide. She tried to resist, claiming conversation interfered with her breathing patterns, but he seemed determined to find a way to make her talk, even if it was only to challenge whether the bandstand really was the site of an original Roman temple.

But inside her consulting room, the floods still lingered.

Sonia Wozniak's face was grey, like her mood. 'The clearing-up's messing with my head more than the actual flood, if I'm honest. Have you been into a flooded house? You know what it smells like?'

Tara nodded. She'd helped rake the mud out of houses, and the smell had been stomach-turning; she'd had to stop to retch every so often. The lingering aftermath of water that had filtered through sodden fields, through drains, through drowned vermin: a reek of decomposition that clung to the inside of your nose long after you'd left.

'Well, I feel like I can't stop smelling it,' Sonia went on, 'everywhere I go, even now everything's clean. It got everywhere. *Everywhere*. Even the tiniest little speck on something, and I had to throw it away. Precious things. Josie's baby stuff. We started off trying to bleach things but Chris just got a skip in the end. I cried, Tara. I just sat down on the steps and cried.'

'I'm sorry. That must be very hard.'

'My partner's OCD's off the scale,' Sonia went on. 'He's obsessed with what might have been in the water. Parasites, germs, chemicals, dead things. I don't think we'll ever be able to go back.' She wiped her eyes and stared out of the window.

'Are you still at your mum's?'

She nodded bleakly. 'I can't bring the kids home. All their toys are in the skip outside. I have to walk past it every day. That's our life.'

Tara was conscious of her phone buzzing on the desk. She always had it set to silent during sessions. As usual, her first thought was: *Phil?* followed by a series of calculations: seven weeks since he'd dropped Sybil off at her house 'just for a few nights'; two weeks since she'd watched him lever himself off her bed and saunter naked into the ensuite, whistling the theme from *Top Gear*.

But unusually, Phil vanished, to be replaced by a new possibility: Dad.

This time Tara's stomach did a proper anxious roll, followed up with a patter of panic in her chest. She glanced at the phone out of the corner of her eye. He hadn't replied to her email yet. Maybe this was it.

'Tara?'

Sonia was glaring at her.

'Sorry, Sonia, I was just . . .' There was no excuse for getting distracted during sessions. It was the one thing she could promise her clients: her focused attention. 'Last time we discussed a self-care plan. How's that going? Getting enough sleep's so important.'

'I wish. We're on my mum's sofa in a sleeping bag. It smells of mice.' Sonia looked exhausted. 'Sounds stupid now, but I'd literally just bought everyone new bedding in the sales. Really nice stuff, I'd been saving up for it.'

Impulsively, Tara reached behind her desk. 'Listen, I was going to take this down to the crisis centre in case someone needed it, but would you like this bedding? It's new, hasn't even been out of the packet. I've got a duvet in the car, if you want that?'

'Really?' Sonia peered into the bag, then looked up, overwhelmed. 'You're sure?'

'I'm clearing out my mum's house. She had an interiors business.' Two hours Tara had spent 'sorting' the previous night, and she'd barely emptied one tightly packed cupboard of pillow cases, duvet covers, linen and 800-thread-count cotton. It was the fourth cupboard she'd tackled, and still she'd found almost nothing personal. No photos, no school reports, no hoarded hand-scribbled cards or tiny stuffed school-trip teddy bears. Twenty scented candles, though. Tara wondered if she should have donated them too, to help with the smell, or if it would come across as flippant.

'This is amazing, thank you.' Sonia hugged the bag to her chest. 'You didn't get any flooding up your way, then?'

'No, we're on a hill. Didn't reach us.'

'Lucky you.'

Tara nodded. Lucky her.

She checked her phone as soon as Sonia had left, but didn't recognize the missed-call number. That didn't mean it wasn't Phil, of course. He frequently rang from numbers she didn't recognize; 'I'm on the office mobile,' he'd say airily by way of explanation.

There was no message. Was it Dad? Should she phone him back, just in case?

Tara put her phone down, then picked it up again. Then put it down. What did he want? What would she say? What would *he* say? She needed to be in a calm space, when she'd had time to plan her responses, so they were dignified and memorable. Ideally when she knew what *he* was going to say.

An embarrassingly loud rumble broke her train of thought, and she checked her watch. It was ten past three. She'd worked through her lunch break, and the sandwiches she'd packed for lunch had been eaten long before her second client arrived at half past ten.

Food first, she decided, and headed down to the kitchen to forage for snacks. It was Harry's turn to provide the Cake of the Week, and thanks to the note propped up next to it, inviting colleagues to guess the 'surprise mystery ingredient!', there hadn't been any takers so far. Cake of the Week was a popular tradition in the Wellness Centre, especially since the vegans and sugar-refusers felt they had something to prove to the chocolate-addicted. Most cakes didn't last beyond the first socially acceptable coffee break of the day; if it got to three and no one had braved the first slice, Jacqueline snuck in, cut a piece and carried it away at arm's length, to spare everyone's feelings.

This would have to do, thought Tara, eyeing Harry's oily green icing with some suspicion, and cut into it with the big knife.

As she was psyching herself up to swallow the first lumpy forkful (cornflour? Courgettes? Piccalilli?), her phone rang, and automatically, rather than eat the cake, she put down the fork and answered the phone instead.

A familiar voice said, 'Hello, Tara, it's Dad. Is this a good time to talk?'

The fluttery feeling returned. Tara glanced at the old clock that loomed over the tea urn, for reassurance. 'Um, it depends what you want to talk about. I'm at work. I've got a client at half past.'

Was her hand shaking? Her knees felt wobbly. All the effort of sounding unbothered was going into her voice. She was glad her dad couldn't see her. The hot-water urn was reflecting a red shape where her face was.

'OK, well, I'll make it quick. I just wanted to say thank you for your email and to apologize again. I can see now how unfair it was. I really am sorry if you felt ambushed. That's the last thing I meant to do. The very last thing.'

Tara had half expected the apology – Mum had always said Dad did a good apology – but she hadn't expected it to sound so contrite.

'You're right, I should have called ahead,' he went on. Tara noted, in a distant, rational corner of her brain, that he didn't take the easy route of blaming Toby for not tipping her off. 'But it was really good to see you and I appreciated the cup of tea.' He paused. 'And what you said in your email about your mum – that she was loved and happy. I'm glad. Glad to know that too.'

Again, the emotion in his voice took Tara by surprise. This wasn't the Dad she'd been expecting. The selfish bastard who did what he liked, never bothering with an actual apology when an expensive bunch of flowers would do the job. Tara's mouth had gone dry. Weirdly, now *she* felt bad for upbraiding him.

Which is exactly how he gets away with it, sighed her mother's voice in the back of her mind. Or was it her own counselling training?

'Tara? Are you still there?'

'Yes. Yes, I'm here. I'm just . . .' Just what? She didn't know.

'Another thing – I've been thinking about these floods, and I was wondering if there was anything I could do? I mean, with this community action group you're involved with? I can put you in touch with a grant hunter, for a start – Jake's brilliant at tracking down funding and charities and whatnot, to get projects up and running. And if you needed someone to have a look at that village hall that was affected – Troutbridge, wasn't it? – we could send someone to assess the structural damage.'

'Wow,' said Tara. Even the way he was talking about it, so positive and upbeat, felt light years away from the growing weariness overwhelming the volunteers now. They were tired, and mostly out of their depth, especially on matters of building work, as well as conscious that there was almost no money available to help the people turning to them for answers. 'We'd appreciate any help. But there's no budget,' she added. 'We can't pay you.'

'Don't worry about that. We've got a company commitment to provide a certain number of hours pro bono for community projects. There wouldn't be any charge. I can send you a link to our website, you can see some of the things we've been involved with. We built an outdoor community kitchen last year: sustainable vegetable beds, solar panels for the ovens – that sort of thing. Playgrounds are another popular one. We do a good playground!'

It sounded too good to be true. 'Is there a catch? If I say yes, do we have to be in a documentary?'

'Ha! No! No catch. I just want to help. I admire what you've done, Tara. It takes a lot of energy to rebuild after flooding. And I know expertise and time are sometimes more useful than cash.'

Tara stared at Harry's greasy cake, already crumbling on the plate, its mystery ingredient still undetected. Dad's voice hadn't changed, unlike his physical appearance. When she saw him again, that too would be less strange. The real ghost was the man in between, the man with her dad's face who'd lived most of Tara's life in a different family, in a different place. Still her dad, but with no interest in anything she'd done, anything she'd achieved.

And NOW he's proud of you? Her mother's voice again, eyebrow arched.

She'd left it too long to reply.

'It's just a suggestion,' said Keith breezily. Too breezily, maybe? 'If you don't think it's a good idea . . .'

Tara thought of Sonia's wrecked house. The food bank. The people without beds, without pets, without the comfort of their homes. She'd be churlish to refuse help, just because she wasn't sure of her dad's motives. Wouldn't she?

'It's a kind offer,' she said. 'But you need to speak to Alice, she's the parish council contact.'

'Brilliant,' said Keith, 'send me her details.'

As she walked back to her room, two things occurred to Tara. One was that her dad hadn't mentioned Toby once – neither to dob him in for not warning her, nor to ask how he was – and the other, as the cake began its quick retreat up her throat, was that Harry's secret ingredient was probably spinach.

Tara had one more appointment before the end of her working day: the Wilsons, a disastrously matched couple who'd been on the verge of divorce before the floods, but who had now achieved an unexpected rapprochement after spending two weeks in emergency accommodation without any of the things (his road bike, her parents, an unemptied dishwasher) that used to give the other the red mist. The floods, Tara conceded, had done more to bring them back together than she had.

She was packing up her bag when there was a knock on the door, and Jacqueline's head popped round.

'Good time for a word?'

'Of course.' Tara put her bag down as Jacqueline was already making her way in, heading for the sofa. 'Cup of tea?'

'Peppermint, please. Kasia's advised me to give up caffeine after lunch and I must say I'm feeling the benefits! You should try it!'

'Ha ha ha!' said Tara, which was as polite as she could manage off the top of her head.

As she flicked the kettle on under her desk, Tara rapidly considered the options: something to do with David?

Had he tipped Jacqueline off about her driving to work? Had Harry's cake been declared unsafe to consume?

'I see you've got your own kettle in here!' Jacqueline observed, sweetly.

'Well, for clients, really. And sometimes there's a bit of a crush in the kitchen and I don't have a lot of time . . .'

The kitchen was big enough to host a low-key wedding. They both knew the reason Tara's kettle was there was so she could avoid mingling.

'And sometimes I'm in the zone and don't feel like chatting,' Tara admitted, under the pleasant scrutiny of Jacqueline's gaze. 'Don't want to seem rude. You know what it's like. I need my coffee. I don't have time to get into a discussion about caffeine after lunch. Well, not until my workload eases off a bit! Ha ha!'

'Well, yes. Although sharing our opinions is what makes this such a vibrant place to work, I always think.'

Bollocks, thought Tara, hunting for the herbal tea bags. This was going to be about the Magic Divide, wasn't it? Had Emily been bitching about dowsing again? It wouldn't be the first time Jacqueline had had to tell Emily to 'share some professional respect' with the unicorn fringe. Was there a discreet way she could slip on Hero's crystal bracelet? It was gathering dust in her drawer – conveniently one of the 'hollow spaces' Hero had been talking about fixing. She slid it on as she pulled out the peppermint tea, and whatever the black bits were dug into her wrist.

But Jacqueline didn't seem to want to talk about that. 'How are things? There's so much going on for you right now, I feel we should be checking in with you a bit more.'

'Oh, fine,' said Tara guardedly. Did Jacqueline mean

her mum dying? Or just the floods? When you put it like that, she thought, there was quite a lot.

'Getting plenty of rest?' Jacqueline reached out for the mug of peppermint tea Tara was offering her. 'And support? Because as Kasia was saying just the other day, self-care is such an important—'

On cue, Tara's phone rang and she turned it over without looking at the screen.

'Sorry, Jacqueline, self-care?'

'Self-care and boundaries between—'

It rang again, and Tara clicked it to voicemail with an apologetic look. 'Keeping busy works for me,' she said, which was true.

Jacqueline sighed and gave her the familiar 'Are you sure you've told me everything, Alfie?' look that had been so effective in her previous career. Tara didn't bite; there were things Jacqueline didn't need to know.

'So!' She sipped her own mug of peppermint tea. It was basically hot scented water. 'What was it you wanted to chat about?'

'As you know,' said Jacqueline, settling back on to the sofa, 'I've been juggling home and work recently too.'

Tara nodded. What was Jacqueline talking about? Was it her husband who'd had the knee replacement? Or her son? She kicked herself: she *never* used to forget this sort of detail, but lately the pressures of work had developed unsettling sinkholes in her brain.

'I'm *so* sad it's come to this,' Jacqueline went on, 'but I've been advised by the specialist that I have to scale right back – apparently stress is a major factor in irritable bowel syndrome.'

'Ah yes,' said Tara quickly. IBS. She knew it was

something medical. 'So I've heard. The coffee probably doesn't help either.'

Jacqueline gave her an 'Exactly!' look. 'But it leaves me with an *impossible* choice. Do I reduce my practice hours, or step back as Centre Director? I can't do both.'

Tara continued nodding, although now her brain was flipping through a *Guess Who?* version of the rest of the staff, trying to recall who it was who'd had the knee replacement. She made an effort to focus. Jacqueline seemed to be asking her for advice.

'Your own health has to come first, Jacqueline,' she said. 'Oxygen masks, planes, and all that.'

Jacqueline sighed. 'That's what Paul says.'

Paul was Jacqueline's husband; from what Tara could remember of him from the last Summer Party, he spoke entirely in management jargon.

'So, strictly between us,' Jacqueline leaned forward, 'what would your feelings be, were the director's role to become vacant, as it were?'

'What?' Tara was caught on the hop: she hadn't expected Jacqueline to sacrifice her team-leader role for her counselling, which was, at best, the therapy equivalent of a supermarket Lemsip. 'Me?'

She nodded. 'Obviously it's got to be advertised externally, but my greatest wish – as a team member myself – is that the board appoints someone from within our community. Someone who *understands* the dynamics and history of the Centre. Someone who truly cares. And can also operate spreadsheets.'

Tara's heart beat faster. She had often daydreamed about changes she would make to the Centre, if she were in charge. Mainly tactical changes to personnel – a bit like Fantasy Football, but with more psychoanalysts and fewer mistletoe therapists. 'What would it involve?'

'Oh, you know what I do, more or less!' Jacqueline waved her hands. 'Admin, reporting to the trustees, talking to the accountants, allocating clients to the right counsellor . . . Of course, the time you can allocate to your practice is limited, but to compensate for that there is, of course, a salary.'

Tara realized her hands were shaking. She put down her mug before she spilled her own peppermint tea. A salary. This was the answer to her house problem! If she had a salary, she could get a mortgage. If she could get a mortgage for Toby's half of the house, she could give him what was rightfully his and stay on in an architect-designed dream home she'd never otherwise be able to afford. Everyone was a winner.

She took a deep, shuddery breath and glanced at her wrist. Maybe there *was* something in Hero's crystals.

Jacqueline leaned forward to indicate she was imparting something she strictly shouldn't. There was a reason, Tara realized, this conversation wasn't happening in Jacqueline's own office.

'One thing I feel I should mention, off the record.' Her eyes darted towards the door. 'The trustees are very committed to the holistic nature of the therapy provision here. If you went for the Centre Director role, you'd have to persuade them you'd be fighting for the *whole* centre.'

Tara sat up straighter in her chair. 'How do you mean?'

'I think it's fair to say that you rather *lean towards* one branch of the Centre's practitioners over the other.'

'No, I don't!'

'Oh, *Tara*. Hand on heart, you don't really believe that

94

Hero and Anji and our more . . . esoteric colleagues are quite on the same plane as the traditional counsellors.'

That was the thing about Jacqueline: she had a way of making you feel not exactly guilty, but as if you'd let yourself, and the school, down. Tara started backpedalling. 'Well, obviously my own practice is theory-based, but I've always said, as long as the client believes in the benefits of a course of therapy then . . .'

'. . . you'll overlook the fact that you think it's a lot of tosh.'

'What? No! I fully respect their training and commitment to . . . alternative belief systems.'

Had that sounded convincing? Tara wasn't sure.

Jacqueline fished out her tea bag with the purple biro she always seemed to have about her person. 'Even angel therapy?'

Tara couldn't stop her eyes rolling. 'Angel therapy' was Anji's latest offering, and proving depressingly/wonderfully popular. 'Come on, Jacqueline. If there *are* such things as angels, don't you think we should be encouraging them to sort out the Middle East? Or liaise with the crystals to eradicate flu viruses? Instead of wasting their time consoling someone from Yarrold whose cat's gone missing?'

'Tara!'

'I'm sorry.' She kicked herself; this wasn't Emily sitting in front of her. Or Bryan. 'I didn't mean that to sound dismissive. My aim's exactly the same as everyone else's here – engaging clients in positive thought and helping them to create strategies for a happier life. Via whichever route works best for them.'

'I'm not saying I agree or disagree with you, but you have to take a different stance when you're representing everyone.' Jacqueline looked over the edge of her mug. 'It's not just you; I've noticed there's a bit of what we used to call playground division going on. Hence my new strategies to foster a bit more team spirit.'

Tara's heart sank. They'd been here before. The last 'team spirit' challenge had involved the various therapists drawing each other in charcoal. Emily hadn't spoken to Kemi, Anji or Kasia for six months, and a hurt Bryan had gone on a juice cleanse that had had unpleasant side effects for everyone.

'Besides,' Jacqueline added, 'everyone benefits from having their belief systems challenged from time to time. You can get stuck in your own rut. This peppermint tea, for example – it's made a real difference to my IBS.'

Tara noticed the jagged chunk of rose quartz dangling over Jacqueline's bosom. She wondered which crystal was best for IBS. Apache tears? Wasn't that about protecting voids?

'So, anyway, have a think. I haven't mentioned this to anyone else, and I'd be grateful if you could keep my stepping back between ourselves. There'll be an announcement in the next fortnight or so.' Jacqueline gave her a stagy wink. 'But I wanted to give you the heads-up. Perhaps have a think about how you might, ah, jumble things up a bit.'

'Of course,' said Tara, but her mind was already doing sums.

Chapter Seven

Tara hadn't intended to join the official committee set-up in the aftermath of the flooding, but somehow the group WhatsApp of lead volunteers had morphed into a formal arrangement once money started flowing in from various sources, and here she was, at ten past six on a Wednesday night, back in the meeting room of Longhampton town hall with a cup of lukewarm tea and a council-branded notepad in front of her.

'Are we all here?' Catherine Chambers from the Citizens Advice was minuting the meeting. She was wearing the exhausted expression of a woman who'd already spent a long day untangling problems. 'Can we crack on?'

The chairs, arranged in a UN-style horseshoe, were full apart from one seat, next to Tara.

'Diane said she'd be late but to start without her,' said a woman from the council. 'Food bank emergency.'

'We'll make a start,' Catherine decided. 'There's a lot to get through.'

And there was. Thirty-two people from Watling Avenue were still in temporary accommodation, unable to get back into their houses because of structural damage; the council was taking longer than hoped to get the debris cleared from several streets; there were no skips left in the whole county. Potholes, overflowing drains, abandoned dogs, subsidence in the graveyard: the list went on. Not much of it was quickly fixed.

'Tara, I've got more requests for counselling, I'm afraid.' Catherine passed her a list of names. 'We've had a rush in the last few days. You did warn us this might happen, once people got over the initial shock.'

'The second wave, as it were.' The bearded police liaison officer whose name Tara could never remember grinned, pleased with himself, and Catherine tutted half-heartedly.

'I'll see what I can do.' She ran her eye down the dozens of names and contact details and wondered how on earth she was going to fit these people into her diary. Time to appeal to the other counsellors at the Centre to volunteer a couple of sessions a week. Maybe the angels could turn the standing water on Watling Avenue into disinfectant. Or gin.

'Anyone else got something to share?' Catherine looked around the chairs. 'Something positive would be nice,' she added plaintively. 'Before we get on to the financial stuff. Which is – spoiler alert – not good news.'

'Well, yes. Actually I've got some very good news to share with you.' Alice Roberts, the parish council representative, shuffled her papers and turned pink.

'Jolly good. We're all ears.'

'Troutbridge Memorial Hall,' she began, and immediately there was a sympathetic groan around the room.

Troutbridge was generally agreed to be the nicest village in the area: one church, four farms, a handful of houses, a pub and a lovely old pre-war hall, used by everyone from NCT mums to spiritualists. Its prime position near the River Martle meant it had been badly affected by the floods, and in the storm that had appeared midway through the rain, as a sort of half-time interlude, an ancient elm had been blown down right on to the Memorial Hall, revealing the oak timbers of the roof like a whale's skeleton against the sky. Tara had felt particularly sad about it: she'd gone to Brownies there, and Ruth had been a regular at Pilates on the parquet floor. It smelled of institutional sage-green teacups and beeswax polish, dust and raffle tickets. The sort of comfortingly Sunday-teatime smell you couldn't recreate in a new building.

As Alice said 'Troutbridge', a funny feeling stirred in Tara's stomach.

'Poor Troutbridge,' murmured Catherine.

'I know, I know. Well, it turns out that the Memorial Hall was somewhat . . . underinsured. Which is a big problem, given the extent of the damage.'

Another glum murmur ran around the table. Underinsurance was something else they knew too much about.

'I thought you said you had good news!' joked the bearded policeman. The new vicar – Louise Hopkins – muttered, 'Give it a rest, Andy,' and Tara remembered he was called Andy Lewis. His beard was the only memorable thing about him.

'Well, this afternoon I had a phone call from a construction expert who's offering to assist with the rebuild!' Alice looked up, her eyes bright. 'His company commits to partnering with one community project per year, and he's offered to come out and assess the whole repair programme, with a view to taking it on.'

Community project. Construction expert. Tara's throat

dried. This had to be Dad. There couldn't be *two* architecture firms offering to help.

'Of course,' Alice went on, 'it would mean *we'd* have to get the necessary permissions moving with the planning department . . .' She looked over at Peter Headley, councillor in charge of building control, who opened his mouth to start his usual spiel about the slow-moving cogs of local government but then shut it, seeing the assembled faces glaring as one at him.

'We'd be mad to put anything in the way of an offer like that.' Rob Lloyd, the local MP, leaned forward. As local politicians went, he wasn't too bad; he'd waded through rivers of slurry alongside the rescue teams, even when the camera crews weren't there. Rob didn't just talk about doing things, like a lot of people; he did them, even if it meant treading on a few toes in his brand-new Hunter wellies. 'Applications can always be fast-tracked, if funding's in place?'

Peter Headley clicked his pen. 'We're in uncharted waters, process-wise. Procedure has to be followed but—'

Rob cut him off. 'Great! Thanks, Peter, we'll take that as a yes. This would be a good news story for the whole community.'

'So who is this white knight in shining armour?' asked Louise the vicar. 'Someone local?'

Butterflies fluttered in Tara's chest. She wasn't sure if she should say something or keep quiet. She turned her phone over on the table and realized it was still on silent. She'd missed two calls. One from her dad, one from Toby.

Now they called her.

Alice consulted her notes. 'It's an architecture firm based

in London, but there's a connection with the area – I think the founder is from here originally? KPH Associates is the name of the firm. I did a quick search online and it's won lots of awards, for, um, eco builds and another one for a hotel, I think, and they worked on something to do with the London Olympics? I mean, it all sounds proper.'

Proper. Yes, Dad was definitely proper. Tara had checked the website herself, to make sure the pro bono stuff wasn't a convenient lie (it wasn't), and this time she'd seen the website with different eyes. The slick international consultancy was her father's. Teams and teams of people worked for him. He was a set of initials, a brand. That was *her* dad.

'Apart from which,' Alice was going on, 'I know Troutbridge parish council have been struggling to find anyone available to even do a quote before September, so even if he magics up some builders to fit some new toilets, this is literally a godsend.'

Tara watched the reactions round the table: surprise, relief, curiosity. Not one of them knew she was connected to him. Not one of them was thinking, *Does this man have an ulterior motive for this act of generosity?* – apart from her. Catherine Chambers was already looking up KPH Associates on her phone, and, going by her expression, was impressed.

Tara took a deep breath and tried to see this from Rob's perspective, or Alice's, or any of the Troutbridge residents missing their weekly yoga or life drawing. It was a dream come true. But now their excitement was real, and the offer was there on the table, all she could see in her mind's eye was the treehouse.

Dad had promised to build a Peter Pan treehouse for her and Toby while they were away on a half-term break with Mum in London. Tara had told her friends at school that they could come round and play in it, even shown them the drawings he'd sketched out for her on his special drawing pad. It would have working shutters, with heart shapes cut out, and a rope swing for Toby, and a promise of some contraption to winch Branston up, if he wanted.

The days in London had passed *so* slowly. They'd talked about the treehouse for the entire train journey home, then ran into the house from the taxi, jumping with excitement to climb up into its leafy frame, only to find Dad asleep on the sofa, smelling of whisky, Branston lying unwalked next to him, tell-tale crisp flakes sticking to his muzzle.

Her mum had said, 'Oh dear, I don't think Daddy's feeling well,' in such a calm voice Tara felt it in the pit of her stomach like a knot.

Back in the meeting room, twenty-five years later, Tara felt that knot of anxiety twist in her stomach again. It had taken a long time to live down the treehouse debacle. Jodi Richardson had been particularly cruel.

Dad wouldn't do that again, though, would he? This was so public. He was *accountable*. And it wasn't for her, it was for the community.

But still she could see Mum's face in the back of her mind; saying nothing, implying everything with one slow shake of her head. She'd done her best to manage Tara's expectations when it came to her dad, especially after he left. *I just hate to see him hurt you, Tara.*

Tara looked up at the committee but they were

102

talking amongst themselves, discussing options for the hall. Every single person looked more cheerful than they had done five minutes earlier. Brighter, as if Keith's spontaneous generosity had flicked on a light bulb inside them.

The treehouse was twenty-five years ago, Tara reminded herself. *And Dad's not doing this himself. He'll send a team. They won't get pissed and forget. They're professionals. And there's social media these days. You can't mess anything up in private any more.*

'I think that's a terrific offer.' Louise Hopkins looked round the room for agreement. 'I find it incredibly heartening that people who don't even live here have seen what we've been through and feel moved to help.'

'What's in it for this company, though? Publicity? Tax write-off?' Peter Headley's irritating pen-clicking increased in volume. 'I've never met a builder who'd do something for nothing.'

'He's not a *builder*, Peter. This man I spoke to is an architect. And he told me he has happy memories of Troutbridge Memorial Hall.' Alice consulted her notes and delivered the final blow. 'He says he took his daughter to Brownies there. So there's a personal angle. I think that's lovely.'

Tara opened her mouth to correct Alice: Dad had never taken her to Brownies. *Mum* had driven her there straight from work, still in her good coat, with Branston slobbering in the back, ever eager for an outing.

Rob Lloyd was looking at her with a raised eyebrow; she closed her mouth without saying anything. Had he made the connection? Hunter was a common enough surname.

Peter wouldn't give up. 'There'll be a catch. Get it in writing that he won't be charging us. I had a builder who—'

Rob turned his attention to his left. 'Peter, honestly – I live just outside Troutbridge, and I've got first-hand experience of how much the local community's missing that hall. Not just Brownies but the knitting club, the dancers, the gardening clubs, baby groups. They're holding meetings in houses to try to keep things going, but we need to get it up and running again. They need to believe life is going back to normal. People do offer pro bono work, you know. It's not always about money.'

'So it's a yes?' Alice's pen was poised over the agenda. 'I'll call him and set up a meeting ASAP?'

'I think so,' said Rob, looking around the room. 'Can't see why not? Anyone? Great. What's next?'

There was a gust of fresh air as the double doors from the hall were pushed open.

'I am *so* sorry I'm late, folks!' Diane appeared in a swirl of scarves and layers, and headed to the spare seat, grabbing a biscuit as she passed the plate. 'What have I missed?'

'I'll fill you in at the end,' said Alice, as Diane scraped her chair back and plumped down. 'We've got a fair bit to push through. Um, next up, it's another plea for accommodation from Janet. She says she's sorry to ask again, but does anyone know of any spare rooms – or anyone with a holiday let, even – we can offer to the Watling Avenue families? Some have got teenagers doing exams and it's a nightmare for them, with revision and so on.'

Everyone made sympathetic noises, particularly Diane. 'It's so hard on the youngsters,' she said.

Tara murmured too, but felt embarrassed. She had spare rooms *and* a garden studio that could sleep two (dogs allowed). She knew she should offer; she wanted to help. But the rooms were still full of her mother's belongings, familiar and unfamiliar possessions she'd barely got round to sorting out, and she couldn't bear the idea of strangers coming in.

It was a crap excuse, and she knew it. She pretended to check the agenda, and hoped her guilt wasn't showing. Between Keith's unexpected intrusion, and now the mental image of strangers unpacking in Mum's spare room, her skin was prickling as though she had heat rash.

'Tara? You OK?' Diane peered over her glasses.

'Yeah, fine.' Tara looked up. 'What's next, Catherine?'

At the end of the meeting, Tara was caught by Rob Lloyd, who wanted her to speak to one of his elderly neighbours.

'She's of the generation who find it hard to ask for help,' he said, pulling on his hoodie. It had Longhampton Rowing Club on the front and LLOYD on the back. He also had, Tara knew from various flood-based shifts, a Longhampton Rugby Club polo shirt, a Longhampton Cricket Club baseball cap, and a Longhampton and District Young Farmers' Club gilet. 'But I sense she needs to talk and I think you could winkle it out of her.'

'I'll do my best,' she said. OK, so it wasn't a no, but wasn't a yes, or a promise. 'Give me her details.'

Rob smiled. He had nice blue eyes. They weren't as

blue as Phil's but that was probably a good thing. 'Thanks, Tara. None of this is going unnoticed, believe me.'

'I don't think—' she started, but was interrupted by a hand on her shoulder and a jangle of bracelets.

'Tara!'

She turned. Diane had finished 'catching up' with Catherine and her grimly set jaw suggested she needed to 'catch up' with Tara too.

'I'll be in touch,' said Rob. 'Night, Diane! Amazing effort on the food bank, by the way – sterling work.'

'Thanks.' Diane generally didn't have time for politicians but even she was sometimes lulled into a smile for Rob. Now, though, her attention was focused exclusively on Tara.

'Everything all right, Diane?' she asked tentatively.

'Not really. I've just been talking to Catherine – have you filled her in on who our miracle-building benefactor is?' She pushed her glasses up her nose and looked at Tara as if she couldn't quite believe what she was saying.

'Does it matter?'

'Yes. Yes, I think it does. She needs the whole picture.'

'Of what? His qualifications?' Something righteous about Diane's fury put Tara on the defensive. 'I have no idea what he's like as an architect. But if he was a bad one, I don't think he'd get much work.'

'You know what I mean. About what an unreliable, selfish arsehole he is.'

Tara looked round, but no one seemed to have overheard, despite Diane's rather emphatic delivery. 'Diane, this isn't about Dad as a person. It's about him as a building expert. Troutbridge parish council needs help. Why shouldn't he be the one to help them?'

Diane tossed her marmalade curls. 'You're very naive, Tara. He pops up, out of the blue, volunteering to repair a village hall in a town he hasn't been in since he walked out twenty-odd years ago. Why's that? Men like Keith — there'll be a reason.'

'Not necessarily. He's done a lot of civic projects, and he knew about the floods in Longhampton because he was already in—' As the words left her mouth, Tara knew she'd said too much. Her face was definitely saying too much.

Diane put her hands on her hips, an eloquent gesture. 'He's been in touch, hasn't he?'

'If you must know, yes,' she admitted. 'He was doing something in the area last week and he came round to see the house.'

'The house? Not you?'

'He didn't know if I'd be there. He was worried the tree in the back garden might have blown down.' It sounded lame, now she said it. Of course he knew she'd be there. But she pushed on anyway. 'We . . . talked. It was awkward, obviously. But he knew what I'd been doing with the floods, and he seemed interested in what's been happening locally. The community effort, you know.'

He was perfectly pleasant, Tara found herself wanting to say. *Charming, even. I didn't want him to be, but he was.* But she got the feeling that would only set Diane off. She'd seen her agitated before, usually during General Elections, but not like this.

Diane seemed to be struggling with herself internally, then stopped. She touched Tara's arm, her voice sadder. 'Tara, love. Why didn't you tell me he'd been here?'

Because I know you hate him, Tara thought, but instead she said, 'I wasn't sure how I felt about it myself. I'm still not sure how I feel.' She ran a hand through her hair, suddenly self-conscious. 'He mentioned this idea of pro bono work to me earlier in the week, and I said he should approach the parish council but that in principle I didn't think it was a bad idea.'

Diane's cynical eyebrow made Tara uncomfortable.

'*Is* that so bad? I mean, they need help.'

'I suppose what I'm saying is . . .' Diane massaged her head with her short gold nails. 'This might be free to Troutbridge – and it's a nice gesture, I'll give him that – but there'll be a cost somewhere. I'm just worried you'll be the one paying it.'

'How do you mean?'

'Well, Keith's assuming a lot, isn't he? He's pushing his way into this, just like he pushed his way into Ruth's— into *your* house without asking. You'll be grateful to him – *owing* him something – which puts him in a position of power. Because at the end of the day, this is about power.'

'And it's completely impossible that my own dad might want to do something kind? To try to get to know me as an adult?' Tara heard her own voice, and it was weak and plaintive.

Diane had unusual green eyes, clear and youthful, and she wasn't afraid of holding someone's gaze until her point had been made. Tara knew Diane usually saw straight into the heart of a problem – which was why this hurt so much now. Was she missing something? Something that Toby would once have told her?

'Is it?' she repeated, miserably.

Diane's expression softened. 'You remember your dad, Tara. The man you wanted him to be. But I remember someone who only *ever* put himself first. Someone who hurt other people. I don't want to let him hurt you again.' She paused. 'Your mum would say the same, if she was here.'

'But how well did *you* know him, Diane? You only know what Mum told you. People are different in a marriage. Maybe he's changed. People do change.'

'Ruth told me things about your dad, things I can't easily forget.' Diane fidgeted with her glasses. 'Listen, Tara, I've met a lot of men like Keith over the years. They like to think they're maverick one-offs. It's usually one of the first things they tell you, how unique they are, what *mould-breakers*. But the sad truth is, they're all exactly the bloody same. Exactly the bloody same. And leopards do not change their spots.'

Tara ignored the fact that 'maverick' and 'one-off' was also how Phil had described himself on their first date. Twice.

'Well, maybe doing what *I* do,' she retorted, 'I want to believe in the power of people to make changes. Maybe he's waited until now out of respect for Mum.'

'Tara . . .'

She lifted her chin. 'And I hope I'm big enough not to put my own feelings ahead of everyone who uses that hall.'

'Oh, by all means let Keith do his generous charity thing. Make sure he delivers everything on that score. You just don't have to let him into your life.' Diane looked at her shrewdly. 'Tell him to come and do an inspection, send his plans, get the hall rebuilt. And he can stay in a hotel, in Birmingham. Deal with Alice. Not you. See what he says then.'

'I will.' Tara realized that she'd gone from being very uncertain at the start of the conversation to having her mind made up for her. 'I'll call him first thing in the morning and tell him exactly that. Thanks, Diane.'

Chapter Eight

Tara had another bad night's sleep. This time she was back at Brownies, Branston anxiously trailing her round Troutbridge Memorial Hall as the dark waters of the River Martle crept steadily over Brown Owl's knee socks, floating the battered papier-mâché toadstool that she'd completely forgotten about until it bobbed past the also forgotten form of Karen Lord, Pixie Sixer. Everyone was ignoring Tara's increasingly urgent attempts to evacuate the hall before the tree fell, and she'd woken feeling more exhausted than when she'd gone to bed.

Morning weariness wasn't unusual – even before the flooding, Tara's mind tended to knead relentlessly at the day's problems long after her body had switched off – but her first thought on waking was the reason for her queasy nocturnal joyride through childhood memories: Keith.

Despite what she'd said to Diane, in the cold light of day Tara wasn't so sure she'd done the right thing. She'd been naive, stupid even, for not seeing the publicity angle first. Diane's clear-eyed reaction flipped everything – and kept flipping it, over and over. One moment she felt bitter, furious that Dad wasn't interested in *her* at all, just what profile opportunities she could offer; the next moment loneliness crashed over her, overwhelming her with shame that she'd been taken in so easily, even now. Worst of all, she couldn't pinpoint exactly how she felt. Did she care? Was she angry, hurt, suspicious, afraid? Tara knew the questions she'd ask a client to help them explore their true feelings, hooking the slippery fish of truth from the confusing shoal of denial and delusion, teasing it out so painlessly they barely noticed. But it turned out that skill was like tickling: it didn't work when you tried to do it on yourself.

The filter machine dripped and the smell of coffee spread through the kitchen. Tara leaned on the kitchen counter and stared into the garden, where Ruth's favourite rose bush had recently erupted into bloom. The white roses gleamed like wedding dress satin in the pale sunshine.

Mum, thought Tara, remembering Ruth meticulously selecting which flowers to clip: two steps back from the bush, head tilted, secateurs raised, the flowers removed with a surgical snap. Every other day Ruth stuffed the silver bowl in the hallway with luxuriant sherbet-scented tea roses, a blowsy delight in Keith's clean modern house. Toby had Ruth's knack of making flowers sit right, the same way he could hang the right picture in the perfect spot, or place the unexpected splash of colour in a room. Tara didn't. As the child of two artists, she felt cheated on the creative front. Toby was a quick learner: he'd absorbed Ruth's little tricks before he bailed out at eighteen, while all Tara had absorbed was an appreciation of high thread counts and Ruth's recipe for whipped feta dip – which Tara suspected was Diane's anyway.

I should have asked her to show me what to do with the roses while I had the chance, she thought, aching with regret. It was the small losses that punched way beyond their size. Papercuts on her heart.

The bush rustled, throwing a shower of petals up into the air and on to the gravel, and a frightened blackbird shot out, closely followed by a determined Sybil.

Tara tried not to see that as a sign. She poured her coffee, added three sugars, and picked up her phone. She needed to get this out of the way before she could think about it too much.

'Tara!' Keith picked up on the second ring and sounded wide awake. 'How are you?'

'I'm well, thank you,' she replied automatically. 'Look, I just wanted to speak to you quickly about this community project.'

'Ah, yes. How did the meeting go? I gather it was last night?'

'Yes, it was.' Tara tried not to think of Diane's contemptuous expression. Or of the treehouse. It was hard, with her dad's voice in her ear, sounding just like Dad. 'Everyone's really excited. Alice is contacting you today to discuss next steps.'

'I'm so pleased to hear that!' He did sound pleased. 'You know, I've always believed, as an architect, that buildings are *much* more than physical constructions — they're where people live their lives, where communities develop. At times like these, it feels right to use what building skills we have to repair those spaces, so people can get on with repairing their lives. It's the small community projects that give me the most satisfaction, to be honest.'

Tara turned away from the window, and her mother's rose bushes. That *sounded* great, but Keith had, after all, walked out on his own small community project, leaving a wife, two children and a very sad dog inside it.

113

'So, with any luck we can get going soon,' he went on, and Tara felt the nerves in her body surge with stress, tingling at her extremities.

'How soon?'

'Well, I've got nothing much on over the next few months, so I'll shoot for a meeting for the end of next week.'

The end of next week? Suddenly it felt very real. Diane's words came back to her: make him keep his distance, don't let him push his way in.

'Dad.' Tara's heart was racing, but she tried to keep her voice steady. 'If you do this, please promise me one thing.'

'If I can.'

Outside, by the bird table, Sybil was stalking an oblivious pigeon. Tara turned away. 'Promise you won't let them down.'

'What do you mean by that?'

'This hall means a lot to these people. Please see it through.'

'Well, if you check the website, I managed to stick it out to the end of Wales's newest multimedia art space,' he said evenly. 'It's a village hall, Tara. It's not the Sagrada Familia.'

'I mean, if something else comes up, something more important . . .' Tara heard herself backtracking, to her own private horror. 'Please don't leave us hanging now everyone's so excited.'

'I won't, Tara. I promise.'

This wasn't coming out right. She sank her forehead on to her free hand. There was no way she'd allow one of her clients to fudge an important communication like this. Two or three times a day she gently stopped a client from talking themselves out of a decision, and helped them grasp the scary flaming torch of their truths, instead of dropping it out of fear. But now, she couldn't let her own fears out, in case . . . in case what? Despite everything, she didn't want her dad to see how much this meant to her, and how easily he could hurt her again.

This is about me, she wanted to yell. *This is about not letting me down.*

Keith's voice broke the silence, familiar and unfamiliar at the same time. 'Do they know I'm your father?'

'I haven't said as much. Although I guess some might put two and two together.'

'It sounds as if you don't want them to know.'

'I'm not sure I do.'

'Why's that?'

'Lots of reasons,' she said shortly.

'I promise you this,' said Keith. 'By the time we've finished on Troutbridge village hall, you'll want everyone to know. How's that?'

He's missed the point, she thought, with a childlike wrench of disappointment. *He's completely missed the point.*

Half an hour later, Tara was cruising slowly down another of Longhampton's premier residential streets, looking for a spot to hide her Mini between the Range Rovers and Volvos, bargaining with the universe.

If she could find a space, and fit into it first time, she could text Phil.

It had been three weeks and two days now since they'd last spoken; the longest silence so far, and Tara's attitude had slipped from nonchalance to irritation and was now sliding into concern.

She slid her car into a gap in two elegant movements – Tara liked parallel parking, she was good at it – and hated herself for the way her heart bounced as she dug through the mess of paper hankies and pens and receipts in her handbag to find her phone.

Justifying Phil to her conscience was an endless system of rationalizations, balanced precariously against Justin's shortcomings. Yes, she and Phil might only get together a handful of times a month, but every time they did it felt like their third date, i.e. matching underwear and flirtation. And Phil was actually a good boyfriend. He could *do* things, unlike Justin, who just moaned about being too busy or too important to grapple with life's minor snags. Phil dealt with waiters, mice, parking wardens, fuse boxes, bad weather, PMT, all with unflustered confidence. He never made promises, but he never broke them either. And he was inventively, flatteringly good in bed. The flipside to this was a lot Tara didn't know about what he did on the other twenty-five or so days, but they were usually too busy tearing off each other's clothes to engage in deep discussion about the future, which Tara found surprisingly easy to live with after Justin's micromanagement.

Sybil had been the step change. Getting a pet together – well, sort of – that had to mean something. You didn't trust your cat with just anyone.

Tara stared at her message: **Hey, Phil! How's things? Sybil misses you – why don't you come over for . . .** Her finger hesitated over the screen; it was very easy to slide into innuendo with Phil.

It was already ten to nine. She couldn't sit here thinking lewd thoughts all morning. She got out of the car,
juggling the phone and her keys, still deliberating about
how to finish the sentence without an obvious double
entendre.

'Tara!'

She jumped back, stumbled and swung round, looking to see who'd spotted her.

It was David. On the other side of the road, waving.
Well, he was raising his hand in a formal greeting. The
sort of cheery wave a post-war detective sergeant might
give to a bright young vicar's daughter. He was only
missing his bicycle.

Tara considered pretending she was just admiring the
car, but spotted her Mulberry bag on the back seat. Bollocks. Could she style it out? Could she leave the bag
there for a few hours, come back later and . . . ?

Her red purse peeked jauntily out of the top. *Yoo hoo!
Nick me!* it said.

The very next lamp post even had a police notice about
bag thefts on it. No, she couldn't leave it. Damn.

And now David was crossing over, and in a few strides
he was right there next to her.

'Good morning!' he said cheerily.

Tara pocketed her phone, beeped the car back open
and grabbed her bag. 'OK, you've got me,' she said,
swinging it over her shoulder. 'Busted.'

His eyes twinkled. 'Oh? How so?'

'You know how so. Have you been waiting to catch me
out? And don't go fake-innocent on me,' she went on. 'In
the kitchen that time with Jacqueline. You were all
hint-y.'

David pretended to look conspiratorial. 'Is this where I should extract some sort of deal from you in return for my silence? Make you offer to bake my office rota cake?'

'You could. But it would be a bit mean.'

'Why? Do you have a particularly awful secret ingredient?' He raised an eyebrow again. 'Leeches? Copydex? Sultanas?'

'Don't give me ideas.' Surreptitiously, Tara checked her phone to make sure she wasn't accidentally pocket-calling Phil – it had been known – then set off down the street.

'I wasn't stalking you, by the way. I only saw you the once before today.' He followed her, his long stride easily keeping up with her quick pace. 'Was it an emergency this morning? I'll overlook it if it was.'

'No,' said Tara. She found it hard to lie to David. Presumably he was doing some sort of low-level hypnotism on her now. 'I just like driving. It's my quiet time. My me time.'

'Do you have a nice drive in?'

'Yes, actually, it's quite picturesque . . .' Tara was about to describe her route in from her old house, the one she'd shared with Justin, which went through a series of pretty black-and-white villages, the oldest church in the county and, unexpectedly, a llama farm. She stopped herself: it was clear from their lunchtime walks when she'd dangled some Justin-based conversational hints that David had no intention of revealing more about his hypnotic past, and that was the only reason Tara ever wanted to talk about Justin again. She didn't really want David linking her with him in his mind.

He was waiting for an answer. 'Well, no,' she admitted, 'it's not a long drive now. But it's the principle.'

'So where do you live?'

'On Malvern Road, going out of town? Just up from the Methodist church.'

'What, seriously? That has to be barely a mile from here. It's quicker to walk than to find somewhere to park.'

'No, it's—'

'Tara, if you're finding parking spaces on the Poets' Streets, you need to tell me your secret. I live in Southey Avenue – round the corner.' He indicated another street of white-fronted villas behind the one they were on. 'And I can never find anywhere to park. It's why I walk everywhere.'

Tara made a note not to park in Southey Avenue again. 'Well, good for you.'

'Yes, it is. Tremendously good for you.' He said it so seriously, she couldn't take offence. 'And fascinating too! Did you know there's a miraculous well on Coleridge Street? Apparently, the water was part of the monastery's spa treatments. Well, not a spa, exactly, I suppose – more of a . . . last-ditch leprosy treatment.'

Tara shot him a side glance. 'No local history before breakfast, David.'

'Just trying to make the walk interesting,' he said, falling in behind her.

Tara kept her eyes fixed on the road ahead, but mentally started sweeping up and down the local streets, trying to remember if she'd seen any ancient wells. She wasn't even aware there'd been a monastery, let alone a miraculous spring. Although . . . Bishop's Road. Huh. That was the annoying thing about David. He got her brain working.

'Do you want to tell Hero?' she asked, despite herself.

They were almost out of the residential terraces, and nearing the outlying shops of the high street. A lone hi-fi specialist, a Polish grocery. Tara tried to steer him down her usual shortcut through an alley full of bins, but David had already set off on the long way round and was fishing in his pocket for his pedometer.

'Come on,' he said, when she grumbled, 'if we'd started our pedometers back there, we could have got a thousand steps in before lunch!'

'Oh, good. So I can have lunchtime off?'

'Absolutely not! Don't you want to beat Lionel and Emily in the Step Challenge?'

'Of course I do,' Tara admitted through gritted teeth, because she did.

After three weeks of Jacqueline's 'teambuilding' Step Challenge, Team Eminel were leading the star chart by a clear margin of 45,000 steps, despite Lionel the homeopath's dodgy hip and his lifelong opposition to what he called 'the tyranny of shoes'.

'We're never going to overtake them if we don't find some extra steps somewhere,' David continued. 'I saw Emily in the park yesterday, whipping the poor chap on. I didn't realize anyone could move so fast in Birkenstocks.'

'Well, that's Emily for you. She could start a competition in a flotation tank.'

'What I don't get is why she picked *Lionel*,' David mused. 'They don't seem particularly friendly?'

'She didn't pick him.' Tara was distracted by the buttery smell of fresh croissants drifting from Juliet's Bakehouse. 'Jacqueline engineered the pairings.'

'Engineered?'

'Oh, it's one of her missions – trying to build bridges

between the traditional counsellors and the alternative therapists.' The croissants were on a two-for-one deal. How bad was it to have croissants for lunch? If she skipped breakfast? 'I mean,' Tara carried on, totting up the calories, '*we're* only paired up because we were last back from lunch and the numbers aren't even, otherwise you'd probably be striding out with someone who thinks you can cure cancer by putting a fragment of a crab claw under your pillow.'

'Ha!'

Tara was jolted out of her croissant-gazing by the sound of David's unexpectedly snorty laugh, and realized she'd probably said a bit too much.

'So there's some tension? In the Centre?'

Tara hesitated, unsure of how to reply. David was on the Credibility side of the chasm, surely? One of Us, not Them? What could be more Establishment than David's wall of qualifications? His books?

And yet . . . although she was secretly starting to enjoy David's dry sense of humour, there was definitely a shrewdness behind his affable exterior. It wasn't just book-intelligence; he did seem to 'get people', as Kasia had pointed out. David seemed to see things in people they didn't even see themselves.

'I believe,' she replied, carefully, 'there's room for a broad spectrum of methodology under the umbrella of therapeutic intervention.'

'Really? As someone once muttered in my direction, "In English?"'

They were at the Wellness Centre door now – the walk had gone much more quickly than normal – and David was holding Tara's gaze with that quizzical, look-into-my-eyes-not-around-the-eyes directness, as if he was waiting for the *real* answer. Feeling herself slipping into another inappropriately honest comment, Tara blurted out one of Justin's meaningless space fillers. 'It is what it is, isn't it?'

She couldn't break their gaze. Now she looked closely, David had unusual eyes – a delicate tiger-striped hazel, the colour of the polished oak staircase – that seemed to see right inside her. And one or two pale brown freckles on his nose that she hadn't noticed before. He smiled, as if he could hear her thoughts, and Tara visualized fuzziness in her head. *Fibre glass. Packing chips. Bubble wrap.* What were you meant to do to fool hypnotists?

Wordlessly, David held the door open for her and Tara swept in, not entirely sure how the conversation had ended. Inside, Chloe the receptionist was obscured by a huge bouquet, with several therapists crowded round it.

'They're for you, Tara!' Judith announced before anyone else could, and the reception committee swung round to catch her reaction, which was not positive.

Tara wasn't a fan of bouquets. They never boded well, in her experience. Generous bunches of flowers had arrived on a regular basis throughout her childhood, usually just before or just after Dad went away for a few days; Mum seemed miserable or furious as she dismembered the arrangement into a vase, not swoony with delight like women on the television. The open-plan downstairs of the house was always filled with roses and dahlias from their own garden, so Dad's hothouse bouquets ended up in Tara's room, where she had to look at the slowly wilting lilies and wonder what was going on. Luckily Justin hadn't been one for sending flowers – or doing anything controversial enough to need to apologize florally – so it hadn't been much of a problem in her adult life.

Dad, she thought. *He thinks he's overstepped the mark so he's sent me flowers to apologize.* The last bouquet he'd given Tara was on the day of her graduation, and she'd had to leave them with her old next-door neighbour.

'White roses,' Hero informed her, solemnly, 'are a magical symbol of innocent love and new beginnings. It's a beautiful gesture. Although totally unjustifiable in an air-miles sense.'

'They're from that posh new florist on the high street,' Chloe added, more pragmatically. 'Must have cost a fair bit, bunch that size.'

'Have you got a secret admirer?' Bryan wagged a finger at her. He was the worst for gossip. By a *long* way.

Tara stared at the arrangement. Had Dad got off the phone and straight on to the florist? She could picture him doing that.

Although . . . maybe they were from Phil? All right, so a phone call would be a much better way to apologize for his silence, but maybe the card would include directions to some romantic boutique hotel? Her stomach fluttered traitorously.

'Must be from a client,' she said, as calmly as she could. If Bryan's intrigued expression was anything to go by, the watercooler rumour mill would be whirring off its axle by lunchtime.

'A client that *fancies* you!' Kemi purred.

'No, they'd have sent *dog* roses,' Hero corrected her. 'Meaning pleasure and pain. Or maybe tuberose, for dangerous pleasure.'

Chloe gave Hero a side eye, then turned back to Tara. 'Aren't you going to see who they're from?'

'Haven't you already peeked?' Tara lifted the huge bunch off the desk.

'Morning, David!' Chloe added, spotting him collecting his post from the pigeonholes behind them, and Tara caught a quick glance pass between Hero and Chloe. David was already popular with Chloe and the reception team, most of whom were dog lovers.

'Morning, all!' David waved his post in a crisp salute, then, unseen by the others, raised his eyebrow in passing at Tara as he went up the stairs to his room.

'Tell us who they're from at least, Tara!' Hero protested as Tara gathered up her bag and flowers and, after a subtle delay, followed him up the stairs.

Tara didn't respond because she didn't intend to open the card until she was safely on her own.

To her surprise, the flowers weren't from her dad. The card read, *Thinking of you always, Pumpkin. All my love, Big Phil xxxx*.

Tara sank back against her desk, feeling conflicted. Every now and again, Phil sent her generous presents: a bottle of champagne here, some fancy chocolates she'd mentioned she liked there. He'd once sent her a pair of silk pyjamas so nice she still hadn't worn them. The problem was, he never called her Pumpkin, or referred to himself as Big Phil. He called her Taz, and himself something a lot worse than Big Phil.

Either he'd forgotten what he called her or, more likely, somewhere Pumpkin was opening a card reading something she wasn't expecting *at all*.

Tara was surprised by how crushed she felt. It was one thing to have suspicions. Another thing to have someone drag your suspicions out from the back of your mind where you were studiously ignoring them, and force you to examine them properly. And then to examine yourself.

She had to face it. The reason she and Phil never got beyond that three-date feeling was because there was nowhere else to go. And it wasn't just Phil putting her in that box: she was letting him do it. A shiver of shame crawled across Tara's skin, and she rammed the flowers in the wastepaper basket as if they were covered in ants. But they looked obscenely wasteful, stuffed in the bin, and she stared at them crossly, knowing they'd catch her eye all day.

Who could she give them to? Kasia?

She retrieved them with a sigh and marched out into the corridor, but even as she lifted her knuckles to knock on Kasia's door, Tara realized she'd then have to explain *why* she was giving them away, and probably get a dose of well-intentioned life coaching in return. Could she leave them in reception 'for everyone to enjoy'? No, they'd just be a focus for discussion. Or put them in the kitchen? Or throw them out of the window?

Tara stared down into the velvety, expensive roses, and wished she hadn't allowed herself to start developing proper feelings for a man who, if you snapped him in half, probably had Bad Break-Up written through him like a stick of rock.

On the other hand, she definitely had a good reason to call him now.

'For God's sake, Tara, this is so *tacky*!' she spat at herself.

There was a discreet cough from down the corridor.

David had just opened his door to a woman with a shaggy black dog in tow. All three were staring at her, and not bothering to hide their curiosity.

Tara swallowed.

'The flowers. Still quite tacky. From the . . . flower food,' she said lamely, and slunk back into her own room, Phil's roses under her arm.

She had five minutes before her first appointment of the day: Jeannie McAllister for her introductory assertiveness coaching. *Take your own medicine*, she told herself, and dialled Phil's number.

When it went to voicemail – as it had done the last two times she'd called, and left not-very-cool messages – Tara closed her eyes. 'Phil, can you call me, please? There's something we need to talk about.' The outrage was already draining pathetically from her voice. 'Hope you're all right. It's been a while!' (*Why, Tara, why?*) 'Um, I'm fine. Sybil misses you. So do I.' (*Oh God.*) 'Bye.'

She looked at the flowers on her table. Jeannie – or as she was now going to be, 'My lucky hundredth new client!' – was going to get a really nice surprise.

Chapter Nine

On Friday afternoon, Tara had parked up outside the Memorial Hall for the big 'meeting with the architect from London', and was debating whether to check in with Toby for some last-minute advice about how to handle it.

On the one hand, she really wanted the old Toby's perceptive, big-brother (even if just by ten minutes) take on things; on the other, she wasn't up for another hurtful radio silence, even if he was clearly very busy driving an electric car through scenic areas of Vancouver Island, going by his Instagram Stories this week.

Other than an ambiguous thumbs up in response to the party photo she'd sent, Toby hadn't offered her any support about this weird reappearance of their father. Tara assumed it was because he wanted nothing to do with Dad either, but, unlike her, he was self-assured enough to state his boundaries. She'd poured out her heart in a couple of long WhatsApp messages about the miserable struggle keeping her awake most nights – loyalty to Mum versus her grown-up curiosity and professional investment in the power of change – but she'd deleted them before she'd sent them. Maybe Emily had been right: sometimes the act of writing to someone was enough.

At least with this new possibility of a salaried job, the issue of the house was on hold for the time being.

Tara's thumb hovered over the message on the screen. **Dad's here. What should I do?** But before she could do anything, a brand-new Mercedes swept into the car park with a crunch of gravel and reversed into a space right outside the front door.

Tara's head bounced up. She'd never seen the car before, but the plates were personalized: KPH 58. Dad was here. Instantly, she felt nauseous, and was annoyed with her body for not managing to be cooler.

She watched in her rear-view mirror as her dad – or rather, this older man, this *version* of her father – jumped out of the Mercedes, followed by an assistant in his twenties, carrying a leather satchel and a heavy laptop bag. They were both wearing boots, ready for the site inspection, but Keith (he was definitely in Keith mode, that much was clear) looked every inch the consultant, with more than a hint of the old glamour: horn-rimmed Ray-Bans, a linen jacket over creaseless chinos, the afternoon sun catching the healthy gleam of his thick silver hair.

Tara's stomach turned over slowly as the ghosts of long-ago summer Dads gathered in the back of her mind. He'd never worn shorts, always chinos; never flip-flops, always red deck shoes. He looked smarter now than when she'd seen him in the garden; he was here to impress the committee, not just her. It was a professional performance and she wasn't sure whether she wanted to be part of it, not with everyone watching. Maybe it was a mistake to be here at all. It was only the second time she'd seen her father in twelve years. Had he seen her? Should she slip away? Could she?

Tara fiddled with her phone until Keith and the assistant had gone inside and then took several deep breaths, in through her nose, out through her mouth. She could smell her own perfume. Had she put on too much?

You can do this, she told herself. *Just be cool.*

Then she opened her door and crossed the car park on wobbly legs.

Inside the tiled foyer, under the scaffolding and plastic sheeting, it was a full turnout – Rob Lloyd, Catherine from the Citizens Advice, obstructive Peter from Planning, Alice from the parish council, and a few faces she hadn't seen before, including a red-faced woman in a ceremonial chain who she assumed was the Mayor, though they hadn't met before. Rob was already deep into introductions, working his way down the line as if it were a royal garden party, or a very strange wedding.

As Tara got nearer she could hear Rob's enthusiasm, and the low tones of her dad being charming and modest. '. . . really exciting . . . everyone very keen to talk about plans . . . chance for real community interaction. Alice, you've already spoken to, of course . . .'

'Alice! How nice to put a face to the voice at last. Thank you for emailing those plans so the team could get across this straight away – put our guys to shame with those notes!' Keith shook Alice's hand and Tara guessed he must have given her his full charm beam too, because a pink blush immediately spread across Alice's open face and she glanced at the floor with a shy smile.

Oh, Alice, she thought, with a protective shudder. *No, don't, honestly.*

Rob carried on introducing and Keith carried on shaking hands and chatting, and a similar effect spread from person to person – apart from Peter, who retained the supercilious semi-sneer he wore to make himself look like a proper politician, and not a retired electrician. There was a discernible air of excitement in the foyer, and Tara had to admit it came from her dad: Keith seemed to emit what Hero would probably call positive energy, reflected in the reactions he was getting.

But with each introduction, each smile, each hand-shake, Tara's heartbeat quickened a little more. *Don't mess this up. Don't let them down. Don't let me down.*

They'd reached the last person – 'Sue Salter, our redoubtable Countryside Recreation Officer!' – and Tara was about to make herself known when someone bustled in from the toilets, shaking the water off her hands, and joined the line with a meaningful sniff. Tara felt herself recoil: it was Diane.

When Keith reached Diane, she pre-empted the intro-duction and the offer of his hand with a brisk, 'I already know Keith.'

'Oh?' said Rob, surprised.

'Yes, we go back a long way. Diane was friends with my ex-wife, Ruth,' said Keith. He was polite but the warmth had gone from his voice. He turned, and saw Tara hover-ing in the doorway. A smile broke over his face and it disarmed her: Tara smiled back automatically, then quickly adjusted her expression into something more neutral.

'Tara! Perfect timing, as always. Keith, this is Tara Hunter, our counselling superstar. Oh.' Rob noticed the smiles and his brow creased. 'Do you two . . . ?'

Keith hadn't opened his mouth, but Tara heard herself saying, 'He's my dad.'

Before Keith could say anything. Before Diane could

say anything. Before she'd even checked with her brain as to whether she should say something.

Oh, very cool, Tara, she thought, annoyed with herself. *Very cool indeed. Now you've managed to make a drama out of it.*

Toby would definitely have handled this better.

There was a ripple of surprise through the group.

'So, is *this* why you're here?' Rob flipped his finger between Tara and Keith. 'Tara, you kept this very quiet!'

'Not entirely why. I wanted to help. I'm glad I *can* help.' Keith raised his hands. 'I've got some great memories of living round here. Longhampton gave me my start in my career, and I'm glad to be able to give something back. But it *is* thanks to Tara, really, that I've got this opportunity to get involved.' He inclined his head towards her in acknowledgement. 'She spoke so movingly about the tremendous, *generous* way the community leaped into action to help those in need, I felt the least I could do was to support that effort with some practical assistance.'

Tara frowned at him. *Don't make this sound as if we chat regularly about my volunteer work.*

'Oh, Tara's been incredible,' said Rob. 'Not just in the thick of the floods, but ever since. She keeps us all going.'

'Hear, hear,' muttered Catherine and Diane.

'Couldn't have done it without her,' Alice piped up.

'Oh. God, no. *Everyone's* gone above and beyond,' Tara insisted. 'It's just been a case of all hands to the deck.'

She could feel her face heating up. Where were these awful clichés coming from? Why did she feel about fourteen again?

'Anyway! Time is of the essence!' Keith clapped his

hands together. 'Shall we get going while the light is still with us?'

He'd done his homework, Tara had to give him that. As Alice explained the damage caused by the falling tree, now removed and reduced to innocuous chunks behind the hall, and the effect of the creeping damp of the river water on the foundations, Keith asked question after question, listening intently to the answers while his assistant, Conrad, zapped the walls with a laser measure, made voice notes into his phone and scribbled in a leather notebook.

'So tell me, Alice, who uses this space?' he asked. 'What sort of activities would you *like* to see here going forward? Paint me a picture of your ideal week in the life of this hall . . .'

And, 'Rob, did I read it was founded by public subscription? Is that a fundraising option now?'

Even, 'Peter, you're the expert on local planning process – what other development work's in the pipeline?'

They picked their way through the piles of muddy leaves into the main hall, which smelled of mould, and slowly Keith moved to the front, leading them like a flock of ducklings. He pointed at the arched windows, at the warped parquet flooring, at the commemorative plaques, and asked questions that gave everybody the chance to offer a nugget of insider knowledge, some of which even Tara hadn't heard before.

Tara let Alice and Rob steer the discussion; there was a limit to how involved she wanted to be with this. She paused by the stage, framed on each side by red velvet curtains, stained at the bottoms as if they'd gone wading into the river. It was smaller than she remembered. Once upon a time, the stage had seemed daunting – a towering height with nothing beyond it but darkness, a muttering, shuffling sea of invisible judgement.

It had been a joint Brownies and Cubs gang show. She'd tap danced on the end of a line with the other eight-year-olds too shy to perform in a herd smaller than four, while Toby had dressed up as Elton John and belted out 'Saturday Night's Alright For Fighting' with a commitment that would have got him on *Britain's Got Talent*, had it been around back then. She'd overheard Brown Owl – Tanya Horrock's mother, Dawn – telling someone it was hard to believe she and Toby were twins, and the someone suggesting Toby had got his dad's flair. She remembered not knowing what that meant (his flares? His flare?) but sensing from Brown Owl's giggle that it wasn't a straightforward compliment.

We were a family then, she thought, as if she was seeing the four of them on a small television screen. *Me and Toby, and Mum and Dad. Symmetrical, me and Toby dressed in the same colours, boy and girl, Mum and Dad.* Her stomach caved in with longing, and the family vanished.

'And that's the stage where I recall there were some dance recitals, eh, Tara?'

She spun round.

Keith was standing right by her. He hadn't said it loud enough for everyone to hear – he wasn't making a point – but the glance made it clear he wanted her to know he remembered.

She looked over to see what was happening with the rest of them; Rob and Alice were explaining something about the kitchen area to Conrad and he was sketching

Lucy Dillon

something, frowning as they added extra details. Everyone was engrossed in correcting him.

Tara turned back. She felt vulnerable, separated from the herd.

'Yes, the gang show,' she said. Dad had made it to this particular show, and had clapped so hard, and whistled so she could make out his applause, even though she couldn't see him. It had felt like the sun rising in her chest.

Or had she known it was him because she could also hear her mother saying a little too loudly, 'For God's *sake*, Keith'? That was how the story had been told later. But she remembered the sunrise feeling clearly: Dad was there. He was there, and he was clapping, and in that moment she didn't really care if Toby was the one with the flair.

'How did it go?' Keith frowned, pretending to think. 'Keep young and beautiful . . .' He mimed some slow windscreen-wiper jazz hands. 'It's your duty to be beautiful . . .'

Tara stared at him, amazed that he'd remembered. That was exactly what she'd sung. In a black leotard, black tights and a red swimming cap; the ideal costume for eight cripplingly shy girls. They looked like a row of matches. She hadn't thought about it in years and years – that feeling of paralysing awkwardness, spiked with adrenaline.

'That's right,' she said. Then added, 'Somewhat off message these days, of course.'

'Of course.' He winked. 'You were the best tapper, though. In your red tap shoes. You used to practise on the tiles in the back kitchen, didn't you?'

'It drove Mum insane.' Her cherry-red tap shoes, with the red ribbon laces. Treasured until they were at least a size too small and gave her stabbing pains when she

134

shuffle-kicked. A lump formed in Tara's chest. The tap dancing had stopped at about the same time as Keith had left; Ruth didn't have the energy to drive her and Toby all over town after school. Or rather, Ruth was full of energy, but not the right kind, and neither Toby nor Tara felt brave enough to bring it up. Toby had negotiated lifts to football and Scouts from his friends; not having as many friends, Tara had focused on her homework instead.

She struggled to keep the memories from spilling out on to her face. 'Anyway, we weren't exactly The Rockettes. Karen Lawson had a plaster cast. So.' She smiled tightly. 'Have you seen everything you need to see?'

'I think we've covered the essentials.' If Keith was hurt by her refusal to wander further down memory lane, he didn't show it. 'Don't want to keep everyone too long on a Friday. Conrad? Have we got everything we need?'

'Yup! Just uploading . . .' Conrad was perched on the edge of the stage, percussively entering data on his laptop, with every electronic device linked up to it.

'It's just for preliminary drawings,' Keith explained, as the others slowly gravitated back towards him. 'Somewhere to start. We'll try to get something over to you in the next week or so, and we can start talking.'

Rob Lloyd hove into view behind them with Peter, who obviously wanted to add one last detail. 'Keith, before you go, Peter has a quick question about that app you were using to calculate, um, whatever it was you were calculating . . .'

'Amazing what they can do these days,' said Peter. Which was about as close to a compliment as they were likely to wring out of him.

Tara could see Diane talking to Catherine by the door;

she kept shooting suspicious glances in Keith's direction while Catherine gestured on, oblivious.

'Excuse me,' Tara murmured and crossed the hall.

'If we're done?' Catherine checked her watch. 'Got to pick up Evie from cricket, then get Aaron on the way back – non-stop, isn't it? I'll see you next week, Tara! Thanks for getting your dad involved! Very secret squirrel of you!'

She'd gone before Tara could put her right, leaving her alone with Diane. And Tara got the distinct feeling from the ominous way Diane was shoving her shirtsleeves up her freckled forearms that she had Thoughts to Share.

'I see he's got them eating out of the palm of his hand,' Diane observed.

'Apart from you.'

'Not so much, no. But then he's not really aiming his charm cannon at me, is he?'

Tara liked Diane so much, and respected her even more, which made her attitude hard to deal with. 'He's here to assess the hall for damage, Diane. He doesn't need to charm anyone. But since you mention it, if he's got Peter on side . . .'

Diane made a disparaging noise. 'Peter's anyone's for a laser tape measure.'

'Can't you just give him the benefit of the doubt and see what happens?' Tara dropped her voice. 'I doubt he's going to be spending a lot of time here – you met Conrad, I bet he'll be leading the team, not Dad. This is just the meet-the-team PR moment. You won't have to see him again after today if you don't want to.' *In fact, there's no reason for you to be here at all*, she added silently.

'It's not about me.' Diane inspected her over the top of

her gold half-moon rims. 'I'm looking out for you, that's all, love.'

'I'm a big girl, Diane. And this is about the community, not me. Don't,' she added, as Diane opened her mouth to contradict her. 'Please?'

Keith was heading over, Peter still chatting with an animated expression that Tara had never seen before. Diane shook her head. Her earrings jangled disapprovingly. 'Just remember your mum. OK?' And she stalked out into the foyer.

For an awkward moment, Tara wasn't sure whether she should just slide away herself, but it was too late: Peter was excusing himself, and there was Keith.

He smiled. Tara managed a half-smile back. Her pulse was still jittery, as if it couldn't decide whether it was safe to relax or not.

'I think that went well,' he said easily. 'What a great bunch of people. Very inspiring.'

'Yes, they're . . . really great.'

Keith glanced to see who was in earshot and dropped his voice. 'I thought you didn't want them to know I was your dad?'

'Changed my mind. I think it's best to be honest from the start.' Tara tried to sound more breezy than she felt. She'd guessed he'd ask why she'd blurted out the one thing she'd asked him not to mention, and had had time to come up with a good reason while Alice and Keith had been discussing the accessible toilet provision. 'Then everyone knows where they stand.'

Keith shrugged, and a damp strand of silver quiff detached itself from the main crop. A little of his glow had worn off after nearly two hours inside the damp hall. He seemed more like her dad now than the celebrity architect. As he pushed it back, Tara saw the familiar glint of his gold signet ring in the early evening light. Another memory slid into focus in her mind, sitting reading in his studio while he worked, and talked, and drew, and clinked ice into his crystal glass.

He spoke, and jolted her out of the memory. 'Well, I agree . . .'

'Good.'

'. . . because now I'm allowed to be publicly proud of you too,' he added.

Tara flushed. 'I didn't do anything more than anyone else here. They're just being kind.'

'There's no need to be modest, Tara,' he said. 'You're allowed to be proud.'

Tara had never found accepting praise easy, even though, ironically, she knew from therapy she was a bit of a gold-star junkie. What else was she supposed to say now? Her mind had gone blank. The others were leaving, discreetly letting them have a moment or two to talk, probably assuming they'd be catching up on normal family chit-chat.

As she was thinking how best to extricate herself without a handy child to pick up or gym class to attend, Tara realized she was walking to the door with her father. She had no idea how he'd done it – like an expert dancer steering a novice without them noticing – but even as the thought was registering in her mind they were back out in the car park, breathing the cut-grass smell of summer air, their steps mirroring each other on the gravel.

Keith had been talking about the hall – technical stuff to do with equipment they could send to dry it out 'so we can hit the ground running' – and broke off. 'Everything all right?'

Tara looked at him. Was it?

'Tara, I think we can do something really special here,' he went on. 'Not just repair what's been damaged, but make it even *better*.' His eyes twinkled with good humour. 'Something everyone can be proud of.'

'I hope so,' she said, because she couldn't think of anything simultaneously literal and profound.

Keith smiled, and slipped his sunglasses out of his top pocket. 'Would you do me a huge favour, Tara? I've never met a committee that didn't have some inside track, and it would help me enormously if we could have dinner beforehand. I don't need to know where the bodies are buried, so to speak. Just . . . whether there are any bodies.'

'OK,' she said. The words came out without thinking, but the sky didn't fall in when she said them. She could always cancel.

'Thank you.'

Tara stepped back before he could try to kiss her goodbye. To his credit, Keith didn't flinch, but just smiled. Sadly? She wasn't sure.

'I'll be in touch,' he said.

And there he was, thought Tara, as he headed to the car. Dad, back in her life. It was as easy as that.

Chapter Ten

'When was the announcement about the homebrew competition? Was that on the Summer Party poster? Because I didn't see it.'

Self-conscious already in her Summer Party outfit, Tara stared in horror at the array of multicoloured bottles lined up on the table nearest the canapes. They ranged from a startling yellow to a murky green, in a variety of recycled containers. It looked like a sample selection from the UTI clinic in Sodom and Gomorrah.

'It was on the invitation. Great British Brew Off. But it's *optional*,' Jacqueline added. 'No one expected you to join in, not with your current workload.'

Tara wasn't even sure she'd seen an invitation. Verbal invitation, yes, but a proper one . . . That might explain how the Summer Party had crept up on her so quickly this year. She raked through her memory. It might have got lost in the admin pile, now rammed in the third drawer down in her desk. She'd left a tiny stack of paperwork for show in the in-tray. Tara had a reputation for efficiency in the office, which was, these days, largely down to her desk having more drawers than anyone else's.

'I mean, it's wonderful that you've dressed up!' Jacqueline added. 'Very . . . festive!'

'Oh, this? It's vintage.' Mindful of Jacqueline's tip-off

about looking more like a team player, Tara had made a creative effort with her outfit, raiding Ruth's jewellery box and throwing a couple of striking perspex necklaces over her usual black dress. She'd also brought a bottle of wine, which she intended to drink herself rather than risk the usual paint-stripping plonk on offer, plus the 'secret recipe' trifle that was chilling in the office fridge, the hundreds and thousands slowly bleeding into the Bird's Dream Topping. Like the necklace, it was authentically eighties.

'I honestly didn't realize about the homebrew,' she added. 'I'm sorry, Jacqueline.'

'Don't worry,' said Jacqueline brightly. 'We've got plenty, as you can see!'

Tara counted the bottles. There were twelve on the table. There were sixteen therapists. Well, that left four other people who hadn't joined in, she reassured herself, but then Eithne leaned in between them with a polite, 'Scuse me!' and deposited another purple flask.

'Oh, thanks so much, Eithne – what's that?' cooed Jacqueline. 'Plum brandy? No? *Aubergine* brandy? How very unusual! Have you had a nibble yet? Do try the blinis . . . And Cressida too! Hello, Cressie! What's this?'

Bryan's yoga teacher wife nudged an olive oil bottle full of yellow liquid between a sloe gin and a damson aquavit, and glared at Tara. Cressida was convinced all women were magnetically attracted to her truculent husband, despite his plaque and his mid-century views on vegans.

'I didn't notice the homebrew requirement either, I'm afraid,' said David. He appeared behind them, dressed in a shirt patterned with tiny birds and navy chinos, and offered a bottle of wine to Jacqueline – decent wine, Tara noted, as Jacqueline unwrapped it. A Californian Chardonnay in a bag from the local wine merchant's. 'Is it too late to pretend I made this?'

'Au contraire, David – it's *ideal*, because you two can be our judges!'

'Oh, er, no, that's really, um . . .' said Tara, at the same time as David said, 'Actually, no, I don't know the first thing about . . .'

'You don't need to. Just decide which tastes the nicest!' Jacqueline reassured him – as if *that* was the criteria for winning. 'We'll have the competition before the gong bath and then everyone can relax!'

Tara automatically glanced at David as Jacqueline mentioned 'relax' and 'gong bath' in the same sentence, and was relieved that he flinched at exactly the same moment as she did.

'Oh *dear*.' Jacqueline lifted her gaze towards the corner of the room where Kemi's son had set up his decks to play inoffensive party music. 'Is Emily having another go at Angelo? I told her, we can't listen to k.d. lang *all* night. We're supposed to be having fun. Do excuse me, you two . . .'

David waited until Jacqueline was out of earshot and muttered, 'Did she say gong bath?'

Tara reached for a smoked salmon blini, then grabbed two. Might as well line her stomach for the compost-liqueur assault to come. 'That's what those yoga mats are for, so we can lie down and let the therapeutic sound-waves of the gong bath wash over us.' She nodded at the stack of purple mats by the window. 'Bryan's wife brought them.'

David looked dubious. 'I'm not really a yoga mat person.'

'It'll be fine,' Tara assured him. 'In a gong bath, no one can hear you scream.'

'I thought that was scream therapy.'

'I suspect it's much the same thing.'

They stood and gazed round the room, where the therapists and their partners were milling with drinks and plates of food. The Centre's WAGS/HABS were a mixed bunch: some seemed normal enough, whereas some had grown, like dogs, alarmingly like their partners. Most of them seemed on edge, as if they weren't sure if they were having a conversation or an assessment.

'Nice bunch of people,' observed David, neutrally.

Tara opened her mouth to say something cutting about Cressida, then decided against it. Tonight she was going to be positive, a team player – Jacqueline's ideal new Centre Director. *Think of the mortgage, if nothing else*, she told herself. *Visualize yourself in a steady, salaried position, paying for the house, healing Longhampton and clearing your conscience at the same time.*

He raised an eyebrow at her, tempting her into an indiscretion.

'Yes,' she said, equally blandly. 'They're very nice people.'

The five blinis and two mushroom mini quiches Tara managed to grab from the canape table weren't nearly enough against the corrosive power of the homebrew on offer. But then a full Sunday roast and a whole roasted piglet wouldn't have stood a chance against the combination of spirits she and David were forced to taste, one after another, while the assembled brewers eyeballed them from the far side of the banqueting hall, and Kemi, Emily and Roger danced somewhere in the middle. Emily kept checking her pedometer every so often, which rather diluted the impression that she was having fun.

David sampled his way manfully through the first four bottles, until they reached bottle five, a purply-blue liquid with a hand-illustrated label announcing it to be Midsummer Gin.

'I *think* I like this one,' said Tara, taking a second sip from the shot glass. 'It's quite . . . floral.'

'Yes.' David had almost finished his glass. 'Rather wildflower meadow-ish? Poppies and cornflowers and sunlight and long grass. Not freshly mown grass, *long* grass.'

She looked at him with surprise. He was taking another sip, so she did too.

'It tastes cerulean blue, like an evening sky in June,' he went on unexpectedly. 'Who made this one?'

'Ah-ah!' Jacqueline waved her clipboard playfully. 'I can't tell you that! How many out of ten?'

'Oh, nine for me.' David looked at Tara. He'd undone a button on his shirt and his constant nervous ruffling had made his brown hair break free of its usual debonair neatness. He looked quite contemporary, for once. 'What do you think?'

She took a fourth sip, amused. This one was actually very drinkable. 'I'll say, eight point five.'

'Tough crowd!'

'Come on, we're not even halfway through. Don't want to over-score in case there's something even better.'

'I am *so* glad you two are enjoying this,' said Jacqueline, marking the scorecard and pouring the next samples. 'Now, next we have a Nutmeg Distillation, whatever that is.'

Tara reached for the glass, sipped it, and suppressed a gag. 'This one is . . . Christmas and America and the colour copper,' she announced, before David could get in.

He took a matching taste. 'Yes, definitely America and copper,' he said, 'but I'm also getting dry leaves and a touch of . . . gingham?'

'Gingham! Gosh, how interesting!' said Jacqueline, scribbling away. 'Marks?'

David's eyes locked with Tara's, each waiting for the other to go first.

'Four,' said Tara at the same time as he blurted out, 'Three point five.'

He raised an eyebrow. 'Great minds.'

Ha! He's getting tipsy, thought Tara. *Oh God. So am I.*

'Next!' David replaced his shot glass on the table with a brisk clunk. 'Is it me, or are they getting a bit more palatable as we go on?' he asked in an undertone that probably wasn't quite as under as he'd intended it to be.

Mrs Bryan and Judith glared at him from the canapé table.

'And here's a Dandelion Tincture,' said Jacqueline, filling a new set of glasses, and Tara grinned as David closed his eyes to appreciate the bouquet properly.

It took them another thirty minutes to work through the remainder of the bottles, at the end of which there was a clear winner. And, in Tara's opinion, a clear five-way tie for last place, two of which she felt should be poured straight down an outside drain. If only to clear it of fatbergs.

David was by now smiling vaguely at nothing, and his hair was pointing in different directions. 'I'm not drunk,' he said. 'I just didn't realize gin could taste so nice. I'm *not* drunk.'

'Sure you're not,' said Tara, but had to concentrate on the words herself.

'People? Hello? If we could turn down the music for a moment, we have a winner!' Jacqueline waved her arms, and the assembled home-brewers instantly abandoned Angelo's dance floor and swarmed to the table.

Emily gave Tara a knowing look and made a 'did you pick mine?' gesture, but Tara shrugged helplessly: how the hell was she supposed to know which of the bottles was Emily's?

'And first prize goes to the lovely Midsummer Gin, which I can reveal was made by . . .' Jacqueline whisked the bottle off the envelope it stood on. 'Hero! Congratulations, Hero, come up and receive your prize!'

'Hero?' muttered Tara. She was feeling unsettlingly floaty now, but not drunk, exactly. More warmed from inside, as if she were full of sunshine. No, not sunshine, pearly moonlight.

Jesus. I need water and carbs ASAP, she thought with a lurch of panic, but the jug on the table was empty, and Bryan and Judith were already clearing away the buffet in preparation for the entertainment.

Hero had dressed for the party in a diaphanous star-spangled navy gown, silver chains and bare feet. She had long toes, Tara noted, as if from a distance, and a very pretty rose-gold pedicure. She looked like Stevie Nicks's granddaughter from Surbiton. 'Thank you so much!' she said, namaste-ing David, then Tara.

'Wh't's *in* that g'n?' David's usual eloquence seemed to have deserted him.

'I can't reveal my secrets!' Hero tapped her nose stud mysteriously. 'But I'm glad you like it!'

'It's not drugs, is it?' Emily looked furious. 'You didn't say we could put *anything* in it!'

'No drugs, just the magic of the solstice,' said Hero, and wafted serenely away with her bottle of champagne.

Emily scowled.

'Wonderful!' said Jacqueline, clapping her hands together. 'Now, if you'd all like to collect a yoga mat from the corner of the room, it's time for our very special party treat . . .'

'I might grab a glass of water from the kitchen first, if that's OK.' Tara began to sidle away as the crowd surged back towards the yoga mats. 'Do start though, I'll just slip in at the back.'

'*Will* you?' Jacqueline gave her a pointed look.

'Yes! Absolutely!' Tara was already at the door. 'Can't wait!'

Five minutes in the loo checking her phone for messages (still nothing from Phil, or Toby), and another five washing her hands very carefully, was plenty of time for the gong bath to have got well underway, Tara estimated. The corridor was quiet and she tiptoed into the kitchen, where she knocked back two big glasses of water, picked up the bottle of wine she'd brought, and went straight out on to the iron fire escape that overlooked the back of the high street. It was high enough that she could see beyond the rooflines to the pale lights in the park, and the bandstand, lit up in candy-floss pink for charity.

Tara poured herself a large glass of wine and took a big sip. She wasn't drunk. She felt calmer than she had in a long time. Open. Mellow. Lovely.

'Ahhhh,' she breathed, and leaned on the railing.

There was a giggle above her head and she nearly slipped over the side, spinning round to see where the voice had come from.

'Sorry, sorry!'

She looked up and was startled to see David hunched on the flight above her, his sleeves rolled to his elbows and another button on his shirt undone. He was clutching an empty pint glass – probably an emergency rehydration measure. 'David? What are you doing here?'

'I'm not a yoga person.' He shook his head like a dog with something in its ear. 'Can't take my shoes and socks off in public.'

'Not even for the sake of the Centre?'

'I did a godawful retreat in Italy about five years ago. With free dancing. I made a promise to myself. Never again.'

'Really?' Tara was intrigued by the panic in his pale eyes. 'What *happened*?'

'We had to pretend we were going through the birthing process ...' David mimed being wedged in a confined space; Tara spluttered childishly at his panicked expression.

The kitchen door opened and someone walked in. 'Tara? Tara?'

They both froze. It sounded like Emily.

David put a finger to his lips in a 'Sshhh!' gesture and pointed at the space next to him on the steps. Silently, Tara removed her shoes and tiptoed up to where David was sitting, one step at a time.

She heard someone else – Cressida? – yell, or rather slur, 'Can you get me some water too, please? I'm feeling a bit . . .' The tap ran, someone muttered, and the steps faded away.

Neither spoke for a moment, then just as Tara opened her mouth to say, 'Do you think we should go back down?' the unmistakeable sound of a gong began booming from the floor below and the pair of them cringed backwards into the metal steps.

'Should we . . . ?' she said, as he said uncertainly, 'They're not going to miss us, are they? I mean, if they're really into it?'

'Better not interrupt them by coming in late,' Tara agreed, refilling her glass. 'Wine?'

'Probably shouldn't, but go on.' David held his pint glass out with an urgency that suggested all the wine in the world couldn't take away the mental image of what would be going on below them. 'I'm feeling a bit strange, to be honest.'

'Strange how?'

'I don't feel *drunk* . . .'

'We established that earlier.'

'But I'm definitely not sober.' David seemed to be exploring the inside of his head. 'I feel . . . drugged? I've never taken ketamine but this is what I imagine it's like. Like I'm trapped inside a well. But in my head.'

'That's exactly how I feel!' Tara pointed at him. 'Is elderflower a hallucinogenic? I know nutmeg can get you stoned. Lionel's wife once misread teaspoons for tablespoons in some biscuits he brought in one Christmas. The place looked like Woodstock by teatime.'

David giggled. Giggly drunk David was very different

149

from the David who now met her at the corner of Shelley Street most mornings, to add pedometer steps and point out Edwardian postboxes.

Unbuttoned, thought Tara randomly. *He's unbuttoned.* Literally and . . . she furrowed her brow. What was the word?

'You're funny,' he said.

'Thank you.' The compliment felt nice. 'You're funny too.'

'No, I'm not.' David shook his head. 'I am many things, but I'm not funny.'

'But you were in a comedy group,' said Tara, and he frowned just as she realized she didn't want to bring *that* up. The last person she wanted joining them on the fire escape right now was the spectre of Justin Biggins. 'You're obviously an excellent counsellor,' she added.

'Oh, prrthhh.' He wafted his hand modestly.

'You are. You've got a waiting list. Chloe told me.' She frowned. 'She probably shouldn't have, though. GDPR and whatnot.'

They were sitting close together on the step. Tara turned to look at him properly. David might be intimidatingly qualified and a creepy hypnotist in a past life, but out here they were just two escapees from the gong madness. An unexpected urge to be very honest swept over her.

'How do you do it?'

David squinted back at her. 'How do I do what?'

'How do you manage to get results from people so quickly?' She was vaguely aware of speaking but it sounded like someone else's voice. 'You've made breakthroughs with clients who've seen *all* of us over the years, and you've just . . .' She tried to snap her fingers, but couldn't make her fingers connect.

She tried again, then again, then sighed and gave up.

'Just a new face,' said David. 'New person often gets results.'

'No.' Tara frowned. 'No, it's not that. It's something you do. You've got a . . . thing.' Might as well ask him. 'Is it hypnotism? Is that what you're doing?'

David waved a dismissive hand in front of his face again, and Tara felt weightless, as if she were falling from a great height. Maybe there was no secret, no magic trick: maybe David was just very good at what he did. Because he was qualified, a proper psychotherapist, unlike her. She listened, made accurate notes, and referred people to helplines. Not the same.

That's what they'll ask in the interview for Centre Director, she thought, with a flash of fear. *Why don't I have more qualifications? They'll talk to Eric and find out I'm way behind with my supervisions, and that I haven't had any grief therapy for Mum, and even Jacqueline will realize I've been busking it from the beginning. And they'd be right. I need more. I need qualifications.*

'Are you all right, Tara?'

'What is it, David?' she said, gripped with a need to know. 'I've seen you with the clients as they leave and I've seen the expression on their faces. Like they suddenly understand themselves. You know how to help them. You *fix* them.'

'Tara, most people know what they have to do before they come. I just guide them towards the answer. But I love it when you see the penny drop. It's an amazing thing to do, helping people help themselves. A privilege.'

'And can you do it on yourself?'

'What?' David's eyes locked with hers and Tara was suddenly afraid she might cry.

'Because I can't.'

'You can't *what*?' he asked softly.

This was awful. Awful. Tara knew she should shut up but she couldn't. Was he doing it to her now, his mystery technique? The words were leaking out.

She turned away and stared into the iron railings. *Now I feel as clueless as them.*

'Tara . . . ?'

'My life is such a mess, David. My dad . . . my boyfriend. Well, he's not my boyfriend. I mean, he is . . . but he probably isn't.' She gripped her head. 'I miss my brother so much. And the floods! I can't make them not happen.' The thoughts were clear in her mind. Why weren't they coming out in order?

I wish I could do what you do, she thought, and for a horrible moment didn't know if she'd spoken it aloud.

There was a long pause, then David spoke. 'Do you really want to know how I help people? Really?'

Tara nodded without turning her head.

'It's the dogs.'

'What?' She frowned. 'What . . . so you, I don't know, you . . .' She struggled to think of what he might do with the dogs and couldn't.

'I listen to them. I ask them what the problem is. And they tell me.'

Tara turned to look at him. 'Seriously?'

She wasn't sure which bit of that sounded more mad. That he asked the dogs, or that he thought they told him.

Dr David, holder of many degrees and diplomas. Telling her he got his amazing results by talking to dogs.

He smiled tentatively, and Tara realized he was joking.

Oh. Disappointment nipped her. She'd been honest with David – *way* too honest – and he was trying to lighten the mood with a joke. Probably out of sheer embarrassment at what she'd confessed.

'And how do you talk to them?' she said, playing along with it.

'I don't know, I've just always been able to.' He looked tipsy, a bit wild-eyed, but earnest. 'You ask from here . . .' He thumped his chest over his heart, connecting on the second attempt. 'If they want to reply, I hear them in my head.'

'You hear voices in your head,' she repeated slowly. 'The voices of dogs.'

'And cats. I know, I know. It sounds insane.'

No more than the Angel Gabriel offering Anji second opinions on divorces. 'And what do they say?'

'Sometimes they say, "She scares me". Sometimes they say, "He cries at night". Sometimes they have no idea whatsoever that there's a problem.' David paused. 'Not every animal is very smart. Like humans.'

'And cats?' What would Sybil say about her, Tara wondered – or Phil, her supposed owner? What had she noticed about them?

David seemed to be giving it proper thought. 'Cats are more objective than dogs. They're not as invested. I mean, they like their owners but they're more . . . observers.'

'Figures.' Sybil was a flatmate, not a pet. A flatmate

who didn't care for her late nights. 'I don't want to think what my cat would be saying about me. She's very . . . aloof.'

He shrugged. 'They're hunters.' He thought for a second, then his face lit up. 'Like you!'

'Me?' She frowned, not understanding. 'I'm not a hunter.'

More like stupid easy prey.

'Tara Hunter.'

'Oh. No, I don't think so. My dad maybe. Not me.'

'Really? How so?'

Tara opened her mouth, then closed it. Too much. Her head was thick with a purplish drunkenness, and although she wanted to tell David – she had a funny feeling he'd understand – it was just too complicated. 'Nah. Don't talk about stuff like that at work.'

'OK.'

She turned to him, and was distractingly shaken by how beautiful David's oak-brown eyes were. A gingery warmth flowered in her chest. Tara reached out a drunken finger and touched his nose, calmly, first time. 'I never, ever mix work and home. Firm lines.'

He removed her finger from his nose, kissed it without thinking, and placed it back on her knee. 'OK.'

They sat in silence for a few moments that stretched into longer moments. Tara wasn't sure what she was supposed to say. Had he just kissed her finger? Had she imagined that?

Without warning, an overwhelming hopelessness swamped her, so sharp that tears sprang into her eyes. Forget mixing work and home – she didn't *have* any 'home'. Phil was a disaster waiting to happen. Toby, the only person who truly understood why she was as she was, had run hundreds of miles from her. Mum was gone. Dad was here, but she didn't know why, and she didn't trust herself to enjoy his company for fear of what might go wrong. And at work everyone thought she was so competent, so *in control*, but right now it would only take one tricky client, one bad morning, to reveal that she was flailing round in a bigger mess than any of them.

She felt David's hand on her arm. Was she crying? A tentative squeeze. Then his arm around her shoulders. It was strong, and warm. Comforting.

If I turn my head, she thought, *he might kiss me.*

Then a more startling thought: *I might kiss him.*

'Come on,' he murmured. 'It's not that bad.'

'It is.' She bit her lip. The pebble of guilt that lay permanently at the pit of her stomach was swelling into a boulder, crushing and indefinable. It usually did when she drank. 'It's much worse than you think.'

He leaned and said quietly, into her ear, 'Tara, tell me if I can help? We're not . . . technically . . . at work now?'

David's breath tickled her neck. It smelled of gin, and wine, and flowers. Midsummer and the colour lilac and foxgloves and silver stars. Tara shook her head slowly, from side to side, and the edge of her ear connected with David's warm lips. A tingle of electricity ran across her bare skin.

Don't let yourself be hypnotized. Be strong. Fill your head with bubble wrap.

But her skin still tingled and prickled, and Tara ached to turn and let David's lips graze her cheek, then her mouth.

Don't add to the mess.

She said the right thing. 'We should go down to the gong bath.'

David didn't seem keen to move. Tara could feel him next to her, his face still close, though she couldn't see him. 'Are you sure?'

'Yup.' She wiped a tear away quickly. 'Better go now.'

'Because . . . ?'

'Come on,' she said. And wobbled determinedly down the stairs to the kitchen.

Chapter Eleven

Tara was no stranger to a hangover, but the mornings after the Wellness Centre's parties were always particularly grim. It was something about the combination of cheap alcohol mixed with undercooked vol-au-vents and the looming fear of having said something she shouldn't without even knowing.

She rolled over in bed tentatively, very conscious of her brain inside her skull. A nasty smell of vomit hung in the room, and for the first time in many years Tara wondered if she'd blanked out a section of the evening. The part where she ate an entire bowl of cold stir-fry and threw it up over the duvet.

Once she prised open her mascara-crusted eyes, however, it became clear that the vomit wasn't her problem. Rather, it was her problem to deal with, but she could cross random puking off her list of things to feel bad about.

Sybil was curled up so tightly on Tara's discarded dress that her head was invisible. She looked like a very sad puddle of black cat. All around her were lumpy pools of yellow puke. Tiny flecks of it speckled her fur. When Tara moved, she didn't shoot off into the corner as she normally did, but made a muffled noise that was so far from her normal empress attitude that Tara felt a real pang of concern through her hangover.

'What the hell, Sybil?' She went to throw back the duvet then realized that would be a terrible idea, given the pools of sick on it.

Instead she reached out a shaky hand for her phone, and started Googling local vets with Saturday opening hours.

When Phil had dropped Sybil off in her cat basket – along with two tins of Sheba and a grisly chewed-up catnip toy with no eyes – he hadn't exactly furnished Tara with a user manual. She and Sybil were already sort of acquainted from the handful of times she'd stayed over at Phil's flat in Kidderminster, which was currently, he explained, full of builders, one of whom had nearly squashed Sybil with his toolkit. Tara would, Phil said, giving her the melting look he was so good at, be doing him and Sybil a huge favour if she could look after her for a while.

'Cats are amazing, so low maintenance,' he'd insisted, brushing off her panicky questions about jabs and vets and what she should do if Sybil malfunctioned in some way. 'They just sort themselves out.'

That was his attitude to most problems, and such was his confident stance in the world that they generally did.

Tara, on the other hand, couldn't bear a teetering washing basket or an unpaid bill. Reliability was everything to her, something she nurtured and prized in herself, as proof she wasn't really her father's daughter. She'd never owned a pet as an adult and her memories of Branston were, she realized after a few weeks in charge of Sybil, viewed through the soft-focus filter of childhood, in which dogs never pooed, and the top shelf in the bathroom mysteriously self-generated loo rolls like the Elves and the Shoemaker. She had a vague memory of accompanying her mum and Branston to the vet's when he was booked in for some operation her father refused to support, but other than that, she had no idea what you were meant to do if your family pet vomited over your bedlinen.

Unlike Phil, however, Tara's first reaction when her cat did malfunction was to panic until she'd found someone who could tell her how to fix it.

'It sounds as though she's just eaten something she shouldn't,' the receptionist decided, after a series of questions about Sybil's habits that made Tara feel like a neglectful owner because she couldn't answer half of them, not really having known Sybil long enough to be on intimate terms with her digestive history. 'If you want to bring her in, the vet can have a look.'

'Great.' Tara had a few gaps between her Saturday appointments, and the vet's wasn't too far out of the town. 'Should I bring in a sample of the vomit?'

Sybil finally lifted her head and gave her a look. Her eyes seemed a bit less yellow than normal but she still managed to look disparaging.

'Just bring the cat,' said the receptionist.

Tara took two paracetamol with yet another pint of water, and drove slowly to work with a reluctant Sybil in her basket in the footwell.

'Now, this is only for a couple of hours,' she told her as she lifted the basket out. 'Try to get some sleep and please don't vomit in my office.'

The mood in the reception area was glacial, with

several people waiting for the first appointments of the day: a middle-aged couple, a teenager staring at the floor, and three people sitting together in a tense and barely contained way that suggested they'd arrived together to get a professional verdict on a family row. Out of the corner of her eye, Tara spotted a couple with a German Shepherd at the far end of the corridor and it jogged a thought loose from the party debris in her mind.

David. She stopped short, Sybil's carrier swinging in her hand. David had told her at the party the previous evening that he talked to the dogs in his appointments.

He said what?

Through her headache, Tara had an unsettling flash of David gazing down at her from his seat on the fire escape: those clear eyes looking straight into her mind, the strange confessional impulse she'd had.

What had she said? *Oh God.* She'd admitted to David Dalloway that her personal life was a mess, and that she didn't think she could help anyone.

Why had she done that? What was in the gin? Tara's chest tightened with a stifling, knotting sensation. He wouldn't tell anyone, would he?

'Tara? Are you all right?'

She looked round: Chloe the receptionist was leaning over the desk to offer her a glass of water.

'What's that for?'

'You just looked . . . like you might faint?' Chloe lowered her voice. 'Everyone looks rough today. Bryan's called in sick, and Anji nearly threw up in my bin. I *told* Jacqueline she should have got more food to soak up the homebrew. Sandwiches don't cut it with that stuff. You need serious carbs. Like, mashed potato or something.'

'Good tip for next year. Thanks.' Tara waved away the water and struggled to get her mind working.

She needed to talk to David. She needed to make it clear that she'd been speaking under the influence of mind-altering homebrew, and that he should disregard anything she'd said. And definitely not tell Jacqueline.

'Is that your cat?' Chloe made a cooing noise. 'Hello, puss-puss.'

There was a thunderous rumble from the basket, then a flash of claw, and Chloe withdrew her finger rapidly.

'That's Sybil. She's not well,' said Tara.

As she spoke, an unnerving image of David's face, very close to hers, on the fire escape swam into her mind and her cheeks burned. Well, at least he'd been talking equally embarrassing nonsense. He probably wouldn't even remember what she said, if he was at the point of telling her he talked to dogs.

That was a small comfort.

'Can you take messages for me if anyone calls?' she asked Chloe. 'I've . . . got some stuff to sort out before my first client.'

'No problem,' said Chloe. 'I'll say there's a bug going round the Centre.'

Tara's thoughtful silences in the Johnstons' session turned out to be useful for everyone involved. Martin Johnston finally had time to speak, and Bryony was so thrown by Tara's minimalist new approach that she assumed it was part of the therapy and actually listened to what her husband was saying.

Tara herself spent at least half the hour trying to think of the best way to open the conversation with David, without sending him running straight to Jacqueline with accusations of workplace bullying to add to her admissions of failure.

When she'd shown the Johnstons out, she gave up and knocked on David's door. Best thing to do was to get it over and done with.

'Hello!' His hair had flopped over his forehead and he was drinking a cup of mint tea very carefully, holding it with two hands. 'Why did no one warn me about the gin?' he groaned. 'I only had two. *Two.*'

'You had more than two,' said Tara. 'And there were at least fifteen entries in that competition.'

'Yes, but we only had sips,' he protested. 'It can't have been more than a glass in total.'

'And then there was the wine. On the balcony, remember?'

'Oh yes. The wine.'

He glanced at her and there was a momentary flash of something else: a guilty camaraderie. 'Well, at least we missed the gong bath.' He paused. 'Didn't we?'

'David, I barely remember getting home,' said Tara. 'There's something we need to talk about.'

He put down his cup of tea. 'Did I say something inappropriate? Everything goes a bit blurry after the one that tasted like spiced pound coins.'

Tara closed the door behind her, and perched on the chair opposite his heavy Victorian desk. Not the client chair; the spare, in-between chair that was mainly used for coats and by other therapists who didn't want to sit on the therapy couch.

'Why do you think you said something inappropriate?' she asked, trying to keep her voice non-accusatory.

David's eyes darted back and forth. 'Well, because I never know whether you're supposed to tell people they're looking nice these days, or whether that's objectification or . . .'

'What? No, it's about something we discussed.' Tara straightened her spine, trying to make herself look more dignified than she felt. 'We had a bit of an . . . under-the-influence conversation.' She paused. 'About work.'

David stared at her with an unreadable expression in his brown eyes, and Tara stared back, and for that moment she would have given anything to be able to get inside his head, no matter what a hypocrite that would have made her on the involuntary mind-control front.

He swivelled on his chair and touched his temples with his forefingers. 'Yes, I think the gin might have led us to, um, admit things that we might not necessarily . . .'

'Yes. It was the gin,' she agreed, quickly. 'The gin.'

Or *was* it? Wait. Had he hypnotized her?

David stopped swivelling. 'You haven't mentioned what we discussed to anyone else?'

'God, no! Of course not. And I'd rather you didn't either.'

'No, I don't think I'd share it with other colleagues. They might think it was a bit . . .' David didn't finish, but looked up at her. Tara braced herself to see the judgement in his eyes, even disappointment that she wasn't all she was cracked up to be, but instead there was a flicker of vulnerability. Uncertainty as to what *she* might say next.

An edgy, chess-playing silence filled the room, as they each waited for the other to carry on.

A revelation belatedly hit her. David wasn't talking

about her drunken confession. He was nervous about what *he'd* said.

'David?' She leaned forward. 'Do you mean that stuff you told *me* about you talking to dogs?'

He flinched and, too late, Tara realized she'd just revealed her own hand.

David was obviously less hungover: he spotted her mistake and swiftly adjusted tack. 'As opposed to you and your burnout?'

'I never said I was burned out . . .' she started automatically, then gave up. Her brain wasn't up to fencing this morning. 'You told me you communicated with the dogs in sessions, and got them to snitch on their owners. You were winding me up, right?'

Several moments passed.

Then David said, quietly, 'No.'

Tara sat back in her seat, flummoxed: if David was mentally ill, then she needed to treat these revelations carefully. 'I read those links you sent to me about pets in therapy. I understand why people feel a sense of being held to account by a third party, even if it's a silent, er, non-human one. So are you saying you interpret the client's reactions and those of the animal together and reach a conclusion based on . . .' Tara struggled; this wasn't the best morning for careful analysis of anything. 'Based on their body language?'

'There's an element of that, yes.'

'But are you saying you go further than that? You communicate with the dogs themselves?'

He watched her eyes, searching for signs of judgement, then nodded. 'Yes.'

'David? Is this . . . ?' Tara abandoned her attempts to

be unflappably professional. 'Who put you up to this? One of the holistic healers? Is this because of what I said about the crabs under the pillow?'

David frowned. 'Remind me what you said about the crabs under the pillow?'

She raised her hands. 'I'll be honest – I don't know what to say. No one's ever told me they could talk to animals before. Well, not someone on *our* side of the table.'

Outside, a dog barked on the street and she said, 'Don't!' before he could say anything.

David still wasn't denying it, though. He could have rowed back easily, pretended it was just a joke, but he didn't. He was gazing at her, and she really didn't know what to make of it.

'OK,' she said. 'Show me. Let me see you do it.'

'I can't let you sit in on a session, Tara. You know it breaks client confidentiality.'

'Well, this puts me in an awkward situation. Because, taken at face value, it sounds as if you're suffering from a mental health condition that I'd normally have a duty of care to refer to a specialist.'

David's phone buzzed. 'That's Chloe, checking in my next client,' he said. 'Can we . . . talk about this later?'

'I think we should. When are you free today? I need to take Sybil to the vet's at eleven and I've got two appointments this afternoon, three till five.'

'Sybil?'

'My boyfriend's cat. She's not very well.'

David eyed her cautiously. 'Is she here with you now?'

'She's in my room in her carrier. Why?' She paused, and a thought occurred to her. 'Do you want to talk to her?'

'Why not?' He glanced down at his desk diary. 'What are you doing after you bring her back from the vet's?'

'Nothing.'

'OK,' said David. 'One o'clock it is. I'll bring my sandwiches.'

'So, where do you want her?' Tara lifted the cat basket from under her desk and placed it on the coffee table between the sofas. 'Does she need to be out? She's stopped being sick. Apparently it was something she ate.'

Sybil glared out from between the bars of the basket with her usual inscrutable gaze.

'She's fine there, and . . .' said David, then paused as if he'd been interrupted.

'What?'

'Nothing.' He indicated the leather sofa where Tara's clients normally sat. 'Do you want to make yourself comfy over here?'

She'd started to settle herself in her usual consulting chair. 'That's the clients' sofa.'

'I know,' said David, and indicated it again.

Tara hesitated, then moved. The sofa was softer than her chair, and she had to make an effort to sit up straight. It was a nice view: straight over to the cathedral, with the blue sky cut into paperchain peaks by the pointed roofs opposite. She'd never seen the room from this angle. The scalloped mouldings along the edge of the ceiling were rather pretty.

David settled himself on her chair. He seemed quite high up.

I need to get a lower chair, thought Tara. *It's quite intimidating from this angle.*

166

'So . . .' He blinked a couple of times. 'What a lovely cat. How long have you had Sybil?'

Tara's chest relaxed, and she realized she'd been expecting David to ask her about her childhood. Usually when she sat on a therapist's sofa she ended up talking about her parents. Never fun. She made an effort to drop her shoulders from their current position somewhere around her ears.

'What? Living with me? About two months.' Sybil was sitting up in her carrier, staring out as if she knew what was going on. 'Although I've known her a bit longer than that.'

'Uh-huh. How much longer?'

Immediately Tara felt herself squirming. When did you date a relationship from? First date? First night together? First time you meet his parents? Because they weren't quite there yet. But they were definitely in a relationship; it just wasn't appropriate for her to be advertising it over social media.

She knew she was fudging it. 'Er, maybe . . . a year.'

'OK. She's a very beautiful girl.'

His soothing hypnotherapist tone was starting to annoy Tara. How on earth could David even see Sybil? She was a black cat in a dark cat basket. 'Are you trying to butter her up? Because I can tell you it doesn't work. I've tried.'

'Not at all.' He tapped his pen against his notebook. 'Just an observation. What would you say are the things you like best about Sybil?'

Tara struggled to think. 'I don't know. She's . . . pretty low maintenance. I'm assuming she scares the mice away from the house with her cat smell? And Hero would say she's lucky. Black cat crossing my path several times a day.'

'That's it?'

'What? What else can she do? Cats aren't exactly spark-ling conversationalists. And they never get the shopping in. Bloody freeloaders.'

'Most pet owners talk about companionship, or the cute personality traits their cats have.' He drew vague cir-cles in the air with his hand. 'How they picked them out from the other cats in the . . .' David's voice trailed off as if his attention had been caught somewhere else.

'I didn't pick her out,' said Tara. Was he even listening to her? 'I did tell you that I'm looking after her for my boyfriend. He's got builders working in his house – Sybil was getting in the way, so he thought it was safer for me to look after her.'

David didn't speak but tilted his head in a 'go on' fash-ion. Tara, marooned on the confessional clients' sofa, heard herself adding, 'He's having an attic conversion.'

She closed her mouth tightly. She didn't want to give David easy cat-reading clues; she hadn't told him how much she enjoyed hearing Sybil purr at night, or the haughty voice Tara supplied for her when she demanded her dinner. Or that the act of asking her to look after his cat had felt like a Significant Moment for her and Phil, which was the main reason she'd agreed.

'OK. I see. OK.'

Tara deliberately switched her gaze to the basket, where Sybil was now sitting upright as a statue against the grille. Was Sybil ratting her out about the worming pills she'd slipped into her food?

David laughed under his breath, to himself.

'Is she telling you what's wrong with her?' she asked semi-sarcastically. 'Because if it's something other than mild digestive upset, I want my forty quid back from the vet.'

'There's nothing wrong with her,' said David, without looking up. 'She ate something she shouldn't have in the garden.'

'Good guess. Can you be more specific?'

'Well, she's not clear about what it was originally. It was a bit . . . decomposed once she bit into it. A thrush, maybe.'

'She can tell the difference?'

David was writing on his notepad with his fountain pen; it scratched against the paper. He paused, added another couple of lines, then ripped off the page and folded it in two. As he handed it to her, Tara was reminded of an old-fashioned doctor writing a prescription. Or a magician doing a trick.

'I don't want you to read that until you get home,' he said. 'Promise?'

'Promise,' said Tara, although she wasn't sure why or what she was promising.

'Great!' He flashed a quick smile at the cat basket, then at her. 'Thank you for letting me meet Sybil – she's a lovely cat.'

'Thanks,' said Tara, watching him stroll out of the room. Somehow David seemed a lot more confident than he had a few hours ago, and far more confident than he had on the fire escape last night.

She looked back at the grille of the cat basket. Sybil had gone to sleep.

At half past five, Tara sat in the car outside her house, and took David's note out of her bag.

It had been burning a hole since she'd hidden it there, but for reasons she couldn't quite admit to herself she'd committed to her promise and waited until she got home to read it.

She unfolded the paper, already guessing what David could have gleaned from their chat. He had smooth cursive handwriting, with looped Ds and Fs; Jolyon the long-since-departed graphologist would have had a field day, she thought. The therapists – including Tara; she wasn't ashamed – had queued up to have Jolyon 'do' them ('These Cs indicate a strong creative side . . . this long tail suggests you have untapped emotional depths . . .' etc.; Jolyon had even found something positive to say about Bryan's scary all-caps printing), until he had to leave under a cloud after Jacqueline's signature was forged on the Majestic Wine invoices.

David had written three things on the paper.

1. Sybil is getting better food from your neighbour two doors down. Scottish lady?
2. Sybil likes you but thinks you need to sleep more. Your phone (something that flashes?) keeps her awake in your room.
3. There are no builders in your boyfriend's house.

Tara had started to smile at the first – she'd long suspected Sybil of supplementing her diet, but that was such an easy guess. What cat *didn't* eat at several houses? Although it was an unexpectedly Sybil touch to add the little burn about the food being better – another lucky guess, she thought.

And the second – of course David was going to say

Sybil liked her! And it was obvious she wasn't sleeping from the constant bags under her eyes. And who didn't keep their phone in their room?

This was actually quite disappointing. She'd at least hoped for revelations about Phil.

But as Tara read the third point, her smile froze. Because there was absolutely no way David could know that about Phil unless . . .

She stared at the words.

Unless Sybil had told him? But then how would Sybil know something different from what Phil had told her? She was a cat.

There are at least three levels of madness right there, she told herself. *Get a grip.*

David was just guessing. But why would he focus on the builders? Why not just throw in a third stab in the dark, like . . . *Sybil says you drink too much coffee?* Why tell her something like that, something that might have repercussions?

Unless he was winding her up, pointed out a voice in her head. For 'banter', like the lads in the college bar. David did have form for that type of thing.

She felt cold.

Tara looked down into the footwell, where Sybil's basket was wedged in tightly. The cat was sitting up; her yellow eyes were trained straight on her.

They stared at each other, and for a deeply unsettling second, Tara felt as if Sybil was trying to tell her something.

'Don't be so bloody ridiculous,' she said, and wasn't sure who she was speaking to. Herself, or the cat.

171

Chapter Twelve

Tara resisted the temptation to call Phil for a whole day and then cracked. She hadn't phoned him again about the flowers – because her conscience knew that conversation should only end one way – but Sybil was a shared responsibility.

The call went to voicemail after some ringing tone that she wasn't sure was even British, and Tara didn't want to leave another needy message, so instead texted him a photo of Sybil in her carrier.

Just to let you know Sybil's had a bit of an upset tum and had to go to the vet. She's fine now, though! That was OK, wasn't it? Updating him on his cat wasn't needy. **How's the building work going? Let me know when I can come and see the finished masterpiece! Miss you. xxx**

That *was* a bit passive aggressive, she thought, ten seconds after she'd pressed send. But it was too late. The message had gone.

It didn't entirely surprise her that no reply was forthcoming. What did surprise her was the £100 that appeared in her bank account a few days later, with the reference SYBIL VET.

But no mention of the builders.

*

Tara's workload gave her the perfect excuse to avoid David, and everyone else in the Wellness Centre who might have seen her drunken behaviour at the party, for a few days.

There had been a couple of moments on Monday that made her wonder if her and David's simultaneous disappearance had been noted. She'd spotted Emily sidling up to Bryan and Lionel while they were reheating their lunchtime soup, moving in a similar way to Sybil when there were blue tits on the bird feeder, and conversation between Kasia and Bridget, the art therapist, had ceased abruptly when she walked in on Tuesday. Tara kept her head high, thought of the Centre Director job (Jacqueline had hinted that the advert was 'imminent'), and said nothing.

As for David, she really didn't know what to do. Part of her wondered if she should inform Jacqueline that her star therapist was delusional, but knowing what she knew about David's past, Tara couldn't rule out the possibility that it was a joke. And if it was, she ran the risk of looking like a snitch *and* humourless. And what if Jacqueline had put him up to it, as a sort of management test? Her brain wasn't up to the complications. Tara politely excused herself from their lunchtime walks by pleading a hideous backlog of paperwork – which was true enough – and was even more confused by how much she missed his breezy tour-guide routine.

By the time Thursday evening rolled around, Tara was finally ahead on her to-do list, but feeling lonelier than she had done in some time. To the point where she was almost looking forward to seeing her dad again for their arranged dinner date.

Keith had suggested eating at The Swan, Longhampton's nicest hotel on the edge of town, where he was staying overnight. It wasn't somewhere Tara had been before, though she'd been aware of its gala opening a few years ago: her mother had been there a few times for lunch with friends, and had decreed it 'persuasively comfortable', which was high praise.

As far as Tara herself could make out, parking her car next to Keith's Mercedes, The Swan was everything a boutique hotel was supposed to be; it was an elegant country house with a gravel turning circle, and a fragrant mass of climbing roses over the broad door, plus a five-star Tripadvisor rating discreetly posted in the stone porch.

Keith was in the lounge when she wandered in through the lobby. The physical shock of seeing him was lessening a little each time; not so much a shock now as a frisson of surprise at seeing something unfamiliar in a familiar setting, like a red London bus on Longhampton high street. He was chatting to a woman with a silver tray under her arm, a staff member, she assumed. Keith seemed relaxed, his arm extended over the back of the squashy velvet sofa, the other hand holding a crystal glass at a casual angle. The woman, a few years older than Tara, was glowing under the spotlight of his attention, laughing at whatever story he was telling her, pushing her short blonde hair behind her ear at regular intervals.

Tara watched from the door for a moment, soaking up the details of their interaction before they noticed her. Mum had always said Dad could charm the birds from the trees, which sounded to the young Tara like a nice thing. It had been a few years before she'd understood what Ruth meant, and by then a different picture of her dad had replaced her childhood memories. Then, after Ashley and her Corsa, Tara had noticed every waitress, every friend's mother, every friend, on the infrequent occasions when he took her and Toby out as teens, watching like a hawk, just like her mum had. It didn't make an already tense situation any easier.

Keith made the waitress laugh, and he smiled himself as he finished his drink. Now she looked closer, the interaction didn't strike Tara as particularly flirty, just someone enjoying a pleasant chat with a stranger.

Or maybe he just likes talking to people, Tara thought.

Mum had tried her best not to let her own feelings colour their memories, not always successfully. She wasn't a bitter woman, Tara knew now, just someone trying to protect her children from the same pain she'd suffered. Putting that aside was going to be hard, but Tara had to try. The problem was, how did she get to know her dad as he was now, without judging him for what he did then? The night before, lying awake with her brain going round and round in circles, Tara had even started preparing a list of questions to ask, then realized she wasn't sure if she wanted to know whether he had a girlfriend, whether he'd married again. Whether he'd had more children. That question in particular gnawed at her. She wanted to know – and she didn't.

'Tara!' Keith had spotted her and was waving.

An acidy feeling crawled in Tara's stomach. A weird first-date, exams, driving-test feeling. But at the same time, her heart beat harder to see her dad right there, smiling at her so his dark eyes crinkled when he got up and kissed her cheek. This time, she let him.

'What'll you have?' Keith patted the sofa next to him.

'Gin and tonic? Glass of wine? Libby's just gone to get the gin menu.'

'Just Diet Coke for me, I'm driving.'

'You should try one of these fancy new gin-free gins.' He indicated his empty glass. 'Very good. You can barely tell the difference.'

Dad drinking low-alcohol gin? 'Seriously?'

She wondered for a moment if he was joking, but it seemed he wasn't when he nodded.

I must tell Toby that, thought Tara. Pigs did fly.

'Isn't this a lovely spot?' His gaze travelled around the lounge, which was decorated in chalky shades of green. It *was* nice: soft armchairs and a marble fireplace filled with candles in tall hurricane lamps, deep sash windows with draped curtains framing a view into a garden of rose beds and fruit trees. The bedrooms were probably gorgeous, she thought wistfully. She and Phil were no stranger to a four-poster.

'This dining's a new venture for them,' Keith went on. 'Libby was telling me one of her friends worked in London at Chez Bruce, he's trialling a chef's table in the conservatory. It's only been going a couple of months but she says they've had some very positive feedback from customers.'

'Yes, someone at work had a special birthday dinner here.' Bryan had raved about it, relating exactly how much it cost, course by course, until Judith had piously told him he ought to make an equal donation to the food bank and all hell had broken loose.

'Good for them, I say.' Keith topped up his glass with water from the silver jug on the table, offering her the bowl of cashews. Tara couldn't get over her dad drinking water at cocktail hour. He'd always poured a whisky at 5 p.m. on the days when he'd worked from the studio. Even now, the smell made her think of him, and of bonfires and medicine; metal and fire. 'End of the day' drinks. He'd pour Tara a Diet Coke in the same heavy glass, clonking an ice cube in to match his. 'Great to see people trying to make a go of it, especially with everything that's happened lately. Do you know Libby and Jason?'

She shook her head, embarrassed. Dad had been in Longhampton about ten minutes and already he knew the names of the hotel owners, their business plans and where their chef had worked. 'I've been pretty busy. With the floods.' It came out a bit martyred.

'Of course you have. Ah, the gin list! Thank you, Libby. Now, this is the one I had, so many herbs it's practically medicine . . .'

Libby – Keith introduced them, charmingly – recommended a garnet-coloured aperitif which Tara had to admit was more than palatable, and then showed them to their table for two, by a window looking on to the garden.

'So!' Keith smiled, filling the sudden silence as though they'd just been admiring the place settings. 'How are you—'

'How did it go at the council meeting today?' she blurted out, before he could ask her something personal.

'Very well! Did I tell you our archivist came up with some old photographs of the original building? I thought it might be nice to incorporate a little history into the design.'

'It would.' This was easier. 'What sort of details would you choose?'

'Those terrific old oak beams should be centre stage,' he said straight away. 'I've already had a long chat with the lead carpenter, and he's happy about the way everything's drying out. I sent some extra dehumidifiers down there to speed things up a bit.'

'So I hear,' said Tara.

Alice had updated the flood volunteer WhatsApp in a flurry of excitement to inform everyone that 'a crack team of tradesmen' had pulled up in a van to install industrial dehumidifiers in the hall, and start scaffolding the exterior. The way she described it, you'd think they'd leaped out of the back like the A-Team. Going by the photos, they certainly hadn't leaped out of the van and put the kettle on in the way the local builders typically did.

'Did you know there was a magnificent original fireplace in there?' he went on. 'Beautiful feature, God knows why it had been boarded over. Anyway, we're going to restore that, commission a new oak surround, find a way of making that a focal point again. We'll find the right local craftsmen, obviously,' he added, before she could speak. 'The whole point is to involve the community in making something for themselves.'

It was clear that he was enjoying himself. Keith's handsome face was animated as he described the particular wood the original builders had used, and Tara noticed that he referred to various people by name – not just Rob the MP, or Alice, but the local joiner, Andy, and his lads, Dan, Tyler, Hugh.

'Have you been doing anything else, apart from researching oak beams?' she asked, only half joking.

'Not a lot.' Keith moved his napkin as the starters

arrived on a wide tray. 'The office is thrilled – they've been trying to get me out from under their feet for months. They think it's Christmas.'

Tara had ordered scallops, Keith the Jerusalem artichokes, and as she lifted her fork to start, a young waitress came rushing back with the wine menu.

'I'm sorry,' she said, red-faced. 'I completely forgot to give you the wine menu. Can I get you anything to have with your meal?'

Keith looked over at Tara. 'Tara? A small glass? I can get you a taxi home?'

She shook her head, and to her surprise, he said, 'We're fine, thank you. Maybe some sparkling water for the table?' and handed the menu back.

'Don't abstain just because I'm driving,' she said, choosing a bread roll carefully. 'You can take politeness only so far.'

'Ha! Actually, I don't, these days.'

'What?' Tara didn't mean it to sound so rude. 'You don't *drink*?'

Keith shook his head and pared some butter off the beautifully moulded Tudor rose pat. 'I haven't for a while now.'

'How long?'

'Ten years or so.'

Tara knew from work that the 'or so' was an affectation. It was probably ten years, two months and three days.

'Why? What happened?'

He shrugged. 'I just decided, one morning, that enough was enough. I needed to grow up. I had responsibilities.'

Tara stared at him. He'd had responsibilities thirty-two years ago and it hadn't stopped him drinking two bottles of whisky every weekend, according to Mum. 'Any responsibilities in particular?'

He paused, bread halfway to his mouth, and acknowledged her wounded expression with an apologetic shake of the head. 'I hear what you're saying. I'm sorry. Of course I had responsibilities to you and Toby. I should have grown up sooner. But it's like they say, the moment finds you – I was—'

'I don't need to know the ins and outs.' The words snapped out. 'I mean . . . well done.'

Keith put the bread down carefully. 'I had to take a couple of runs at it, but I'm happy with how things are now.'

'Good,' said Tara. It came out a bit tightly.

How would her mum react, hearing Dad was teetotal? A sharp pain went through Tara's ribs because she'd never know the answer to that question.

She'd roll her eyes, interjected a voice in her head. *And make a show of biting her lip, and then change the subject.* It sounded like her mum's voice. Her 'Come on, don't be gloomy, Tara' voice.

'You know, life has a way of offering you silver linings,' Keith went on. 'It's a bit like the fireplace in the hall – that only came to light because of the floods, we'd never have found that if the floor hadn't been taken up. And for me, I only met Sarah because we—'

'No,' said Tara. Her fork slipped from her hand and clattered to the plate, too loud in the quiet dining room. 'Sorry?'

'If you don't mind, I don't want to talk about . . .' She stopped, conscious of how brattish that sounded. *I don't want to talk about anyone except you and me.*

180

There was a silence, in which Tara almost retracted what she'd blurted out. But Keith seemed to understand.

'OK,' he said easily. 'Let's talk about you. Have you got any plans to go away this summer?'

'No, work's still mad,' said Tara automatically.

'But you've had a hard year. The floods, your workload.' Keith paused, then added, 'Your mum. Can you take some time off in the autumn, maybe?'

She shook her head. 'I used my holiday allowance to cover the volunteering.'

'That's no good. You need time to process. Time to look after yourself, not everyone else.'

Tara looked out of the window and swallowed down the lump in her throat. That tone was so familiar; not a memory, something lodged so deep inside her that she couldn't remember knowing it. Her kneejerk reaction was to say, *And what gives you the right to tell me that?* but there was concern in his voice. He meant it, one adult to another.

They didn't speak for a moment. A very long moment.

'Is anyone looking after you?' It was lightly asked but she could hear genuine concern.

'I don't need anyone to look after me.' Tara's defences rose again, and she smiled too brightly, scraping the last smudges of pea puree round the plate. 'I'm managing perfectly well on my own. Believe me, I've got *all* the books and a crystal therapy bracelet.'

'And Toby? Are you helping each other?'

Tara placed her knife and fork neatly together, unsure what to say. Her brother. Her twin. Yes, what was her brother doing to look after her?

'He's very busy,' she said loyally. 'It's not easy, when we're in different time zones.'

'Ah, yes. The king of Instagram. He's a funny guy.'

'He's done incredibly well,' agreed Tara, ignoring the opportunity to tell Keith who Toby got that from – an opportunity she sensed had been lined up. 'I love his photographs. I think he got his eye from Mum.'

Keith acknowledged it gracefully. 'I think he did. I always assumed you'd be the writer, though. Wasn't that the plan, once upon a time? That you'd be the family hack?'

It had been. Secretly, she'd planned the post-graduation Europe trip as if she'd been commissioned; it would have been her portfolio – food review here, vignette there, travelogue everywhere. But she'd let that dream go.

'I don't think I'd have been tough enough for journalism.' Tara wondered if she'd have turned out like Toby if she'd been the one to make the break, if she'd developed his thicker skin and quicker wit. Or whether he'd always been like that, and that was the reason he'd gone.

'I'm sure you would.'

'Childhood dreams,' she said, with a bleak smile that vanished like a ripple. 'I prefer what I do now. Helping people. Fixing problems.'

'Do you remember those little red books you had? The sketchpads that you'd write down your stories in?' Keith leaned back, savouring the memory as if it were a fine wine. 'I wonder where they are now. Did you keep them? Are they in a cupboard at home? I think you interviewed me once. God, I'd love to read what—'

'Dad,' said Tara suddenly, unable to bear it.

'What?'

'Stop it.' She didn't want to tell him Mum had cleared

the house out of everything like that. She couldn't bear to give him reasons to see Mum in a bad light, even though she suddenly yearned to see those books again too.

'Sorry.' The waitress came back to remove their plates, and bring the main courses. Quail for Tara; trout for Keith. 'This looks tremendous,' he said, as she checked they had everything. 'Compliments to the chef!'

The pause was like a reset. While the plates were being cleared, Tara had shuffled through the neutral conversation topics in her head and come up with, *So, what's happening about the redevelopment of Turville Court?*

But before she could ask it, Keith leaned forward and said, 'Tara, I just want you to know that I look back on those years with you and Toby, and . . . I have happy memories of being a father. It wasn't your fault that the marriage part didn't work out. I never wanted you to think I left because of something you did.'

'I never thought that,' lied Tara, just to deprive him of his Bono moment. 'I thought you'd left because Mum kicked you out.'

But of course she'd blamed herself. In the back of the last red notebook was a list of things she must have done or said to make Dad leave. Even Toby had thrown away the Tamagotchi that had annoyed Dad with its incessant bleeping. The house had been so quiet for months afterwards as she and Toby tried to eliminate any irritating behaviours that might push Mum away too.

Keith's eyes were searching her face, and Tara knew he didn't believe her. Should she tell him the truth? She remembered how he'd always been the one she'd admitted the bad stuff to, not Mum. Even though Mum was kind and fiercely loving and capable of reducing class teachers to quivering wrecks, Dad always made Tara's nightmares go away. After he left, there were definitely things she hadn't told her mum, not wanting to add to her pile of worries.

'If you liked being a dad so much, why didn't you try harder to see us?' she retorted. 'Why didn't you make more of an effort to keep in touch? You only had one birthday to remember.'

'I did,' he said simply. 'Presents every birthday and Christmas, without fail.'

Tara didn't want to say, *You're lying*, because it was such an ugly thing to say across this beautiful white table, with its delicate water glasses and silver cutlery. She let the silence speak for her.

Mum wouldn't have kept presents from them. That absolutely wasn't her style. She didn't exactly *encourage* them to see their dad, but she definitely wouldn't have stopped them, if he'd tried.

'Your mother was understandably protective of you and Toby.' He fiddled with his glass. 'I wasn't a great husband. She had her reasons for wanting to protect you two. With the benefit of hindsight there are . . . things I could have done differently.'

'Don't turn this on to Mum.' One step forward, two steps back. 'If you're suggesting there's a cupboard full of your presents in the house, I can assure you there isn't. And I left home fifteen years ago – I'm not exactly hard to track down.'

Keith sighed. 'As I say, there are things I could have done differently.'

Tara looked at him. He was being very honest, but there were careful gaps. Not just the things she didn't want to talk about, but other secrets she sensed he was skating over. Did she want to know what?

She really wasn't sure.

Chapter Thirteen

'. . . and then Rhys.' Sian Bannon blew out her cheeks with a despairing sigh. 'Jesus. Rhys.'

'Rhys isn't coping well in the temporary accommodation?'

Sian fixed Tara with a dead-eyed look. 'He set fire to his bedroom curtains while we were asleep.'

Under the desk, Tara circled her wrist, which was aching from taking increasingly disturbing notes about the Bannon family and the issues arising from their third move in four weeks. Dylan, the youngest, had got them ejected from Sian's sister's place, after he smeared the bathroom, landing and two bedrooms with, well, something awful ('He was only showing his cousins what the house looked like when we went back . . . '); Mared had traumatized her grandma's cat by trying to 'teach it to swim' in the bath. And now Rhys had set fire to the curtains in the emergency accommodation the council had found for them.

Tara was doing her best to help Sian. She'd already given out-of-hours support in dealing with insurance and coping with recurrent nightmares, but the junior Bannons needed emergency intervention from child psychiatry experts for what sounded like PTSD. And maybe a fire prevention officer.

She wrote *David?* on her notes. He'd responded to her kitchen noticeboard plea for volunteers to donate a few hours' counselling, and from what he'd said about his clinical work, he was more equipped than she was to deal with Rhys and his lighter. Maybe between the two of them they could stop the Bannons burning down their next property.

Tara tried to strike a positive note. 'Still, the council are moving ahead with repairs, aren't they? It won't be long before the house is signed off and you can move home. Maybe Rhys will—'

'No.' Sian stared straight at her. 'I'm not going to lie to you, Tara, Rhys has always set fire to things. It's what he does. Gareth – my husband – he used to be able to talk some sense into him, but to be honest, he's not dealing with this well at all.'

'No?'

'He's drinking again. And – I'll put my hands up – I'm not at my most patient right now. We're not setting the kids a good example,' she added with a mournful frown, and folded her hands protectively over her stomach. Sian was six months pregnant but every time Tara saw her, she seemed ten minutes away from going into labour.

'If Gar could just get back to playing his drums again, I think it would help,' Sian went on, 'but the arsey bitch next door to us in the council place wouldn't let him even set them up. I told the housing officer, he needs a release, he does.' She bunched up her lips. 'Otherwise he finds other stuff to wallop.'

'But in the meantime . . . ?'

'Meant to be speaking to the housing officer again this

afternoon.' Sian's face darkened. 'I just want somewhere I can relax.'

'I know what you mean. Right!' said Tara, with some effort. 'Let's break this down into manageable chunks, shall we?'

After dealing with three of Sian's manageable chunks and referring her to specialists for the rest, Tara had been looking forward to a lunchtime power nap on her sofa, but David knocked at ten to one, and once she'd unloaded about the Bannons and he'd agreed to see Rhys, it felt only polite to agree to join him 'for some fresh air' in the park.

Outside, the summer air was soft on her face, and the sensation of striding out in time with David eased Tara's thoughts away from the office. The only fly in the ointment was the circular David-Sybil-Phil niggle in her mind, but fortunately David spent the first ten minutes talking earnestly about transference theories, until he sensed she'd tuned him out.

'I see your dad was in the paper this week,' he said, as they marched past the newsagent's. The *Gazette* board outside declared 'Work Begins on Hall Rebuild', which was something of an understatement, given the speed of operation now Keith's team were in charge.

'Chloe?' No client had passed the threshold without Chloe showing them that week's *Gazette*. 'She might not have mentioned it to you, but that was her mum, you know – with the spade?'

'*Everyone* had spades, as far as I could see. And hard hats.'

It had made a classic front-page photo: Keith, surrounded by representatives from every community group with an interest, waving spades and wearing yellow hard hats, even the baby from the Tea 'n' Tots Baby Group. In addition to pointing out her mum, Pat, chair of the Troutbridge Crafters' Circle, Chloe had told everyone who didn't already know that the star architect was none other than Tara's dad.

'I could tell you were related, even before Chloe pointed him out,' David added. 'Definitely a family resemblance there!'

Tara side-eyed him as they powered down the long entrance to the park, heading towards the bandstand. 'In what way?'

'You've got the same eyes, very striking. Sorry, have I said something wrong?' he added. 'Are you two not close?'

'Not really.' She was trying not to pant, which was making long sentences a problem. It also meant she was revealing more than normal. 'Parents divorced when I was ten. I barely know him.'

'Would you like to slow down?' he asked courteously.

Tara shook her head. 'No, s'fine.'

'And are things going as you expected?'

'I'm not sure – what I expected.' Her chest had tightened, even trying to condense the Dad situation into words.

'Are things going as *he* expected?'

It was a good, if wrong-footing, question, and Tara was genuinely trying to work out what the answer to it was when she became aware of her phone ringing in her pocket.

She pulled it out, already braced for another call from Sian Bannon, but the name on the screen made her say, 'Oh my God!' out loud before she could even think.

Phil.

Tara stopped dead, swiped to answer and put the phone to her ear, leaving David marching on ahead, oblivious. 'Phil?'

'Hey, gorgeous.'

Tara's whole body melted downwards in one lustful swoop at the sound of Phil's voice in her ear. *Stupid treacherous body.*

'How you doing?' he asked, without a shred of irony. He sounded so close, and so casual, as if they'd seen each other just the other night.

'I'm fine. No, I'm not. I'm . . . Where are you?' Too late, Tara realized she'd planned to be distant when Phil finally called, not incoherent.

'Back home. Listen, sorry for the radio silence,' he breezed on, 'but we need to catch up. I've missed you and your beautiful . . . self. You around next weekend?'

'What? Um, yes.' Her head was a jumble of 'FLOWERS – Sybil – where have you been? – FLOWERS – dignity – WHO IS PUMPKIN?', jostling like hysterical shoppers trying to shove their way through a tiny door into the January sales.

'Fantastic. You choose a time and place and I promise you I'll make up for being such a bad boyfriend. Hopefully by being a very, very bad boyfriend . . . What?' The phone was muffled, presumably by his hand going over it, and some conversation raged out of earshot.

'Wait! You can't just . . . Phil!' Tara didn't care if people were staring. Her heart was racing too fast. Until she'd heard his voice and felt the sudden explosion of colour through her whole body, she hadn't realized how much she'd missed him. The last time she'd experienced such an instant dangerously out-of-control rush was when she'd given up coffee for Lent and celebrated Easter with a triple espresso.

'Sorry, gorgeous, I've got to go.' Tara could hear the wink in his eye, the sexy promises in his smile. 'Just text me – I'm yours, wherever whenever, OK? So long as it's next Saturday.' And then he hung up.

'Oh, for God's sake.' Tara stared at the phone, adrenaline still pinballing around her body. What had just happened?

And then she fell over the man with the dog.

It was a Corgi on a long extending lead – the owner was engrossed in an audiobook so hadn't noticed just how far the lead had extended – and no one was hurt, but Tara was sent flying to the floor, skinning her bare knees in the process. The moment hung in the air like a cartoon – the dog walker's shocked face, her slow crash to the ground – then, without warning, Tara burst into tears of shock. Big, chest-heaving, shoulder-shaking sobs, the 'falling over in the playground' sort that wouldn't be stopped.

David, ten steps further down the path, turned, horrified, and hurried back to help her to her feet. 'Tara, what happened? Are you OK?'

'I'm . . . fiiiiine,' she roared, too loud, trying to speak on a sobbing out-breath.

Heads were turning in their direction; the dog owner finally yanked out his earphones and apologized, then quickly dragged the Corgi back down the path towards the bandstand, away from the red-faced woman gasping and weeping like a small child.

David helped her up gently, producing a white hanky which Tara used mainly to hide behind, mortified.

'Did you hurt yourself?' he asked, and she shook her head, then wondered if she should have nodded because then she'd have a legitimate reason to be howling like this.

The sobs refused to stop. Tara covered her face with her hands, trying to hide her ugly-crying toddler face, and now she felt David's hands on her shoulders, steering her towards a bench. She heard him say to someone, 'She's fine, honestly . . . just shock . . .' and then she was carefully pushed on to the seat. Where they sat, in silence, his arm around her shoulders, until the sobs subsided into hiccups. It took ten embarrassing minutes, even though Tara had stopped crying after five.

Every time David started to ask, 'Are you all right?' she had to hold up a hand to indicate yes, but that she couldn't talk.

'How about . . . now?' David asked eventually.

Tara took a breath and didn't hiccup. She nodded OK, tentatively.

'If you need to get something off your chest . . .' He paused.

It was too humiliating. But what was the point in hiding now? Thanks to Hero's gin, and maybe his own hypnotic powers, David already knew more about Tara's shambolic personal life than anyone else. Well, apart from her cat.

Tara stared out into the park, Phil's words still in her ear. Why did it suddenly hurt so much? She'd been happy for her and Phil to be a grown-up casual thing, congratulating herself on keeping him at arm's length. Something had changed. Now her chest was aching as if she'd been punched, just from hearing his voice.

'David.' She had to force out the question. 'When you were . . . talking to Sybil, why did you say Phil didn't have builders in?'

'Phil as in . . . ?' He raised an 'on your phone just now?' eyebrow.

'Obviously.'

He took a deep breath. 'The way animals communicate is by showing me pictures – Sybil showed me a man I assumed was your boyfriend leaving her at your house, with her mouse. Then she showed me her house, and . . . there were no builders.' He hesitated, as if he wasn't sure whether to say something, then decided not to.

'And what about me? What did she really say about me? Be honest.'

'She shared an image of you being . . . sad.'

Was that Sybil . . . or David's impression? He hadn't mentioned it before. 'And how exactly would she judge that?'

'She's not judging. She watches you like you watch telly. Animals are incredibly observant – well, they have to be, to fit into our ludicrous human set-ups. But they're not mind readers. They don't *know* any more than we do, they're just sharp on human behaviour. I just open up a channel of communication, and they share what's important to them.' David seemed to realize at the same time as Tara did that his arm was still around her shoulders, and moved it away with an awkward squeeze.

She felt the absence immediately. Was it too much to ask David to put it . . . yes. Yes, it was too much.

They sat in silence for a few moments, and then David

193

said, 'I know you said you like to keep clear boundaries between work and home life, Tara, but if you ever need someone to talk to . . . I don't just talk to cats.'

It was tempting.

'Honestly, no, I'm fine.' Tara wiped her eyes with the edge of her finger. 'Just . . . been a long week.'

'It's been a long few *months*.' He meant her mum. They hadn't talked about her before, but David's expression was gently sympathetic. 'Most people would be nervous wrecks.'

'And that's you or Sybil speaking?'

'It's *you* speaking.' David looked her straight in the eyes. There was a challenge in his expression: not to lie to him, not to lie to herself. And that being honest wouldn't be so bad. Suddenly, Tara understood why David's clients opened up like flowers.

She *was* sad. Phil's lying had made her sad, not his absence. How 'in the way' could a cat be? What was going on? Why was she letting him get away with treating her like this? And why – why? – was the thought of David knowing this about her making her cringe inside?

'The thing about Phil is that, it *sounds* bad, but actually we're—' she started.

'Hey! Stop slacking!'

It was Emily's voice, in top PE-teacher form, and Tara jumped with a guilty start. As did David, and probably several lunchtime joggers.

Tara swivelled to see where Emily's voice was coming from and spotted her on the other side of the lawned area, hands on hips, glowering at a panting Lionel, four steps behind her. He was bent over, struggling to get his breath back, a deep red heart of sweat forming on the back of his Aertex shirt.

'Should Lionel be that colour?' David's brow furrowed. 'Should we go and *help* him?'

'I don't think he'd want us to see him like that,' she said, and patted her own knees. 'Come on. Let's get out of their way before they spot us.'

'Are you sure you're ready to go back?' He looked concerned. 'We could nip through the rose gardens and just walk on the other side of the park for a bit.'

'I'm OK. Really. Come on.' Tara bounced to her feet. 'We can get the defibrillator warmed up for Lionel.'

But even as she made conversation about the local plague pits on the way back, Tara had made up her mind about one thing: she was going to end it with Phil.

By the end of Keith Hunter's first week, when the official plans were presented to an open meeting, there was a palpable air of anticipation in the town hall.

Keith's assistant Conrad had set up a slick display to showcase KPH Associates' vision for Troutbridge village hall; the repairs marked in pale grey, the proposed adjustments in a darker colour. What could be saved from the original structure was being made safe by workmen; beyond that, KPH Associates proposed extending the kitchen to make it viable for event hire, removing the ramshackle extension and replacing it with a lighter, glass-encased space, adding facilities for Flicks in the Sticks cinema nights and a mezzanine cafe space. There was a computer simulation alongside the drawings: silhouettes of people doing yoga and tap dancing on the refurbished stage, as well as standing around drinking coffee in front of the renovated fireplace.

The presentation, Tara had to concede, had been

impressive but completely focused on what the community needed to start living again. Living, and growing again, stronger than before.

'As you'll see in the notes, we've considered green options to reduce running costs . . .' At Keith's nod, Conrad passed out glossy pamphlets. 'And Alice is liaising with our office about additional grant applications to supplement current budget projections.'

'I can't believe you've turned these plans around so quickly,' marvelled Catherine. 'I haven't even had a call back from my builder about our blocked drains yet.'

Everyone was gazing at the outline plans on the board with tremendous interest, but only Tara was aware of one tiny, important detail. Dad had done these himself, not farmed them out to some in-house team. The explanatory pencil notes on the drawings were in his distinctive handwriting: neat and crisp, halfway between printing and joined-up. She'd loved it as a child because it didn't look like 'adult' handwriting. He wrote his As in the typewriter style and his Ds were like musical notes. Every written comment was perfectly sized and spaced, the faint, sharp pencil lines pinning an imaginary construction halfway to reality on the paper.

Keith caught her eye. *He knows I know he drew this up himself*, she thought.

He raised an eyebrow, and she nodded, very slightly.

'So – when can we start?' Rob asked.

'Repair work's already underway – it's like for like, so that's within guidelines. As for the work covered by planning permissions . . .' Keith deferred to Peter from the planning department. 'It depends on what we find, and what magic my friend here can work.'

'Peter?'

'I'll see what I can do,' said Peter grudgingly. But even Tara could tell he was going to make it happen.

The meeting dissolved into smaller groups, with people lining up to ask Keith about various elements of the proposal. Tara watched out of the corner of her eye, while half involved in a discussion about a fundraiser for new stage equipment.

Keith was in his element. A little sharper than everyone else, a little more definite. He had a distinguished look with the silver hair, she decided. New Dad was overwriting Memory Dad in Tara's mind.

'Plans look incredible!' she said, when he finally made his way over.

'Don't they!' Keith beamed. 'I think this is going to be one of my favourite projects.'

'Good!'

'While it's in my mind, Tara – Erin's reminded me that I need to give my expenses receipts to whoever's in charge of finances. Who would that be?' His eyes twinkled. 'I'm under *strict* instructions not to let them mount up like I normally do. Erin rightly pointed out that my usual trick of dumping eighteen months' worth in one go mightn't go down very well.'

'Your expenses,' repeated Tara. 'Um, did you actually clear what they were going to cover?'

'Nothing outrageous, just accommodation. That's usually what happens on projects like this. Erin spoke to . . .' Keith pulled a face. 'Lisa-Marie?'

'Yes, Lisa-Marie Hill.' Tara hadn't seen the parish council accounts but she knew they just about covered the basics in a good year, let alone one as disaster-filled as this. They had the budget for a Nice Celebratory Meal, not several nights at The Swan hotel.

'It's just that . . .' she started, then stopped. This wasn't her problem. This was for Keith to sort out. Or Conrad, or someone else.

Except it was. She was the one who'd brought Keith here. Indirectly.

Keith seemed to read her face. 'Look, if you're worried about how much it's costing, Libby's done us a special rate. And Rob's very keen to get me involved in some other local projects so it makes sense if I'm here for a few days at a time, throughout the month. I'll only bill them for days I'm working on the hall.'

Tara ran her hand through her hair. 'Dad, I don't think they've got *any* sort of cash available right now.'

This is not your problem. This is not your problem. If he wants to look like a tit then that's his problem.

They stared at each other.

'I suppose there is one other option,' said Keith.

'What?'

'The studio.'

Immediately Tara thought of Diane, and her prediction. *Keep him at a distance.*

'Well, isn't that a good solution?' He raised his palms in frustration when she didn't answer. 'Didn't you say your mum had been running it as an Airbnb? Presumably it's set up to be self-contained? You can charge whatever the going rate is. Bound to be less than The Swan! Well, I assume so . . .'

'I don't think that's such a great idea.'

'Why not?' Keith's eyes locked on hers; Toby's eyes,

dark and keen. He pushed his hair off his forehead in an impatient gesture and an odd automatic panic shimmered through Tara. 'I wasn't going to mention it, but I did have a slightly awkward conversation with someone who assumed I was staying with you anyway.'

So that would make The Swan hotel bill even more of a shock. Tara struggled with her conscience. Charging him to stay in the studio would at least maintain a boundary, but . . . of course she couldn't charge him. How weird would it look, if she was deliberately creating an expense for the council instead of letting her own dad stay in her holiday accommodation?

'Let me talk to Alice,' she said, and Catherine appeared at Keith's shoulder and whisked him off to talk to the chair of the town's trade association.

As it turned out, Alice found Tara before Tara found her.

'Tara, I've got a massive favour to ask.' Her eyes were even bigger than normal. 'It's not for me, but I said I was seeing you tonight and that I'd ask you . . .'

Tara touched her arm, glad to be reassuring. 'If it's about the counselling waiting list, the good news is that some of my colleagues have offered to—'

'No, no, it's not about that.' Alice glanced around and dropped her voice. 'This is *strictly* confidential, but we're trying to find somewhere for a family from Linnet Close – they've been asked to leave their temporary accommodation because of an . . . incident, and there's nothing else available. Jess on the housing team is desperate.' She took a deep breath. 'I told Jess I'd ask . . . is anyone staying in your mum's Airbnb place at the moment?'

Linnet Close. Why did that ring a bell? And then Tara remembered: that was where the Bannons' house was. Pyromaniac Rhys, Gareth and his drum kit. Tara fought not to let the horror show on her face. 'Is this the Bannon family?'

'Yes! I mean, maybe.' Alice's eyes darted from side to side. 'How did you know that?'

'I'm their counsellor.'

'Oh.' Alice looked temporarily flummoxed. 'Oh. Have I broken some confidentiality thing? Ugh. I never know. But that doesn't have to be a problem. You wouldn't be talking to—'

Tara made a snap decision. 'I'm sorry, Alice, but some-one's already in the studio.'

'Who?'

'My dad.'

'Your dad?'

Tara nodded. 'I was going to talk to you about it tonight – he's been staying at The Swan. I think he thought the council would pay his accommodation expenses.'

'No! Oh God, how much?' Alice's expression confirmed Tara's fears about funds.

'Um, a lot. I thought it would be terrible if we ended up spending thousands on his accommodation when the money could be used on something more immediately helpful. So I said he could stay.'

Alice's shoulders slumped, then rose again. 'Well, I suppose that solves one problem – thanks, Tara, for offer-ing that option.'

'My pleasure,' said Tara automatically, because her

inner counsellor was banging her head on her imaginary desk. One way or another, this probably wasn't her finest hour.

Dad was back in the house, just as Diane had predicted.

Chapter Fourteen

Tara's decision to meet Phil in the IKEA cafe just outside Birmingham should, she reasoned, signal loud and clear her decision to end their relationship. Not even Phil's sexy magic could work surrounded by meatballs and flatpack wardrobes. And there would be no lingering. Straight in, The Conversation, then out.

Once she'd made up her mind, Tara felt surprisingly positive about it. The only downside – and it was a big downside – was having to return the one gift of Phil's that she really valued: Sybil.

She struggled hard with her conscience. It had to be a clean break, she told herself. She couldn't give Phil a reason to phone for check-ins. More to the point, she couldn't give herself a reason to keep in touch.

Sybil's last supper at Tara's house was luxurious – a whole tin of pilchards and half a pack of Dreamies – though, typically, she'd shown no sign of gratitude. When she'd stalked on to Tara's best cashmere cardigan at bedtime, Tara hadn't chucked her off as she usually did, and Sybil reciprocated by decamping to the bed in the middle of the night, waking her up with some loud purring and spiky kneading, perilously close to her ear.

I'll miss this, Tara realized, lying very still to avoid being clawed in the head, as the morning light filtered through the curtains. Then she blanked her mind to everything but Sybil's throaty purrs, just in case Sybil was picking up her guilty, sad thoughts.

Tara wasn't the only one up and about early on Saturday morning. As she was fastening Sybil's carrier properly on to the back seat of her car, Keith appeared, a vision of summeriness in an open-neck shirt, sunglasses dangling from his top pocket.

'Good morning! Where are you off to?' Keith beeped open his Mercedes, then frowned, seeing Sybil's basket. 'Not the vet's, I hope? Everything OK with my furry friend?'

The speed with which Sybil had taken to Keith was outrageous. 'She's fine.'

'Good!'

Keith seemed to be waiting for an answer and Tara didn't really want to give him one, so she smiled as if she had, and headed back into the house.

She took a little longer than she needed to, wiping breakfast crumbs off the counter top, filling the dishwasher with wobbly hands, and when she returned the Mercedes was still there, but there was no sign of her dad.

Tara slid into the driving seat and put on her shades. She didn't want to discuss today's mission with him. She didn't even want to think about it until she was there and it was happening, as there was every chance she'd bottle it.

'Come on, Tara, you can do this,' she said aloud. She plugged in her phone, already tuned to a motivational playlist of break-up songs, and turned the key in the ignition.

Nothing happened.

She turned it again, and this time heard a faint clicking, then nothing.

'Damn.' Tara squeezed her eyes shut. The protective layer of patience between her outer calm and the churning lava of nerves inside her was very thin right now. *Very* thin.

There was a brisk knock on the window.

Keith was crouching by the side of the car, making a 'wind it down' gesture.

Tara tried but nothing happened. Because – as she now realized – the Mini's battery was flat.

How symbolic, she thought.

Reluctantly she opened the door. 'Something the matter?'

'Not with me, no. But I think your battery's dead,' he replied, helpfully.

'I *know*. But I can't see how. I only drove it last night. It was *fine*.'

'Did you leave your lights on? Door open?'

'Of course I didn't leave . . .' Tara spluttered with outrage, then spotted the interior light switch. Still on. She stared at it, then threw her head back against the seat in frustration.

She *had* to see Phil today. If she didn't, something stressful would happen at work that would make her crave some no-strings distraction, or else he would find a way to charm her off her high horse. He'd done it before. Tara groaned.

'Not to worry,' Keith went on easily. 'Got any jump leads?'

'No. Have you?'

'Ah. I did in my old car. Not this one. Where were you off to?'

Proof he wasn't a proper dad, thought Tara. All dads had jump leads somewhere. And screwdrivers, and stepladders. 'Birmingham,' she said without opening her eyes.

'Really? What for?'

'I don't want to answer that.'

He didn't rise to her snappy tone. 'I mean, is it important? Do you need a lift?'

Tara tilted her head just enough to see her father's expression. It seemed genuine enough. Or at least, as genuine as the concern he showed to the village hall team.

'Pretty important, yes,' she conceded.

'I'm having lunch in Bromsgrove, so I can drop you off at the station, or if you and Sybil need a lift all the way, I don't mind taking you.'

Tara weighed it up. It had to be today. She wouldn't put it past Phil to turn up on her doorstep, or send more flowers to work. She couldn't get to IKEA on the train, and carting Sybil around on public transport wasn't fair on either of them.

But on the other hand, did she really want to be trapped in a car with her dad for ninety minutes – what if there was traffic? They were getting on well enough, but there were still things she didn't want to talk to him about, *personal* things, and she was on edge enough as it was without having to come up with endless non-Mum, non-new life, non-upsetting topics of conversation. You could only have so many conversations about *Line of Duty*.

'Tara?' Keith's tone had changed. 'You're not . . . having the cat put down, are you?'

'No!' She sighed. 'If you must know, I'm meeting my boyfriend to end our relationship. I have to give Sybil back. She's his, after all.'

'Oh. You never mentioned a boyfriend?' The tone was overly casual.

'No. I didn't.' She sighed. 'I'm not sure he was ever . . . exactly my boyfriend.'

'Well, then you need a lift, don't you?'

Tara closed her eyes again. *Bloody hell*, she thought. *What has my life come to?* 'I don't think it looks very empowering, getting a lift from my dad to dump someone.'

'You can drive, if it makes you feel any better?'

Tara took two, three deep breaths, and considered the next few weeks, if she didn't do this now. Was it the lesser of two evils? He was more of a lodger than her dad. And it was quite a dramatic statement of trust, letting her drive his brand-new Mercedes.

'Fine,' she said. Then added, 'Thank you,' automatically.

Tara's consumer rights training had made her an expert on the small print of her car insurance but Keith didn't appear particularly uptight about letting her drive, even before she showed him the clause in her documents that proved it was fine. Unlike Justin, the human satnav, he seemed happy to let her get on with it, and contrary to Tara's fears, he didn't start listing the Christmas presents he'd supposedly sent once she was trapped next to him, either. Instead he quizzed her about where the independent wine merchants were, and if there was 'a decent Asian supermarket' anywhere near Longhampton. Tara didn't know, but she let him blether on about artisan quince paste and furikake while she drove, because it prevented her from thinking about Phil and what she was going to say to him.

It was only when Tara accelerated recklessly on to the

motorway that Keith touched on the reason for their journey.

'So this bloke . . .' he asked casually, as she wafted past a Range Rover, 'how did you meet him?'

Tara considered which of the various versions of meeting Phil to tell her dad. She'd finessed the truth a few times, depending on who was asking. Although, given that the relationship was entering its final hours, what was the point of lying?

'We were on the same speed awareness course. He came in late, and the only space was at my table. And can I just say, for the record,' she added, 'I wasn't speeding *dangerously*, I was doing thirty-four in a thirty. The policeman was hiding behind a hedge.'

'Well, well. I didn't have you down as a speeder. Let me guess – your mum taught you to drive?'

'No, Diane did. But there was nothing wrong with Mum's driving.' They both knew that was a lie. Ruth attacked the road as if the car was on fire and she was driving it away from an exploding building and a herd of cattle, also on fire.

Tara flashed a look at her dad, and he took the hint.

'So I'm guessing this Phil was caught speeding too? How fast was he going?'

'A hundred and twelve on the M6.'

'A hundred and twelve?' Keith whistled appreciatively. 'Don't you automatically get sent to court for that?'

'Apparently not.'

'Lucky bloke.'

'Well, he's got the gift of the gab. And one of his friends specializes in traffic law.'

Tara's stomach still gave a little ripple remembering

Phil catching her eye while the instructor was writing up their admissions of guilt on the whiteboard. *Late for work. Distracted by kids. On the phone.* He'd winked, and whispered, 'Third time here – slow learner, me!' He was so Not Her Type, but as Phil leaned towards her, something about the intimacy of his smile, as if they were the only two people in the room, grabbed her in a way that overrode her brain entirely.

Justin had been a logical choice of boyfriend: sensible, qualified, ambitious. Phil was a physical shock, a magnificent, exhilarating, inevitable plunge over the waterfall. She'd told herself as they were flirting over tea that she wouldn't give him her number. She'd told herself, driving away, that if he called, she definitely wouldn't pick up. She'd told herself, on the way to their first date, that she'd leave after two drinks. And so on.

Oh God, thought Tara, seeing her lust-fuelled antics through someone else's eyes. *Surely having a womanizing father should have given me antibodies to men like Phil?*

'So what happened? You bonded over your shared love of speeding?'

The silent disaster movie was still playing out in front of Tara's eyes. The flirt-fest first date. Then the second. Then the dirty weekend away. Phil's jokes, his easy enjoyment of everything around him, the way his attention put her in a personal spotlight. 'We just clicked,' she said.

Tara gripped the wheel so hard she accidentally changed the radio station.

Keith changed it back. 'Nothing wrong with that. Everyone likes a click now and again.'

'It wasn't ever meant to be . . . a relationship. I mean,

Phil's good fun, he makes me laugh, but I don't want to end up like . . .' Tara stopped herself, self-consciously. 'It's been going on too long to be this casual. He travels, he's away a lot for work. We don't really talk about the future. I think it's better to draw a line.'

'Fair enough,' said Keith. 'You deserve someone who plans their future with you in it.'

Tara stared at the road ahead, refusing to rise to the irony of that comment when they still had at least half an hour to go.

They drove on for another mile, and eventually Tara said, 'Dad?'

'What?'

'Have you been on a speed awareness course?'

'One or two.'

Of course he had.

'I do a lot of motorway miles.' He waved a hand. 'It happens. I'm not a dangerous driver.'

That's what Phil said, thought Tara. *And everyone else on the course.*

And me.

Maybe I'm like Mum AND Dad, she thought with a flash of despair.

'Getting a bit close to that lorry, love,' said Keith.

Tara found her way into the IKEA car park and parked in a space miles away from the entrance to avoid scratching the Mercedes's paintwork.

They sat for a moment while the car turned itself off. It was ten to eleven. Tara took a deep breath and ran through the coaching she'd have given a client facing the same situation: set your intention, calm your breathing, visualize . . .

'Before you go – I think you should keep the cat, Tara.' Keith's voice broke the silence, and she turned in surprise.

Keith was staring out of the car at something she couldn't see, and didn't seem to want to turn back.

'Why?'

'Because you look after her properly, and this Phil sounds like the kind of selfish bastard who doesn't.'

'And how do you know that?'

Keith gave a heartful sigh and shook his head. 'I left Branston.'

Tara was about to say, *Stop making this about you!* when she saw the expression on Keith's face and the words died on her lips.

It had been awful, Branston's broken heart after Keith left. It didn't matter how many slices of toast Tara slipped him, or how often they let him sleep on their beds, Branston was sad for ages after. At least Dad had taken her and Toby to the Hard Rock Cafe a few times, offering them vague explanations about how he and their mum were 'better apart' until they'd decided they didn't want to see him.

'He used to walk backwards and forwards from the studio to the back door constantly,' she said, twisting the knife. 'Looking for you.'

Keith wiped a hand over his face. 'Tara, I didn't want to leave him. I loved that dog. I often thought about him. I don't get the impression this bloke has the same kind of attachment to Sybil.'

'Bloody hell.' Tara stared at her father, choked. She'd never really considered that leaving Branston might have been a wrench for him. 'Why are you doing this? How can you even talk about this, about Branston, when you know what I'm about to go and do?'

He seemed genuinely remorseful. 'I'm sorry, Tara. I know it's bad timing but . . . when else could I say it? Please. You'll only worry about her.'

'OK.' She let out a long breath. The unexpected flood of memory had winded them both. 'I won't give Sybil back.'

Tara turned to look over to the carrier on the back seat. David had raised her expectations; she half expected to see Sybil's grateful face pressed up against the bars, pleased at having successfully transmitted her wishes to a human. But there was just a quilted expanse of fur pressed against the wires – the cat's curled back rising and falling with a faint snore.

She spoke without turning back. 'We loved Branston. He was a good dog.'

'He was the best.' Keith looked, if not on the verge of tears, then on the verge of deep thoughts. 'So, what – shall I meet you here later this afternoon? How long do you need?'

Tara had a sudden 'edge of the diving board' lurch in her stomach. 'I suppose . . . long enough to be clear, but not long enough to talk myself out of it. How long do *you* need?'

'I'll fit in with you.'

She closed her eyes. This was one of the very worst ideas she'd ever had. If not *the* worst. Everything her dad touched instantly became a million times more emotionally stressful.

'Just call me when you're done,' said Keith. 'Now go and get on with it.'

'Right,' said Tara, and opened the door without looking back.

Phil was sitting in the cafe, with a coffee and a tiny green cake, talking intently on his phone. When Tara appeared he ended the call immediately, and got up as she pulled out a chair.

'Hello, Taz.' He smiled, making no secret of his approving up-and-down glance. 'I've missed you.' The fact he didn't add 'you beautiful creature' somehow underlined his sincerity.

Tara raked Phil's appearance for clues as to where he'd been for the last month. His cheekbones seemed more pronounced, and there were some faint shadows under his eyes. But his thick honey-blond hair was as she remembered it, pushed back off his handsome face in that slightly eighties way. If anything, he looked a bit sexier. Thinner, and sexier.

Tara had nursed some theories: best case, on a lucrative-if-shady freelance contract overseas. Worst case, on honeymoon. Somewhere in between, hospital, but for something embarrassing like a minor nose job.

He reached his hands across the table, his blue eyes locking with hers. 'Do you want to move this conversation upstairs?' he murmured. 'I have some bedroom requirements to discuss.'

A contrary desire tugged in the pit of Tara's stomach and she placed the bag of Phil's stuff on the table before he could get into his stride.

'Phil, this isn't working for me any more.' She steeled herself. 'Thanks for the flowers that were meant for your wife, but you can go back to her now – and tell her to leave me alone.' It was what she'd planned to say when she was lying awake in the middle of the night: go in there with a depth charge and see what floated to the surface.

He looked momentarily shocked, an expression Tara had never seen on Phil before. It made him look a bit bovine. 'Zoe's been calling you?'

Tara's heart sank. 'So you do have a wife.'

'Well, she's not technically my wife.'

'You are such a cliché.'

'It's not what it sounds like, I promise . . .'

'And so is that. Got any more? Does she not understand you? Are you staying together for the kids?'

Tara stared at the distant display of meatballs behind Phil's head. They were unrealistically glossy. Somehow it was a fitting punishment that this should be happening in such a family-orientated, wholesome Scandi environment.

What had happened to her brain?

There had been a moment when she'd almost convinced herself that all that was needed was a frank conversation about how yes, this had started as a fun thing, but now the rules needed to change. Phil was obviously scared of commitment. Maybe he was waiting for her to admit she wanted more.

But now he'd confirmed her worst suspicion, she had no option but to end it. Tara braced herself to hear the truth. 'Where have you been?'

'What do you mean?'

'I mean . . .' Tara shook her head. 'No, I can't make it more straightforward. You tell me you're going away, total silence for nearly three weeks, then out of the blue, you call. Was it work? A holiday with your not-wife?'

'Ha ha.' He rubbed his face. 'Does it matter?'

'Yes!' Tara stared at him. 'I've been trying to get hold of you for *weeks*. I've been worried. Why wouldn't you tell me? Unless you've been in *prison*?'

Phil stared at her, and an awful realization dawned on her.

'Oh God. You have.'

'Not prison-prison, Tara, nothing *bad*.'

She covered her mouth in horror.

His wounded expression changed to a wicked grin, and he pointed his finger at her. 'Got you going there, didn't I?'

Her heart was pounding in her chest. 'Jesus, Phil.'

He reached over the table, circling her wrist with his fingers. 'Sorry, sorry, Taz, didn't mean to freak you out. It was just a joke.'

'It's not funny.' She snatched her hand back. 'Where were you?'

'I was . . . on holiday.' He shifted in his seat. 'In the Bahamas.'

'With Zoe?'

A pause. 'Yes.'

'Your . . . fiancée?'

He nodded, and had the grace to look ashamed. 'She booked it. She, um, proposed while we were out there.'

'And you said yes?'

He widened his eyes. 'What else was I meant to say? She did it on the first night.'

'Oh my God.' Tara leaned on the table, covering her eyes with her hands for a brief moment or two of blissful darkness. Part of her wished Phil *had* been in prison. At least there'd be an outside chance he hadn't done it.

She felt his finger stroking her bare arm. 'I'm really sorry, Taz. I didn't know what else to do. I was going to tell you. I was going to—'

'Shut up.' She pulled her arm away. 'Answer me one question and don't even think about making up some bullshit. Have you got builders in your house?' Her flashing eyes dared him to lie.

'What?' Slowly he withdrew his hand.

'Why did you leave Sybil with me, if you didn't have builders?' Tara already knew the answer.

He mumbled towards his coffee. 'Zoe's allergic to cat hair. But I did want you to look after her . . .'

'Why?'

Phil looked up, and seemed genuinely miserable. 'Because you're so good at looking after things.'

'Shades in the rain? Scared you'll be recognized?'

'I've got a headache,' said Tara shortly, as she got into the air-conditioned passenger seat of Keith's car.

An hour shuffling around a primary-coloured labyrinth of bookcases and plastic colanders waiting for your dad to collect you wasn't the ideal way to process a broken relationship. But at least there were unlimited Daim bars and Swedish coffee. Maybe too many.

Keith checked his watch. 'Do you want to go for a drink till it passes?'

'No, I want to get out of here. I want to go *home*.'

Tara was horrified to hear her voice wobble, and turned her head away before he spotted her face crumpling. She'd been fine till she'd seen him there, waiting to collect her. Some part of her subconscious recognized her dad, making her want to bury her head in his chest; the stronger part of her brain yelled that he had no right, that she should maintain what dignity she had left.

'Tara?'

The concern in his voice – the bloody fatherly concern – was too much. 'No!' It came out as a wail. 'Just . . . don't. Don't feel sorry for me. And don't hug me!'

Keith had started to extend a tentative hand but withdrew it. 'OK. You've done the right thing. It's never easy.'

'Isn't it?'

'No. It's not.'

Tara had a sudden thought: *Sybil!* She swung round to look at the back seat. Poor Sybil had been trapped in her carrier all day: she would be absolutely furious.

But the back seat was empty.

Tara swivelled back. 'Dad? Where's Sybil? What have you done with the cat?'

'I took her home,' said Keith.

'When?' Tara tried to calculate the distances in her head; he must have driven back to Longhampton and turned around immediately. And put his foot down too.

'I'm no cat expert, but I didn't think she'd appreciate being in a basket for four hours.' He shrugged in a 'you got me' manner and added, 'And also to get her out of the way. I didn't want you changing your mind. Or this Phil character demanding her back.'

'But what about your lunch?'

'Rearranged for next weekend.'

'You cancelled your lunch to take a cat home? Why?'

Keith sighed. 'At the risk of sounding like a Hallmark

card, Tara, it felt like the right thing to do. I wasn't there for any of the other boys you've broken up with. And Sybil's a nice cat.'

Tears flooded her eyes. 'Shut up.'

'OK. Not what I was expecting but . . . fair enough.'

'No, I mean, shut up, or I'll start crying again.'

They sat in silence while Tara struggled with herself. Eventually she managed a croaky, 'Thank you.'

'You're welcome.' Keith rubbed his hands together. 'Have you eaten? Shall we find somewhere for a snack?'

'Can we just go home?'

'Of course,' he said, then added, 'I seem to remember there's a certain drive-through McDonald's where we might be—'

'Don't push it,' said Tara. 'I might be getting driven home by my dad but I'm not eight.' And she slid down the seat and folded her arms.

As the motorway miles passed under her listless gaze, Tara tried to analyse how she felt. The guilty weight pressing down on her shoulders had gone but there was a new hollowness spreading through her chest, and not even the knowledge that she'd done the right thing made it any better.

No more Phil. No more midnight phone calls, no more spontaneous sexy weekends away, no more fun, no more flattering moments of feeling more interesting than she really was.

Just flood damage and depressed clients and bills and the probate nightmare still to sort out.

He preferred someone else to me, she thought, twisting the knife. *I wasn't enough.*

Keith didn't try to instigate conversation. He was humming along enthusiastically, if not quite in tune, to a song by The Cure, and it dislodged a memory from a deep part of Tara's brain. A car journey on a summer evening, that fresh new-car smell of Dad's silver Saab, mint-green Clarks sandals tinged with rusty blood where they'd rubbed her heels raw, squabbling with Toby in the back seat, then snoozing, then half waking up to Toby snoring and Mum and Dad singing in the front to Spandau Ballet, and a feeling of absolute security that covered her like a blanket as the car sped home to their warm house and waiting dog. Safety. Love. Completeness.

She didn't know where the memory had come from, but Tara reached out not for the lost family, but for that feeling of everything in the world making sense and requiring nothing from her. It was such a comforting memory that, without warning, she slipped into sleep.

Chapter Fifteen

The positive response Tara had had from her kitchen noticeboard plea for help with the flood counselling went some way to restoring her dented faith in human nature. Rather than offering hazel twigs to heal the damp, the counsellors had come up with some genuinely helpful sessions.

Bridget was running a 'craft and craic' hour twice a week in the town hall for those who just wanted to be around other people, and Anji was helping her out. She arrived with a patchwork knitting bag and sat beatifically creating a host of four-ply angels at an admirable speed, while patiently listening to whatever the service users wanted to talk about. Tara had joined in, after Anji had got her started with a simple pattern, and found that knitting was a great way of taking your mind off things. And also that the Angel Gabriel was in charge of water.

David offered to help with Tara's drop-in counselling service alongside the craft hours, and his advice was, naturally, in high demand, particularly with the older ladies. There was already a small queue of them, patiently waiting with their handbags on their knees to see him.

'No offence, Tara, but my friend Lillian saw Dr Dalloway and she said he was lovely,' Elsie Cogan said apologetically.

'You're lovely too, mind,' added her sister, Dorrie. 'And we appreciate everything you've done for us. Especially these social nights. Never met so many nice people!'

'Thank you,' said Tara.

'We should flood more often!' agreed Elsie. 'Between you and the River Martle, you've finally got us out the house!'

The Cogans were two elderly sisters whose midnight evacuation from their terraced house had stirred up memories of wartime Birmingham. 'We're putting on a brave face, bab,' Dorrie had told her the night they were rescued, although the chattering teacup and saucer in her arthritic fingers said otherwise. Tonight, they were at the front of the line of orange chairs, their Yorkshire Terrier, Sukie, on Dorrie's lap instead of a handbag.

'Better make a start, then!' said David, and courteously ushered them behind the discreet grey screen.

It was still light when the session came to a close at six thirty, and Bridget suggested a quick drink at the pub on Bishop Street with tables outside.

'I don't know about you, but I need a vodka,' Anji said, with a determined look in her eye that made Tara wonder if she'd jumped to conclusions about vegans.

She'd glanced at David, hoping he'd say yes, and he did. As a thank you, she got the first round in, then David offered to get the next, and then Bridget said she had to get back to put her ferrets to bed.

Anji left soon after, and David and Tara were left with the bottle of wine.

'Might as well finish it, eh?' he said, and shared it between their glasses.

Tara fiddled with the stem of the glass. Now they were on their own, she wanted to tell him the good news about Sybil but that would mean telling him about finishing with Phil, and somehow that made her feel strange. Even thinking about Phil curdled her mood; now the grief had worn off, an unexpected anger had revealed itself underneath.

'Good news on Mrs Murray,' David told her, turning the bottle upside down in the cooler. 'Simba came home last night. Bit of his ear missing but otherwise none the worse for his two weeks in the wild. She brought him in to say hello!'

'Hooray!' The thought of Sybil going missing now filled Tara with real panic. 'They've no idea where he's been? What he's been up to?'

David tapped his nose. 'What happens in Much Larton stays in Much Larton.'

'And what about Mrs Cartwright? Has little Bobby turned up yet?'

'No, sadly. I think we're turning a corner, though, in terms of her general outlook. She's coming along to the next craft drop-in – she's going to be a crochet coach.'

'Poor Mrs Cartwright.' Tara had only seen Joan twice before David had taken over her counselling but she already felt as if she knew Bobby, his likes and particularly dislikes, which were legion. He'd been Mrs Cartwright's sole companion for eight years. 'It must be heartbreaking for her, not knowing whether he's alive or dead. He had his own china plate, you know.'

'Cats usually find someone to feed them,' said David. 'And they can always hunt.'

'Not Bobby. He can tell the difference between Waitrose and Tesco own-brand cat food.'

A thought occurred to Tara. It went against her position of polite neutrality on the topic of David's 'gift' but she felt she owed it to Mrs Cartwright to ask. 'David, when you do this communication . . . do you have to have the animal physically in front of you to talk to it?'

He gave her a wary look. 'Is there an answer that will sound more crazy or less crazy, in your opinion?'

'I think we passed that point some time ago.'

He sipped his wine. 'Then, no. I don't have to have the animal in front of me. I can just tune into them. It's an energy exchange, like telepathy – distance isn't an issue.'

'OK, well in that case, why don't you just ask Bobby where—?'

Before she could even finish her sentence, David was shaking his head emphatically. 'No. No, that's not something I do, sorry.'

'How do you know what I was going to say?'

'Lost pets. And no. Sorry.'

'But why not?' Tara turned on the bench to look at him. 'Surely that's the most useful thing you could do with . . . your ability? Especially now – we've got a whole list of pets that went missing during the floods. Even if Mrs Cartwright knew the worst, she'd be able to stop worrying.'

'I'm really sorry, but no.'

'But why not?' Well, because he couldn't do it, obviously. The wine had gone straight to Tara's head, so she added, recklessly, 'I mean, if you're *serious* about being able to do this and not—'

'If I'm not what?' David looked affronted.

'Well, if you could stop an old lady crying her heart out every day about the only friend she's got left in the world, surely you'd want to. I would.' She slumped back in her seat, taken aback at how disappointed she felt. David could pretend all he liked, but clearly it was just about reading the person, not the animal. Making people think their cats could understand their relationships.

Tara mentally kicked herself for being so gullible. She'd started to warm to the idea of David sensitively counselling small animals. She'd even let him probe into her private life, via the medium of Sybil. How stupid must she have looked, getting emotional when he guessed the builders were an excuse for Phil to offload his cat on to his bit on the side? *Ugh.* Was it *that obvious* to everyone but her?

'So, what is it, then?' she went on, more to punish herself than him. 'Cold reading? Psychology? Or is it *hypnotism*?' She glared at him. 'Hmm?'

'What are you getting at?' David narrowed his eyes.

The atmosphere tipped, and Tara knew there was no way back from this.

She shook her head, dismissively. 'I know about what you used to do at university. I'm sure it was *hilarious* for you lads at the time, making people look stupid for everyone else's amusement, but you have no idea how—.'

'No, no.' David tried to shut her down. 'I don't think you've got the right end of that particular stick.'

'Haven't I?' She glared at him, not wanting it to be true. '*Hypno Dave*?'

He groaned and rolled his eyes. 'Tara, it's not—'

'Not what it looks like?' she half roared. Her heart was pounding, all her humiliation channelling into one convenient direction. 'You have no idea how sick and tired I am of men saying . . . of people saying that to me right now. News flash – it's always *exactly* what it looks like.' Tears had sprung into her eyes, and when he tried to pat her arm, she spun away, nearly knocking over her wine glass.

Tara got up to leave, and David tried to grab her arm to stop her; she shook it off as he immediately dropped it, embarrassed, then once her bag was on her shoulder, Tara realized she didn't want to leave. Their eyes met, awkwardly.

'Sit down and I'll explain,' said David, so she did.

'I'm not denying that I did, on occasion, at university, perform a bit of stage hypnotism. And yes, on occasion I made some rugby players – who were not known for their sensitivity towards other people, I would add in my defence – the butt of the joke, for a change. It's not one of my CV highlights. I stopped doing it altogether when someone very like you, someone whose opinion mattered to me, took me to one side and told me I was being a cock. And I realized she was right. So I stopped doing it.'

He said it in a matter-of-fact way but his ears were a tell-tale red.

'And, if you must know,' he went on, with a visible wince, 'I did not call myself Hypno Dave. That's just what Justin and his mates called me.'

Tara raised a cynical eyebrow. 'Did you have a better name?'

'Of course not.' He corrected himself. 'Well, one rag week I did an event as Doctor Hypnoticus, but that was a joke.'

'That's actually worse.'

'I know.' He shrugged. 'How long have you known?'

'A while.'

David said nothing, but Tara knew what he was thinking (ha!): did she think worse of him for it? Affronted adrenaline was still charging through her, and she felt somewhat stranded on her high horse. Although for once it was him making the embarrassing revelation, not her. He was handling it with much more dignity, though.

'People can only really change when they see what they were doing was wrong,' he said simply. 'And I did.'

His words hung in the air between them.

'I'm sorry,' she said. 'I shouldn't have said that. I'm . . . I'm too wound up about other things. Other . . . people.'

To his credit, David didn't ask what, but he'd probably worked it out for himself. Tara couldn't bear to humiliate herself by telling him he'd been right about the builders. She was much easier to read than a cat anyway.

'You want to know why I don't do missing pets,' he said, by way of reconciliation. 'I'll tell you.'

'I'm all ears.' Tara leaned back in her chair, watching him.

'When I was growing up, we had a dog, Bruno. I thought everyone could chat to him. You know, when people come home and the dog brings a toy – "Hey, Bruno. Is that toy for me? It is? Wow, thanks!" And I would wonder why they weren't responding to what he was saying, because whenever *I* said, "Hey, Bruno!" I could hear him saying, "This duck needs a wash." So I did whatever he asked, and he loved that, because no one else ever actually listened to him. We were best mates. I was ten and he was a Terrier-Lurcher-God knows what – we didn't have deep conversations. I didn't realize it wasn't normal until my dad told me off for making things up. But I loved that dog. He was my best mate.'

Tara smiled, but David wasn't smiling; she already knew – and she knew he knew – that he was skirting around the painful part of the story, the way clients did, padding around the sting with anecdote.

'Anyway, you know what's coming.' His stare became more fixed on the bottle in front of them. 'When I was thirteen, I was camping with the Scouts, and there was a thunderstorm. Bruno didn't like thunderstorms. He used to hide under my bed hours before they started. Animals can sense the electricity in the air, it upsets them. Soon as I heard the first clap of thunder, I got that horrible, heavy worry, right in the pit of my stomach. I knew something was wrong. When I got home, Bruno wasn't there. Mum was in tears, Dad was in a foul mood. Apparently Bruno sneaked upstairs to hide but Dad found him, and dragged him outside as a punishment for going upstairs. And at some point, there must have been a huge lightning flash and he ran for it.'

'Oh no.' Branston hated thunder too. He would try hard to be brave but couldn't stop whimpering.

'They couldn't find him. They'd been out looking for hours. But I could hear Bruno's voice in my head, begging me for help.' David bit his lip. 'He was terrified, and in pain. He'd broken his leg, I think, and he didn't know where he was. He tried to tell me, showed me pictures of trees, but I couldn't understand where he meant. I searched and *searched* for him, everywhere I could think of, talking to him in my head, reassuring him I was coming, even though it was almost unbearable, getting his terror and his pain coming back, but I kept going until . . .' His voice cracked, and he stopped for a long second. 'Until I couldn't hear Bruno's voice any more. I couldn't hear him. He'd shut himself down. It's what animals do, when they can't cope with pain, or stress – they shut down. To protect themselves.'

This time David stopped for a lot longer, and blinked, hard. He was pushing his thumbnails into the pads of his fingertips, so hard that the skin around them turned white.

'Did you find him?' Tara asked.

'Eventually. He was exactly where he said he was – beside a willow tree, in a ditch by the golf course. I carried him home, trying to talk to him all the way, but he'd gone.' David stared ahead. 'The worst thing was, when I tried to tell my mum about it, my father sent me to a psychiatrist. Things weren't . . . great for a few years after that.'

Tara grabbed David's hand and squeezed it. After a second, his fingers squeezed hers back, a strong grip. A ripple ran between them, more comforting than words. They sat in silence for a while. Tara didn't know what to say, but she believed him. She recognized the vulnerability of someone who's said more than they meant to and realized what it sounds like, spoken aloud.

'I'm so sorry, David,' she said. Whether it was all in his mind or not, his pain, twenty years on, was written in his hunched shoulders, his wretched expression.

'No, *I'm* sorry. But that's why I don't try to connect with lost animals.' He forced out a smile, but it was bleak. 'The responsibility is . . . horrible. It's selfish, I know. I'm not proud of it, and I'll do everything I can to help in any other way, but not that.'

Tara hadn't expected this, especially not without half a bottle of Hero's Midsummer Gin under their belts. There was a confessional atmosphere between the two of them, as fragile and unexpected as a soap bubble floating down the main street.

'Do your parents really have no idea you can do this?' It seemed churlish to do anything other than support him.

'We've never discussed it as such. Mum's good with animals – she claimed the same birds came to our garden every year. Dad, definitely not. He's Scottish, a Free Presbyterian, very strict on what he calls woo-woo nonsense. Won't even have horoscopes in the house. So, no. As far as they're concerned, talking to dogs is just something I grew out of, like an imaginary friend. I didn't want another dog after Bruno, and we didn't get one. I closed down that side of me for a long time.'

'So what changed?'

'Ha! Well. Funny story, actually.' David's mood lifted a little and he ran his hand through his hair. 'My ex wanted a rescue dog. Trial run for a baby, she said. So we adopted Churchill, a Spaniel cross. One night I was walking Churchill round Clapham Common and, out of the blue, he asked me when the other nice man was coming round to play again. The man who played with Imogen. My ex.'

'No!'

David shrugged. 'Yes. I hadn't picked up any communication from dogs for years so Churchill must have *really* wanted to talk to me. I think the boyfriend was more fun to play with than I was. Churchill seemed particularly keen on the pigs' ears he brought too. It wasn't all Immy's fault – I was studying, and working long hours. She deserved better. But I took the hint, we split up, and lo and behold, she married pigs' ear man.'

'Churchill went with her?'

'He did. Fickle little sod.' David stretched out his long legs under the table. 'But the silver lining was that Churchill made me think about what he was picking up, what our relationship looked like from his perspective. And from that, what sort of negative impact destructive human relationships have on pets. It sent me down a different rabbit hole . . .'

'Appropriate.'

'. . . of research, most of which has been useful and fascinating, and here I am. Ten years down the line.'

Tara nodded but her brain was industriously filing away snippets of information. David had an ex. Called Immy, now married. He'd lived in south London, ten years ago. This was a veritable deluge of information.

'And . . .' She was about to ask, artlessly, if there was a girlfriend on the scene now, when he slapped his hands on the table, ending the conversation.

'Anyway, enough work talk for tonight! I need to make a move – you probably do too.'

'Yes,' said Tara, and felt a tang of something like disappointment.

She got a taxi home – David insisted he'd prefer to walk, and she didn't argue.

There was a light on in the studio and Tara thought, *Oh, Dad must be back*. He'd been away for a few days now; he hadn't said where he was going, and she didn't think they were at the point where she could demand to know his movements. She presumed he was checking in with his other life. She still wasn't quite ready to hear about that.

Tara dumped her coat over the banister and hung her

bag up, flipping through the takeaway leaflets in the pile by the door.

Since the IKEA trip, they'd shared a couple of takeaways from restaurants that Keith 'wanted to try out', claiming he needed help to sample the menu properly. Tara had graciously gone along with the excuse. They ate halfway between their houses, outside on the patio area Ruth had created, then went their separate ways. It was . . . nice. It was starting to feel like the start of something.

Tara scanned the leaflet from a new Nepalese place that was meant to be good. *I wonder if Dad wants to split a takeaway*, she wondered idly.

She wandered into the kitchen, texting him as she went.

Do you want to go halves on a

But before Tara could finish the sentence, something moved in the garden and caught her eye. She stopped dead in her tracks.

There was someone in the back garden.

A young girl in a white T-shirt and blue jeans, sitting on the grass in what was left of the late evening light. Her hair was plaited in a thick black braid that hung down her back, and her head was bent in deep concentration over the book she was reading. She looked – to Tara's inexperienced eye – to be about ten.

There was a dog lying next to her, a chunky yellow Labrador fast asleep against her long legs.

Tara's mouth dropped open. *Branston?* And if that was Branston, who was the little girl?

Chapter Sixteen

Tara stared out across the kitchen as if the window was opening out not on to the garden now, but the same garden held in a bubble of time twenty years ago.

She couldn't move. She could only just take tiny sips of breath into her lungs. Was this real? Or was she somehow looking backwards at herself?

The girl in the garden was as still as a photograph, and there was an eerie déjà vu about her pose: her dark head was bent over a book, as she read with the same intense concentration that Tara had seen in old photos of herself. One thick black plait hung down her back like a plumb line; a faint frown creased her high forehead. She sat cross-legged, and the paleness of her knees showed through stringy rips in her jeans. Next to her, the Labrador lay with its broad head on its paws, eyes shut, dozing in exactly the same way Branston had slept next to Tara, in the summer evenings when she'd read Agatha Christies in the rose garden until the sun faded into dusk and the yellow light on the pages was cast from the upper-storey studio windows behind her, and Mum had yelled at them both to come in because dinner was on the table getting cold.

Tara's tongue clacked against her dry mouth. Was that *her*? Her in the summer before Dad left, when they were a normal family, and she and Toby had no idea it was the last holiday they'd have together? Had Dad's return re-awoken this unhappy ghost of herself? Was she hallucinating what she couldn't change?

A hot magenta sunset streaked the sky, dappling light through the big silver birch, and the wine she'd drunk with David seemed to detach her brain from her body.

I was so small, Tara realized suddenly, gripped with an urge to hug the ten-year-old Tara to her chest and throw herself against the changes looming as the season turned. *I was so SMALL. I knew NOTHING. How could he leave me? How could he walk away from us? And Branston. Was Branston's sadness stuck in this limbo too?*

Hot tears blurred Tara's eyes, and she felt a longing so painful it seemed to rip her heart through her whole body.

And then Sybil streaked across the garden like a smear of darkness, and the dog's head jerked up, and he started barking. Sybil – a very real Sybil – had already clattered through the cat flap in the back door by the time the dog made a paltry attempt to go after her, but in jumping up, he spotted Tara in the kitchen and started barking with a more focused effort.

As the dog bounced up, the girl dropped her book with a yelp, and turned to see Tara too.

They stared at each other in mutual shock.

It wasn't a ghost of herself, but a girl who looked a lot like she had done at that age. Same wide mouth, same freckles on the same milky skin turned a painful pink by too much sun. The same thick hair and the same long, skinny limbs Tara had had, until puberty struck and her hair was cut in a fury of 'no more plaits' and the limbs rounded out and everything else caught up in a rush. Her eyes were very different, though. Not dark and expressive like Tara's – or rather, Keith's. They were big and round and pale blue. And anxious.

Tara put her hand over her heart. It was hammering so hard in her chest she wondered if she was having some kind of cardiac episode.

The girl's big eyes stretched with anxiety and she looked around, hugging herself, not seeing whoever she was hoping to see. But she didn't try to run away.

Tara struggled for an answer other than the very obvious. Could it possibly be one of the Bannon kids, booted out of their latest accommodation? Or some other flooded-out local child? Had Alice tried to get hold of her in an emergency, and left the child in the back garden? No. There was no way Alice would do that. And she was clutching at straws, in any case.

The girl was looking around her more urgently, on the verge of tears.

Tara was the adult here. She had to deal with this.

With a deep breath Tara walked across the kitchen, opened the bifold doors and strode over the grass, trying to look friendly. The dog was bouncing around her, and the girl shouted, 'Lloyd! Lloyd! Lloydie!' but he ignored her, making a beeline for Tara.

'I must smell of cats.' Tara crouched down and let the dog sniff her hands. He was like Branston, but not Branny. Same yellow velvet coat but a flatter head, a fluffier tail. 'This is Lloyd?'

'Yes,' said the girl.

The dog wagged its tail, amiably. He wasn't much of a guard dog.

'Hello, Lloyd. Nice to meet you. And what are you called?'

Again, the girl's eyes flicked from side to side, as if hoping someone would pop up, but no one came.

'I'm Tara,' said Tara, remembering too late that modern kids didn't go revealing their names and ages to strangers who talked to their dogs. They'd had several Lunch and Learns about child protection. But she wasn't at work now. She was in her own garden. 'You don't have to tell—'

'I'm Molly.' The eyes squinted up at her, solemnly. Familiarly.

Tara stared at her. It was deeply unsettling.

She glanced down the garden towards the studio. The lights were still on upstairs but there was no sign of Keith through the big windows.

'Molly?' She tried to make her voice neutral, kind. 'Why are you in my garden?'

The girl looked down at her feet, then up at Tara. Her pointy face was tight with anxiety and Tara realized Molly didn't have an answer. The poor kid didn't know what she was doing there.

'Molly! There you are!'

Tara stood up. Keith was striding across the lawn, his hair dishevelled and his clothes unusually rumpled. For the first time since he'd arrived, he looked all of his sixty-four years. Molly jumped up and ran over to his open arms.

When he picked Molly up and hugged her, a quick comforting hug that she was a little too big for but clearly was used to getting, a sharp pain pierced Tara's heart and made her inhale with surprise.

Keith put Molly down, and carried on to where Tara was standing, frozen. Molly trailed after him, her eyes still wide with tension but not as fearful as before.

'Sorry, sorry, I had to make a couple of phone calls.' His eyes darted back and forth between Tara and Molly. 'Have you two introduced yourselves already?'

'Sort of,' said Tara.

If Keith detected the coolness in Tara's voice he ignored it, and instead said, with a rather theatrical gesture, 'Tara, this is Molly Hunter, my *younger* daughter. Molly, this is Tara Hunter, my *older* daughter.'

Just like that. He made it sound as simple as that.

But it wasn't simple. Tara bit her lip. For so long she'd been the *only* daughter: not that much, but something to hold on to; not only special and unusual as a twin, but her dad's only daughter. It was stupid, but it was the reason she hadn't wanted to ask about his life between leaving and coming back; she preferred, in her head, to imagine that he hadn't felt able to replace the family he'd left behind. Here was the proof that he had.

'Hello,' said Molly carefully, and held out her hand to shake. She didn't seem anywhere near as thrown by the appearance of a brand-new sister. She also seemed quite well versed in formal adult introductions.

There wasn't much Tara could do other than take the cool hand; being out-mannered by a ten-year-old wasn't a good look.

'Hello,' she managed, and Molly gave her a brave smile that made Tara feel worse.

Keith looked between them, scanning their reactions, then, when there were no tears, he clapped his hands together. 'Excellent! Now, I don't know about you ladies but I am absolutely dying for a drink. What's it to be? Cup of tea? Double espresso? Diet Coke? Scotch and soda?'

'Cup of tea,' said Molly. 'It's too late for espressos!'

It sounded like a running joke. *Silly Daddy.*

'Cup of tea it is,' he agreed. 'Tara? Cup of tea for you?'

He'd set off walking towards the studio, and Molly and the dog were following obediently.

Tara watched them, frozen to the spot.

After a few steps, Keith turned back, and said, 'Tara?' in a way that made her feet move, despite the protest from her brain.

Inside the cool downstairs room of the studio, Keith sent Molly to the kitchen to 'give Lloydie something to drink'.

His eyes followed the little girl as she skipped off, the dog at her heels; Tara watched him watching her, and felt as if she was falling through a trap door, and hated herself.

'Oh *man*,' murmured Keith under his breath, as if he'd forgotten Tara was there.

'What's happening?' she asked, in a stiff voice that sounded like her mother's stiff voice. 'If you wouldn't mind telling me?'

Keith ran a hand through his hair. 'Sorry to spring that on you. Not the plan, as you might imagine. Molly's my daughter, she's ten. Sarah, her mum – well, that *is* a bit more complicated . . .'

Surprise, surprise, observed a waspish voice in Tara's head.

'. . . but we do our best to co-parent her between us. Sarah works as a make-up artist, mainly films and telly. I try to see Molly when I can – she comes to me for holidays and a weekend here and there. Time out, as it were. For both of them! She and Sarah are very alike, both very independent women . . .'

Tara stared at her father mutely. The emptiness in her chest was deepening with every new detail, scooping her out inside. She tingled with a strange, childish resentment that she'd have found shameful, had she been able to step away from it, but it was clinging furiously to her legs, very much like a furious, jealous ten-year-old, in fact.

She and Toby had never had a proper holiday with their dad after he walked out on them. Not one. A few weekends in London when they were teenagers – staying in hotels, which was pitched as fun and grown-up and cool, not weird and nomadic – but after that, nothing. On a couple of occasions there'd been an unexpected, too-generous cheque 'for holiday money' that she'd actually been too embarrassed to spend on the modest weeks away they'd had in the Lakes or Scotland (Toby sulking in his room, if he deigned to come). But that wasn't the same as taking time off from his incredibly important job to be with his actual children.

Molly was different. Keith *made* time to see her. A bitter shiver of something cold and irrational whistled through her.

You are being ridiculous and unfair, Tara reminded herself. *Jealous of a ten-year-old? Seriously?*

Yes, she thought. *Yes, I am.*

'I'll be honest, this wasn't planned – Molly was supposed to be staying with me next month for her summer holiday,' Keith was explaining. 'I'd booked Center Parcs but, um, there's been a bit of a hiccup on the Sarah front . . .'

'Really?'

Keith nodded, opened his mouth, but before he could speak, his expression abruptly shifted. 'It turns out,' he went on, his tone suddenly two pitches jollier, 'that the film Sarah was working on in Dublin needs her back for reshoots, so she had to hop on a plane this afternoon and head over there.'

'Wow,' seethed Tara. 'How glamorous.'

'Yes, well, that's the thing about Hollywood, as Sarah often tells me – it can be terribly unpredictable and demanding.'

'I suppose she's very used to unpredictable and demanding by now.'

Keith blinked and did a double take, as if he was suddenly seeing someone else in Tara's place. 'Fortunately, she's a very understanding woman.'

Tara let that one go. 'And how long will Molly be staying?'

'Sarah wasn't sure about dates. But what the heck – it's the summer holidays, and Longhampton's a lovely place, with lots to do . . .' His eyes were trying to signal something. 'It's not a problem, is it?'

That was the final straw. Tara stared at him in disbelief. A *problem*? After twenty years, Dad had finally come back to spend time with her, to get to know her as an adult and maybe, eventually, when she'd tested him enough to start trusting him again, he'd get to know the confused child he'd abandoned. Hadn't they almost reached that point?

But now, suddenly, there was another child. This child, though, he *made time* to see. He *made time* to co-parent.

And he'd brought her here, to her house. To Mum's house. What was wrong with him?

A rush of white noise in Tara's ears drowned out any attempts at rational thought.

'Tara?'

Tara put her hand to her mouth to stop herself saying something she might regret, and as she stepped back, she felt something brush against her leg. She spun around in shock. 'What . . . ?'

The Labrador was standing right behind her. And standing about ten feet behind the Labrador was Molly.

Tara forced her face to smile, although she was still raging inside.

'Were you talking about me?' Molly asked. Her voice was high.

'No! We were talking about supper,' Keith lied, easily. 'I know it's a bit late, but do you fancy something to eat? Tara? Would you like to join us for a nibble? I can rustle up some cheese on toast?'

'No.' It came out sharply. A splinter of glass in the genial atmosphere that Keith liked to create around him.

Immediately, habitually, Tara threw out excuses. 'No, I'm sorry. I've been working all day. I need to . . . I need to feed Sybil. Get things ready for tomorrow.'

'Of course.'

Molly was watching them with her wide-set blue eyes. Slightly too big for her face. Slightly too old for her face too.

'Goodnight, Molly.' Tara raised her hand, as if her words weren't strong enough to get her meaning across. 'Nice to meet you. And Lloyd.'

And she walked out of the studio, across the lawn,

through the bifold doors that her dad had installed in their kitchen, and poured herself a big glass of wine while Sybil watched her from the velvet love seat.

Then Tara curled up on the sofa, and cried and cried.

Tara went through the motions of going to bed at eleven but it was pointless because there was no way her brain was going to sleep. Her head throbbed and pounded, rerunning the events of the evening, and slowly the tears solidified into something harder: indignation and anger.

She threw back the sheets and grabbed her phone to call Toby.

When he didn't answer, she called again. And again. And again.

I need you, Toby, she thought fiercely, forcing her words like distress flares into the night sky. *I need you now, so don't you dare ignore me.*

He picked up on her fifth call.

'Hey, Tara – you OK? What time is it with you?'

'I don't know.' She glanced at her watch; the moon was throwing a silver light into the room, bleaching the furniture into monochrome. Sybil was a featureless black comma on the bedside chair. 'Ten to four. Doesn't matter, I need to talk to you about Dad.'

'Dad? What's happened? Is everything OK?'

'No.' Tara closed her eyes. Where to start?

'We've got a sister,' she said. 'Dad has a child with a woman called Sarah. A make-up artist. She's called Molly and she's ten and he's brought her here. Here! To our house. No warning, nothing. He didn't even have the courtesy to tell me she existed, let alone ask if it was all right for her to stay! I came home from work and found this little girl in the garden. She was sitting there reading a book, with a dog. Looking like . . . looking like me.' Her voice broke as the words finally ran out.

Silence whistled down the line across the Atlantic.

Say something, Toby, Tara willed him. There was a time when she wouldn't even have had to explain this. He'd have known. He'd have understood and supplied the words she didn't have, just as he did in the months after Dad left, still a jump-cut collage of memories in her head, when Mum was either livid or devastated or worryingly silent, and Toby had to make them supper or find the school trip money in jars and drawers.

Tara didn't want to prompt Toby now. She didn't even want to speak, afraid she might cry again. She was also terrified that in her general rage with the world, awful, un-take-back-able things might launch themselves out of her mouth about Toby abandoning her all over again, going straight back to his life in America after the funeral when her soul was howling out for his support here. Someone to remember things with. Someone to reassure her that they'd been happy once, that Mum had loved them and they'd loved her enough too.

Now, though. Now was his chance to redeem himself. *Come on, Toby. Say something.*

But there was nothing.

Tara cracked. 'Toby, are you on mute?'

A heavy sigh. 'No, I'm not. Tara, listen, I'm not excusing Dad, but did you give him a chance to tell you about Sarah and Molly? Or did you blank it out?'

Tara's mouth fell open. 'You *knew*?'

'Yes,' said Toby. 'I knew. I tried to tell you when I came over for the funeral but you didn't want to hear then either.'

The betrayal took the breath out of Tara's lungs. She sat down with a thud.

When, she wanted to say. *Why. Why?*

Toby didn't wait for her to speak. 'I bumped into Dad at a hotel launch in Dubai about eighteen months ago. He'd designed one of the suites, but I hadn't noticed – my fault for not reading the press release. I saw him in the lobby, doing an interview and . . .' He paused. 'It seemed ridiculous to ignore him, when I was supposed to be interviewing him anyway, so we had a drink and just . . . talked. I realized he wasn't some ogre. He was just a man I knew *of*, but didn't really know. Like a distant uncle. He was OK.'

Tara tried to process the words. It was such a huge fact to have existed between them, invisible for so long. 'Why didn't you tell me?'

'It was before Mum died. I knew what you'd say.'

'Did you?'

'Yes, Tara,' said Toby, infuriatingly patient. 'I knew you'd go spare. You've never been able to hear a bad word about Mum – and fair enough, she needed someone to have her back – but you have to admit that it made you pretty unreceptive to different viewpoints.'

'No, it—'

'Look, I'm not judging you. Mum needed her version of what a bastard Dad was to be true so that everything else in her life made sense, so . . .' Tara could hear the shrug down the phone. 'It is what it is. She lived the life she wanted to live.'

'She lived the life she was left with,' Tara snapped back.

'There you go. You see what I mean?'

In her dark bedroom, her old childhood bedroom

transformed in every possible way since she'd left home, Tara stared out of the window towards the studio. The lights were all off – or was there one light still on, somewhere downstairs? Was Dad still up? Or had he left it on for Molly, in case she needed to find the bathroom in an unfamiliar house?

'But I thought things were OK with you and Dad?' Toby went on, more gently. 'I got a message from you the other night, saying you'd both found a great new Japanese delivery place.'

'So you read my texts then? You just can't be bothered to reply?'

'Oh, Tara . . .'

Her mind was zig-zagging. 'So, is that what all this was for? Buttering me up so he could bring Molly here?'

Toby didn't bother to hide his incredulity. 'Why would Dad deliberately arrange to look after a ten-year-old kid in the middle of a big work project? Maybe – just maybe! – it really is a massive fuck-up and he's trying to do the right thing.'

'Maybe he expects me to look after her.'

'I doubt that.'

'Why?'

'Well, he barely knows you. You might be an absolutely crap babysitter.'

He said it in such a deadpan, Toby-ish way that Tara was pushed off of her self-righteous track. 'Shut up.'

'Yeah, yeah.' There was some noise on the end of the line – someone shouting. 'Look, I've got to go, I've got a deadline. Take some melatonin, get some sleep.'

'I've run out.' It had been Toby's one useful post-funeral gift to her: a huge bottle of prescription-strength melatonin to get her through the sleepless nights after Mum died. 'You'll have to send me some more.'

'I might be able to *bring* you some more,' he said unexpectedly. 'There's an outside chance I might have a couple of commissions in London next month. Someone's dropped out. I could pop over.'

Pop over to London. Toby's entire career had been building up to making comments like that.

'OK. Well, I'll be here.' She stared out of the window towards the studio. 'With Dad. And our half-sister.'

'Be the bigger person, sis,' said Toby. 'Make them breakfast. Speak soon.' And he hung up.

Across the garden, the full moon was making the lawn look like a beautiful skating rink. Smooth and inviting, as if you could swirl from patio to studio in a series of lovely arcs. *Hero would probably have something to say about the moon*, thought Tara. *It's probably significant. Revelations and women and what have you.*

She looked one more time at the soft light in the studio, and with a sigh, tucked her feet back under her mum's fine Egyptian cotton sheets and tried to fall asleep.

Chapter Seventeen

'. . . and as far as I know, they're having breakfast in there now. He's probably doing his famous scrambled eggs.'

Tara finished and slumped back in the chair. The cappuccino in front of her had lost its froth some time ago. Probably about twenty minutes ago, around the point where she was 'explaining' how her own brother felt it wasn't a problem that their dad had brought his replacement daughter and her replacement dog to her childhood home.

Her throat was bone-dry with talking non-stop. Dad's transgressions sounded satisfyingly worse – which made her own reaction feel less infantile – and pinning down her feelings with words was, as Tara told her own clients, the first step to taking back control. Once you'd articulated what was hurting you, you could begin to work on it, shuffling the broken pieces into a better order. Making sense of it, restructuring everything with yourself back at the centre.

A familiar pause settled over the table: the tiny interval in which the momentum shifted from one person to the other. The problem was temporarily suspended in the air, its messy trail contained in the silence, no one's weight to carry just for a moment.

'OK.' Emily blinked hard. 'Wow. That's a lot. Don't

take this the wrong way, Tara, but do you think you should really be here?'

'What, in this cafe?' Tara looked round. It was several doors down from the Wellness Centre but was the fourth or fifth choice of most of the therapists, thanks to the expensive coffees and the terrible acoustics that left you vulnerable to bellowing something personal into an unexpected silence.

'No,' said Emily patiently. 'I mean, should you have come into work today?'

'You think I should be at home? Making breakfast for them?'

'No, should you be seeing *clients* today? You need to talk this situation through with your supervisor at the very least – I can't see how you can just put something so . . . personally disruptive to one side.'

Tara sipped her cold coffee, pretending to consider her words. Emily was right, of course: ethically, she had an obligation to protect her clients from her own issues. And for once, she had already done the right thing on that front. 'I called Eric this morning, but his secretary said he's in Greece for a fortnight, and he's mad busy after that so . . .' The fact that her supervisor's secretary didn't recognize her name said everything about how very overdue Tara was with her supposedly regular supervisions.

'What about your own therapist? Could they not give you some interim advice?' When Tara didn't answer, Emily added, 'You *are* getting some support with this, aren't you?'

'It's only happened recently,' muttered Tara. 'And I've been busy.'

Emily opened her mouth, then closed it again. She seemed to be struggling to process such a torrent of surprising information about her colleague. 'Wow. Tara. I had no idea you had all this going on as well. No wonder you're stressed out.'

I shouldn't have told Emily, thought Tara suddenly. She really hadn't meant to, but the manic energy had got the better of her. Tara's plan was to suggest a casual catch-up coffee before work, and then – again – ask Emily about her hypothetical client, but the truth had started spilling out the moment they'd sat down in the cafe, a couple of tell-tale 'I's, and now Emily was regarding her with undisguised concern.

Undisguised concern wasn't one of Emily's natural expressions; she prided herself on maintaining a completely neutral face, in order to let clients speak freely and without judgement. But right now, Tara had never seen Emily look so shocked and appalled – and, if she was being honest, fascinated. Emily looked as if she'd just seen a five-car pile-up on the M25, but with a zebra driving one of the cars.

Oh God, thought Tara, realizing the extent of her mistake. *I should have waited and told David. David already knows some of this. Why didn't I just talk to David?*

Because she didn't want David to see this unedifying side of her.

'You definitely need to talk to someone,' Emily was insisting. 'I can ask my own supervisor if she could squeeze you in? She's really good. And look, if you need to go home to process, go home. Jacqueline will understand. Bryan had the day off when Scotland got knocked out of the Rugby World Cup. And Anji claims she needs three days off every year to mourn the passing of Amy Winehouse. Three days! Every year!'

'To be fair, she does claim to get a lot of her spiritual guidance from Amy.'

'That'll be why it's usually the first three days of Glastonbury, then.'

Tara could only imagine how frazzled she looked when Emily changed her tone to out-and-out sympathy. 'Speaking as a friend *and* a counsellor, Tara, I'm telling you to go home, take some time to get your head around this. Now. Don't try to work today. It's not fair to your clients.'

'I can't. You've seen my schedule for this week.' Tara shrugged helplessly. 'I've got people who've already had to cancel and rearrange twice.'

'Then they can wait a little bit longer. I've only got two appointments this morning, I could cover for you – if it's appropriate?'

It wasn't, not really. 'Thanks, Emily, I appreciate it. But I'll be OK.'

Emily remained unconvinced. 'So what's going to happen next? How's your dad going to take care of Molly if he's on a building site? Has he got childcare lined up?'

These were also very good questions that hadn't occurred to Tara. 'And there's another very good reason why I'd prefer not to be at home this morning. Oh, speak of the devil . . .'

Her phone was ringing. **Dad mobile.**

She turned it over on the table with a slightly unworthy frisson of power. Let him see what it felt like to be ignored when you really, really needed to talk to someone.

That didn't make her feel better, though. It gave her

the same guilty-sick feeling that she got immediately after 'treating herself' to a whole chocolate orange in one go.

And – Tara couldn't help noticing in that quick glance at her phone – Toby hadn't called back to check in with her. The emotional ground beneath her feet started to shift again, and she had to make a conscious effort to pull herself back.

It's not like your house has been flooded and you've lost your family's photo albums and your wedding dress. It's not like you've had to borrow money you can't afford, or comfort your child through nightmares.

Tara straightened her spine and forced out a bright smile. 'Wow. Is that the time? Need to get a move on! I'm getting a croissant to take into work. Want one?'

'No, thanks,' replied Emily, but the despairing look that accompanied said a lot more.

The rest of the morning passed slowly. Emily had been right. Every few minutes an intrusive thought would break through Tara's concentration, distracting her from the client's dialogue: had Dad been there for Molly's birthdays? All of them? Had he given up drinking because of her? That one really stung. Dad didn't care enough about her and Toby to quit drinking, but suddenly—

'Are you listening to me?'

Chrissie Tyler smacked her hand on the table between them and Tara jumped.

Chrissie was incensed, but then she always was. 'I can get ignored at home, you know! Yes, I'm boring! My life is shit! But I'm paying you to *listen* to me.'

Tara coughed. Would it help to point out that Chrissie

was actually getting this counselling free? Probably not. 'I'm sorry, Chrissie, I—'

'Unprofessional.' Chrissie pointed a finger over the table, then jabbed it for emphasis. 'I'll be speaking to your boss.' Then she marched out before Tara could gather herself.

Tara sank back into her chair. Brilliant. She'd started to make some headway with Chrissie's anger, and now this.

She leaned on the desk, cupping her aching eyes in the palms of her hands. Molly popped into her head instantly: the glance over her shoulder as Keith had shepherded her back to the studio, her pale heart-shaped face caught in the dying evening light. A little owl-face. Curious, sad.

I should have talked to her, thought Tara. That would be the adult, sensible thing to do. Not leave home first thing to avoid the situation altogether. Running away was what Dad did. What Toby did. Not what she and Mum had done.

But I'm not running away, she reminded herself. *I'm here at work, helping people, where I'm paid to do something good for others.*

But that didn't feel right either. Neither option felt right.

So what was she supposed to do?

There was a knock on Tara's door and she sat up, too quickly. Chrissie, back to apologize? Or Jacqueline, already here with a bollocking?

It was David. 'Coffee?' he asked. 'And just to tip you off – Kasia's put a cake in the kitchen and I swear the secret ingredient is crack cocaine, so if you want some I'd get in there fast before Bryan hoovers up the lot.' He winked.

Just seeing David gave Tara a reassuring sense of the world shifting back on to its moral axis. He would know the right thing to do. But – she winced inwardly – she'd already told Emily. She couldn't tell everyone. Damage limitation.

'Come on,' he urged, with a pretend hup-hup gesture. 'Bryan's got his special plate out.'

Maybe they could get some cake and sit on the fire escape and she'd find a way to ask him what to do. Tara pushed herself away from the desk and followed David to the kitchen.

'Everything OK?' he asked, as they walked down the corridor. 'You seem a bit quiet today.'

It was almost as if he knew what she was thinking. 'David, can I talk to you about—?'

The door they were standing outside suddenly flew open and Anji appeared. 'David! Just the man! I need someone tall to pin up my dreamcatchers.'

'Dreamcatchers?' asked David innocently. 'I thought they were classed as cultural appropriation now?'

'What? Are they?' Anji looked horrified. 'Tara?'

'I don't know,' said Tara. She wasn't in the mood.

'Let me have a look,' said David, with a mildly reproachful glance in Tara's direction. 'Mine's a black coffee, two sugars, demerara. And get me another slice of cake. Don't tell anyone.'

'OK,' said Tara, and headed into the kitchen.

Kasia's cake was indeed very moreish – the note next to it explained it was her mother's original Polish recipe with no fewer than three 'secret ingredients' – and Tara was cutting two generous slices when she sensed a warm presence behind her.

'Tarara-boom-de-ay!' Jacqueline's small hands clasped her shoulders. 'So glad I caught you. I need to talk to you about . . .' She stopped when Tara turned round, and said, 'Gosh. Are you all right? You look drained.'

Such candour was very out of character for Jacqueline: normally she framed any enquiries about colleagues' health in such discreet terms it was hard to work out what she was actually enquiring about. Earlier in the year Tara had had a whole conversation about the best place to get seafood in the UK before she'd realized Jacqueline was subtly suggesting she take some time off.

'Um, just . . .' What was the point in lying? Especially if Chrissie had already made good on her threat to report her ineptitude. 'Bit of family turbulence. Nothing to worry about.'

'Oh, you poor thing. As if you haven't had enough family turbulence this year,' said Jacqueline. 'Can I ask what's happened?'

Tara bit her lip. She couldn't very well not tell Jacqueline, now Emily knew. She turned to spoon coffee granules into her mug. 'My father's brought my half-sister to stay.'

'I didn't know you had a half-sister?'

'Neither did I until last night. It's come as a bit of a shock. I mean, a surprise.' *Downplay it, downplay it.* But her hand wobbled, spilling sugar over the work surface. 'Whoops! Sorry, I'll just clean that up.'

Now she looked, it wasn't even sugar. It was salt.

Jacqueline's eyes burned on Tara's back as she wiped the counter.

'Anyway!' she went on. 'We had a great time at the craft session last night. It's a good idea – I might start making a flood blanket. Or we could do one between us here? A few squares each, mixed media?'

'Tara, I'm not going to tell you what to do, but in a client-centred workplace such as ours . . .' Jacqueline started, and Tara turned around like a schoolgirl caught smelling of cigarette smoke.

It turned out Jacqueline's reproachful gaze was surprisingly effective.

'I'll go home,' said Tara.

'I think that would be for the best.'

The house was peaceful when Tara got back; no sign of activity in the studio windows, no note in the letterbox from her dad.

She felt relieved but couldn't help being curious about what was going on at the bottom of the garden. Although, was 'curious' the right word? What was Dad thinking, bringing Molly to *this house*? Was there really nowhere else to go? Didn't Sarah have parents, or friends?

Tara didn't enjoy examining her less generous instincts.

Sybil was sprawled out on the kitchen counter, meditating in a pool of warm sunshine; she didn't get up when Tara dumped her bag on the chair, but flicked a tail in welcome, more like a dog than a cat.

Now Tara was home she wasn't sure what she was supposed to do. She drank a cup of tea and made a half-hearted attempt to book an appointment with a family counsellor from the list Emily had emailed her. She started with the only one whose name wasn't familiar from local networking events.

'They're good,' Emily had added reassuringly, 'and properly qualified.'

253

They were so good that none of them had any availability for a fortnight at the very earliest, and after the fourth phone call, Tara booked a phone appointment and gave up for the day.

She looked around the house for something useful to accomplish, and her eye fell on the latest Sindy doll waiting to be posted to the winning bidder on eBay.

It was a rare Free Wheelin' Sindy ('Wheels that really MOVE!') still in its box, like nearly all Ruth's collection, and had made enough to pay the quarter's electricity bill. Tara had refereed a convoluted argument between her conscience and the pile of bills the house seemed to generate all on its own, and concluded that if Ruth hadn't spent her savings on Sindys, Tara might not now have to sell them to pay the council tax too.

She started to gather everything she needed – cardboard box, Sellotape, her laptop – and tried to stop her gaze from flicking towards the garden, and the studio. It was impossible, of course. Question after question popped up in her mind, and all the answers were down there. In the studio.

For a second – a heart-stopping second – she thought she saw Branston on the lawn. Patient, loyal and loving Branston, waiting for her.

She shook herself. Not Branston. It was Lloyd, Molly's dog. He was sitting in the garden by the picnic table, staring up at the studio as if the sheer force of his gaze might bring his people to the window.

Tara carried on encasing Free Wheelin' Sindy in bubble wrap and when she looked up to find the packing tape, the dog had revolved on the spot and turned his attention to her.

His brown eyes were confused, furrowing the smooth space between his ears.

Where has everyone gone? his sad expression seemed to say. *Why have they left me in this garden? Why does it smell of cats when there is no cat?*

Tara got a grip of herself. What, she was now verbalizing dogs' thoughts? *Stop it.* Too much time with David.

Tara scribbled a note to go in the envelope, then looked up and the dog was in exactly the same pose, gazing at her with even more mournful eyes, but fifty metres closer to the house, as if he had zoomed in on casters.

Sybil had assumed an upright position on the counter, glowering at the invader. Her tail flicked imperiously, a warning of hissing to come.

'No need to panic, Sybil,' said Tara aloud. 'He's not coming in. You stay there and glare at him while I get some more Sindys.'

When she returned with a 1984 Masquerade Sindy, complete with fan, mask and every ball-related accessory Sindy definitely wouldn't still have had she been allowed to attend a bunk-bed ball with a nine-year-old owner, the dog was right up against the window, pleading silently to be allowed in.

'Oh, for God's sake,' said Tara, and at the sound of her voice, the dog lay down, gazing at her from over his paws. He panted, showing a long pink tongue. It was hot outside. Tara forced herself not to wonder if there was a water bowl out somewhere. Surely Dad would have remembered to leave some water out for him?

She tried to ignore Lloyd as she photographed the boxed Sindy from different angles, and then started writing the description. But it was hard. Branston popped into her mind. How he'd sleep across her feet while she read. How soft his ears were, how his armpits smelled of hot digestives, how comforting it was to feel the weight of his head on her lap when she was sad . . .

Tara wasn't even aware she was walking across to the bifold doors, but before she knew it, the dog was in the kitchen and Sybil, disgusted, was halfway up the stairs.

'Lloyd?'

He wagged his tail and gazed at her, panting. Tara filled up a glass salad bowl at the tap and put it down just outside the door, and the dog submerged its face in the cool water, lapping gratefully until the patio slabs were splashed dark. The sheer relief of his frantic gulps made Tara feel bad for taking so long to let him in – and also annoyed yet again with her dad.

So much for being a devoted dog owner.

The heat had intensified, and when Lloyd lay down on the cool tiles in the shade of the kitchen, Tara didn't have the heart to move him outside.

Instead she went back to her photographing and eBay listing, and was so absorbed in finding exactly the right way to describe the shoulder covering on Masquerade Sindy's outfit that the sudden knocking on the window made her jump.

Molly was standing on the other side. Lloyd leaped to his paws, his tail circling with joy, and started bouncing up and down against the glass.

What else could she do? Tara went over and opened the door.

'Lloyd!' cooed the girl as the dog launched himself at her.

'Hello,' she said. 'Did no one leave any water out for him? He was *very* thirsty.'

'Daddy said he'd be OK. We just went to the hall to see if the workmen had started the windows. The windows are beautiful! They've got stained glass apples!'

'I don't think it's safe to leave Lloyd in the garden on his own. Someone might steal him.' Tara didn't want to scare Molly but honestly, how thoughtless was Keith? Had he learned nothing in the last twenty years?

Instantly, her excitement vanished. 'Really? Would they?'

Tara changed tack. 'Where's . . . your father?'

'Our father' sounded wrong. Like he was God. 'Keith' sounded wrong. 'Dad'. No, Molly had said 'Daddy'. He'd clearly opted for a name change second time around. Rebranded himself.

'Daddy?' Molly clarified.

Tara nodded. Daddy. Now she thought about it, he'd been Daddy to her and Toby too, till they were six. Toby had been the one to knock it on the head.

'He's getting the shopping out of the car. I wanted to make sure Lloyd was all right.'

As Molly spoke, Keith appeared in the garden, struggling with shopping bags. He was flustered, less like his debonair work self. His hair was messy, and he looked hot. A multipack of crisps fell out of one bag and Tara thought she could hear the clinking of bottles. A nameless shadow crossed the back of her mind.

'Are those your dolls?' Molly had reached out for Masquerade Sindy and was inspecting the box. 'This is really old!'

'It was my mum's,' said Tara, trying to work out how

to describe Ruth in relation to Molly, before remembering they were no relation at all. *She* was the link here. 'It's from 1984, it's very rare. And worth quite a lot of money,' she added, as Molly's small fingers explored the faded packaging. 'So please don't open it!'

The words came out sharply and Molly put it down.

'If it's so old, why is it still in the box?'

Keith was staring at them from the middle of the lawn.

'Because . . . it's worth more if it hasn't been played with.'

Molly screwed up her nose. 'That's weird.'

Yes, thought Tara. If she was honest, the dolls made her feel sad: they were designed to be given lives by little girls exploring their imaginations, not trapped for ever in their boxes, elegant ankles bound with sandwich ties. What it said about her mum didn't bear close examination. Any other psychotherapist would have a field day.

Out loud, she said, 'It's an antique. It's about the same age as me.'

Molly stared at Masquerade Sindy, then at Tara, then back at the Sindy. Her mouth dropped open.

'I'm thirty-three,' said Tara. 'I was joking.'

Lloyd saved them both from having to find an answer to that by barking at Keith, who was standing by the window. He'd abandoned the shopping in the middle of the lawn and seemed to be waiting for the right moment to interrupt.

Tara gestured for him to come in. Because . . . why not?

'Tara, I was hoping to catch you!' he said. 'We found an excellent fishmonger, didn't we, Molly? And I got rather carried away with the scallops.'

'They're my favourites,' Molly informed her, counting on her fingers. 'Then steak, then gumbo.'

'Very grown-up taste you have,' observed Tara.

'Scallops were your favourites too,' Keith added. 'I seem to remember you eating twenty in one go up in Skye.'

'Snap!' said Molly, pointing at her.

Her hesitant smile undermined the precocity of her dining habits. If it had been someone else's child, Tara would have laughed, charmed.

'So,' Keith went on, 'then we found a very good deli – Longhampton's really come up, hasn't it? – and I thought I would cook them with some pea puree and some black pudding and some . . . um . . .'

'Pancetta,' Molly prompted him. 'And pea shoots.'

'Pea shoots and pancetta, yes. So would you like to join us? We'll be eating about seven, in the garden.' Keith smiled hopefully, and although Tara knew she was within her rights to tell him she'd rather eat her own toenails, it was very hard to do that in front of a child.

No, not hard. Basically awful.

Tara wished she could ring David, just to hear him say something ridiculous like, 'I'll check in with Lloyd and see what the real story is,' but . . . it would cross a line. They'd got very close to the line recently, talking about their lives but only during work hours; this would defi-nitely cross it. On the other hand . . .

'Please?' said Molly. 'I think Lloyd really likes you.'

David would probably say yes.

'OK,' said Tara, against her better judgement. 'Seven o'clock.'

259

Chapter Eighteen

The picnic table between Wye Villa and the studio had been decorated with enthusiasm while Tara was getting changed, and the design notes pointed to Molly as the project manager.

The spokes of the big umbrella had been wrapped with fairy lights, which also glinted around the backs of the wooden chairs and among the rose bushes. Fat crystal globes lurked in the flower beds like generously scattered handfuls of crystal balls, and jars of red roses and LED fireflies clustered around the table. The flowers, Tara noted, were not snipped from her mum's rose bushes, but were stiff hothouse blooms from whatever supermarket the rest of the decorations had come from.

Thoughtful, conceded Tara.

'Do you like it?' Molly came rushing across the lawn, carrying a glass bowl of salad. She had changed for dinner too, into a long pink dress with streaks of gold and silver sequins like spangled seaweed. She'd undone her plait and the loose hair rippled down her back. With her pale arms and big blue eyes, Tara thought she looked like a mermaid.

'It's very sparkly,' said Tara. 'Did you do it all yourself?'

'Yes!' Molly looked shyly pleased. 'You sit here.' Molly put the salad in the middle of the table and pointed to the placemat with a gold T on it. 'And I'm here, and Daddy's here.'

'Wow. It looks like a very special occasion.' Not only new placemats but new glittery glasses, new golden side plates. Even the cutlery was rainbow metallic, not the dishwasher-safe IKEA set from the studio.

Good job she'd said yes to dinner, thought Tara. How had Keith sold this to Molly? Had he assured her Tara would be just as excited as she clearly was?

Molly beamed. 'Daddy wants to know what you'd like to drink, please?'

'Oh, just . . . whatever you're having.' Tara knew she'd need wine to get through this, but presumably that wouldn't be available. Would it be making a point to bring her own, from the kitchen?

'I'm having elderflower pressé.'

'That sounds lovely.'

Molly disappeared again, and Tara sat down. Sybil was glowering at her from the bedroom window, and when Tara made eye contact, Sybil turned her head and vanished.

Lloyd the Labrador pottered amiably across the lawn, also dressed for dinner, in a floral collar. He wagged his tail at Tara and lay down on the grass near her, his eyes raised expectantly at the table.

'Don't worry, I should think you've got a bowl with an L on it,' Tara told him.

He beat his thick tail three times on the grass in response.

'Dinner is served!'

Tara turned her head: Keith and Molly were approaching, bearing trays. Molly's tray contained large glasses of sparkling pressé, and Keith's contained the bowls of scallops. No wine.

Molly opened the dinner conversation like a pro as Keith handed out the bowls. 'I like your house, Tara. Have you lived here your whole life?'

Tara glanced at Keith. How much had he told her about his first family? 'Um, no. I lived here until I went to university.'

'With your brother Toby, and your mum, and your dog, Branston,' Molly supplied.

'Um, yes. And him.' She nodded at Keith. 'Until I was about your age.'

It took tremendous self-control to keep her expression neutral, but Molly's reaction was one of pleasure, as if she'd got the first set of Hunters neatly stuck in an album.

'What's the nicest house you've ever lived in?' Molly asked.

'Hmm.' Tara didn't want to say 'this one', even though it was true. She pretended to think.

'Didn't you live in a rather amazing chapel conversion for a while?' Keith speared a scallop. 'Where was that?'

'In Haversley.' Tara was surprised Keith remembered. 'Only for six months. And it wasn't amazing, it had *mice*.' And possibly a ghost, and definitely no carbon monoxide monitor. 'How come you remember that?'

'I remember you telling me about it – when we got together, ah, for your graduation. No, can't have been. Your twenty-first? In London, anyway.'

Typical, thought Tara, that the flat was more memorable than their meeting. 'I think you rang me,' she corrected him. 'You missed my twenty-first. And you were *at* my graduation.'

'Ah yes, of course. Lots going on back then, details are a bit blurry.' Keith seemed momentarily uncomfortable, then recovered. 'Yes, I was curious about how they'd managed it – converted churches are so tricky. Magnificent space but you need a trapeze to appreciate most of it.'

Tara hadn't thought about the creaky chapel flat in years. Mum hadn't wanted her to move out, but Diane had talked Ruth round. 'You need to be your own person,' she'd told Tara. 'Not your brother's twin, not your mum's daughter.' She'd been right; the minor thrills of independence made up for the fact that her friends were starting jobs in London and Manchester. It didn't quite make up for the hurt of Toby's promised visits home being delayed. And delayed again.

Still, she'd had Mum.

'Did you really have a trapeze?' Molly asked.

'Tara has many hidden talents.'

'I do.' Like *he* would know. 'Plate spinning. Tightrope walking. Sawing people in half.'

Molly was watching their faces, turning from one to the other, following the quick exchange of words, struggling to understand the current of unspoken ones beneath. A faint, uncertain smile twitched at the corners of her mouth.

She grabbed at the pause in the adult conversation. 'Then where did you live?'

'Me?'

Molly nodded.

'Um, then I lived in a village called Much Larton in a

tiny cottage that had been a pigsty a hundred years ago. That was . . . nice.' It hadn't been nice. It had still smelled, subliminally, of pigs. 'And then I moved into a bigger house in Hartley with my . . . with Justin.'

'Justin,' Molly repeated solemnly. 'Justin what?'

'Justin Biggins.'

There was a pause.

'And what happened to Mr Biggins?' asked Keith conversationally.

'Well, we lived together for a bit, and we, ah, thought about getting married, but decided not to.'

Molly made an 'Oh, dear' sad face that she'd obviously learned from an adult.

Keith topped up her glass with the sparkling pressé they were all, it seemed, drinking. It probably made Molly feel very grown-up but Tara couldn't shake the feeling of being at a kids' birthday party.

A double gin, she told herself, *the second you set foot in that kitchen.*

'So, now you're back in the house – are you staying?' Keith asked casually.

'I haven't decided. There's a lot to consider.'

Bryn the estate agent had left another message that morning, claiming that he had 'several' potential buyers lined up, inspired by the local paper's fangirlish profile of Keith Hunter, saviour of village halls and also designer of luxury hotels. Two were apparently willing to go over the probate valuation price by a significant margin, sight unseen. Could she call back at her earliest convenience, if she'd come to a decision about selling?

Tara hadn't called back yet. Her heart wanted to stay, more so every time she sipped her morning coffee in the garden and inhaled the glorious perfume of Ruth's red roses, every time she soaked in the indulgently re-enamelled antique bathtub, and watched the candlelight flicker on the silvery fishscale tiles covering the wall. But her head kept pointing out that 'Toby's half' was getting more expensive by the week. She'd been through her accounts several times, and couldn't get around the fact that she needed the Centre Director job, or a lottery win. Ideally both.

'It's a big house for one person, I suppose.' Keith tried to read her face. 'But you could rent out the studio? Or work from home? It'd make a wonderful private practice room.'

Tara shrugged. Was this leading somewhere?

'What does Toby think? Guess he's happy just to leave it as an investment, is he? Can't go wrong with property.'

Tara looked away, uncomfortable.

Molly was shelling a prawn with quick, practised movements, expertly peeling off the shell in one go. She seemed so at ease in this adult conversation, far more so than Tara could ever remember being, even though she'd passed around her fair share of canapés at Ruth and Keith's drinks parties. She felt a tingle of envy, and then wondered whether Molly's adult assurance was actually anything to be jealous of.

'Are you still in the same room you've always had here?' Molly looked up, head tilted curiously, a gesture very like Keith's. 'Is it *exactly* the same?'

Tara started to say yes, when she realized only the view was the same. And yet it still felt exactly like her room.

Keith mistook her hesitation for emotion. 'Tara's only been back here for a few months, darling. Her mum lived here on her own for a long time. It's not the same as your room at home.' He glanced at her, to check he'd got it right.

'On her own? Wasn't she lonely?' Molly started, but Tara said quickly, 'No, she wasn't lonely. Her best friend lived upstairs. And my room's totally different to the way it was. My mum loved decorating, she was always changing things around. My old room's probably been four different colours since I was your age. Maybe more!'

'My room is *exactly* the same,' said Molly firmly. 'Mummy's not allowed to move anything. Ever. She's promised.'

'You might want to one day, Molly. You might fancy a change!'

'But Dad . . .'

'Never say never, sweetheart,' said Keith, and Molly pouted.

Tara reached for her glass, but it was empty, and Keith pounced on the opportunity to change the subject.

'The tide's out – can't have that!' he said, reaching for the jug. 'Who wants some more pressé?' He'd already stood up, so the question seemed to be answered. 'I'm going to get some more. Don't you two talk about me while I'm gone.'

Silence fell between Molly and Tara while he walked over to the studio. Then as Tara was racking her brains for a suitable topic of conversation, Molly started chattering away again.

'Mum and Lloyd and I have always lived in Waldegrove Road. Dad lived with us until I was two but I don't remember that.'

'Don't you?'

'No. It's all right though. He comes and visits and it

means we've got a spare room for if friends want to stay over.'

'I see.'

'And I never want to move anyway.'

'Tell me your favourite things about your room, then.'

'My rainfall shower,' she said, counting on her fingers. 'Then my daybreak light, then Lloyd's bed. It's exactly the same as mine, but smaller. Oh, and my balcony – we grow sunflowers on it. Do you want to know what else we've grown in the garden?'

'Yes,' said Tara, because she got the feeling she'd be hearing about it anyway.

After they'd finished eating, Molly went back to the studio to feed Lloyd and bring out the pudding.

They both watched her go, Lloyd trailing at her heels, then Keith turned back to Tara and pretended to look exhausted. 'Sorry about that. Molly is *not* afraid of questions! Kind of goes with the territory – lots of actors, film people. Always talking about themselves.'

'She's certainly not shy.'

'You could say that.' Keith took a big sip of pressé. 'But not in a bad way. I mean, she's precocious but she's not spoiled. Molly's a good kid.'

Tara scrutinized his face. He seemed proud of Molly, and it gave her a weird curdled feeling that she didn't like. A stupid feeling, because Molly *was* a good kid. Had he talked about her and Toby like that? Did he ever mention his grown-up children now, when he talked about his family?

'So what are your plans?' she asked briskly.

'My plans?'

'Well, everything's full steam ahead at the building site, as far as I know. And I thought you had meetings this week. Are you postponing that while Molly's here?'

Keith leaned back in his chair. 'She'll be fine tagging along with me. She came out to Sweden last year. And building sites are interesting places. Always something going on.'

'If you're a plasterer.'

He laughed. As dusk fell, the solar lights had started to come on around them, flickering like fireflies in the roses. 'Don't worry, my attention won't be diverted from Trout-bridge. Alice has already offered to find me a reliable sitter – one of her friends' teenagers.' He paused. 'And I thought maybe you might—'

'No!' Tara raised her hand. 'Whatever you're about to say, don't. I am far too busy to babysit, and even if I wasn't, it's not . . . not something you spring on people.'

'No need to snap. I just thought you might want to. I thought you'd be offended if I *didn't* ask.'

'How do you work that out?'

'Because after years of bitter experience, my rule of thumb is that most women will want the exact opposite of what my original instinct was.' The smile that accompanied it was self-deprecating, but it was too smooth for Tara in her current mood.

'You mean you don't know me well enough to guess right,' she said, and felt bad as soon as the words left her mouth.

'That is also true.' Keith shrugged. 'But believe me, I wouldn't—'

'Because this is getting to be a pattern, Dad.' The

words were coming out of nowhere. 'First you turn up in my garden. Then you get involved in my work. And, what – now you've decided Molly and I need to get to know each other? What's going on?'

Keith didn't reply immediately. He massaged his temples, as if trying to order his thoughts. He glanced down the garden towards the studio, and dropped his voice. 'Tara, I've tried to explain several times, and I understand why you've resisted, but there are things about Sarah you need to know. Things that would throw a different light on to this whole situation . . .'

'. . . but which are entirely from your perspective.' Tara held up her hands. She didn't want to hear that Sarah was hysterical, unreliable, over-emotional – accusations she knew he'd levelled at her mother. Unfair accusations. Her mother was none of those things. 'I do *not* need to know. And she isn't here to defend herself.'

'I get that, but for Molly's sake? Sarah's—'

'No, you listen.' Tara's throat felt raw. 'I thought this was *our* chance to get to know each other. I thought you wanted to spend some time with me, so we could maybe start again and build an honest relationship. I was actually happy about that. But now you've sprung this on me and it changes *everything*. I don't know Sarah. I don't know this little girl . . .'

'But that's it. Molly's just a little girl.' Keith gazed at her, and Tara could feel herself being reeled in by the intensity of his dark eyes. 'I understand why you're furious. You have every right to be. But please, do one thing for me – believe me when I say I had no idea Molly was going to be here. I'm just doing anything I can to make a bad situation better.' He raised his hands, defending himself from her furious glare. 'Do it for Molly, if nothing else.'

Tara opened her mouth to argue further but was stopped by the sound of happy barking.

Molly was walking down the garden with a huge chocolate caterpillar cake on a tray, Lloyd bouncing and leaping around her. It wasn't – Tara glanced at her dad, concerned – it wasn't Molly's birthday, was it?

'Ah, pudding!' he declared, as if they'd just been chatting about the weather. 'Marvellous!'

Molly put the cake in front of Tara. Either she was allowed birthday cake whenever she liked, or Keith had no idea. 'You can have the first slice with Colin's face, Tara,' she said generously.

Tara had sent the first message before she'd even grabbed the bottle of wine out of the fridge.

Hey Toby. I need to talk – can you ring me, please?

There was no immediate response, so she texted again, typing awkwardly with her left thumb while pouring the wine with her right. This time she didn't bother with her usual pretend casualness.

I need to talk to you right now. This is urgent.

He must have detected the anxious emotions coming across the Atlantic because three dots appeared almost immediately.

2 mins. On a call.

Tara clicked crossly around Toby's website while she waited for him. His latest feature was about the five best hotels in the Pacific North-West to 'recolonize your happy place'. All five hotels looked like heaven's guest room: huge white beds, tranquil treatment rooms with towel flowers, shadowy indoor pools fit for a Roman emperor. Toby had painstakingly crafted two hundred words about each one, and only used the word 'luxurious' three times.

What a life, Tara thought. *The biggest effort he puts in is finding synonyms for 'luxurious', and he doesn't even manage that all the way through.*

Toby's call was taking a long time. Tara carried on clicking through to the hotels, then to the areas themselves. Seafood shacks, turreted Victorian mansions hidden amongst lush fairytale forests, friendly neighbourhood coffee shops with house-roasted beans and buttery pastries, snowy resort hotels with hot chocolate and sled dogs. Peaceful places where you could sink into the quietness and be whoever you felt like being that day.

Her eye skimmed the copy; it wasn't Toby's feature, but another journalist, a woman about her own age who'd gone to the mountain-top lodge for a month's therapy after a drawn-out divorce. (*I left like a snake who'd shrugged off a skin that didn't fit any more, and emerged into the light with fresh new scales, a gorgeous new pattern. I even moved in a different way. I was ready to start again.*)

Tara let the idea unfold in her mind, picturing herself standing on the mountain top in the unbroken snow, a stranger to everyone she met, undefined by her job, or her mother, or her clients. Who was stopping her running away to reinvent herself? If she sold the house, she could afford to do her Interrailing but in style this time. No fear of running out of money in Prague, or sleeping on crispy hostel sheets. Ironically, Ruth would be giving Tara the trip she'd denied her twelve years ago, but a million times more luxuriously.

Her WhatsApp was ringing; Toby had finished his call.

'Hey,' he said. 'So what's the problem?'

Had she said there was a problem? Or was he just anticipating them, now Dad was around?

'Just . . . Dad.' She groaned, thinking back to her irritating evening. 'He's presuming *so much*. Like, I've just had supper with him and his daughter—'

'Our half-sister,' he corrected her. 'Molly.'

She took a big gulp of wine. 'I keep forgetting this isn't quite as new to you as it is to me.'

'Don't be like that, Tara,' he said reproachfully. 'It's not you.'

'What's not me?' She eyed the bottle, then topped up her glass.

'Sarcasm. That's *my* thing. Stay in your lane!'

'Maybe I want a go in your lane.'

'Listen,' he said, before she could tell him more about dinner. 'I was going to call you tonight anyway – I've got some good news. Those commissions I was talking about came through, so I should be in the UK from the fourteenth.'

Tara forgot her irritation in the surge of relief that followed his words like a rainbow. Toby was coming back! He'd put everything in perspective. He'd know what to do, how to finesse this odd new situation. 'That is brilliant. How long are you staying?'

'A week? Not sure how long I'll be in Longhampton, though – I'm trying to line up as much work as I can while I'm over. I'll do my best.'

'OK, but try, won't you?' Tara's eye was drawn inextricably towards the notebook by the phone, the one with the notes from the estate agent and the solicitor. And the man at the bank who'd 'run some numbers' for a mortgage on Toby's half of the house. 'There are some things we need to discuss. About Mum.'

No need to mention it now, she thought. *It can wait till he gets here. By then I'll know what's happening with work. I'll have a plan.*

'Sure,' said Toby, and she thought his voice changed slightly. 'Yeah, there is some stuff we need to talk about.'

She frowned. What did he know? Had he spoken to the solicitor? Or had he read her mind?

'Like what? About Dad? Is there something you haven't told me?' Tara put her glass down. 'He hasn't got *more* children, has he?'

'No, nothing like that.' He laughed. 'Just . . . It's a long time since we had a proper chat, that's all. Nothing that can't wait until I see you, though. I'll let you know when I've booked flights,' he carried on, as if he had another call to be getting on to. 'I'm looking forward to it!'

'Me too,' said Tara. She felt warm inside at the thought of a proper chat. Warmer still that Toby had missed talking to her.

She caught sight of herself in the night-time reflection of the bifold doors. The reflected Tara looked as if she was presenting an aspirational cookery programme, in a gorgeously styled kitchen set.

I can't sell this house, she thought. Not even for a round-the-world voyage of a lifetime.

But it didn't stop her dreaming of mountain-top lodges, and an endless ballroom where everything was covered in fairy lights and she was waltzing around and around in the comforting arms of a man whose face was always looking over her shoulder, out of sight.

Chapter Nineteen

The advert for the Wellness Centre Director job, when it appeared the next morning in Tara's inbox, sounded significantly more dynamic than the role Jacqueline was currently inhabiting.

Someone on the board of trustees had hunted out a solid corporate job application template (*we are seeking an exceptional candidate . . . a disruptive yet effective approach to facilitating change . . . multi-disciplinary experience in motivational strategy*) but someone else had then zhuzhed it up with a generous sprinkling of angel dust (*a passionate ally and advocate for a full spectrum of ideologies . . . open-minded, holistic and reactive . . .*). The overall effect was *The Apprentice*, but covered in essential oils.

Tara scanned it for the part that mattered most to her: the salary range. And to her relief, it was within the bracket that would make the mortgage on the house work, with enough spare to pay the heating bills. *Yes!* She was so grateful to whatever universal force had made that happen that she sent a heartfelt prayer to the angel in charge of career development and personal finance.

The application form seemed straightforward enough, until Tara came to what looked like the longest tiebreaker in history: *Please outline, in no more than 1,000 words, an occasion on which you have made a significant contribution*

*to the mental health and/or community spirit of your local
community.*

Jacqueline couldn't have made it easier for her to
answer, and Tara knew it was her chance to shine. Her
experience of direct action during the floods was exactly
what they were looking for – she'd spent hours doing
everything from human-chaining heirlooms to safety, to
PTSD counselling.

The only problem was, now there was so much riding
on the job, the words refused to come.

'Do you need some help blowing your own trumpet?'
Diane asked her, when Tara told her about the job while
the committee meeting was winding down into tea and
biscuits. 'I think *your* problem is fitting it into a thousand words.'

They were both in a good mood. It had been a fun
meeting, for once. Plans had been submitted for the children's playground outside Troutbridge Hall, which had
led to some jovial reminiscing about roundabouts versus
monkey bars, and then the mood boards had arrived to
illustrate possible colour schemes for the kitchen and
communal areas. Decisions were now being made that
gave them hope that the hall would soon be a living community space again. Nobody could get excited about
insulation, not even boring Peter from Planning, but
swings in the shape of apples were a different matter.

'Would you have a look?' Tara trusted Diane. Her gram-
mar was meticulous but her honesty was even more so. 'I've
always had a mental block about job applications – probably
from Mum telling Toby not to show off all the time.'

'This isn't showing off. You're the best person for the

role.' She nodded at Tara's phone, where the job description was still open. 'I can see you making a real success of this outreach project they mention.'

'I know. I've already got some ideas to present about that. I want to be involved with it even if I don't get the job.'

You are going to get the job. You are going to get the job.

'So what's the problem?' Diane gave her a shrewd look. 'You could do this job standing on your head. You know what your mum would say now if she was here?'

'No.' Of course Tara knew. She wanted to give Diane the chance to tell her, though.

'Confidence is the difference!' declared Diane, with a flourish. 'And that's the truth. She would be so proud of what you've been doing. *So* proud.'

Tara smiled, and for a moment Ruth was there, held between them like a hologram in their memories. Sharp-eyed and red-lipped, quick-witted and kind, feeder of birds and wearer of scarves, Arpège and Clarins night cream. Mum was there every time Tara talked to Diane. She wondered if something similar happened for Diane too.

Mum would have stood behind her while she typed, thought Tara, sipping her tea and suggesting more eloquent ways of saying, *I organized the whole damn thing*. And then probably leaning over and typing it for her.

'Speaking of your mum,' said Diane, 'I've thought about something else I'd like as a keepsake.'

'You can have anything, you know that.'

'Ruth had a couple of huge crystal vases,' Diane went on. 'She used to put lilies in them – I'd love those for my new flat. I'm going to buy myself lilies every so often, in memory of her.'

'She'd like that. And I found that necklace,' Tara added, 'the rainbow one you were talking about? There are some earrings too. She'd want you to have the set.'

'Ah, come here, Tara.' Diane opened her arms and Tara hugged her. For a moment, she felt completely safe again.

Mum would be glad Diane's keeping an eye on me, thought Tara, her nose buried deep in her pillowy shoulder. Diane *cared*. She was the woman who'd helped her with the Maths homework that had Mum baffled, the patient driving instructor, the proud seventies feminist influence, the trustworthy voice of common sense.

'Do you want to pop round one night and pick the vases up?' Tara asked. 'They're quite heavy.'

'I'm away most of this week on a course,' said Diane. 'Maybe next weekend? Would that be all right?'

'Of course,' said Tara. 'Any time. You're always welcome.'

A few days later, the arrival of the house insurance renewal and the last quarter's gas bill, both in the same post, sent Tara back to her eBay account, this time with a couple of Sindys and a dramatic semi-precious necklace that she'd never seen her mother wear, and therefore had no qualms about selling.

The marble kitchen counter was a perfect backdrop for the citrine and sodalite collar, still in its original box, and Tara was so focused on capturing the intricate detail of the fastener that she didn't hear the first three knocks on the window. The fourth knock – when Keith and Molly hammered in unison and Lloyd barked too – caught her attention.

'Quick favour, if it's OK?' Keith hustled Molly and the dog inside; Molly hopped up on to the kitchen stool next to Tara, and Lloyd sniffed the air where Sybil had been, four seconds previously. 'Lily's coming to babysit Molly but she's been held up, and I need to be in a meeting . . .' He checked his watch. 'Damn, now *ten* minutes ago. OK if Molly hangs out here till Lily rocks up?'

'Lily?'

'Lily McQueen,' Molly informed her, swinging her legs. 'She's nice. She works at the bookshop. She has two mums, two dads, two older sisters and a little brother.'

Family details seemed to be critical to Molly.

'I see.' Tara glared over her head at her dad. He'd kept a slight distance since her outburst over supper. 'I'm actually in the middle of something . . .'

'So I see.' Keith eyed up the necklace. 'Is that your mother's necklace? That was an anniversary present.'

Tara leaned on the counter in a half-hearted attempt to shield it. It hadn't occurred to her that some of these pieces might have been gifts. Did that make a difference? 'This is just a quick thing. I've taken the morning off to finish a job application . . .'

'What for?' asked Molly.

'A job,' said Tara, and Keith raised an eyebrow.

'What kind of a job?'

'A trapeze artist.'

He raised an eyebrow again but didn't probe further. 'Lily won't be long, literally ten minutes. Let me know if you want a hand with your application . . .' He mimed swinging from a trapeze but he was already strolling out – down the hall towards the front door, not back

279

through the garden. 'I'll be back about two – have a think about what you'd like for tea, Molly!' he added, with a 'ring me' gesture towards his ear.

And then the front door opened, and he was gone. Infuriatingly.

Tara turned back to see Molly running her finger along one of the textured amber beads.

'Why don't you wear this?' she asked. 'If it was your mum's?'

'Because it doesn't suit me. My mum suited jewellery like that. She was very elegant. She used to wear white shirts, then something like that on top.'

'What did she do?'

'She was an interior designer. She said she had to look stylish for work, so people would trust her to make their houses stylish.'

Molly seemed to be processing this information carefully. 'So what relation is your mum to me?'

'None.'

'But you're my half-sister.'

'Yes, I am,' said Tara. 'And Toby's your half-brother.'

'And Lloyd is *your* half-dog.'

'I wouldn't go that far, Molly.' Tara put her phone down. She wasn't going to get this necklace listed any time soon, she could tell. 'Do you want a cup of tea?'

'Yes, please!'

Tara put the biscuit jar on the table, and made them both a cup of tea.

Molly nibbled a chocolate digestive (Tara had no idea about whether this was bad or not, and it wasn't as if Keith had left instructions) then said, 'Tara?'

'Yes?'

'What star sign are you?'

'I'm a Pisces.'

'Ooh.' Molly's face lit up. 'That's why you're a counsellor! Because you're empathetic and caring, and you have a natural desire to help people!'

'Not exactly,' said Tara. She'd already had the full character assessment from the short-lived astrologer at the Wellness Centre, Roddy. It had been part of his interview process; Jacqueline had been starry-eyed, literally, about his description of her astral blessings. 'I'm a counsellor because I never got round to finishing my legal training to become a family law solicitor. There was a job going as an advisor and I like helping people so . . . it went from there.'

She drifted into it, in other words. Totally Piscean, according to Roddy.

Molly nodded as if she'd said something very profound.

'I'm not a proper Piscean, anyway,' Tara went on. She wished her brain would retain information about the EU or world religions, instead of silting itself up with this nonsense, but it was impossible. 'Apparently I've got Taurus rising. That makes me predictable and fond of steak.'

'And wine.' Molly nodded, affirmingly. 'And luxury. But in a good way. You seek comfort over risk. And you might have problems with your neck or throat.'

'How do you know all this?' It was startlingly close to what Roddy had said. And he'd self-published three books about how to run your life using this gobbledegook.

'I'm really into astrology,' Molly explained. 'Mum's friend Angelina is teaching me how to read charts. She's a shaman. And a kinesiologist.'

'Wow.' What else could she say to that? 'And do you know everyone's star signs?'

She nodded. 'Daddy's a Leo, and Mummy's a Scorpio, with Pisces rising, and her Moon in Cancer.'

Was that good? Or a terrible combination? Tara had passively absorbed some basic astrology from the never-ending astro-analysis in the kitchen between Hero and Anji and Kasia, who claimed to be able to 'divine' people's star signs from their faces. She usually left before they could start on her 'fishy' face.

'It's not the greatest combination.' Molly sighed. 'If I knew what time Daddy was born he might turn out to have a better rising sign. Do you know?' she added hopefully. 'He says he doesn't, and that Grandma Hunter wouldn't either.'

'Does it really matter?' Tara asked kindly. 'Dad is who he is. It's not as if he's suddenly going to turn into a more reliable person once we've pinned him down to a Capricorn ascendant.'

'Capricorn would work! Or a Taurus ascendant, like you! I've got my book in the studio, I can check the times. Tara?' She glanced shyly down at the counter. 'Do you think *you* could ring Grandma Hunter? Dad says she won't remember, but she might if you ask her.'

Bloody Dad, thought Tara. Clearly he'd swerved the unpleasant task of explaining why Grandma Hunter might not recall minor details like that; she'd been living in a care home in North Yorkshire for the past ten years, with advanced dementia and Parkinson's disease.

Molly was gazing hopefully up at her, and Tara sensed there was a lot that Molly wanted to know about her family, but hadn't been able to find out. Was she the right person to ask, though? There were huge gaps in her own knowledge.

'I haven't spoken to Grandma Hunter in a long time. She's not very well. She's forgotten a lot of things.' Tara hadn't visited her in the care home. *There'd be no point,* as Auntie Jane had told her briskly, in her Christmas card. *Mum thinks I'm her own mother and that Linda is Margaret Thatcher, so it would only be upsetting.* Tara had been ashamed of her relief at the reprieve.

'How old is Grandma Hunter?' Molly's hand stretched out for her bag. 'When's her birthday?'

Tara sighed. Had Molly even met her grandmother? 'Ninety-three,' she added, so Molly could work out her star sign. 'February the fourteenth, nineteen twenty-eight.'

'Do you know what time she was born?'

'I don't even know *where* she was born.'

Molly was scribbling away in a spiral-bound notebook Tara recognized from the previous evening. It was black, spangled with silver stars. 'And do you know when Grandpa Hunter's birthday was?'

'No idea, sorry. Maybe Dad can help you find it online when he gets home?' *And then you can fill me in on the details,* she added to herself.

Molly chewed her pen, thoughtfully. 'It would be good if Grandpa Hunter was born in . . . late May. A Gemini. Or maybe late September, so he'd be a Libra. Were they happy?'

Ugh. What a question.

Tara started to say yes, of course they were, then stopped herself. Instinctively she wanted to be honest with Molly; it didn't sound like her dad was being as honest as he should.

'I don't know much about them, I'm afraid. They lived in London, so we didn't see them very often when I was younger, and then after Dad left, Mum . . . My mum tried to keep in touch, for our sakes, but obviously, it was a bit awkward. We fell out of touch.'

'That's really sad.' There was a pause. 'I wonder if that was because he was a Scorpio? That's a bad match for Aquarius.'

Tara put her mug down. Where was Lily McQueen when you needed her?

'Molly, I know astrology's fun,' she began, 'but you're not taking it too seriously, are you? I mean, it doesn't mean people *have* to behave in certain ways. Or that certain things will *definitely* happen. We're our own people, aren't we? We decide who we are, and what we do. Not some silly planets.'

'But it explains some things really well.' Molly ran her finger along the vintage package of the Sindy-doll box. The thirty-year-old plastic crackled ominously beneath her touch. 'Things that people don't want to tell me.'

'Oh, Molly, that's . . . that's what adults can be like, I'm afraid. I'm sorry.'

'No one tells me anything,' she said quietly, and Tara felt a wrench in her heart, because the exact same words had come out of her own mouth when she was about Molly's age. She'd whispered them into Branston's long-suffering ears, and he'd grunted as if he was sympathizing.

Lloyd, Branston's doppelgänger, lay sleeping in the warm pool of sun by the garden doors. His ears twitched at the sound of Molly's voice. Tara was glad that Molly had Lloyd, at least. Lloyd couldn't give her worse advice than Keith did.

'So what star sign are you?' Tara asked, because she sensed Molly was desperate to tell her.

'Guess!'

'Oh dear, I thought you might say that. Um . . .' She pretended to think. Molly was ten, and she looked a young ten so presumably she'd had a birthday quite recently? She hadn't mentioned a party or presents, though. It was the end of July now, so . . . Tara made a wild stab in the dark. May? What was May? Taurus or Gemini?

'Well,' she said solemnly, 'you're curious and articulate, and you're always taking notes, and you have very sharp eyes for detail . . .'

Molly beamed, flattered at the small things Tara had noticed.

'So, I'm going to say you're a . . . Gemini?'

Her face fell. 'No.'

'Oh.' Tara was surprised by how bad she felt. 'I'm not as expert at this as you are. Can I have another guess?'

Molly nodded, but while Tara was struggling with dates and stereotypes, the doorbell rang.

'Let me just see who that is,' she said, getting up. 'I'll be right back. I'm still thinking!'

The person on the step was a young woman with brown Heidi plaits and a 'Books are My Bag' tote over one shoulder.

'Hello,' she said uncertainly. 'I'm looking for Keith Hunter? I'm Lily, the babysitter. Have I got the right house . . . ?'

'You have!' The word 'babysitter' jarred with 'Keith Hunter' in Tara's head; the girl standing on the step was probably, in hindsight, about the same age as Ashley, in whose Vauxhall Corsa Keith had exited their lives all those years ago. It suddenly occurred to Tara that she herself wasn't much younger than her mother had been that night.

Lucy Dillon

She pushed away the unsettling thought, and opened the door wide. 'Come on in, Molly's just here.'

Molly was inspecting the Sindy doll in her box and put it down guiltily when Tara showed Lily into the kitchen.

'Hi, Molly!' said Lily, and Tara was relieved when a happy smile appeared in response on Molly's face. She lifted her wrist to show Lily a skinny cotton bracelet and Lily clapped her hands: 'Yay! It survived the shower!'

'Lily showed me how to make friendship bracelets last time,' Molly informed Tara. 'She's really good at them.'

Lily shrugged modestly and then her phone rang. 'Oh sorry, it's my mum, I just need to . . .'

'Sure, take it, no rush.' Tara glanced at Molly, still fiddling proudly with her bracelet. *That was me*, she thought, as if seeing herself in an old home movie with her own friendship bracelets; she and Toby had matching ones. *As clueless and curious and vulnerable as Molly. I knew nothing. And now I'm Mum's age and I've learned more but I still don't really understand.*

'Is your mum having fun on her film set?' she asked Molly, to shake off the strange sensation of detaching from her own life. 'Must be very exciting working with film stars! Is there anyone famous there?'

Molly abruptly turned her attention back to the trapped Sindy doll. 'I don't know.'

'Oh, does she have to sign those non-disclosure forms?' Tara made a lip-zipping gesture, and Molly nodded.

'What else has she been up to, then? Does she get any time to visit anywhere? Ireland's a *very* fun place . . .'

Again, no reply. The change in Molly's mood was odd, and Tara felt rather concerned for her. What was wrong?

She misses her mum, stupid, said a voice in her head.

286

You don't need to have a Child Psychology diploma to see that. She's only talked about her family since she walked through the door.

Tara stepped forward and gently removed the box from Molly's hands. She'd started unpeeling the vintage tape with her sharp nails. 'Molly? I'm sorry if I said the wrong thing. It's OK if you're missing your mummy – you'll be chatting with her soon, though, won't you?'

Molly lifted her anxious eyes to Tara. 'Mummy hasn't called me yet.'

'What? Oh no, I'm sure . . .' Tara stopped herself. 'Really? She hasn't just phoned Dad and he's talked to her instead? Has she texted?'

She shook her head.

How long had Molly been here? It had to be well over a week by now. That was shocking. How busy was Sarah that she couldn't even text? How unfair was it for Molly to have two parents who put work before basic parenting?

Or had Keith forbidden her to call during 'his' time? Tara had dealt with divorcing couples like that. No one ever 'won', especially not the children. Poor Molly.

'I think this Sindy is sad,' Molly said to the doll, casketed in the box. 'She's even older than you and no one's ever played with her.'

'All fine!' Lily appeared in the kitchen doorway. 'My mum! Honestly! She's been running a shop by herself for years and she still needs me to talk her through the wifi! Right, Molly!' She held out her hand. 'What do you want to do this morning? Shall we make some more bracelets or would you like to learn how to knit? I brought my knit kit!'

'Bracelets.' Molly slid off the stool, but Tara couldn't push her worry away so easily. What on earth was happening on that set that there was no time to call a child?

'Call me if you need any supplies,' she said to Lily. 'I'm here all morning, working.'

'Will do.' Lily smiled. She seemed wholesome, friendly. Not the kind of teenage Jezebel who'd run off with someone's father one Hallowe'en.

Although, Tara conceded with refocused hindsight, other people might reserve their scorn for the sleazy forty-something father of two who'd run off with a teenager. Who was Dad's age at work – Douglas the osteopath? Lily and Douglas? She shuddered.

Molly was hovering by the doors that led out into the garden. Outside, Lloyd was already bouncing around, woofing energetically at the apple tree – from whose branches Tara suspected Sybil was hissing profanities.

'It's been nice chatting,' said Tara. 'Thanks for keeping me company.'

Molly smiled, then, as if she despaired of Tara ever asking, said, 'Leo. I'm a Leo too, like Dad. August the seventh.' And she turned and ran down the lawn after Lloyd.

The kitchen felt too quiet, now Molly had gone, and Tara flicked on the kettle to distract herself.

As it was boiling, she reached for her kitchen calendar to jot down Molly's birthday for future reference and suddenly realized August the seventh was next Saturday.

Chapter Twenty

Tara finished her thousand-word essay – working title, 'Things I Did in the Floods' – just after two o'clock in the morning on Saturday.

She sat and stared at the screen of her laptop, glowing in the dark of the kitchen, and rubbed her itchy eyes.

Yellow sticky notes of everything she'd organized, assessed or suggested over the past few months were scattered around the table: not just the dry agendas and to-do lists, but the details for every person who'd sat in her office or hunched on a plastic chair in the town hall, and poured out their frustration with partners, financial demands, fears for the future that they couldn't share elsewhere. Each one with the same chorus: grief, for what had been lost. Her job – and she wasn't sure she'd always managed to do it – was to convince these people that not everything *had* been lost. That there was still tomorrow and the day after, and that there were still things to smile about, seeds of hope to plant in the mud left behind.

Tara's thousand words finished with one of those seeds of hope that had stayed with her for weeks: Jenson Hall's birthday party.

Jenson and his family lived by the river on Dorstone Road. He'd only just come out of hospital after a bike accident that had left him with complex fractures and a programme of extensive rehab. The Halls had planned a treasure hunt party for his whole class – and, of course, everything for the afternoon was stored in their cellar.

Rosie Hall had come for help cleaning up the house, but broke down when Tara asked how the family was coping. Between the volunteers, they'd managed to throw the party, and in the end, it had been a bittersweet ray of sunshine in a gloomy time. Tara remembered Rosie's hand squeezing hers so hard the bones nearly cracked.

You made everything go away for one afternoon, Tara, wrote Rosie on the other side of Jenson's thank-you card. *That was the best present.*

Birthday parties were important to children, thought Tara, staring at what she'd written. You never forgot a birthday party that you didn't get to go to, or a party cancelled because of measles or some grown-up 'issue' that was never properly explained.

Or a Swiss roll with candles hastily stuck in the top because someone forgot to collect your ballerina cake, and because someone else refused to go out and get another, on principle. You remembered something like that for years.

Tara stared at the screen and the words blurred.

'You don't have any plans for next Saturday?' she repeated carefully. Not because she hadn't been clear the first time, but to give Keith a chance to redeem himself.

The smell of toast and the sound of singing in the studio kitchen reassured Tara that she'd managed to sneak across the garden without being spotted by either Molly or Lloyd. She hovered on the doorstep, ostensibly to drop something off before she left for work.

'I want to say . . . no?' Keith's eyes darted from side to

side in the hesitant manner of someone unused to oper-
ating without a PA. 'I've got a meeting at Perryfield on
Friday but, ah . . . Saturday, no. Why?' He brightened.
'Are you planning something? A road trip?'

Tara's shoulders dropped. He didn't even realize why
he was such a let-down. Despite the 'new dad' trips to
buy party plates and gold forks, he still needed reminding about minor details like birthdays. She was surprised
by how disappointed she felt. 'You've forgotten it's Molly's birthday?'

Keith had the grace to look horrified. 'I knew it was
coming up, but . . .' He wiped a hand over his face. 'Well
then, yes. I suppose a party's in order, isn't it?'

'Isn't that what you normally do?'

'Parties are Sarah's domain – she loves organizing parties. Always very elaborate, lots of balloons and whatnot.
Calligraphy invitations, even for the kids. She's done a
course . . .'

Yet she can't make time to text, thought Tara. *What a
pair.*

'So what's happening this year? Is Sarah coming here?
Are you going there?' It dawned on Tara that they still
hadn't established exactly how long Molly was staying.

He looked evasive. 'I don't know. I don't think so.'

'Well, can you find out? It's Molly's birthday!' Tara
dropped her voice; if her half-sister was anything like her
and Toby, she'd have international-level eavesdropping
skills when it came to adult conversations. 'And she says
her mum hasn't been in touch with her since she got
here. Is that true?'

It wasn't any of her business, not really, and Tara was
aware that ten-year-olds sometimes leaned towards an

emotional truth rather than a strictly factual one, but Molly's lost expression still haunted her conscience. Something wasn't right and although Tara still squirmed away from the details of Keith's personal life on her own behalf, *someone* ought to be asking the questions Molly couldn't.

Surely Sarah would want to know exactly what was going on here, whether Molly was OK, what was planned for her birthday?

'Shall we have a tea party?' said Keith, before Tara could find the right words. 'Here? In the garden? Would that be nice?' He glanced sideways to check Molly was still occupied.

'But what about her friends? What about her mum?'

Keith raised his hands. 'Would it not be more weird if I had a list of ten-year-old girls in my phone to invite?'

Tara couldn't argue with that. 'Fine. You, me and Molly it is, then.'

Poor Molly.

Sybil had registered her displeasure at Lloyd's arrival at the other end of the garden by spending more and more time lurking in the rose bushes at the front of the house, leaping out at unsuspecting birds when Tara was stacking the dishwasher or parking her car.

Tara was almost positive she was doing it to scare her as much as the birds. There was always a bit of side eye involved afterwards.

Sybil's dramatics felt rather ungrateful to Tara, since she'd splashed out on a complete vaccination and micro-chipping appointment at the vet's, at the end of which she was presented with a record card in the name of Sybil

Hunter. It made Tara feel as if she'd adopted a game sep-
tuagenarian line dancer, not a cat, but as she carried
Sybil's basket back to the car on Monday morning, she
tried to tell herself there was a faint glow of appreciation
emanating from the depths of the wicker shell.

Microchipping was a step further than Phil had ever
bothered to go for his beloved pet, she now knew. As the
vet nurse had scanned Sybil's back for signs of an existing
chip, Tara had experienced a shameful flicker of hope
that there would be a beep – and a reason to contact Phil
from the moral high ground, to let him know she'd be
changing Sybil's details. Tara had no idea whether Phil
worried about Sybil, or her, since she'd blocked him on
every single channel of communication more to protect
herself from late-night texting than anything else.

Tara had come to terms with the fact that Phil had
decided to do the decent thing, and stick with his not-
wife, Zoe. It had now been three weeks since their IKEA
break-up and so far there'd been no avalanche of roses to
the office, no planes trailing banners reading 'I've Been a
Dick, Tara, Please Forgive Me' over the skies of Longhampton. Tara knew she was being ridiculous, but a tiny
part of her couldn't believe that was it. It felt as if she'd
been forced to leave a predictable film ten minutes before
the end: she knew how it would play out, but there was
still the minuscule chance of a twist.

It did occur to her, as David sat stroking Sybil in her
office later that morning, that she could go direct to the
horse's – cat's – mouth and see if Sybil had some hotline
into Phil's shady brain, but she wasn't sure how that conversation would start.

David was filling in ten minutes before heading down

to the Lunch and Learn meeting, today starring Douglas the osteopath and his step-by-step guide to creating a spine-friendly work space. Neither Tara nor David was looking forward to it much: Douglas was waging a one-man campaign against laptops which, as Emily pointed out, was a bit like Father Christmas sounding off about Amazon, given that his entire client base suffered from Laptop Hunch.

David's face visibly lit up on spotting Sybil's basket by the window and she'd seemed pleased to see him, rubbing her head against his chin and flicking her long tail around with enthusiasm.

'She only does that with men, by the way,' Tara pointed out. 'She's just as flirty with my dad, so don't feel special.' She'd told him about Dad, and Molly, in the end; he'd texted her to check she hadn't gone home because she was ill, so it seemed only fair to explain. He hadn't offered any advice, but he'd listened. David's thoughtful listening made Tara feel better than most people's advice did.

'She seems in good form,' he observed. 'No repeat of her unfortunate vomiting incident?'

'None whatsoever. But then again, I have no idea what the people two doors down are feeding her.' She glanced over to see if he'd registered the reference to his list of three things.

'You never asked them about it?'

'I wasn't sure how to phrase it, to be honest. "My friend's been chatting to my cat, and apparently you've been feeding her?" You can get a reputation for that sort of thing, you know.'

'And the item with the flashing light keeping her awake?'

'I leave my phone downstairs. It was a phone, by the way. Nothing more sinister.'

They both knew what was coming next.

'And the builders?'

The question hung in the air.

'There were no builders.'

'Sorry to hear that.' David scratched Sybil's ears. She closed her eyes and pushed her head into his hand, fully in love.

And Phil. Ask him about Phil. It was an open goal, the topic already broached. Tara juggled the words in her head: what could she ask that wouldn't make her sound desperate? *'Is my ex thinking about me?' 'Does my ex miss me?' 'Does Sybil miss Phil?'*

Tara tried to sound casual. 'Sybil's here because I took her to get microchipped today. Turns out Phil never bothered chipping her. My ex, Phil,' she added, in case he'd forgotten.

If it sounded clumsy, David didn't show it. 'Sorry to hear he's now an ex.'

'I was wondering if Sybil knew . . . I mean, if Sybil could . . .' Tara frowned. The words wouldn't come out of her mouth.

David's attention was fixed on the cat; Sybil was patting his face tenderly with her paw and making funny chirrupy noises that Tara had never heard before. In fact, Tara had never seen Sybil interacting so positively with a human being. There was clearly something about David that Sybil could see. Something patient. Something understanding.

Am I going insane? Tara wondered. *Or is he talking to my cat?*

David looked up and caught her watching him. A

295

flicker of connection passed between them and Tara felt ashamed that she'd even been thinking of asking David to ask Sybil about Phil. Firstly, because – and she was aware of how mad this rationale was – why would Sybil care about Phil, the man who'd given her away? And secondly, because she suddenly didn't want David to know that she still secretly thought about Phil. She didn't like what it said about her.

What did it say about her? It was a very confusing thought.

'You've got a dog living at the other end of your garden now?' said David.

'What? Um, yes.' She'd told him that, hadn't she? When she'd told him about Molly arriving. Tara couldn't remember the conversation precisely, but she must have done.

David stroked Sybil's ears and didn't speak for a moment or two. 'It's a big yellow dog?'

'A Labrador, called Lloyd.' Was he pretending this was coming from Sybil? *If I told him Molly had a dog, I'd have told him what breed it was*, thought Tara. *No reason not to.*

He laughed. 'She says they all look the same to her.'

'Rude.'

David hadn't finished. 'Sybil says he's fine as long as he's in the garden but she doesn't like it when he comes in her house.' He paused. 'She doesn't like the way he follows you around. I think she's jealous.'

Tara felt smug at the idea of Lloyd following her round; she was growing rather fond of him too. He reminded her more and more of Branston, the way he leaned against her leg as a sign of high esteem. 'Tell her she's being ridiculous – poor Lloyd's only been in the house once or twice!'

'Nothing poor Lloyd about it, apparently. Sybil thinks he's taking liberties. She's quite a character, isn't she?'

'As cats go.' Tara watched David's face as he communicated – or pretended to communicate, whatever he was doing – with the cat. She reminded herself that she should either be annoyed, if it was an act, or worried, if he seriously thought he could communicate with animals, but the truth was, she had no idea what he was doing. David's whole face seemed to lighten, losing its usual grown-up composure, and Sybil did seem engaged with him. Tara's curiosity grappled with her professional instincts. What had Sybil noticed from the garden wall? What did she think of Molly? Did she like her? Could she see the family resemblance?

Sybil abruptly swivelled her head in Tara's direction, eyeing her in an accusatory fashion, and Tara had the unsettling sensation that there was a conversation going on that she wasn't part of.

'Sybil's showing me . . .' David hesitated, the same way Tara had hesitated before, as if there were words that were sticking in his throat. 'Um, not sure whether I should say this really.'

'If it's another complaint about the food, tell her to cut out the middle man and get on to Tesco head office.'

'It's not about the food. It's about you.'

'Go on.' He was guessing. Playing for time.

'She says . . .' David looked up at her. 'She's showing you as being much happier now. And she's showing me herself happier too.'

Tara's heart pulsed in her throat. It was partly because

what he'd just told her was weirdly intimate, but also because David's brown eyes were locked on hers, and there was a vulnerability in his gaze that was also protective, and out of nowhere, Tara had the strangest feeling of being completely safe, completely at home in this—

The atmosphere was broken by a knock on the door, and Kasia's head appeared round it.

'Are you coming down to Douglas's laptop lecture?' she said, without much enthusiasm. 'Jacqueline's announcing the winners of the Step Challenge – Chloe says there's prizes. Better not be that foot spa that keeps doing the rounds on the raffle,' she added darkly, then looked between the two of them, as if noticing something for the first time. 'Sorry, am I interrupting?'

'No!' Tara spoke too loudly. Her face felt hot. 'No, we're coming down now.'

'Nice cat,' said Kasia, and Sybil glared at her, then stalked back into her basket.

In order to ensure full attendance at her meeting, Jacqueline had cannily seeded rumours of the Step Challenge results amongst the most gossipy members of the Wellness Centre team, and then even more cannily reserved the announcement until *after* the lecture about correct chair adjustments and DVT.

Tara forced herself to focus on Douglas's collection of lapel badges as he droned on, conscious that with her job application now in the system – and applications closed – her enthusiasm for every aspect of the Centre's programme was under scrutiny.

She wondered how many other people in the room

had applied for Jacqueline's job. Bryan, maybe? He was always pontificating about what changes he'd make if he was in charge, starting with the banning of instant coffee. Emily? Emily would love to wreak changes, much like Bryan, but it was hard to imagine her wanting the paperwork. And she'd have mentioned it.

David?

Tara couldn't study David's expression as he was sitting next to her, but she sensed he was concentrating on Douglas's talk – genuinely, too, not for show, like her. A few weeks ago she'd have assumed David would not only apply for the job, despite his newness, but that he would get it. Now, though, Tara was sure he'd have told her.

Jacqueline was fidgeting with something in a glittery bag: presumably the prize for the Step Challenge. Had it really been six weeks since they'd started? *At least we won't have to spend our lunch breaks marching around the park*, Tara thought, but was struck at once by another thought: she was going to miss walking around the park at lunchtime with David.

It wasn't that they'd used the time to find common professional ground, as Jacqueline had intended. It was the small talk that had slowly turned them from colleagues into friends: their pretend reality-show commentary about the people with dogs and the imagined secret lives of joggers they only saw once a week. Their friendship had built with every lap of the bandstand. Even David's Fascinating Facts about the area, thrown out at random for her to bat away with a roll of the eyes, were a running joke. She'd started to wonder if he researched them especially for her.

Will he miss it too? Tara wondered.

'. . . although of course I can't help with *all* types of wrist pain,' Douglas concluded, as if leaving a pause for laughter – which was not forthcoming. Instead there was a momentary pause, in which thirteen lots of attention shifted abruptly from the buffet, the open window, Jacqueline's bag, having registered that the talk was over.

Jacqueline clapped heartily to prompt the others. 'Thank you so much for that useful advice, Douglas. And now,' she said, steaming past the usual questions, much to everyone's relief, 'the moment you've all been waiting for. I have been *astounded* by the efforts we've made as a team in the name of fitness and health. Between us, we've covered over a million steps – yes, one million! – and I feel we've benefited from the fresh air and exercise. And, I hope you've had as interesting conversations as I've had!' She glanced over at Kemi, who'd been her walking partner. 'Thank you, Kemi!'

Kemi smiled without showing her teeth. Tara suspected Kemi now knew far more than she'd ever wanted to about container gardening.

'So. In the spirit of the Olympics, I've decided to award bronze, silver and gold medals to our most active team members. Without further ado, in bronze medal place . . . Chloe and Hero!'

Chloe and Hero wove through the chairs towards Jacqueline to collect their prize. David leaned towards Tara's ear and muttered, 'A million steps? Really?'

His warm breath tickled her neck. She leaned sideways and muttered back, 'Well, if everyone *else* fiddled their steps by a couple of hundred per week . . .'

'Are you accusing me of cheating?' he whispered in faux-outraged tones.

'No, of course . . .' She turned her head and found

David had leaned in closer than she thought. The closeness of him, and the conspiratorial glint in his eyes, made her jump and she almost missed Jacqueline saying, '. . . David and Tara!'

'What?'

Everyone was clapping, and David was hustling her towards the front.

'There you go!' Jacqueline handed them a bag which was surprisingly heavy. 'Congratulations! So many steps! Well done! And now, the winners! Who are . . . Emily and Lionel!'

Tara swerved to avoid Emily barrelling up to the front with Lionel trailing behind her, in a fitting tribute to their walking pattern over the past weeks.

'What did we win?' she asked David, once they were back in their seats and Jacqueline was running through the Any Other Business.

David lifted out two bottles of Hero's Midsummer Gin. 'One each!'

'Oh . . . good,' said Tara, and across the room Hero waved, and then offered a little namaste accompanied by a smile Tara couldn't quite work out.

'We are still going to have the occasional spin around the park?' he said, a little hesitantly. 'I mean, I've just got these new trainers.'

'Why not?' She tried to sound casual. 'I wouldn't want to deprive the joggers making stories up about *us*.'

'Good,' said David.

Tara phoned Toby just before bedtime to ask if he could rearrange his trip, to make it to Longhampton a few days earlier than planned.

'It's Molly's birthday on the seventh and Dad totally forgot. Her mum won't be here either, so the poor kid's celebrating her eleventh birthday with me and him. I'm going to have to find her an amazing cake or she'll be discussing this with her therapist for years to come.'

There was a pause on the line.

'Toby?'

'Is that really your job? Birthday parties?'

'Well, no, but who else is going to do it?'

'Her mum?'

'Her mum's worse than Dad. Apparently she hasn't even called since Molly's been here. Molly's still young enough to care about birthdays – she engineered a whole conversation about astrology just to make a point of telling me when hers was, so I suspect she knew both her parents were going to forget, or mess up somehow.' Tara thought about Molly's face, the tentative glances from under her lashes, checking Tara's reaction, checking her point had got across.

'I just want her to feel special,' she said. 'That she *matters* to someone.'

There was another long pause on the end of the line.

'This is so you, you know, Tara,' said Toby, and she could picture his face as he said it. Amused, but slightly annoying.

'What is so me?'

'You can't resist looking after people. Even when you're simultaneously furious about being made to do it. Amazing how you can do both things at once. Has your therapist ever worked on that?'

Not in so many words, thought Tara.

'This is about being *kind*,' she retorted. 'It's about remembering what it felt like to be ten years old, and pinballed around between fuckwit adults, and stepping in and doing something to make someone feel better.'

'So it *is* really about you.'

'Toby, I've had a long day dealing with people's emotional issues at work,' she said. 'I'm supposed to be at home. Can you just let me know if you can move your dates to be here for Molly's birthday, and ideally bring her an interesting present from America that will make up for the boring birthday she's about to have?'

There was another long pause in which Tara hoped Toby would say something. Something like, *Yes, Tara, I will. And I'll bring you something nice too, to make up for the last few birthdays we've missed.* In an ideal world, he might even add, *It would be lovely to spend a bit longer with you too, actually – can you get some time off so we can do a trip to Paris?*

Toby said, 'I'll make some calls.'

'*Thank* you.'

'You're *welcome*.'

It was the old pretend-annoyed tone they used to use as kids.

'No, *you're* welcome,' said Tara. This could go on for hours. She'd missed it.

Toby laughed. 'Night night, pizza face.'

Chapter Twenty-One

Although the repair work on Troutbridge village hall was powering ahead at a speed previously unknown in Longhampton building history, Keith's absences from the site were becoming more frequent, and Tara had a sinking feeling she knew why.

He claimed that his personal involvement was required on the Turville Court hotel project; it was going to be a big job, he told Tara, with contracts potentially worth millions. This sounded plausible, but why shut down phone conversations about it whenever she approached? Maybe the developer was a woman – no reason why not – but Tara was pretty sure she'd heard her dad refer to his contact as 'Steven', and the two times she'd heard him talking in the garden, a noticeable distance away from the studio, he'd definitely been talking to someone called Niamh.

She'd never heard him mention a Niamh before. There was no one in the office with that name. No one he talked to like that, anyway, with his hands in his hair and a funny expression on his face.

Most suspicious of all, Turville Court was in Perryfield, twenty miles away. That definitely didn't require an overnight stay the night before a meeting.

It could only be one thing. Some woman. Maybe even the one who'd replaced Sarah.

'I've got an early morning meeting,' Keith 'explained', when he asked Tara if Molly could sleep over the night before her birthday. 'Couldn't get everyone together any other day.'

'A Saturday morning? Seriously?'

He shrugged. 'Investors flying in and out – I don't know the details, I just turn up when I'm told.'

Yeah, right, thought Tara. A hotel would definitely be involved, one with a cocktail bar and discreet staff. It was so disappointing. So exactly what her mum would have predicted; so annoyingly as Diane had said: leopards didn't change their spots. One step forward towards a proper father-daughter relationship, two steps back.

Tara itched to challenge him about it, if only to show he couldn't pull the wool over her eyes these days, but she didn't want any bad feeling in the air before Molly's party. The good news was, though, that they would now be three guests – Toby had changed his flights. 'You'll be back by lunchtime, won't you? I planned to start about half three. And you know Toby's arriving on Saturday morning now?'

'Is he? Marvellous. I'll be back as soon as I can,' said Keith. 'I promise.'

'You'd better.' Tara almost added, *Tell whoever you're sleeping with you need to get home for your little girl's birthday party*, but she didn't. She hoped her face said that for her.

Toby's flight landed in Heathrow on Thursday but he didn't arrive in Longhampton until mid-morning Saturday.

He'd come via work: a series of 'iconic British experiences' conveniently located in a straight line from central

London to Longhampton. By the time his hire car – an Aston Martin convertible, which he was reviewing for a separate feature – pulled up outside Tara's house, Toby had already covered his flight plus upgrade, courtesy of five hundred words each on two brand-new London hotels and their afternoon tea offering, a spa in Reading that did coffee-based treatments, Stonehenge and the Pump Room in Bath.

Tara had tried not to be jealous when he'd updated her on the phone. Of either the hotels, or the chutzpah in getting paid to have the ultimate English summer holiday.

Molly's face had fallen when Keith hadn't appeared for breakfast. Her lower lip wobbled, but Tara had swiftly produced croissants and chocolate spread, and reminded her that her half-brother was on his way.

This seemed to distract Molly, and the notebook had discreetly made an appearance as she quizzed Tara about Toby ('Does he have a dog? Where does he live in America? Does he sound like you? Which bits of me does he look like?' – only some of which, disconcertingly, Tara could answer), but when the silver Aston roared up outside, Molly's excitement was swallowed up by shyness and she ran off to 'get something' from the studio.

Tara's own nerves were fluttering in her stomach from the moment she woke up too. The few days Toby had spent in the UK for their mum's funeral were a blur; she could barely remember the funeral, let alone conversations. There hadn't been time. There hadn't been any emotional energy left.

But through the dull ache Tara had instinctively noticed the tiny changes in Toby, whose face she'd once known as well as her own. His voice on the phone was the same, but physically he was a subtly different person, a successful British soap star recast with a Hollywood actor. Tara's eyes, sharper nearly a year on, raked him for more changes: travel had bestowed a golden year-round tan and his shoulders had broadened out under his leather jacket. His hair was still thick and chunky ('My little Dennis the Menace,' Dad used to joke) but streaked prematurely with a few fine silvery threads that she hadn't noticed last time.

Like Dad, she thought. At least Toby wasn't vain enough to colour them over.

'Toby!' She ran down the path, her arms wide open. It was impossible not to.

'Hey, Tarantino,' he said with a grin, pushing the hair out of his eyes and then dropping his bag so he could hug her.

'Does James Bond know you've nicked his car?' she asked, nodding at the convertible.

'Very funny.'

It was a decent hug, lasting several seconds longer than Tara expected. It was warm, open-hearted; Toby smelled the same as ever. She heard 'good to be here, I missed you' in the wordless squeeze of his forehead into her shoulder. Tara hoped he could feel her 'I'm so glad you're here making this house feel more like home'.

'Jeez, it's weird to walk in here,' he said, as they made their way inside. 'It *is* our house, isn't it?'

He hadn't come back after the funeral. Diane was still living there, and Toby had asked to stay with Tara in Hartley. He didn't want to visit their old home, and Tara had been too shaken off her axis by grief to care, let alone ask why not.

307

'Is this the first time you've been here since . . . well, since when?'

'Since I left home.' Toby gazed around, looking for landmarks and finding none. 'She's changed it completely yet something's . . . something's the same. Is it the smell?' He sniffed, then frowned. 'It smells like Branston. Can that be right? Does dog hair have some kind of nuclear half-life?'

'No, it's Lloyd,' Tara corrected him. 'Molly's Lab. Different dog, same smell. Want some tea?'

'Tea! Ha! Tea. Yes, tea'd be great.' He followed her into the kitchen, and froze. 'Woah.'

Tara knew what Toby was feeling. It was disconcerting: the walls and the furniture might be different but the trees were the same, Dad's glass and oak kingdom rising at the bottom of the garden, their old swing still down by the hedge. The house hadn't changed. It had been waiting for them to return. Now Toby was back, it felt as if it had shifted nearer to her memories.

She glanced at her brother; he was standing with a hand over his mouth, his adult cool momentarily lost in a rush of memories. But almost as quickly, he gathered himself and the confidence smoothed over his reaction as if it had never been there.

'I take it that's the dog? And our new sister?' He nodded towards the lawn, where Molly and Lloyd had emerged from the studio and were walking self-consciously across the garden.

'It is.' Tara watched Toby's face to see whether Molly stirred complicated feelings for him too. But it seemed not. Or else he was better at hiding them than she was.

Toby merely raised his eyebrows. 'She's very like you, isn't she?'

'Do you think?' Molly was a lot prettier than Tara thought she'd been.

'Yeah. Got your skinny legs. Got your frizzy hair.'

'Shut up. You've remembered a present, right?' She spoke quickly, trying to pack in the necessaries before Molly arrived.

'Course.' He paused. 'She's not allergic to airline pretzels?'

'Toby!'

'Duh. Of course I've got a present. I'm not stupid. I even took advice.'

'Good. Molly! Come on in!' Tara opened the garden doors and Molly shyly stepped inside. 'This is Toby. Toby, this is Molly.'

'Hey there.' Toby held out a hand, shook Molly's, then gave her a high five, all upbeat transatlantic energy. 'Happy birthday! I hear it's a very special day.'

Molly giggled, and her cheeks went pink. 'This is Lloyd.'

'Hi, Lloyd.' Toby bent down and shook Lloyd's heavy paw, then looked up at Molly. He had Dad's knack, Tara thought, of striking exactly the right conversational note. And he was good with kids; Toby was good with everyone, being very confident in who he was. She felt proud of him. 'Hey, Molly? Is Lloyd Branston's half-brother? They look pretty alike.'

Molly turned to Tara, thrilled by the idea of another connection. 'I never thought of that! Do you think he might be? Like, distantly? Like, aren't all Labradors related?'

'It's not impossible,' said Tara diplomatically. 'Toby

and I were going to have a cup of tea, would you like to join us?'

'Yes, please.' Molly hoisted herself on to a tall stool and swung her bare legs, looking between the two of them expectantly. 'Milk, two sugars.'

Toby pulled out the stool next to her as Tara assembled the mugs and boiled the kettle. 'So where's Dad?'

'Business meeting. One of his developer mates has bought Turville Court and wants to turn it into a Center Parcs for grown-ups. He'll be back by lunchtime,' she added, more for Molly's benefit than Toby's.

Toby, she noticed, didn't query the weekend meeting time. He shrugged and helped himself to a croissant from the pile Molly had been too excited to eat earlier. Maybe 9 a.m. Saturday meetings were normal in fancy hotel world. Or, added a cynical voice in her head, did Toby know something she didn't? Like this mysterious Niamh?

'So what's the birthday-girl timetable?' Toby asked. 'I'm thinking photo shoot, makeover . . . ?'

'I thought we'd have our tea at about half three, with presents?'

'And Dad will be back by then?' Molly asked.

'Yes. Definitely. And in the meantime, I've got some special pottery we can paint!'

'Yay!' Molly smiled her sunny smile, but Tara thought she could detect a glimmer of cloud behind her blue eyes.

I sound like Mum, she thought, *jollying up the mood without really believing in it.* That made her suddenly quite sad.

The summer had already been warm, and as August went on, the temperature had been steadily climbing each day.

When Keith returned just after one, it was almost too hot to sit outside in the direct sun, and Tara put up the big umbrella on the picnic table so Molly wouldn't get burned.

'Must make you feel at home!' joked Keith, giving Toby a big manly bear hug, which Toby returned, plus a side of back slapping.

Tara watched them from the kitchen counter, where she was buttering thin slices of bread for cucumber sandwiches. It had been fine when it was just her and Toby – and Molly – but Keith's return had tipped an invisible balance again.

She knew she was being negative, but she resented the way Toby and Dad were so relaxed with each other. They'd obviously pushed through the awkward conversations months back, and were two stages ahead of her. Plus they didn't have the complicated matter of loyalty to Ruth to get in the way of fun, like she did. And they were already so alike, charming and confident, letting the good-natured joshing wash over each other.

Skinny legs. *FFS*. It was like being thirteen again. For the last ten years, Tara's long slender legs had been her *best feature*.

Molly was observing them with the same hungry expression, her eyes darting between her dad and Toby as if they were the most fascinating television programme ever. Both men were on top form, joking and playing with an excited Lloyd, including Molly in their conversation, chatting about America and the weather and restaurants, as if it was the most natural thing in the world for the four of them to be there.

At least Molly's enjoying it, Tara reminded herself. *This is one hundred per cent more family than she's had up till now. Focus on that. Not what you lost.*

But it was hard, in her mother's house, not to think of Ruth and what she had to let go.

Tara wanted Molly's party to be one she'd remember for the right reasons, and the catering, at least, was pure Instagram. The table outside was set with Ruth's mother's tea service, fine white bone china with forget-me-nots and clovers: she sensed that Molly wanted something grown-up and special, so she'd gone to town with a full Ritz afternoon tea, complete with Granny's articulated tea strainer and silver cake forks and sugar shaker.

'Cucumber, salmon, egg and cress, and ham,' she said, pointing out the finger sandwich selection on the tiered stand. 'And then scones and cream, petits fours, meringues and macarons. The tea's in that silver pot, and there's lemonade in the jug, but if you want something else, just ask.'

'Wow.' Molly's eyes were wide. She kept glancing at Keith, then Toby, then Tara.

'Do you like it?' Tara asked.

Impulsively, Molly ran over to Tara and gave her a quick tight hug which squeezed Tara's heart inside more tightly than Molly's arms squeezed her waist. The bond between them had developed quickly – too quickly, probably. Tara was well aware that children needed slower steps than these, that children with chaotic home lives made reckless attachments – she had her own issues on that score. But she knew that Molly needed a protector. She'd already seen Keith check his phone, frown and put it back in his pocket twice since he returned.

Leopards don't change their spots. Had Sarah been left for a babysitter? Tara pushed the thought away.

Something about the silly adult fuss required for the complicated tea made conversation flow like the Earl Grey. Molly wanted to hear every detail of Tara and Toby's most memorable birthday parties (the funfair one, the fancy dress one) and when the conversation veered too near Ruth, Toby reeled off some outrageous stories of his more recent birthdays that Tara hadn't shared in person, because they'd taken place abroad, thousands of miles away, with people she didn't know. He was a natural story-teller, and Molly's eyes never left his face.

Tara tried to smile in the right places, but inside she wanted to yell, *Did you never think of flying somewhere with me?*

Keith seemed happy to let Toby take centre stage, sipping his tea and diplomatically avoiding any memories that might spoil the atmosphere. He told them about his own birthday parties as a child, some stories that Tara hadn't heard before. Everyone was trying hard to make it as much fun for Molly as they could. They coaxed conversation out of her and she gradually bloomed under the attention of her siblings. At four o'clock, the birthday cake was brought out from the pantry – a lemon drip cake with a fondant Labrador on top – and presents were produced.

Keith, much to Tara's relief, hadn't forgotten. He'd given Molly a silver necklace with an M on it.

Toby helped fasten it round Molly's slender neck, while she held up her dark hair, released from its usual plait into Pre-Raphaelite ripples. As their heads bent together, Tara caught the undisguised emotion in her dad's face. He looked overwhelmed. *Was this how he expected it to go?* she wondered. How had he imagined it would play out – the party, the gathering of his children? In his ex-wife's house?

Toby's present was a pink instant camera.

So was Tara's.

'How did you . . . ?' She boggled at her brother over the pile of crumpled giftwrap, surprised and a bit delighted. It was *years* since they'd done something like that; there'd been a time when they'd regularly get identical test results, or send identical birthday cards. It was a long time since she'd been able to read Toby's mind, or he hers.

He shrugged. 'I dunno. I just thought . . . they've come back in style.'

'I can swap mine for something else,' Tara told Molly. 'Choose whatever you like – we can go shopping tomorrow, if you want?'

Molly hugged the boxes. 'No, it's perfect. I'd rather have two, because you both thought of me and chose the same.'

This is going to be all right, thought Tara, buoyed up on the glass of champagne Toby had brought out for himself and for her. Not for Dad. He didn't even offer Dad a glass, which told Tara they'd spoken about it.

'Squeeze up so I can take a photo!' Molly ordered, and Toby and Keith leaned in close to her, already saying, 'Cheeeeeeese!'

'You smell,' Toby informed her.

'Can we stop this now, please? It's not funny.'

'Well, you do.'

'You both smell,' said Keith.

Tara laughed in protest and Molly took the photo. The

first family photo of her, Dad and Toby for twenty-three years.

They all looked drunk in it, even Keith.

Molly took lots more – Toby had had the foresight to get plenty of film – but Tara noticed that that photograph was the one Keith slid into the inside pocket of his linen jacket.

'I fancy a drink,' said Toby, just after six. 'Anyone else?'

Tara started to get up, but he waved her back down. 'No, you've done enough today. What can I get you? Gin and tonic?'

'That would be nice, actually.'

'No problem. Where do you keep your booze?'

'In the sitting room, on the cocktail wagon.' Ruth had, of course, an original Art Deco cocktail wagon, the only item of furniture Tara was excited about inheriting. She almost didn't want Toby to see it, in case he tried to bagsy it.

'Dad?'

'I'll stick with this botanical non-gin malarkey.' He indicated the bottle. 'Maybe bring some ice?'

They watched as Toby strolled into the house, swinging his arms and whistling.

'Daddy?' Molly had slipped off her chair. 'Daddy? Is it OK if I go inside and read? I'm too hot.'

Keith stretched out an arm and she leaned comfortably into him. 'Yes, of course, sweetie pie. Are you bored of the adult conversation? Are we a bit dull?' He tickled her. 'Are we boring you?'

'No!' Molly giggled and squirmed.

They made a sweet picture, thought Tara. She probed the feelings swirling in her chest; what was the dark edge on the warm affection she felt towards Molly? It wasn't jealousy any more, it was . . . anxiety. An anxiety that Keith was going to let Molly down exactly as he'd let her down, this time with Niamh as the agent of his unexpected departure.

And what about her mother? Where was Sarah? Why hadn't she rung?

Maybe Molly's going to ring her now, Tara reasoned. Maybe that's why she wants to be on her own. So she can separate her loyalties out, play down the fun for Mum.

Toby was coming back with a tray of drinks, pushing open the doors with his elbow. Molly gave Keith a kiss, gathered up her presents and ran down the garden, Lloyd following at her heels. Tara watched her father watching Molly as she went.

This is not your problem to fix, Tara, she reminded herself. But it was so hard not to want to.

'Here you go,' said Toby, distributing the glasses. 'I'll have that drinks trolley, by the way, Tara. What a cracker.'

'It's mine,' she said, not joking. 'I saw it first.'

'Ah . . . that looks like a pretty gin.' Keith sighed. 'Local?'

'Homemade, I think. No label on it.'

Tara had taken two long sips of the very pretty gin and hearing that, nearly spluttered them out. 'Not homemade by me. By a co-worker who's also a crystal healer. You need to go steady with this one. Last time I had a few of these, I ended up having a very odd night indeed.'

'Oh, really?'

'Yes, really.' Tara sipped her drink and let the floral,

midnight-blue, juniper fragrance of the gin roll around her tongue. David's face drifted into her mind's eye. She smiled inwardly. *Poppies and cornflowers and sunlight and long grass.* Was that him, or the gin?

If only I'd met David somewhere other than work, she thought. *If only I'd met him in the park, or at the gym.* Her mind drifted even further, towards his rolled shirtsleeves that sat halfway down his lean forearms, to the hair that fell on to his forehead when he wrote. Where would they be now, if she didn't have to stick to her rules about keeping her private life private?

'Is that the doorbell?'

'What?'

Toby was nodding towards the house; Dad was checking something on his phone. Again.

'I'll go and see,' said Tara, and it was only when she was walking through the hall that it occurred to her that it might be someone very late for Molly's birthday party. Someone who should have been there from the start?

Chapter Twenty-Two

'Hello, Tara,' said Diane. Then she took in Tara's party dress, and the streamers still round her neck. 'Sorry, is this a bad time?'

Too late, Tara remembered their conversation about Ruth's vases. Diane had said she'd come round to get them that weekend.

'Oh, the vases! I totally forgot.' She clutched her head. Why hadn't she looked for them before now? 'We're all in the garden. Come and have a piece of birthday cake while I go and get them.'

'We?'

'Dad and Toby and me. It's Molly's birthday, we've been having tea.' Diane's head reared back, hearing Keith's name, but Tara was filled with a strong urge for everyone to just *get along*. A strong urge, or strong gin. 'We've had a good afternoon. It's been nice. Honestly. Just say hello to Toby. When was the last time you saw him?'

The prospect of seeing Toby seemed to be about as exciting for Diane as seeing Keith.

'You know what, Tara, I'll just wait here,' said Diane, but Tara urged Diane towards the garden, and stumbled back into the kitchen in search of the vases.

*

318

It took her a while to find what she was looking for. Ruth had vases for every type of flower and they were arranged in height order in the floor-to-ceiling cupboards in the pantry, so by the time Tara had climbed up on the stool, found the right ones, and then found a strong enough bag to put them in, Toby had been in and out for another round of gin and tonics.

Tara staggered out with the bags. Diane was sitting stiffly at the table with Toby, and Keith was over by the rose beds, on his phone. Neither Diane nor Toby was saying much.

The air felt charged with freshly snapped words.

Diane got up as soon as Tara appeared. 'Thanks, lovely,' she said. 'Oh, and you wrapped them up. Thanks for the cake, it was delicious.'

'You're not leaving?' Tara looked between them. 'Stay, have a catch-up. Toby, tell Diane about that great spa you reviewed this week. Weren't you looking for a thermal spa, Diane?'

'No spoilers, please. It'll all be online from Monday,' said Toby brightly. 'With links.'

'It's OK. I need to get back.' Diane gave her a pointed look. 'Say goodbye to Keith for me when he's finished on the phone with his new girlfriend.'

'What?' Tara hurried after her as she stalked back down the garden to the kitchen door. 'What new girlfriend?'

'Oh, nothing changes, Tara. I told you. I'd no sooner sat down than the phone rings and he leaps up, not even a "Do you mind?".' Diane sniffed. 'Rude. Just . . . rude.'

'How do you know it's a girlfriend?'

Diane paused at the door and gave her a withering

look. 'I could hear it was a woman. And he answered the phone on the first ring.'

Thank God, at last. Better late than never. 'Oh, that'd be Molly's mum, Sarah. She'll be calling to speak to Molly.'

She shook her head. 'Not Sarah. I remember you mentioning her. Niamh, this one's name is.'

Keith had gone to check on Molly when Tara returned, but Toby had refreshed his gin. He'd used one of the really big glasses too. At this rate, thought Tara, he'd have powered through her whole bottle, and Hero probably only made it when the moon was in Bacchus or something.

'Where does Diane get her clothes these days?' he asked. 'There's an organic yurt compound that wants its main tent back.'

'Why were you so rude to her?' Tara demanded. 'There was absolutely no need for that.'

'I don't like her.'

'Why? She was only ever kind to us. She's really looked after me since Mum died.'

Toby fidgeted with his glass. 'It's not compulsory to like everyone.'

'You just don't like Diane because she's not afraid to say what she thinks. Out loud, to actual people, not on social media. She's done a lot to support people round here. The food bank, for a start.'

Tara could see movement in the long windows of the studio; the main light going off, the smaller bedroom lamp going on. Molly was probably settling down with a book, or was on the internet trying to get a birthdate for Grandpa Hunter.

Maybe Sarah would call now, she thought, and started to tidy the table to distract herself, piling up used plates and cups on to the tray. Keith's phone was lying on the table next to his glass. Tara couldn't stop herself reading the screen. There were eight missed calls and a WhatsApp message from Niamh. **Call me ASAP please.** While Toby was looking elsewhere, Tara slipped it into a napkin and tucked it under a saucer. ASAP could wait till tomorrow. Tonight was for family.

'You can run food banks and still be a hypocrite.' The venom in Toby's voice took Tara by surprise.

'Meaning what exactly?'

'I mean . . .' He turned his head, and his voice changed completely. 'Everything OK, Dad?'

Keith was strolling down the garden, smiling.

'All fine. She's had a great day. Can't stop talking about her new cameras and her tea. Her brother and sister.' His eyes seemed shiny as he sat down. 'Thanks, the pair of you. You made her day. I couldn't have hoped for this, you know.'

'We enjoyed it too, didn't we?' Tara lifted the tray with its covert cargo; it sounded as if Dad wanted to talk, properly, in which case she definitely didn't want some random woman distracting them with phone calls. 'Can I get anyone anything from the kitchen?'

When she came back, Keith and Toby were reminiscing about Branston.

'Toby was just saying how much like Branston Lloyd is,' said Keith, indicating the seat where Molly had been sitting, the one next to him. 'What a prince among dogs.'

'My best friend.' She slid in next to him, keen to

forgive. 'There could never be another Branny. I'd have done *anything* for that good boy.'

'What? You are such a rewriter of history, Tara.'

Toby's voice had a slurry edge. Tara didn't like the sound of it.

'Meaning?'

'Well, when you say you'd have done anything for him . . . are you forgetting the time you nearly got him killed? On purpose?'

'Don't be ridiculous.'

'Come on. We can laugh about it now.'

'I honestly don't know what you're talking about, Toby.'

Toby looked between Keith and Tara. 'You've never heard this story, Dad? About Tara's big scheme to get you to come home?'

'Toby, you're pissed,' she said shortly. He'd always been a bit of a fabricator, adding funny twists to stories to make them more entertaining. Not lying, exactly. But not quite the truth. 'I would *never* do anything to harm Branny.'

'You did!' He pointed at her. 'It was about six months after Dad left, so . . . April? You knew that Branston was pining for Dad, and you knew that if we ever left that gate open in the back garden he'd have a wander off, see if he could find any girls in the area. So, your little brain got whirring . . .'

Something dark stirred in the back of Tara's mind, a half-remembered dream with no faces or places, just an unspecific dread looming larger and larger behind her.

'And one day you came running into the kitchen, going "Mum, Mum, I can't find Branston! I think he's run away."' His impression of her voice was accurate but not very kind. 'And of course Mum was busy, in the middle of something more important, as usual, and she said, "Oh, he'll come back." But he didn't, did he?'

Why was Toby making up such a horrible story? 'Dad, make him stop.'

'You were all, "We should call Dad, we should tell him Branston's run away," but then we got a phone call from a complete stranger saying they were very sorry but they'd just run over a dog—'

'Shut up, Toby!'

'And they'd taken it to the vet's.' Toby raised his voice to cover her protest. 'And luckily for you, I mean, *us*, Branston only had two broken legs and several broken ribs and he recovered. Apart from his limp.'

Tara's heart pounded in her chest. 'I have absolutely no recollection of that whatsoever.'

'Of course you don't. You blanked out lots of stuff that you did after Dad left.'

'Tara, if it's any consolation, I never heard that story,' said Keith.

'Well, you wouldn't,' said Toby, before she could speak. 'Mum made a point of shutting down every avenue of communication, didn't she? Both ways, as it turns out.'

Keith looked uncomfortable. 'Look, it's in the past. There are reasons why . . .'

Toby finished the dregs of his gin. 'I'm going to get another drink.'

'Like that helps!' Tara shouted after him, nearly in tears, and then added, 'Sorry, Dad, no offence.'

'No, I'm sorry, Tara.' Keith had had his head in his hands, but he removed them, so he could look her in the eye. His were bloodshot. 'That's a sad story. You must have been very worried about Branston. And me.'

'I don't remember it,' she insisted. But she knew that didn't mean it hadn't happened. There were cupboards in Tara's head, cupboards where certain things went. Sliding doors that you could shut against even experienced supervisors.

Keith didn't contradict her. Silently, he extended a hand, and Tara took it.

She didn't know what to say, so she said nothing, and they sat there, united in guilty remembrance of Branston's unconditional devotion, until, too soon, Toby returned.

To Tara's horror, he was carrying something.

'Dad, this your phone?' Toby offered it to Keith. 'It's just stopped ringing.'

'Where was that? I've been looking for it.'

'In the kitchen? The ringer was off, I only noticed it because it was flashing in the dark.'

Tara held her breath as he handed it over. Was Toby going to say something? He would have seen the missed calls too. She tried to catch his eye. Couldn't Toby see what Dad was doing? Couldn't he see history repeating itself? Didn't he *care*?

Toby calmly sipped his drink, and refused to meet her gaze.

Tara clenched her fists to stop the energy racing up and down her arms. *I've got to say something*, she thought. *I can't just leave it.*

'Dad?'

He was already scrolling through the messages and didn't look up. 'What, darling?'

'Can you leave your phone alone for one evening?' She

324

struggled to keep her tone calm, adult. 'I feel as if there are strangers muscling in on our time when you're on your phone.'

Keith still didn't look up. 'It's important, Tara. I won't be a second.'

'Please don't tell me it's about work. On a Saturday night.'

Keith was still reading, a deep frown forming on his forehead. He managed a 'hmmph!' semi-laugh in response, which only riled Tara further. What was so important? When she'd just told him how important his attention was to her?

'Dad!'

'It's not work.'

'Then what is it?' Tara could hear her voice rising. 'What is more important than your own children? You say you want to start again with us, and build a proper relationship, but you can't even ignore your phone for *one night*. I've been watching you all afternoon, texting and checking it. It's like everyone else is more important to you than us!'

'Tara, did you hide the phone in the kitchen?' Toby was looking at her strangely.

The gin was making her brain unwieldy. 'Not intentionally – I mean, it was on the tray, I was tidying up . . .'

'You did! Who made you the phone police?'

'Why are you taking his side? Oh, wait – you've probably met *Niamh*, haven't you? You've probably been out for drinks, and—'

'Niamh?' said Toby, and when Tara flushed red, he pointed at her, triumphantly. 'So you *have* been checking his phone!'

'That's not—'

'I take it back, you'd make a crap policewoman.'

'Stop it!' Keith didn't even look up at them. He'd already dialled a number and the phone was by his ear. 'It's not like that.'

'It never is!' Tara's self-restraint snapped. It was so disappointing; she knew what her dad was, but when it came down to it, she'd hoped he'd come up with something grander, more impressive, than the cheap self-delusion she heard week in, week out, on her consulting room sofa. 'You've created a separate reality in which you can shag someone else, and line up another person to deal with the mess.'

'Like Mum,' said Toby.

'Exactly,' said Tara, surprised that Toby was agreeing with her. 'Mum had to clear up the mess you left behind. And now Molly's got to go through what we did?'

'That's not what I meant,' said Toby.

'What?' Tara turned on him. 'Then what *did* you mean?'

'For Christ's sake, shut up, the pair of you!' Keith raised a hand, and turned away. 'Hello? Yes, it's Keith. Thanks for your calls, Niamh, sorry I didn't get back to you earlier but . . .' His expression changed, and he got up from the table. 'Oh.'

He didn't sound like someone talking to a new girlfriend.

Toby and Tara exchanged glances as Keith started walking down the garden, talking inaudibly, clutching the small of his back, a deep frown on his face. When he got to the swing, he stopped, suddenly, and squeezed his forehead as if it ached.

'Seriously, Tara,' said Toby. 'You're jumping to some conclusions. Why should Niamh be a girlfriend?'

'Because . . .' She raised her hands. 'It's *Dad*. Accountants don't call you ten times on the weekend.'

'You don't think Niamh could be someone professional? Like his *doctor*?'

'Why on earth would I think that?' She glanced down the garden, suddenly uncertain. That tone, that look. He wasn't talking to a friend.

Toby shot a quick look in Keith's direction to check he was still talking, then said, under his breath, 'I heard him mention something about a hospital earlier, on the phone, in the garden. Something about results, an appointment. A second opinion. I think Dad's ill. I think that's what all this is about.'

The breath left Tara's body as if a wind had blown through her, sweeping her blood and thoughts and sense away with it.

'*Dad* lined up some of the features I did in London this week. He wanted us both to meet Molly. He's not drinking, he's thinner than when I last saw him, he looks shattered. Isn't this adding up to something to you?'

An otherworldly light show was taking place over the treetops, a storm so far away it was completely silent. Lightning flashed in the distance, throwing veins of golden light across the soft suede of the night sky. It was beautiful, but it struck Tara that it wouldn't be so peaceful underneath the storm. Wherever the storm was centred would be wild and loud and primeval. She felt a heavy drop of something wet fall on her face.

Then another.

Fat drops were falling on the table, the size of coins. It

had started to rain but Tara barely registered the cool change in the air.

'Why didn't you tell me?' she hissed. 'How long have you thought this?'

'I only overheard him today. I mean, I had my suspicions about why he suddenly wanted to build bridges, but I assumed it was to do with Mum dying.' Toby shrugged. 'But think about it. Why would he come here and spend time, *personally*, on some nothing-y village hall in the middle of nowhere?'

'Because he wanted to do something for the community?' Even as she said it, Tara felt the past weeks shifting in her mind; the focus of everything flipped, revealing a totally different picture.

Toby shook his head, as if her naivety was sad and touching.

Keith finished his call and was walking back towards them, his face serious. It was an expression Tara remembered from the death of Simon the rabbit, from her Grandpa Hunter passing away: Keith's serious face was so different from his normal humorous twinkle that he hadn't needed to say a word for the young Tara to burst into tears.

Dread swept through her. What Toby said made perfect sense. Why hadn't she asked more questions? *Dad's going to tell me he's dying*, she thought, and the idea of losing him just as he'd come back – no matter how bad things had been – punched her in the stomach.

She was standing – Tara didn't remember getting up – and so was Toby. The raindrops were falling around them, heavier and heavier, turning the paving stones black outside the circle of the umbrella, but Tara barely noticed.

'Kids, I've had some bad news,' said Keith, as if his face wasn't telegraphing that already. 'Will you sit down?'

Trembling, Tara sank on to the seat. *It could be something fixable*, she told herself. Diabetes. High cholesterol. But everything about her dad's weary body language told a different story. Whatever this news was, it was crippling him from the heart outwards.

'What's happened?' Toby spoke for them both.

'I haven't been completely straight with you. I'm sorry.'

'Dad, whatever it is . . .' she began, then felt a sob close her throat.

Hold my hand, Toby, she thought, but he didn't. He sat staring fixedly across the table, bracing himself.

The silence seemed to go on for ever, punctuated by the dot-dot-dot of the rain on the umbrella over their heads.

Keith pinched the bridge of his nose, then spoke. 'Sarah – Molly's mum – isn't on a film shoot. She is in Ireland, but she's in a clinic. She has some . . . some serious dependency issues, but she's getting herself sorted out. Some friends and I staged an intervention a few weeks ago – it wasn't planned. But it was necessary. That's why Molly's here.'

The night was still, but Tara felt the storm inside her building: it was relief but mixed with something angrier. She tried to ignore it, but it was roaring closer, like the thunder now rumbling only a few miles away.

She tried to push it away, knowing it wasn't a good feeling.

'I wasn't in Turville Court yesterday,' Keith went on. 'I flew out to attend a session with Sarah, as part of her treatment. Sarah seemed stronger. Wanted to know about

Molly's party, what I'd planned. We discussed whether she might be able to speak to her on her birthday. They've got strict rules about outside contact.' He swallowed. 'Sarah's counsellor – Niamh – found her in the grounds this afternoon. They don't know where she got the stuff from, but she's had a very bad relapse. Niamh's been trying to call me all day.'

'Oh.' Tara's heart plummeted. So that was Niamh. Not a girlfriend. Someone who really did need to speak to Keith.

'I've got to fly out in the morning. I'm Sarah's next of kin.' He sighed again, almost a groan, and looked at Tara, then Toby. 'I have to be there. For Molly, as well as Sarah.'

A triangle – Keith–Sarah–Molly. Each other's next of kin.

And we're on the outside, thought Tara. *Me and Toby, pushed out, yet again.*

As soon as the thought went through her mind she was ashamed of it, but she couldn't stop. Thoughts and feelings tumbled out of a place in her head that she'd kept locked up for a long, long time: angry, resentful, childish thoughts.

It was always about someone else. Dad's attention was *always* somewhere else.

'Doesn't Sarah have parents?' she heard herself say. 'Or siblings?'

'Tara!' Toby and her dad were both staring at her, shocked.

'Well.' Tara distantly remembered this shameful feeling from somewhere in her past: knowing you were saying something bad but too lashed on by your feelings to stop. 'Surely you should be here with Molly? You're

330

her father. She needs you. How do you think she's going to feel if you're not here in the morning?'

The pain on Keith's face made something shrivel inside Tara. 'She'll know I've gone to look after her mum. And that I've left her in the care of two people I trust most in the whole world.'

'Of course we'll keep an eye on Molly,' said Toby, with a quick 'shut up' glance at Tara. 'Are you going to tell her what's happening?'

'I'll explain in the morning.' He checked his watch. 'Probably time to call it a night. I've got to get flights booked.' Keith looked up at the night sky, glowing behind the shifting clouds.

The lightning hadn't stopped. The storm was coming nearer.

'Let's get some sleep,' he said. 'Things will look better in the morning.'

'Night, Dad,' said Toby, and with an ambiguous glance at his sister, turned and went inside.

Tara sat in the garden on her own until the fizzing sensation in her veins died down. Her head churned with so many thoughts that everything blurred into white noise, and all she could do was stare at the distant flashes in the sky.

Eventually she went inside, and found the bottle of Midsummer Gin. There was an inch left in the bottom, and she poured it down the sink.

Chapter Twenty-Three

Keith left for the airport at seven the following morning, depositing Molly and Lloyd on Tara's doorstep while she was still yawning in Ruth's embroidered dressing gown, groggy with the after-effects of last night's gin, and also last night's argument.

The words were still flashing back in her head at random intervals. Each time it made her stop momentarily, and wince. Tara didn't recognize the Toby of last night. The last time – the *only* time – she'd seen Toby that drunk was after someone's sixteenth birthday party, when he'd vomited a litre of peach schnapps outside the house at 3 a.m. and Tara had crept down to sluice the steps before Mum woke up. Normally Toby was a genial drunk, like Dad, not mean. And even taking into account the weird effects of Hero's gin, why had he said what he said?

Tara had genuinely blanked out the episode with Branston. Now Toby had dislodged it, fragments were coming back – Branny's limp, a memory of him coming back from the vet's with red bandages – but she didn't recognize herself in it. The mortification was real, though. Lloyd's cheerful pat-seeking was particularly hard for Tara to bear in the cool light of morning.

It had rained all night, and it was still raining now. Big

puddles had formed along the flower beds, and the sky was colourless.

'I'll keep you updated on the plans,' said Keith over Molly's head, in a cheery tone that implied he hadn't told her exactly why he was going to Ireland, a suspicion confirmed when Molly hugged him, and said, 'Give my love to Mummy and tell her get well soon.'

'I will.' Over Molly's head, he mimed someone sneezing which Tara took to mean 'she's got a bad cold', although other interpretations were, she supposed, possible.

Jaded, Tara made a cup of tea and some toast which they ate – still no sign of Toby – while she tried to think of ways to amuse Molly for a whole day. Ideally ways that worked well around a hangover.

'Where's Sybil?' Molly asked, looking for the cat. She liked to make an equal fuss of Sybil so as not to create what she called 'brother–sister rivalry' with Lloyd. If only it was that easy.

'She doesn't like rain. She'll be hiding somewhere.'

'Oh.' Molly raised worried eyes to Tara. 'Indoors, or outdoors?'

'I don't know.' Tara decided not to tell Molly Sybil was no fan of thunderstorms either, and that she'd turned herself invisible. 'Her breakfast was gone ten minutes after I put it down so . . .'

Molly seemed satisfied by that. 'What are we going to do today?'

Sleep? Eat brownie mix out of the bowl? Make lists of drinks that are never allowed across my threshold again? Tara summoned up what little energy she had left. 'How about you help me with some of my eBaying?'

It turned out Molly was handy with a phone camera and didn't mind taking the tedious detail shots from every angle, and then uploading them twice as fast as Tara had managed. With tea and biscuits and the radio on, it wasn't so bad, and between them, they got two Sindys and three vintage necklaces up on Tara's page. After half an hour or so, Tara realized she could tune out some of Molly's complex monologue about Lloyd and Sybil's imaginary relationship, her favourite cereal, astrology, etc., and simply enjoy the low hum of a contented child, wittering on in the knowledge someone was sort of listening.

The happy stream of consciousness continued until Molly said, 'Tara, if I ask you a question, will you tell me the truth?'

'If I can.' She crossed her fingers, hoping it wouldn't be anything to do with last night. Had they been yelling loud enough to be heard in the studio? She really didn't want Molly to have heard the Branston story.

'Is it . . . ?' It was hard for Molly to get out, whatever it was. 'Is it my fault Daddy's gone?' Her gaze remained on the necklace she was photographing.

'What?' Tara felt relief, then sudden sadness. 'No, of *course* not. No, it's nothing to do with anything you've done.'

She was about to say, *How could it be?* and then remembered her own sad list in the back of those red notebooks. Snoring. Lack of piano practice. Not being funny enough.

'Your mum's not very well,' she said carefully, trying to stick to the truth, 'so Dad's gone to be with her. She's being looked after, though.' She paused, unsure whether that had gone in. 'Molly?'

'Uh-huh.' Molly had returned to taking detailed photos of Air Hostess Sindy.

'I'll let you know as soon as I hear from him.'

No reply. Just a close-up of Sindy's shoes. They weren't really suitable for long-haul travel.

Tara hesitated, then put a hand on Molly's bent head. Her 'don't distract me, I'm concentrating' defensive hunch stirred up another memory in the back of her mind, the reading, reading, reading she'd done in the months after Dad had gone. Ploughing through books just to be somewhere else, anywhere else, other than with this strange family that didn't feel like hers any more.

Without speaking, Tara picked up the doll that Molly was photographing and unpeeled the tape that had sealed Sindy's cardboard coffin for forty years.

Molly turned in surprise. 'What are you doing?'

'Let's get her out,' said Tara. 'She's time-travelled here from 1981, let's see what she's got to say for herself.'

Molly watched Tara untwisting the ties, and then smiled and reached for Sindy's tiny flight bag.

It carried on raining for the rest of the morning.

Tara and Molly took Lloyd for a slow walk around the muddy fields behind the house, which Lloyd seemed to enjoy, despite the lack of anything much to chase or sniff. Even the rabbits had retreated in the face of the incessant downpour.

They were soaked through when they made it back to the house. However, a welcome smell of fresh filter coffee drifted down the hall from the kitchen as they towelled Lloyd off in the porch with one of Ruth's Egyptian cotton bath sheets.

Toby was washing up at the big Belfast sink. His hair was flattened on one side, and he had a Moroccan dressing gown thrown over his T-shirt and boxer shorts. The extreme carefulness of his actions suggested it was a great effort not to drop anything, but he'd cleared the counter of the previous night's debris and the kitchen was back to normal.

Now that's an apology, thought Tara. She'd never seen Toby wash up before.

He turned when they walked in, and his face was as crumpled as the rest of him.

'Morning,' said Tara.

'Morning,' said Toby, and looked round to see where Molly was.

'She's gone upstairs for a bath,' said Tara. 'She might be some time. I said she could use any of the toiletries in the cupboard, and her little eyes went . . .' She mimed pinging.

'Good.' Toby wiped a hand over his stubble. 'God Almighty, Tara – what was in that gin?'

'I did warn you.'

'Are you sure it was gin, and not moonshine? Or poitín?'

Tara poured herself some coffee from the jug. 'It certainly brought forth some revelations.'

He put down the porcelain teacup he was rinsing. 'Look, I'm *really* sorry. I don't know why I said what I said. About Branston.'

'You were drunk.' She added milk, two sugars, without turning round.

'Well, I shouldn't have.' He crouched and angled his head so he could see her eyes. 'Can you forgive me?'

Tara wanted to say yes, but she also wanted Toby to see

how much he'd hurt her. It wasn't just what he'd said, it was *how* he'd said it. As if he enjoyed pointing out to her that she wasn't the perfect person she thought she was. 'I'd genuinely blanked that . . . that incident, you know. It was a shock being forced to remember it. In front of Dad too.'

'I can imagine. I genuinely am so sorry.'

She glanced towards the hall, where Lloyd was flopped on the welcome mat. 'I loved Branston.'

'I know that too.'

Tara let the silence extend, to punish him.

'I should probably take a leaf out of Dad's book,' he said, with a forced laugh. 'Stick to the herbal tinctures from now on.'

It was just enough penitence. Tara rolled her eyes, a little too theatrically. 'Of all the things I wish I could call Mum to tell her, it's that. Dad's on the wagon.'

'Fair play to him, he's been on it a good while now,' said Toby, returning to the soapy sink.

'Do you know what triggered that?' It was a bit masochistic of Tara, but she wondered if Dad had opened his heart to Toby, told him that second-time fatherhood had Changed His Life.

Toby shrugged. 'Dunno. Apparently he checked himself into rehab, and he's been going to AA meetings for years now. It's where he met Sarah.'

'Oh? And was she an alcoholic too?'

He stacked the teacup carefully on the drainer. 'Why don't you ask him yourself? Dad's pretty open about a lot of things, these days. He said it's one of the positives about recovery: you have to do a lot of work on yourself to recognize why you make mistakes.'

Tara was familiar with recovery talk. The acupuncturist at the Wellness Centre was a reformed gambling addict and had put them off raffles for life. 'Sounds like you two have had some real heart-to-hearts.'

'We've had a couple of long chats, yes. Not as easy without a couple of bottles of wine to get things going, but we're not kids any more, sometimes you've got to bite the bullet and hear stuff you don't like.' Toby shook the suds off his hands and reached for the tea towel hanging off the brass range rail. 'All part of growing up.'

'Is that directed at me?'

Tara could feel her defences rising, purely at his tone.

'Not necessarily. But you've got to admit you're very good at avoiding conversations you don't want to have.'

Tara remembered this tone of Toby's. The 'ten minutes and twenty years older than you' tone that had irritated her as a teenager. 'That's bollocks.'

'Well, if you didn't know when Dad met Sarah you've obviously asked him nothing about his life. And since he's happy to talk about it, I'm guessing you've actively shut those conversations down.'

She seethed because this was true.

Toby dried his hands carefully. 'I need to talk to you about something while Dad's away. It's about Mum.'

Tara groaned, a teenage noise. 'Whatever he's said about her . . .'

'Hear me out. Dad says he wrote to us, tried to get in touch with us regularly after he left.'

'Yeah, he told me that too.'

'I believe him. I wanted to know if you'd found any letters or anything while you were sorting out the house.'

'I told you, Toby, there's nothing. There isn't even anything from our childhood – no school reports, no teddies, nothing.'

'That doesn't prove anything. She could have thrown the whole lot out.'

Toby always wanted to see the worst in anything their mum did. 'I think it says a lot about how hurt Mum was, that she couldn't bear to have any reminders of what he did to her. And if it turns out Dad was drinking so much he ended up in rehab . . . maybe she thought he wouldn't be able to look after us properly?' Things were falling into place now, making sense. The treehouse, the whisky in the office. Mum's hawk-like observations. 'That explains why we only ever saw him during the day, not for sleepovers. Mum was just being a responsible parent, not this vindictive cow you're making her out to be.'

'I'm not saying that . . .'

'The thing is,' Tara went on, warming to her theme, 'you have no idea what her life was like after you left.' She didn't add, *just like Dad*, even though it would have evened the score from the previous night. 'She never had another relationship after him. She must have found it impossible to trust anyone. I find that heartbreaking.'

Toby poured himself some coffee and took a couple of deep breaths, as if he was trying to reason with a deeply irritating child. 'I'm not saying she wasn't a good mum in many ways, but she wasn't the tragic lonely martyr you need her to be.'

'What do you mean, *need*?'

'Because that's why you felt obliged to stay round here, isn't it? Instead of finishing your law training and going to live somewhere more interesting? I mean, you still could, right? Do your legal qualification?'

He probably thought he was being encouraging, but Tara heard, *You live in a backwater and have no ambition.*

'I might have stayed initially, when Mum had her accident and needed *one* of her children to help her out,' she replied, hotly, 'but it was my decision to stay after that. I like it here. And I'm glad I didn't do my LPC because otherwise I'd never have got into counselling, which I love.'

'You don't need to lock the door to make people stay,' said Toby.

'Do you get all your philosophy from Instagram now?'

He raised an eyebrow.

'Maybe if she'd married again, I might have moved,' she conceded, 'but she didn't, and I can totally understand why. We never discussed it explicitly, but I think she struggled to trust people after what Dad did. She had to throw herself into her work and her shop and this house because she had no one else to—'

'Tara,' said Toby. 'Mum was shagging Diane.'

The words froze on Tara's lips. 'What?'

'Mum was in a relationship with Diane. That was why Dad left – he found out.'

'Did Dad tell you that?' Tara almost laughed. 'That is such a cliché. Women aren't allowed to have a close friendship without men assuming they must be lesbians. Don't be ridiculous. I would have noticed.'

'It's nothing to do with Dad.' Toby was speaking slowly, as if she were particularly stupid. 'The reason Dad left Mum was because she was found in a fairly undeniable situation with Diane.'

'By who?' This was surreal.

Toby was looking at her now with something border-ing on pity. 'By me.'

'By . . . you?'

He nodded. The words hung in the air between them. *By Toby. Diane and Mum.*

'I was supposed to be staying over at Harry Jackson's but his brother got food poisoning so they brought me home early,' he said, in a matter-of-fact tone. 'You were at a friend's. Dad was away. I let myself in, heard some-thing upstairs and . . .' His voice trailed off and he shrugged.

Tara stared. She couldn't picture it. Her brain refused.

'It's not the *relationship*,' he went on calmly. 'Who cares what people do, so long as no one gets hurt? It's the hypocrisy. Mum always maintained what an unfaithful bastard Dad was, even after he'd left. As if she could rewrite history to make it his fault when she was just as bad! I couldn't stand that, especially when you started to repeat things she'd said about Dad.'

'Why didn't you tell me?'

'I tried.' He lifted his hands. 'I thought you had a right to know. Mum unsurprisingly didn't. She basically told me that there were things about adult life I didn't under-stand, that there was no point upsetting you even more and that if I did, it would be on me.' He paused. 'I was ten, Tara. And I *hated* it, by the way. I hated not being able to help you. I hated knowing something you didn't. But I didn't want to take away the comfort you obviously got from Mum so I said nothing. I thought it was the least bad thing to do.'

'But Ashley . . .'

'Ashley had nothing to do with Dad. She just drove him to the station. Although,' he added, with an air of someone making a gesture of fairness, 'it did turn out he'd had a thing with Ashley's mum at one point. Like I say, neither of them were saints. And Dad was drinking, as we now know. So not making great judgement calls. I think one thing we can all agree on is that they were better off divorced. Better for them, anyway.'

Tara's knees wobbled and she sank on to the kitchen sofa.

The world felt tilted. She'd always sensed there was more to her mother than she was able to reach, but this – this! – turned her into a complete stranger. It wasn't who her mum had been.

Mum preferred me to think she was miserable, she realized. *She wanted me to think that, because it fitted her narrative about Dad ruining her life.* The loss – of time, of choices – made Tara feel empty. And what a waste! If Mum had just told her, the distance would have gone, they could have been better friends.

'How did I never see?' she whispered, half to herself.

'Because she didn't want you to, and you weren't looking.' Toby sat down beside her. 'You blanked a lot of what happened when Dad left.'

'I haven't, I remember loads – that first birthday, in Pizza Hut. Dad's red car. Mum crying a lot.' Tara scrabbled around in her memory, desperately trying to grab faces, times, from a period that was blurry, a page with too many rubbed-out words. It was hard to separate what was real memory and what was only stories and second-hand recollection.

This is why I needed proof, she thought, glancing round

the pale surfaces of the kitchen. *Even scraps, just to prove I was there.*

She felt Toby take her hand.

'I tried to tell you a few times, but you never wanted to hear. You just went into a rant about poor Mum and what a user Dad was.' Toby shook her hand up and down for emphasis. It was supposed to be comforting, she guessed, but it came across as patronizing. 'You've got to deal with this properly, in therapy. All of it, not just the bits you want. Hiding from the truth isn't good for you.'

'Don't tell me what's good for me.' The tears were streaming down Tara's face. 'And don't talk about the truth. I was the only one who didn't *know* the truth about our family. The only one! And you *left me* here to live my life in the middle of everyone else's lies. How could you do that, Toby?' She shook her head, as if things might suddenly make sense. 'I wouldn't have minded if you'd kept in touch to make sure I was OK but you didn't! You've been impossible to get hold of for the last ten years. I've spent more time with my dentist!'

Toby looked shifty. 'I thought you were OK. You were engaged, you had a house . . .'

'How could you know I was OK?' Her voice was too loud. 'You reply to one in ten of my messages! Is that because you don't care about me, or because you feel guilty that I've ended up so much less successful than you?'

Toby started to snap back, but then his face fell. 'Tara, please . . .'

'Don't.' She pushed him away. 'I need to be on my own.'

'Tara, it's going to be OK,' he called after her, and she thought she heard him add, 'if you just grow up,' under his breath.

It was good to cry, she told herself, struggling to breathe in between gasping tears. It was a natural release when there were too many thoughts, too much emotion, overloading her brain.

As Tara stumbled towards the hall, she heard something that sent her stomach sinking, even in the midst of her own misery: the feet of an eavesdropper scuttling back up the stairs.

The last thing poor Molly needed was to hear them rowing.

Sybil, she told herself, reaching blindly for the polished banister. *It was probably Sybil.*

Toby, in semi-penitence, made tea, scrambling every egg in the fridge, and giving a subdued Molly extra butter on her toast. Tara ignored the buttery crusts that fell on the floor, and into the mouth of Lloyd. Sybil made a brief appearance at the kitchen door, saw Lloyd and slunk away in disgust. Keith didn't call. It was still raining.

The three of them sat under a blanket on the sofa to watch the Toy Story series, in order, until Molly went to bed, and they switched to *The Crown*.

'Is Dad going to ring tonight, do you think?' Toby asked.

'I've tried a couple of times but no answer.' Tara had checked out the place Sarah was staying; it was upmarket, but strict. 'There are rules about phone usage.'

'Hope Sarah's OK.'

'Me too. Poor woman.' Tara already felt bad about last night's reaction. Of course it was right that Dad should go to her.

'Mmm.'

Neither wanted to start a big conversation. They were too tired. Tara wondered if she should tell Toby about the will, but she couldn't summon up the energy for the complicated legal explanations about what their options were. Not on a Sunday night before a long week at work.

Prince Charles and Princess Diana sulked across the screen in front of them, and Tara ate another biscuit and wondered if the Monday morning astrology report in the kitchen would mention anything about family revelations.

The thought of the Wellness Centre made her feel unexpectedly better. It was somewhere she felt safe. Somewhere positive and supportive, where her abilities were valued. Even Hero's healing crystal bracelet now felt like a kindness.

I'm going to ace the Centre Director interview next week and take charge of my life, Tara decided. She had enough time to prepare the heck out of it – time to learn the statistics Jacqueline loved, to draft an irresistible outreach programme, and to spreadsheet some impressive new therapy directions. Tara had always hated exams, unlike seat-of-the-pants Toby, but having a ton of preparation under her belt helped.

'You know what,' she said, throwing back the blanket. 'I've had enough of dysfunctional families for tonight. I'll see you in the morning.'

*

Upstairs, cross-legged in her pyjamas, Tara opened her laptop to check what she had coming up in the next few days, so she could plan her interview prep timetable.

There was a Troutbridge project meeting on Wednesday; a finish date was now in sight, and Alice wanted to brainstorm grand reopening ideas – an autumn party or a barn dance?

Emails from the Centre, about clients and appointments.

A reminder from the board about her interview on Monday 9th.

A referral request from a GP in—

Wait. Tara's eye skimmed upwards again. Monday 9th? That was tomorrow morning. The interview for the director's role was in her diary as Monday 16th. Yes, there it was, *Monday 16th: interview.*

Her heart sped up. Which one was wrong?

Tara scrolled back through her work emails to find the initial interview invitation. There it was, last week.

> *Thank you for your application for the role of Director of Operations at the Longhampton Wellness Centre. We look forward to discussing the position further with you at 9.30 a.m., Monday 9th August. Please prepare the attached scenarios for exploration with the panel.*

Her heart plunged downwards in her chest as if it were in a malfunctioning lift.

Oh God, thought Tara. *How did I miss that?*

She changed the date on the calendar and immediately got a ping notification.

This event will take place in ten hours.

Ten hours, seven of which she needed for a good night's sleep.

Oh God, she thought, as she scrolled through the hundred-page scenario attachment and the blood drained from her head. *Oh God*.

Chapter Twenty-Four

When Tara woke up the following morning, it was still raining.

Everything was dripping with water as she hurried to the car, with her blow-dried hair tucked into a beret. The trees, the patio furniture, the bird table, all dripping. She was starting to get a bad feeling about so much rain.

Tara didn't take the straight route into Longhampton; she deliberately followed the route she and David sometimes took when they met up at the corner of Coleridge Street and Chaucer Avenue, in case for some inexplicable reason he'd decided to walk and she could give him a lift, but there was no sign of his familiar gabardine mac.

Tara needed David's calming company this morning. As she drove, flashbacks from the weekend kept sliding sideways into her head when she was trying to memorize the notes she'd made on the interview prep lying open on the passenger seat. Even David's trademark running commentary about the traces of Roman wall along the road into the centre of town would have been a welcome distraction from the mental image of Mum and Diane locked in a passionate—

'Just no,' she said aloud. Then added, 'Not that there's anything wrong with same-sex couples,' in case her mother – or anyone else – could hear her.

Another car hooted at her as she drifted slightly out of her lane, trying to read what she'd written about the ethics of Zoom therapy sessions.

The traffic was crawling on account of everyone slowing down to avoid the fresh flooding on the road. Tara sat for ten minutes in a queue for the traffic lights at the bottom of the hill, flipping through scribbled 3 a.m. bullet points on the hypothetical client crises she would have to discuss in under thirty minutes.

Why hadn't she double-checked the interview date? It was such a stupid, careless mistake to make.

She hit the steering wheel with the palms of her hands. *Come on, Tara*, she told herself. *Don't let yourself down.*

The Wellness Centre smelled of wet coats and bad moods, and not even Jacqueline's new Monday-morning flowers could cheer up the clammy atmosphere in reception.

Tara went straight to the kitchen to make herself a strong coffee. She still had time to get her head together before her interview, and a big dose of caffeine might help.

As she slipped out of her office, from the corner of her eye Tara saw David leave *his* office and head straight down the corridor, then down the broad stairs at a brisk trot. He did it rather elegantly, as if to an inaudible Fred Astaire soundtrack.

Tara frowned. Where was he going? And why was he wearing a suit?

Emily was already in the kitchen, stirring her tea and rolling her eyes at this week's horoscope. 'Morning, Tara! You're a Capricorn, aren't you? Fabulous week coming up for you, you lucky old goat.'

'No, I'm a Pisces,' she said, getting her mug out of the cupboard. 'Can't you tell from the gills?'

Emily looked back at the board, then grimaced. 'Oh. Ouch. Well, never mind.'

Tara decided she didn't need to know what was in store for Pisces. As if this week could get any worse.

'David's looking smart today,' Emily observed, as Tara flicked the kettle on.

'Is he?' Tara pretended she hadn't noticed. David was always well put together – tie, jacket, shirt with proper sleeves – but this was . . . smart. A pale biscuit-coloured suit, white shirt, striped tie, his brown hair freshly cut.

'Dressed to impress, I'd say.'

The questions flipped over in Tara's head. Was David going on a date? Did he have a special client? He hadn't said anything. Was the ex-girlfriend back on the scene? Tara was surprised to find herself hoping not.

'I wonder if . . .' Emily said, then stopped theatrically.

'You wonder if what?' asked Tara, since that was clearly her line.

'I wonder if . . .' Emily repeated under her breath, then leaned out of the kitchen door to check no one was about to come in. When she was satisfied that they were alone, Emily nodded towards the staircase. 'I wonder if that was an interview suit? Do you think Dr David's applied for the Centre Director job?'

That was one option Tara hadn't considered. 'No, why would he? He's only been here a few months.'

'He hasn't said anything to you?'

'No.' He hadn't. And she hadn't said anything to him about her application.

Which Tara now realized wasn't the same thing at all.

Emily's eyebrows jiggled again and she put a finger to her lips and stepped out on to the landing, beckoning Tara to follow her. Then she leaned over the polished oak banister, embellished with a range of locally grown carbohydrates, and peered down the stairwell to the ground floor.

David was standing outside the downstairs meeting room, fidgeting with his tie. As they watched, he knocked sharply on the door – a brisk three-note rap – and was summoned inside. The door closed behind him.

Tara's heart dropped in her chest.

Emily turned to her. 'That's where they're doing the interviews, isn't it?'

'Yes. I mean, I guess so.'

'Well, then.' She sashayed back into the kitchen for her tea. Emily loved being proved right. 'He's going for it. Good luck to him.'

It took the final shreds of Tara's self-control not to let her disappointment show. That was that. If David was applying for the role, with his qualifications and his experience and his charm, that was it. He'd probably hypnotize the bloody interview panel into giving him a company car too.

The energy drained from her. Was it too late to go home? She was experiencing a genuine, undeniable family crisis. In fact, Tara argued, some people would counsel that she shouldn't even do the interview in her current mental state. Was it even possible to outline your vision for an outreach therapy programme if there was a real chance that you might be ambushed by a mental image of your mother having sex with the woman who taught you to drive?

'Oh, Tara, don't look like that!' Emily grabbed her arms. 'It won't just be decided on the basis of qualifications! I mean, you've got . . . qualifications too. And you really *know* this area – you've spent your entire career in this town, whereas David's worked in London and Newcastle and Birmingham – big cities with big-city problems. You know exactly how small-town people tick.'

'Are you trying to make me feel better?'

'Yes!' Emily frowned. 'Am I not?'

'Not really.'

'God, I'm sorry.' She looked contrite. 'Do you want a biscuit?'

They looked at the plate by the kettle: a collection of green cookies in the shape of shamrocks. There was a Post-it note stuck to the counter next to it, on which someone had written *THIS IS CULTURALLY OFFENSIVE TO THE CELTIC DIASPORA!!!* in angry capitals.

'Judith?'

'I think so.'

Tara sighed and took a shamrock. Then a second one, along with her cup of coffee. She was going to need all the luck of the Irish now, if that wasn't a politically questionable thing to wish for.

Tara's interview didn't start well. It didn't end well, and there was a period in the middle where she thought it might be going all right, but it turned out she'd been waxing lyrical about talking therapies when in fact the earnest male trustee had asked her about Tolkien therapy. Which she hadn't even heard of.

After forty-five minutes of painful limping around the hypothetical management situations, Jacqueline asked if

Tara had any questions for them, and the only thing that came into her mind was, *Please can I go now?*

In the last-choice cafe down the street from the Wellness Centre, Tara stared bleakly into her collapsing cappuccino. That had been, without doubt, the worst interview of her life, but weirdly, she felt nothing.

Something Tara's supervisor had told her early on in her training kept running across her mind like breaking news: 'Numbness doesn't mean you're feeling no emotion, it means you're feeling too much emotion. You're flooded.'

Tara knew that was true. Finally, she was overloaded. Her brain was silted up with toxic emotions like guilt and shame and resentment and . . .

'Oh *God*,' she said aloud, and rested her eyes on the heels of her palms until everything went a comforting black. She hated interviews, but she'd never failed one before.

Tara could tell Jacqueline was disappointed with her performance. *Surprised* and disappointed, that double-edged schoolteacher reaction. She'd blanked the names of the other two board members sitting on either side of her: the serious man who wrote down everything she said, and a woman with pink hair who stared at her without blinking, as if waiting for Tara to say a trigger word she could pounce on.

The waitress had already circled her table once, checking she wasn't crying by wiping the tables around her. She didn't want to get into a conversation about why her mascara looked like this.

Tara made herself sip her coffee to show the waitress she was fine, and stared out through the window. The rain was relentless. People were hurrying down the high street with

353

umbrellas, their flimsy summer clothes covered up with anoraks resentfully dug out of cupboards. August, so-called high summer, and it was more like October out there, wet and grey and mean. This wasn't summer, thought Tara, not like the turquoise sea and sun-bleached sand of Toby's Instagram account.

In a funny way, thought Tara, at least this unmitigated disaster took one decision out of her hands. There would be no salary-based mortgage now. No mortgage meant no way of giving Toby his half of the house, so Wye Villa would have to be sold. Even though she was still mad at Toby, Tara had decided she couldn't *not* give him his half. She couldn't live with herself if she didn't. She certainly couldn't maintain her comfortable position on the moral high ground.

The thought of her home in an estate agent's brochure made her heart sink with sadness and she immediately tried to buoy it up with positive thoughts.

What's wrong with you? This means you can travel! You can plan that holiday you've been promising yourself for years.

Today wasn't a failure; it was a *sign*!

She started to warm to her task. The universe didn't *want* her to stay in Longhampton. The universe wanted her to have a break, get out of town, find new inspiration, meet new people. Maybe fall in love. She was free to do whatever she wanted to do now – nothing was holding her back. Not Mum, not work, nothing.

A stunned smile broke across Tara's face, and the waitress wiping the table opposite smiled back with relief. Their eyes met, and Tara nodded awkwardly towards the half-eaten cake in front of her. 'Great carrot cake.'

The waitress nodded, unconvinced.

Tara got her notebook out of her bag and began to plan her escape.

No, not escape. Escape was a Keith Hunter thing. What she was doing was planning a structured sabbatical.

Her heart beat faster, but with relief this time, not panic. She'd have to put the house on the market, this week. The agents already had people lined up; the deal could be done in no time.

Her clients. Tara did feel responsibility there, but she was hardly the only CBT therapist in the country. And if she was honest, there were a few of them who could probably do with the break. Nothing wrong with a change of counsellor now and again.

Would David miss her if she left?

The thought pierced the muddiness in her mind, smarting like a bee sting.

She would miss David. She'd miss his relentlessly educational company on the morning walk to work, his thoughtful observations that often made her think harder about her own snap judgements. She'd miss the old-fashioned way he held the heavy Centre door open for her, and the brief scent of soap and ironed cotton and warm male skin that she caught as she ducked under his arm to go in.

Tara checked herself. She was going on holiday, not leaving for ever. And after all this time, it *was* time to leave. That much was suddenly very clear.

Back to her escape plans. Flood committee. There were so many people more organized than her who could take over. Troutbridge Hall was nearly done and—

'Hello, gorgeous.'

Tara's head jerked up, and she blinked in shock.

Sitting in the chair opposite her, large as life and twice as charming, was Phil Shawcross.

'I've been trying to call, but I think you've got me blocked, haven't you? And I don't blame you.' He sipped the black coffee the waitress had brought over with a coy smile. (The waitress, not Phil. Phil was, Tara noticed, unusually careful not to give the waitress a coy smile back.) 'I was on my way to the Wellness Centre, as it happens. You've saved me fifty quid – I was going to book a session with you.' He adopted a serious expression. 'So we could talk.'

'You know I blocked you because I didn't *want* to talk?'

'I guessed that.' He gazed at her earnestly. 'But there are things I need to say, Tara.'

'Oh.'

It wasn't something she would have admitted aloud but seeing Phil across the table was actually very, very pleasant right now. He always had that air of someone who could make a situation better, even if it was just by ordering cake with zero thought for the calories. He was still wearing a little too much aftershave, and she had a bad feeling he was wearing Chelsea boots, but something was different about him. He seemed to care much more than usual about how he was coming across.

'Go on, then,' she said. 'Talk.'

Phil adopted a serious expression. 'How are you doing?'

'Since you ask, I'm having a nightmare day.' Tara never had a problem being honest with Phil. That went with the no-commitment territory, weirdly enough. There was never anything at stake, no need to lie to make

yourself look better. 'I've just screwed up a really important interview.'

Tara didn't tell him about her dad, or Toby, or Molly.
That also went with the territory.

'I'm sure you haven't.'

'No, there's no need to be nice. I made just about every
mistake I could have done.' Sure, she should be icy with
Phil, but after the weekend she'd had, it seemed un-
important. 'But maybe it's for the best. I've decided it's
time for some changes in my life.'

'Me too. Me too, Tara.' Phil reached for her hands across
the table, cupping them in his own. They were warm and
made hers look delicate in comparison, but Tara was surprised by how unmoved she was. They were just nice,
warm hands. She couldn't be bothered to remove hers.
'I've got something I need to say.'

'Really? OK.'

'Um, right. Well . . .' He cleared his throat. 'So.'

Tara suspected she wasn't giving Phil the reaction he'd
expected; he seemed to be mentally throwing discarded
prompt cards over his shoulder as they failed to have the
desired effect.

'Last time we met,' he began, 'I should have said sorry a
lot more than I did. I wasn't thinking straight, a lot of stuff
had just happened. I was at an emotional crossroads, and I
just took the easiest route. But I've spent the last few weeks
really examining my life, and I realized that if I didn't come
back here and tell you what you meant to me, I'd never
forgive myself.'

'Right,' said Tara. 'So – your not-wife threw you
out?'

'No!'

'You mean she's not your wife, or she didn't throw you out?'

'I mean . . .' Phil pushed the hank of blond hair out of his eyes. 'You're confusing me, Tara.'

'No, I get it. You've broken up with the woman who was allergic to the cat you dumped on me.'

'Yes, but—'

'And now she's dumped you, you're here to see if you can pick up where you left off.'

'No!'

Tara smiled sadly at him. It was so much easier when you didn't care. If only she could bottle this feeling and sell it to her unhappy, hanky-shredding clients. 'Come on, Phil. I do this for a living. Just spit it out.'

Phil stared down at his coffee as if gathering his thoughts. It took a while. When he met Tara's eyes after a moment or two, the expression on his handsome face was one she hadn't seen before. He looked uncertain.

'I knew there wasn't a way of saying this that wouldn't make me look like a tosser, Tara. So maybe I'm just a tosser. But the thing is, I've missed you so much. I tried to tell myself that I didn't, but I did. More than that, I missed the person I was when I was with you.'

'Wow,' said Tara. 'Existential.'

He gazed at her, hurt. 'Don't make fun of me when I'm trying not to sound like a plum.'

'Sorry. Go on.'

Phil braced himself. 'When I was with you, I always tried that bit harder. You are such a great girl, Tara.'

'Woman.' *Oh, stop it*, she told herself. *He's trying.*

He didn't even kick back at it. 'Such a great *woman*. You're strong and you're smart and you're bloody gorgeous. Never met a . . . woman like you before. I guess I was just scared of you finding out what a plum I was, if I let you get too close to who I really am, underneath the chat. I think . . .' He swallowed. 'I think I might actually love—'

'Don't say it, Phil.' Tara held up a finger.

He sighed. 'Listen, I understand if you don't want to give us another try – I get that – but I wanted you to know that I've broken up with Zoe. You can't marry someone because they take you on holiday. I decided it wasn't fair to marry her when I was missing you.'

At least he was being honest. That put a different slant on things.

'I've also decided to retrain and do something useful for the community.'

'And what's that?'

Phil beamed. 'I'm going to college to learn how to be a paramedic. Always wanted to drive an ambulance. I reckon they need drivers who can get to the scene of an accident quick smart.'

'Wow.' Tara realized she'd never known exactly what Phil did, beyond 'business consultancy'. He wouldn't be able to go off-radar for three weeks in an ambulance. That's if they even let him drive one, with his points. She decided not to rain on that parade. 'Well, good for you, Phil.'

He looked up, gazing straight into her face with his blue eyes, eyes that could wink her into bad decisions just like that. They were serious now. 'You once told me change is hard, but I'm ready for it. I needed this shock to make me realize what I really wanted. But I'm going on holiday first.'

'Oh.' That was more like Phil.

'Yeah, bit awkward, as it happens. I'd booked the apartment for me and Zoe, as a last-minute thing but obviously that's off. Somewhere in Italy, near some vineyards or something. Seven days, all-inclusive, end of the month. Anyway, I was wondering if you'd like to come?'

He looked hopeful.

'Have I got this right?' asked Tara. 'You're asking me to come on the holiday you booked for the woman you were two-timing me with?'

Phil gazed at her, and there was a glimmer of the old charm under the new humility. 'Come on. I didn't have to tell you the truth, did I? I could have just said, "Tara, I've booked a holiday for you and me in Italy . . ."'

Tara rolled her eyes. She didn't want to be amused, but it was so outrageous she couldn't help it.

'You'll think about it?'

Why not? What else was there to think about right now? Wherever she turned – work, the house, her dad, her brother, the floods – there was stress and responsibility. A week away in the sun with Phil, with absolutely no promises of anything other than vino and a hot tub, was tempting. It shouldn't be. But it was.

'Phil, tell me something.'

'What?'

'Have you been reading self-help books?'

'How did you know?'

'I just . . . I just guessed.'

'I've been seeing a counsellor too,' he said proudly. 'Will you think about it?'

'I'll phone you,' she said. 'Look, I've got to go. I've a lot on right now.'

'Do you . . .' His face twisted with the effort of the New Phil. 'Do you want to talk about it?'

Tara smiled. 'It's OK. I don't.' She pulled her coat off the back of her chair and glanced out at the street. A shallow river was running down each side of the road, swirling into the gutters. Cars swished past, their windscreen wipers flicking thick swipes of rain from side to side. No one looked happy about it.

August. This was *August*. But it wasn't raining in Tuscany.

'I'll call you,' she promised, and headed out into the rain, back towards the office.

She'd only got as far as the deli on the corner when Toby rang.

'Can you come home?' he asked, dispensing with any preamble. 'As soon as you can?'

'What? Is everything OK?' Tara started walking more quickly, avoiding the growing puddles on the pavement.

'No,' said Toby. 'Not really. I need you back here, now. Quick as you can.'

And he hung up.

Chapter Twenty-Five

'You called me home because the babysitter had to leave early?'

Tara stood in the kitchen with her hands on her hips and didn't care if it made her look like a sitcom mother-in-law. She felt like a sitcom mother-in-law.

She'd hared back as fast as the traffic would allow with lurid Doomsday scenarios playing in her head. Molly overdosing on a handful of melatonin; Sarah escaping from rehab and on their doorstep demanding her child; Dad in a car crash; Lloyd run over. Lloyd eaten by Sybil. Sybil with her claws stuck in Lloyd.

But no. Toby had summoned her back because Lily's dad had called round to collect her 'before the roads are cut off'.

'Yes.' Toby looked affronted. 'I need to work. I can't write and look after a child at the same time.'

'And what do you think I was doing until you called me back?' she asked incredulously. 'Macramé?'

Toby didn't need to know she'd been drinking coffee with her ex. It was the principle of it.

'What looking after does she even need?' Tara dropped her voice so Molly – in the bathroom upstairs – wouldn't hear. 'I know she's had a stressful weekend, but that's what boxsets are for. And she reads! Jesus, Toby, I have had *sourdough starters* that required more attention than Molly.'

'You wouldn't understand, you've never had to deliver work to deadline,' said Toby. 'I need to concentrate.'

Tara stared at her brother with barely disguised fury. He'd always been like this, insisting on absolute silence for his GCSE revision which meant she'd only been able to do half as much practice for her Grade 6 piano exam as she needed, resulting in a Merit not the Distinction she'd been predicted. Toby never had a problem stating what he required, then making sure he got it. This wasn't a new thing. Ten years in therapy hadn't got Tara to his level of self-assurance. It probably never would.

'Anyway, you're back now, no need to be a martyr about it,' he said, as if that concluded the matter, and replaced the expensive noise-cancelling headphones on his ears. 'I'll be in the dining room – do you mind keeping it down till I'm finished?'

'Toby, you can't just . . .'

But he was gone.

Lloyd gazed up at her from the sofa. He looked happy. Evidence of his boredom was scattered around – a pair of socks, ripped paper, a knocked-over cup. House rules had clearly gone by the by.

A sudden image of a villa in Tuscany floated into Tara's mind. Warmth, high thread count sheets, wine. Phil.

'Do you want to see my photographs?' Molly brandished a rainbow box at her.

'Yes, please!' said Tara with as much enthusiasm as she could muster.

Molly had used up two films from her new instant

cameras already, and nearly all the photos were of Tara and Toby, Keith and Lloyd.

It was obvious which her favourite was: a blurry selfie of Keith and Lloyd. 'My two favourite people in the whole world,' whispered Molly shyly.

It reminded Tara of another photo of a younger, darker Keith with a younger, blonder dog. Her two favourite people in the whole world too.

Her heart pinched. Where was that photo now?

'And Mum too,' Molly added loyally, and looked pensive.

While Molly was arranging her photographs in order of preference, Tara made a quick call to the office, explaining that she'd be late back for her 2 p.m. appointment.

'Don't worry about it,' said Chloe. 'We're just about to close anyway. The road's flooded so Jacqueline's declared an emergency and sent everyone home.'

'Oh no, is it serious?' Tara looked out of the window at the leaden sky. The trees were swaying silently back and forth, as the rain slid down the windows, puddling in the slate containers. Thank goodness they were on a hill.

'The police are diverting people away from the main bridge, so I think we're in for it.' Chloe sighed. 'You left at just the right time.'

'Good luck getting home,' said Tara, but she was already thinking about Troutbridge. Surely it couldn't flood again, not when they were so close to finishing?

She called Alice, but her phone was engaged and she didn't want to add to her list of woes. Was it worth calling Dad, to see if he had any specialist advice for them?

Tara dithered. Who was his loyalty to, right now?

Her eye fell on Molly, her head bent over the kitchen counter as she started another friendship bracelet from the leftover kit Lily had brought.

No, she thought. *The foreman will call Dad; let him deal with Sarah.*

She moved around the kitchen, trying to make it cosier against the grey day outside, lighting a few of Ruth's thick church candles in the glass lamps, plumping cushions, picking up socks and tea towels, straightening the art books on the glass coffee table. Tidying made Tara feel more in control. She didn't like to admit it to herself, because it was so boring, but it did.

She picked up one of Keith's enamel cufflinks. Molly's pink hair bobble. A rainbow spoon from the studio. Tara felt a moment's irritation at the mess, then thought, *The house is turning back into a family home.* Too late for her, though. Another family would be coming into it now.

'Have you got any clothes for the wash?' she asked Molly, once she'd filled the dishwasher. Every rainy day needed the soft smell of warm tumble-drying. Molly ran to get her muddy trousers and jumper from their dog walk, and while she was upstairs, Tara called through to the dining room.

'Toby? Any laundry I can do for you?'

There was no response.

'Oh dear,' said Tara under her breath. His noise-cancelling headphones also cancelled favours. 'What a shame.'

When Molly had filled her basket, Tara bumped it on to her hip down into the cellar. Ruth had created a basement laundry area where she could iron and listen to the radio, surrounded by lavender bags and shelves of starch sprays and French handwash liquids. It was probably Tara's favourite spot in the house.

But as she put her foot down on the bottom step Tara sensed something was wrong. Her next step, on to the tiled floor, splashed.

In a panic, she put the basket down behind her and gazed around the utility room.

There was an inch of water covering the floor.

What had happened? Tara stepped gingerly over to the washing machine. She had very little knowledge of household maintenance, but she'd heard enough office tales of woe about washing machines flooding, pipes coming loose, that sort of thing, to know it was a fairly regular if annoying domestic occurrence.

At the back of her mind, a voice pointed out that there was another explanation for an inch of water on the floor, but she dismissed it. They were on a hill. It was impossible. This house didn't flood.

All the pipes seemed to be connected, though.

Bloody great, she thought, standing back as if something might reveal itself. *Another huge bill that I don't have any money to pay.*

Tara sloshed back to the stairs, pulled off her soaked socks and ran up to the dining room.

Toby was watching YouTube on his laptop, but when he saw her he pulled off his headphones and slammed the lid shut. 'What?'

'I need you to come and look at something in the cellar,' she said, trying not to alert Molly to any problem. 'Now,' she added, with emphatic eyebrows.

*

366

'The cellar's flooding,' he announced, as they stood on the bottom step. There was now two inches of water covering the floor.

'I know that, but where's it coming from?'

'It's coming from the *sky*, Tara.'

'But it can't—'

'It is.' Toby rolled up his jeans and splashed across to the wine rack, where he started stuffing bottles under his arm. 'We need to shift these before the water gets any higher.'

Still Tara hunted around for a different reason. 'There must be a tap on somewhere? Or the freezer's defrosting . . .'

'You can't be in denial about *everything*, Tara.' Toby returned to the lower wine racks. 'But you can look for a magic spring if you want. And while you're looking, make sure Mum didn't store anything down here that might get ruined by floodwater.'

'Like what?'

'Like, antiques? Valuables? What's in those boxes?' He pointed to a stack of storage boxes in the corner.

'Mobile chargers and Farrow & Ball paint cards,' said Tara. She'd had a cursory look a few weeks ago. 'I only got down as far as the first three but it's all the same.'

'Well, we need to move them anyway.' He boggled his eyes at her. 'Come on, hurry up. This is our house now. Mum and Dad aren't in charge, we are.'

Tara stared at her brother and her stomach curdled. Maybe this was a good time to tell him? Maybe he'd feel relieved not to be responsible for a flooding house. 'Toby, about Mum's will. She didn't—'

'Tara! Taaaara!' Molly was calling from upstairs.

'One second!' Tara called. *Do it,* she told herself, *just tell him now.* 'Mum didn't leave—'

The cellar door opened, and Molly called down the stairs, 'Your phone's ringing, Tara. Please will you answer it? It might be Daddy.'

'Get that,' said Toby, at the same time as she said, 'I should get that.'

Tara headed upstairs, two at a time.

The phone had stopped ringing by the time she'd got to it, and when she saw whose call she'd missed, Tara didn't care that it had gone to voicemail.

It wasn't Keith, it was David.

Tara was surprised to feel annoyed, not excited. Seeing David walk into the interview room had been like a needle-scratch on a record. She'd thought they were friends, but he wasn't. He was her competitor. He could end up being her boss.

She ignored the voice observing that she hadn't told him she was applying either. That wasn't the point.

'Was it Daddy?' Molly asked hopefully.

'Sorry, no. It was someone from my work.'

'Can you try Daddy again?' Her little face. 'Please?'

Tara had called Keith twice that morning and both times the call had gone to voicemail; she'd presumed he'd been asked to leave his phone off, and left polite messages asking him to update her with any news. Tara didn't want to ring again, in case it looked as if something was wrong with Molly, but she looked so anxious that Tara felt she had no choice.

It rang out, six times, and she left another awkward message, feeling Molly's eyes on her the whole time.

'. . . and so you know, it's raining quite hard here still. So, um, drive safely.'

She hung up and looked round for something to distract them. 'Shall we see what's on the television?'

Blimey, today was going slowly if it was still lunchtime, Tara thought, then realized this was breaking news. Scrolling-along-the-bottom-of-the-screen, slowly-getting-worse-and-worse, news.

'. . . *warnings of serious surface water flooding through the West Midlands. We're getting reports of flood threats to the main power station at Tewkesbury . . .*'

As long as there's no bloke in a canoe, we're fine, thought Tara, just as a bloke in a red kayak paddled down the main street in Leominster. Her heart sank.

Molly turned round, eyes huge in her pale face. 'How will Daddy get home? Lily's dad said the roads were going to flood.'

'Lily lives in a different part of town, doesn't she? Maybe he just wanted to be on the safe side. Dad'll be fine. And if the roads do get shut, he can borrow a digger from somewhere. Did I tell you he once did that when Toby and I were little? He drove us home in the floods on a digger!'

I'm using a Dad myth I don't even remember to cheer Molly up, thought Tara.

'Tell me about the digger!' Molly asked, predictably thrilled. 'Did Dad drive it?'

'OK, so . . . you know what, Toby remembers it better than me,' said Tara, spotting Toby emerging from the cellar with five bottles of champagne.

'Ah, the kayak!' said Toby cheerfully, seeing the television report. 'My theory is that the news crews have the one kayak and they take it to all the . . . what are you looking at me like that for?'

Tara flipped over to QVC, the channel least likely to have flooding updates, and said, 'Toby, tell Molly the story about the digger. When Dad drove us through the flood when we were toddlers. You were wearing your frog wellies.'

Toby read the look on her face correctly. 'Well, we were at nursery . . .'

Molly sat back, engrossed, and Tara took the opportunity to slip away to check her own notes about what to do in the event of a flood.

After a panicky call to her friend at the Environment Agency, Tara managed to trace the source of the brackish water in the basement. First to a ventilation brick tucked behind some shelves, then to a small (but rapidly expanding) stream which had appeared in the garden from underneath the hedges, and was now trickling steadily down the basement wall.

'It'll be a blocked culvert overflowing, there's a lot of them near you,' said Morris, darkly. Tara could hear phones ringing in the background; it sounded manic. 'Nothing you can do now, but sit tight, and clear it out when it goes down.'

'How much worse will it get? Is it bad in town?'

'It's not looking good. Do you need me to walk you through the basics?' asked Morris, and Tara was grateful for his help.

Back upstairs, Toby had finished his story and Molly was showing him her photographs, proudly pointing out her favourites.

'Right!' said Tara, as brightly as she could. 'I've had a chat with my friend and I'm going to have to turn the electricity off here, so I think the best thing to do, Molly, would be if you went back over to the studio. You can watch Netflix there.'

'Am I in the way?' Molly asked immediately. 'Can't I help?'

'Best thing you can do is look after Lloyd,' said Tara. 'You're in charge of him! Keep him busy. So, get your things together and we'll go over, OK?'

Reluctantly, Molly nodded.

Back in the cellar, with the stairs covered in Ruth's church candles like a Guns N' Roses video, Toby and Tara moved what they could out of the way of the water.

'Wish Dad would call,' she said.

'Ha!' said Toby, and he didn't need to explain. He passed her a box of wine to add to the pile on the stairs.

'Did you ever think it was your fault Dad left?'

'Yes and no.' Toby paused and wiped his brow with the back of his hand. 'Obviously me seeing Mum and Diane set the whole thing in motion. She told Dad. I didn't. As I got older, I realized it wasn't my fault their marriage wasn't working and they were better off apart. But at the time, yeah, of course I felt responsible. I didn't understand.'

'I wish you hadn't dealt with that alone.' Working together like this, under pressure, had somehow made it easier to talk. 'I'm sorry I didn't hear what you were trying to tell me.'

He shrugged. 'If anyone's apologizing, it should be me,' said Toby. 'I shouldn't have brought up what happened to Branston. I'm not very kind when I'm drunk.

371

But I genuinely assumed you'd have worked through it in therapy.'

'I should have done. I will.'

'What I'm saying is you didn't *need* to block it out.' Toby sloshed back across the floor for another box. 'You were a kid, a distressed kid, and Bran was fine, remember? He recovered and he lived like a king until he was, what, two hundred in dog years? He forgave everyone. He loved us.'

Tara stopped. Her back was protesting. 'It's not as easy to forgive myself.'

'But you're not responsible for everyone else's mistakes. You did what you did because Mum and Dad were messing everyone's lives up. Do you want me to give you permission to move on, Tara? You can let go of protecting Mum and hating Dad, and get on with living your own life. For yourself.'

They stood in the strange softly lit basement, surrounded by boxes and wine bottles, candles and water, and the years peeled back, leaving them looking at the sibling they remembered. Tara couldn't remember the last time she'd had such an honest conversation with Toby.

He was saying the things the voice in her head had whispered over the years, a voice she'd done her best to ignore. Her conscience – or the ghost of that old intuition they used to share?

'Mum left the house to me,' she confessed. It felt more hurtful to tell him like this than by flinging it at him like a thunderbolt, as she'd almost done in the heat of their row. 'I've been trying to find the right moment to tell you but I just couldn't. I can't afford to buy you out, so it's going on the market.'

'What? No! She left it up to you to decide what to do?' Toby laughed. 'That's very, very poor parenting.'

'But the house is worth—'

'Tara, I don't want half the house. I'd rather you kept the cash and did something crazy with it.' He'd started moving across to get the final boxes. 'What would I spend it on? Fast cars and holidays? I get paid to do that already. You earned it. Buy yourself some time.'

She knew he couldn't mean that. He was just being flamboyant.

Like she'd always wanted to be, but never felt confident enough.

Toby turned. 'You deserve it,' he said. 'You deserve to start living. I'm happy to help you with that.'

Tara looked across at her brother, the old Toby in her heart, and she wanted to laugh, but there were tears in her throat.

'Tara,' he said, suddenly. 'This box . . .'

Her phone had started ringing. 'Wait,' she said, grabbing it from the step, 'in case it's Dad.'

But it wasn't Keith. It was David.

'Hey,' he said. 'Where did you go this afternoon? You missed some literally violent shamrock biscuits. There was a hell of a row. I saved you one.'

David sounded totally normal. No mention of the job interview. That also irritated her.

'I had an emergency at home.'

'Oh no. Nothing serious, I hope?'

'We've got a bit of a flood. Water in the cellar.' Toby pushed past her, carrying the last box upstairs to safety.

'Ah. Bad luck. I hear the roads are shut.'

'Uh-huh.'

373

There was a long pause.

David laughed, a little nervously. 'Call me a trained counsellor, but I feel a certain tension. Come on, spit it out, what's up?'

Tara closed her eyes. 'Why didn't you tell me about your interview today?'

This time the silence was on David's end.

'Well?'

'Because I didn't want you to know,' he said stiffly.

He didn't want her to know? Somehow that was worse than anything she'd been expecting him to say.

'And that's it?'

'Yes.'

Toby had appeared at the top of the steps, waving to get her attention.

'Hang on, David,' she said, and put the phone against her shoulder. 'What's the matter?'

'Molly texted me half an hour ago.'

'Is she OK?'

'No, she's gone out. She wanted to be helpful, so when it stopped raining, she took the dog for a walk but it started raining again, and she's got lost.' He raked his hair with his hand. 'And now she's not answering her phone.'

'You're kidding,' Tara started then remembered she'd put Molly in charge of Lloyd. And if he'd whined to go out . . .

'What's going on?' asked David.

'Nothing.'

'I heard that, it doesn't sound like nothing. Are you all right? Can I do anything to help?'

Tara was already scrambling up the stairs, blowing out

the candles, as Toby pulled on one of Ruth's raincoats from the cupboard by the door.

'Say nothing,' he said, as Tara opened her mouth to comment on the bright red parka. 'I didn't pack for monsoon season.'

Something about Toby's big-brotherly focus brought back a memory of the times he'd come to Tara's aid as a child, finding conkers for her, chasing off bigger kids. She'd never had to ask; he'd just been there as if her fear and sadness were his too.

'Well, look, call me if you need an extra pair of eyes,' said David.

'It's fine,' said Tara. 'My brother's here.'

'Right, so where should we start?'

Toby scanned the options outside Wye Villa: the road led down to the town one way, out towards open countryside the other, with a footpath leading off towards fields and woods. Brown streams of fast-flowing water were running down all sides. There weren't many landmarks for a scared eleven-year-old to fix on.

'I'm guessing she's taken the same route we took yesterday.' Tara pulled up the collar of her coat; it was no match against the wind. 'I warn you, it's muddy.'

Toby looked down at his grey suede trainers. 'Oh, great.'

'You could have taken my boots.' Tara set off along the footpath, which was paw-pocked (a good sign) and slippery with mud. 'We're the same size.'

'I'm not wearing my sister's boots.'

'You're wearing your mother's rain mac.'

'She was more stylish than you.'

'If only she were alive to hear you say that.'

Tara joked to downplay her mounting fears, and she knew Toby was doing the same from the apprehensive way his eyes went from his phone to the horizon to his phone, over and over.

Tara texted Molly's phone again – **'Stay where you are, we're coming!'** – but got no reply, and they set their shoulders against the steady rain. Was that a distant rumble of thunder?

'By the way, I think Molly was on the stairs yesterday,' she said, scanning the brown fields for signs of Molly's pink mac. 'When we were . . . having words.'

'Oh dear.'

They both knew what that meant, having eavesdropped a fair few arguments in the same place.

'None of it would have made any sense to her,' Toby pointed out.

But that didn't matter, did it? Rain dripped into Tara's eyes. Adults arguing for any reason was upsetting. Molly barely knew her and Toby, and they were meant to be looking after her. What had Dad said? He'd left her with the two people he trusted most in the world? And they'd let her wander off.

Tara swept the field with uneasy eyes, willing the pink mac to appear. What was Molly thinking now?

'I hope she doesn't think her mum being ill's something to do with her.' She could remember several people reassuring her it 'wasn't her fault' her parents' marriage had imploded. It had only cemented the idea in her mind.

'Molly? Molly!' Toby swung round, spraying his yells into the wind.

Still no text replies. Tara checked her texts, her Whats-App. Nothing. She was too hot now under her coat, her armpits slick with sweat and panic.

'She's going to be OK, isn't she? Toby?'

'We said we'd look after her, and we will.' Toby turned. His black hair was already flat on his head, as if he'd been dunked in the pool. 'This is your lane, remember? The good-at-looking-after-things lane?'

Tara's eyes filled with tears, and her heart wailed, *But I'm not good enough*.

Toby didn't reply. He shook his head, then wrapped his arms round Tara for one quick hug that said everything she needed to hear.

'No time for this,' he said, breaking it off with a final squeeze. 'We need to find this runaway sister.'

The sky was darkening. Tara's legs protested as she trudged through the mud, and Toby's voice was now hoarse. How far had they walked? Two miles? Three? The mobile signal dropped out, then reappeared, only to fall away again.

They carried on taking turns to yell, 'Molly!' and 'Lloyd!' until Toby suddenly stopped and pointed to the far corner of the field, where something small and pink was wandering along the path away from them.

'Molly! Thank God!' shouted Tara.

Molly turned and waved. But there was no sign of Lloyd.

Chapter Twenty-Six

Tara nearly slipped over twice in the rush from one end of the muddy field to the other, and Toby had to grab her by the hood. Molly hurled herself into Tara's open arms and sobbed into her coat.

'It's OK, Molly, we're here.' Tara stroked her hair and mouthed, 'Dog?' at Toby.

'I'm so sorry!' Molly's voice was muffled. 'I'm so sorry!'

'No need to be sorry!' Tara hugged her. 'You got a bit lost. No harm done.'

Toby crouched so he wasn't looming over her. 'Where's my pal Lloyd?' He said it in his kid-friendly voice, but it set Molly off sobbing again and it took another five minutes to calm her down.

'I thought I could be useful if I took Lloyd out for a walk,' she hiccupped heartbreakingly. Rain had soaked her pink coat magenta, and her jeans were crusted with mud. 'He was chewing things, and I could tell you were getting cross with him.' She tried to speak but her sobs were swallowing whole words. 'We were meant to go the way we went yesterday but I got . . . I got lost! The trees look the same!'

'Deep breaths.' Tara rubbed her narrow back. 'Deep breaths.'

'We came out on a road and . . .' Molly struggled. 'There was a fire engine, with its siren on, and Lloyd was scared . . .'

Tara and Toby exchanged dismayed glances over her head.

'And he . . . he tried to run away, and I couldn't hold on to him, and I don't know where he went!' she finished up hysterically. 'What if he's been run over?'

'He won't be run over,' Toby reassured her. 'It's a quiet road, and everyone's at home because it's raining. If anything, he's more likely to . . .'

Tara glared at him.

'Labradors are *excellent* swimmers,' he said.

That set off fresh sobs. Molly clung to Tara, suddenly much younger than eleven. 'He's lost! He must be so scared! It's *my* fault.'

'It does dogs good to have an adventure, now and again,' said Toby firmly, seeing Tara's own lip start to wobble. 'Tara and I will find him. First, let's take you home.'

Someone in a mackintosh was waiting on the doorstep when they arrived back at the house: David.

He was scribbling something on a pad but stopped as they approached.

'I was leaving you a note, I need to talk to you about something. Nice day for a country stroll,' he added, seeing their drenched clothes. 'Or was it a swim?'

He's got the job, thought Tara, her heart plunging. *He's here to tell me he's got the job and he's excited because he doesn't know I wanted it too.*

The strange thing was, even though Toby had said he didn't want his share of the house, Tara realized she cared a lot about the Centre Director role.

379

She'd really wanted it. Not just for the money, but for the team. The projects. The chance to challenge herself, to make a difference.

'Hi, I'm Toby,' said Toby, holding out his hand. 'This is Molly, my sister.'

'David Dalloway.' They shook hands, and when Molly heard Toby say 'sister', she smiled through the last of her tears.

'Molly's been for a cross-country run,' said Toby. 'Unfortunately we're now one Labrador short.'

'Can I help?' David looked between Toby and Tara. 'An extra pair of eyes on the search party?'

Tara knew David could locate Lloyd in an instant – *if* he could do what he said. But she didn't really believe he could. The stakes were too high now; she didn't want him to pretend, and let Molly down.

However, he could always help her look.

'That's very kind of you, David,' she said. 'Why don't you and Toby—'

'Nu-huh. I don't have the footwear for this.' Toby pointed at his ruined shoes. 'You two go, and I'll ring the police or whoever's in charge of finding runaway Labradors these days.'

'Lloyd likes you, Tara – if he hears you shouting, he'll come back.' Molly reached in her pocket and gave Tara some damp kibble. 'He sometimes comes back if I give him treats?'

Then she buried her head in her big sister's coat. Tara bit her lip and threw back her head to stop herself letting out an audible gulp.

'Better go and find this dog, eh?' said David.

*

They took Tara's Mini, in case Lloyd had gone further than the fields they'd already searched.

It was still raining, and the monotonous swish of the windscreen wipers replaced the conversation that normally unfolded between them as easily as a map.

'Pull over,' said David suddenly.

Tara nearly swerved as the Mini hit a pothole under a large puddle. 'What? Have you seen Lloyd?'

'No. Just pull over. This is only going to take a minute, but I need to tell you what I came round to say.'

There was a layby ahead. She pulled over and sat without taking her hands off the steering wheel. Her knuckles were white. This was it: *I'm now your boss.*

David turned in his seat. Tara didn't.

'I had a meeting this morning with Jacqueline . . .'

'I know,' said Tara, staring at the rain. 'And for what it's worth, I hope you've got it.'

'What?'

'The director's job. I hope you've got it. I had a bit of an epiphany while I was in there with Jacqueline – it's ridiculous to consider taking on a project like that when I need some time out. I mean, this year. It's been a lot.' She decided not to mention Phil in her portfolio of emotional crises. 'I've decided to take six months out. Perform a complete life laundry on myself for a change, instead of tackling other people's.'

David was stunned into silence and Tara was pleased she'd taken the high road. The air was so fresh and rewarding up here.

'I understand why you didn't tell me,' Tara went on, encouraged by the inner lightness she felt at making her time-off plan feel 'real', 'but you're probably the best person for the job. I mean, you combine pure psychother-apy with animal communication. Can't get much more holistic than that!'

'Tara, I didn't—'

'Do you mind if we leave it there? My interview was painful.' She checked her mirrors in an exaggerated driving-test manner. 'Can we get back to finding the dog now?'

She indicated to turn back on to the road, but David put his hand over hers on the steering wheel to stop her. 'Tara.'

The physical contact surprised them both.

'Tara, that wasn't an interview. I mean, it was, but it wasn't . . . the one you were doing.'

'So what was it?'

David raked a hand through his hair. 'It was an infor-mal meeting between me and two trustees and Jacqueline, to discuss allegations that had been raised about my practice.'

'What?'

'Allegations that I was mentally unstable and/or delib-erately abusing the therapeutic relationship.' He raised his eyebrows. 'Someone shopped me about the animal communication. It's my own fault, I take full responsibil-ity. I should have made it transparent, instead of just being . . .' He blew out his cheeks. 'Lazy.'

Tara hadn't been expecting that. 'What? Oh, David.'

'Yes, it made for an uncomfortable half-hour. I'm sus-pended, pending further discussions. Jacqueline wanted me to go away and think about what I'd done, and to come back in a fortnight's time and tell them it was all a joke, or that I'm getting psychiatric help. Words to that effect.'

Tara didn't know what to say. *Suspended.*

'You don't think . . .' Her chest tightened. Did he think *she'd* dropped him in it? That she valued Jacqueline's opinion over his trust? 'David, I didn't tell Jacqueline, if that's what you came round to talk to me about.'

He looked at her, and Tara suddenly felt hurt that he seemed to be weighing it up. She didn't want David to think badly of her. His opinion mattered. His friendship mattered. More than she'd realized until now.

'I wouldn't,' she insisted.

His face softened. 'I know it wasn't you.'

'Really?'

'Really. You wouldn't have snitched to the teacher without telling me first. It's not your style.' He paused, then added, 'And we're friends. Work friends, obviously.'

His eyes were locked on hers, searching her face, and she wondered what her own eyes were giving away. Work friends didn't generally drive round the flooded countryside on mercy missions like this.

'Plus you could have checked in with Sybil,' she pointed out.

It seemed to break the spell. 'Absolutely,' he said. 'But right now, she's more concerned about finding this stupid dog you keep letting in her house.'

They slithered round a couple of fields, with no sign of Lloyd, and then Tara's phone rang. She grabbed it, thinking it might be Keith, but it was Toby.

'Molly's hysterical,' he said. 'She hasn't stopped crying since we got back and she's making noises like she's about to be sick. What was that stuff Mum used to funnel into us every time we sneezed?'

'Calpol.' She could hear Molly crying in the background and it went through her like a knife, right under the ribs. 'I don't think we've got any.'

'Brandy? Can you still give kids brandy?'

'No! Don't give her brandy. Just . . . just make her a cup of tea and put a boxset on.'

'Any word from Dad?'

'No, not yet.'

David was giving her the full mind-reading stare when she ended the call. 'Everything OK?'

Tara closed her eyes, but when she did, Molly's ashen face floated up. Tara needed to help her.

'Lloyd means the world to Molly,' she said. 'He's the one stable thing in her life. She's an only child, her mum's struggling with addiction, and her dad's a . . .' She stopped the automatic words spilling out. They were Ruth's words. What did she really think of the man who'd reappeared? A man who was full of problems, but attempting to find some solutions at the same time. Without once bad-mouthing her mother, though he had every reason to.

What did *she* think?

'Dad's trying to be a better father this time round, but I don't know how much he's there. Lloyd's her rock.'

As she spoke, Tara saw another little girl. Another dad and another dog, her two favourite things in the world. She pushed the thought away, but David seemed to understand the pain in her face.

He patted her shoulder. 'We *will* find him.'

Could David somehow connect with Lloyd, wherever he was? She couldn't make him do the one thing he'd explicitly said he'd never do. It was enough that he was here with her, in the mud, searching.

They stood under a sycamore tree by the side of the road. The rain was heavier again and Tara imagined Lloyd sliding in the mud, distressed and disorientated. Had he found somewhere to shelter? Was he hurt? Worse, had some stranger picked him up – and driven him away? The fields were covered with standing water, and it was impossible to see where the swollen streams started and the fields ended. Very easy to fall in. Very easy.

Poor, scared Lloyd. If he was stolen or injured, Molly would blame herself. She'd carry his pain like a scar for the rest of her life. Tara covered her mouth to keep the sob in.

'Right,' said David, without warning. 'I think we should get back in the car and head down the road.'

'Are you . . . ?' Was David seeing what Lloyd was seeing?

But he was walking back to the car, with a determination that made her want to follow him, quickly.

They drove in silence for another mile or so until they came to a tarmacked entrance to a cider orchard.

'The footpaths cross just over here,' he said, pointing to a sign. 'Lots of dog walkers, lots of smells.'

Tara couldn't tell if he was being logical or just pretending to be logical to cover his less easily explained intervention, but they braced against the rain and set off down the footpath, slipping around as they tried to search and call and avoid sliding down the bank at the same time.

Neither of them spoke, other than to shout, 'Lloyd!' and grunt at the mud and the rain. Tara's lungs burned keeping up with David, but something about the way he was striding out made her feel as if they were getting nearer.

They'd walked for what felt like miles – but probably wasn't – when David stopped so abruptly Tara nearly pushed him off the path. He pointed over the hedge into the next field. 'There!'

'Where?' David didn't seem to notice her grabbing his arms to keep her balance. He hoisted her easily on to the higher bank so she could see.

Tara couldn't make it out at first, because instead of a yellow Labrador there was now a chocolate one, merging in with the water and mud, but there he was: cowering and surrounded by water, trapped in a field of sheep. Lloyd.

'Lloyd! Lloyd!' Tara waved, and the dog barked in response, but each time his paws touched the water he shied back with a whimper.

David turned to her. 'Aren't Labradors supposed to be water dogs?'

'He's a city boy. Don't think he's seen a sheep before.'

'Him and me both.'

Tara surveyed the field with zero enthusiasm. It was beyond muddy, bordering on boggy, and there were sheep – which she'd never felt totally comfortable with either, despite growing up surrounded by them.

But who else was going to do this?

Tara took a deep breath. For Branston. For Mum. For Molly.

For herself.

'Right,' she said. 'Let's go and get him.'

'Have you found Lloyd?' said Molly before Tara could even speak. Her voice was scratchy with fear. 'Is he alive?'

Tara swivelled round in the driver's seat to check the state of a mud-encrusted, drenched-to-the-bone Lloyd wrapped in David's mac, on the back seat. His eyes were closed with exhaustion and he was limping badly on three different paws. But he was alive, yes.

David sat next to him, looking equally drenched and shattered. He'd staggered the length of a field bearing the whining Labrador to the nearest point Tara could reverse the Mini without it getting stuck. Which, it turned out, was nowhere near enough for David's lower back.

'We've got him! He's fallen in the river and he's a bit, um, soggy, so we're just taking him to the vet's for a check-up.'

Molly started saying, 'Hurray!' but the word dissolved into tears of relief. A lump rose in Tara's throat. Deep in the hidden folds of her subconscious there was a shift, a balance restored.

She heard Toby saying, 'Is that good crying or bad crying?' over more sobbing, then he'd taken the phone from Molly and was on the line.

'Good job, Sis,' he said. 'I'm proud of you.'

'Call me if Dad calls,' said Tara, and hung up before her voice broke.

She busied herself with the windscreen wipers, but when she glanced in the rear-view mirror, David looked straight at her.

'Tara? Are you all right? You're crying.'

She wiped her nose with the back of her hand. 'Sorry, I'm just . . . I did something similar with our dog when I was Molly's age.' She gulped. It felt like David already knew.

'Branston?'

'Yes. Branston.' Had she told him that? Probably. That was how cold readers worked; you forgot what you let slip. Still, what did it matter? 'I let him out hoping he'd get lost and Dad would come home. He was hit by a car. I managed to blank it completely, but not the guilt. It all merged with Dad leaving and Mum's unhappiness.'

And why I've spent nearly twenty-five years trying to make up for it by wading into other people's problems, she thought, *by shouldering as much responsibility as I could. More and more, and never enough to make it right.*

David's voice from the back was kind. 'You know, I bet it wouldn't even make Branston's top five memories.'

'He had plates in both legs, David!'

'That's not what he remembers. How many more years did he have with you? Eight? He was an old boy when he went. A very happy old boy.'

Tara checked in the rear-view mirror. Lloyd was lying with his sodden head over David's lap, soaking his trousers. David didn't seem to have noticed. He was focused on Tara's brimming eyes in the mirror.

'Yes,' she nodded.

'Well, then.'

It was only much later that Tara realized she'd never told David how old Branston was when he finally went to sleep for ever in her arms, after a breakfast of mashed potato and steak, and a walk around the garden. Probably a good guess, she told herself. A good guess.

Lloyd was limping badly, but managed a brave thump of his tail for George the vet when they struggled into the surgery with him.

'You hauled this big lump across a field?' George wasn't one to mince his words. 'Do you play for Longhampton Rugby Club, sir? And if not, would you like to?'

David massaged his shoulder with a grimace. 'He seemed reluctant to walk.'

'He's a Labrador.' George was checking Lloyd's legs, squeezing and prodding. Lloyd wagged his tail. 'Given half a chance he'd have you carry him round the house.'

'Whatever treatment he needs, just go ahead,' Tara insisted as George checked Lloyd's heart, his laboured breathing, his twig-crusted paw pads. The Sindys could pay for any medical care he needed. She'd cover the rest. Her heart clenched thinking of Molly's voice on the line, so small, struggling with the heavy responsibility of love.

'I don't think that's going to be necessary. He's fine. Come on, you beast.' George gave the dog a gentle but firm prod. 'Up you get. Show's over.'

To Tara's astonishment, Lloyd staggered to his paws, then wobbled over to the food display and started sniffing it.

'Keep him warm and quiet tonight, plenty of water, any change give us a call.' George replaced the stethoscope round his neck. 'But if *you* need a chiropractor,' he added to David, 'I can give you a number. I see her twice a year, after lambing. Excellent. Utterly brutal.'

Lloyd maintained an intermittent limp for effect as they returned him to the car, and Tara clipped him in with the harness the receptionist had sold them on the way out. She wasn't thrilled by the concept of a dog on her back seat, but a tiny part of her liked the idea of being prepared for Lloyd's company. Somewhere in the future.

'Well, the good news? Is that that mac is dry-cleanable,'

said David, and Tara was overwhelmed by a powerful impulse to hug him.

Since there was no one around, and she couldn't work out how to thank him in the right words, she did.

It took them both by surprise how easily Tara's arms wrapped around David's neck, how neatly her head fitted into the curve of his neck. How easily – after a moment's hesitation – David's arms slipped around her waist and pulled her body into his.

It was strange, Tara thought, breathing against the tender spot just under David's ear, that the same tingly, silvery shivers of excitement she'd felt that night on the fire escape were exploding over her skin now, even though she hadn't had a drop to drink. This felt like the right way to express the surging gratitude in her heart.

Gratitude. That was it, she told herself. Relief.

She hugged him tighter, resting her lips against the smooth curve under his strong jaw. More gratefully. Then she dropped her forehead to his shoulder, conscious of where her lips wanted to go next.

'I know what you did in that field, David,' she said into the fine cotton of his shirt, damp with rain and warm from his physical exertions. He'd walked so specifically to the right place. So surely.

'I would never have asked you,' she added. 'But thank you.'

David didn't reply, but he tilted his head so his cheek pressed against hers. For an uncomfortable moment, Tara wondered if his silence meant he was about to admit it was bollocks after all, and she felt oddly disappointed.

But would it matter if he did? They'd found Lloyd. He was safe. Would it change what she thought about David?

'Love has a loud voice.' He sighed, his breath hot across her wet hair. 'Sometimes . . . sometimes it's too strong to ignore.'

Tara squeezed her eyes to hold in the tears.

'It's incredible what we animals will do to come home,' he said. 'When you love someone, you always sense where home is. Always.'

I'll stay here until I've stopped crying, Tara told herself, burying her eyes in David's shirt. *I don't want him to see me crying.*

Although that was a weak argument when he'd seen her crying all day.

David's arms didn't slacken either. The hug had now gone on for several minutes, and if anything, it was evolving into something different.

The rain had started again around them, fine rain, but Tara didn't really notice.

She didn't want to break the hug, because once it was broken, they'd have to talk about it. She didn't want to hear David say he'd felt something different than the sparkling, tingling electricity she was feeling. Because, Tara realized now, there was no way she would be getting on a plane with Phil Shawcross. He was from a different life.

She turned her head and rested her lips against the softness of David's neck again – not a kiss, not quite a kiss – and she heard his sharp intake of breath, then a slow sigh over her hair. Something new shimmered inside Tara, like the solar fairy lights twinkling in the midnight garden.

It rained, and they stayed tight in each other's arms.

Tara sensed David's arms release first and as they did,

she felt as cold and bereft as a city Labrador scrambling out of a cold beck.

I need him to hug me again, she thought. *I* . . .

'David,' she started to say, but got no further as David leaned in and kissed her properly, on the lips.

The kitchen window was brightly lit with many candles when they pulled up outside Wye Villa.

Most of Lloyd's mud had transferred itself to the back seat of Tara's Mini, and the Labrador who emerged on to the slick pavement was already more yellow than the miserable chocolate creature they'd found.

Tara unclipped his lead. Lloyd leaped out, dashed straight up the garden path and scraped at the front door to be let in.

The door was flung open. Molly stood there in her unicorn pyjamas, and opened up her arms. 'Lloyd!'

With a woof of pure joy, Lloyd nearly knocked her over in his frenzy of licking and wagging and barking.

'See?' David nudged Tara as they followed him in. 'Lloyd's forgotten already. And if he hasn't, he's already forgiven her.'

'Well, his limp seems to be cured anyway.'

'Lucky for you. I was going to make you carry him this time.'

Keith was standing behind Molly, and the candle-light made his hair darker. For a surreal moment, Tara thought the years had rolled away to the dad she remembered, the dad she'd dreamed of seeing standing on the steps with his arms open to hug her. Then he moved, and his hair was silvery again, his chin silvery too, his handsome eyes baggy with weariness. But she could see love in his eyes. Love, and relief to see the same reflected in hers.

We all change, Tara thought. *We have to look back at things we don't want to, because it's the only way to see how we've changed.*

'Come on in, my darling,' said Keith, holding out his arms. 'Let's get you a cup of tea.'

Chapter Twenty-Seven

'So,' said Jacqueline, 'I think that's about the size of it. How do you feel this discussion has gone?'

She looked between David on the chair of judgement opposite her desk, and Tara at a neutral angle on the couch of supportive observation.

'It's been very positive for me, Jacqueline,' said David. 'I think you've shown tremendous empathy for my situation, but at the same time, found a way for us to work together towards a mutually acceptable solution. Thank you for accepting my proposal, regards separating my practice. It's an opportunity for growth, and I intend to make the most of this teachable moment.'

Tara shot him a side-look. *Don't overdo it.*

'Good!' Jacqueline looked relieved. 'I *hate* conflict resolution. It's one thing I *won't* miss! Call me old-fashioned, but I just want everyone to get along.'

'Absolutely,' said David.

Jacqueline left a discreet pause of about fifteen seconds to draw a line under the interview, and then leaned forward with an eager expression. 'When do you think you'll be available for these animal communication appointments then? Because my cat is an *awful* sulker. I'm constantly on pins wondering what I've done.'

'I'm sure it's nothing,' said David. 'Cats can be like that.'

'Really? She gives me these looks.' Jacqueline's mouth turned down at the edges, to demonstrate. 'And then sometimes, like this.' Her eyes squinted peevishly.

'Why don't I email you some dates? Any time on Friday afternoons, as discussed – *outside* the Centre.' David smiled. 'And obviously the same client confidentiality applies to my animal clients as my human ones.'

'Of course,' said Jacqueline, and clapped her hands vertically with delight, like a thrilled teenage seal.

'So. Is that everything?' David made to get up.

'Absolutely, yes. Thank you, David, for being so open with us. I hope you know what an important part of the team you are.'

Tara nodded in agreement. 'A very important part.'

'Ladies.' David bowed slightly to them both, and let himself out. The faint sound of jaunty whistling drifted back down the corridor, then faded away. It wasn't the whistling of a man who'd just had a disciplinary. It sounded more like the whistling of a man still enjoying the afterglow of a romantic dinner in Ferrari's the night before.

Tara also got up to leave – not at the same time; she didn't want anyone knowing just yet about what may or may not have been going on with her and David – but Jacqueline motioned for her to sit back down.

'Tara, do you mind? I just wanted a quick word. Off the record, as it were.'

Tara sat down again, bracing herself for one of Jacqueline's 'subtle' interrogations. Had she been at Ferrari's? Tara hadn't really been taking much notice of anything other than David; someone could have walked an elephant through by the time the spaghetti vongole arrived.

'I just wanted to say . . .' Jacqueline tried to look

magisterial, but failed. 'How proud of you I was, on a personal level, when you asked if you could re-interview.'

'I'm grateful for the second chance.' Tara glanced down at her nails. 'I knew I hadn't given it my best shot. I should have explained what was going on, instead of trying to muddle through.'

'It was brave. And honest. And more than that,' she warmed to her theme, 'it showed us that here was someone who understands emotional pressure, someone who can empathize with those struggling in their care.'

'Thank you,' said Tara. It hadn't been an easy call, but Toby had coached her through it, right down to the 'power pauses'.

He'd appeared in her room the morning after the flood, and plonked himself down on her bed the way he always used to, displacing a disgruntled Sybil.

'Phone your boss,' he'd said, shoving Tara's phone in her bleary face. 'David told me how you ballsed up your interview – you need to explain what's been going on here, and ask if they'll see you again.'

Tara pulled the duvet over her head. 'I'd rather eat my own hair, thanks.' *And you don't want the stupid job anyway, remember*, she added to herself.

'You messed up because you were trying to sort everyone else out,' he persisted. 'As usual. But you'd be *great* at running that place. You know it, they know it. At least give them a chance to consider you properly, and then decide if you don't want the stupid job.'

She regarded him through a screwed-up eye. *Stupid job?*

'Are you reading my mind?'

'God, no. I bet it's like a jumble sale in there. Right,

now I've done your careers consult, you need to get up and help me feed everyone. Molly wants boiled eggs and I'm like . . .' Toby mimed extreme confusion, and Tara threw back the covers.

The second interview had gone a lot better. At the end of the following week, Tara was officially offered the role of Wellness Centre Director, which was why she'd been 'tasked' with 'sitting in' on David Dalloway's reconvened disciplinary solution session: David had come up with his own commitment to consult with animals only on Friday afternoons, outside the Centre. Jacqueline had accepted it immediately.

Tara suspected Jacqueline's moon of agreement was ascendant because she'd also accepted Tara's request for a six-month delay to the starting date, in order for her to have a sabbatical.

'What better example for the Centre as a whole than to recognize the importance of recalibrating your life's path, after significant personal upheaval?' she'd said, nodding so hard her moonstone earrings swung.

Tara couldn't argue with that.

The plan was for her to start shadowing some of Jacqueline's decision-making until she left officially for her as yet unplanned break. This was her first meeting. There were more lined up, some involving 'idea showering' the outreach project, and one about a Christmas Bake Off competition. As far as Tara could tell, her appointment had gone down well with the rest of the team. Hero left a bottle of Midsummer Gin on her desk; Tara had asked Hero if she wouldn't mind swapping it for a crystal necklace.

As for her own professional development, Tara had

booked herself on a Blended Families course, Management Skills and also an Intuition foundation. Covering all the bases.

'Now, will I see you for the Lunch and Learn at one? Bryan's going to be talking to us about the importance of making lists and sticking to them.'

Tara paused on her way to the door, surprised. 'That sounds . . . almost useful.'

'I know!' said Jacqueline. 'Doesn't it?'

Sunshine was streaming through the stained-glass window of heritage apples outside Jacqueline's office, throwing bright pools of Egremont Russets and Cox's Orange Pippins on to the carpet. Someone's mint tea was brewing in the kitchen. The colour and the smells lifted Tara's spirits. Everything seemed lighter since the floods had subsided. Her workload, her body, her heart.

Life's good, she thought, smiling at nothing. *Life is good.*

'Where did you find this?'

Diane looked over the top of the wooden box Tara had put into her hands.

Tara curled her legs underneath her on Diane's sofa in the flat on the high street, overlooking the shop her mum had once filled with jade vases and handmade curtains.

'It was in the cellar. Toby and I had to move everything out when it flooded and we found about ten boxes we assumed were junk.' Tara watched Diane's face as she lifted the lid and started sorting through the contents. 'This was in the last box. I'd never have found it otherwise. We'd probably have chucked everything without knowing.'

Tara knew roughly what was inside, although she hadn't looked further, once she'd recognized Diane's handwriting on the envelopes.

Diane's green eyes filled with tears, spilling fatly over her lashes. Carefully she lifted a stack of cards in red, blue, yellow envelopes, tied with a ribbon. A book of poetry. A snowglobe. Little mementoes of happiness.

She pressed her fist against her nose, overcome.

'We thought Mum had thrown out our childhood stuff,' Tara went on, 'but it was there, stacked in boxes. She didn't want to look at it. But she didn't want to throw it away, either.'

The silence between them expanded, swelling with questions.

Was there any point going through them? Tara had been over it so many times in her head. The questions she wanted to ask weren't the obvious ones. They weren't questions, anyway. They were conversations.

Diane raised her wet eyes to Tara's. 'I wanted to tell you. But your mum didn't.'

'Why not?'

She shook her head. 'She had . . . various reasons. I didn't agree with them all. But the affair, if you want to call it that – it wasn't the defining part. It was what got us both out of the wrong marriages. Our *friendship* afterwards was what was precious. Our support and our love and our companionship and our shared experience of life. Female friendship is magnificent, and complex. It's spiritual. Your mum and I were *friends*. You knew that. What else did we need to tell you?'

Out of anyone else's mouth, Tara thought, that would sound disingenuous. But not from Diane, somehow.

'Obviously I wish your parents' marriage had ended differently.' Diane's face flushed. 'You have every right to be angry about that.'

'I *was* angry,' Tara admitted. 'More about Mum and Toby – it was a shocking burden to put on poor Toby. But then I thought about the kind things you did for me, the kind things you still do. And I've reached the conclusion that I'm just not in charge of everything.'

'I'm sorry, Tara. I don't think any of us handled it well.'

She sighed. 'I'm seeing a new therapist. I'll get back to you if there's more arising.'

'And what about the house? Are you still selling? Or will you stay?'

Tara smiled, because she couldn't help smiling when she thought about her plans for their house. 'I'm staying. Toby's going to run the studio as an Airbnb from his laptop. And we're redecorating.'

'Oh?' Diane managed a smile. 'That's brave.'

'There's a bit of flood damage in the cellar so . . .' Tara shrugged. 'Good opportunity to ring the changes. I've been to pick up some colour cards.'

Tara had a particular shade of blue in mind for the kitchen-diner: the hopeful colour of the morning sky, when the storm clouds have passed and the new day, freshly washed and full of sunlight, promises to be the start of something even better.

A few weeks later, Tara put her packed lunch in the car and drove out to Troutbridge, and parked in the newly re-laid car park. It had a cherry tree in the middle, and electric car charging points at one end.

The Troutbridge project's grand opening was booked for the end of October. It would be a family-friendly Hallowe'en celebration with apple bobbing, wrap up the mummy, fortune telling – and 'a spooky barbecue', whatever that meant.

Tara knew it would be a good night, not least because everyone in the village was determined that it would be. The hall represented everyone's renovated hopes and dreams: dried out, repurposed, ready to send out new shoots. Keith's design had taken the bones of the modest building and opened its heart out to the sky, creating something solid with oak timbers that would deepen and darken with time, but at the same time filling it with glass and space and light. It was a building that would grow into its own landscape. Outside there was a community vegetable garden, and wildflower beds for bees, and a few small wooden boats positioned in the young new trees which would, as they grew, eventually lift the boats high up into their branches like arks, to celebrate the magical re-rising of the hall after the floods.

Nice touch, Dad, Tara had thought as the young oaks were dug in. *Very holistic.*

Inside, her favourite new addition was the exhibition space running down the long wall of the open corridor, ready for the community to tell their stories. The first display was the saga of the local floods: 'After the Rain', told by the people who'd lost wedding albums and washing machines, the older residents who'd been rescued in dinghies, and the schoolchildren who'd learned about dinosaurs in the sports hall while the school was hosed out. It was the story of loss and destruction, but also of community spirit and kindness, generosity and humour in the face of crisis.

It was Tara's idea. She'd asked each of her clients if they could write something about their experience, or share a photograph that summed up how they felt about the night of dark waters. She'd had some interesting responses.

The Bannon family had gone for a dramatic crayon interpretation of events, including the pyromania incident and their grandma's cat's near-death experience. After intervention from David, Rhys was responding to counselling, and Sian had had her baby without further complications, other than Gareth buying a drum kit to celebrate.

Grace Jordan and Harrison shared a photograph of Harrison's miracle guinea pigs, Fluff and the still twitchier than normal Peppa, Noah's Ark survivors. Dorrie and Elsie Cogan, the elderly evacuee sisters, made paw prints of Sukie the dog. And Mrs Cartwright provided a photograph of her cat, little Bobby, who eventually resurfaced in Yarrold, six months and four kilos later.

And, of course, now Tara had some experience of her own to share.

Her contribution was a photograph Keith had taken of Tara and Toby in their wellies, trousers rolled up, carrying Molly through the last of the water in the cellar. They were laughing, and Lloyd was on the stairs behind them, his mouth open in a silent bark. A 'do you remember?' story, linking the three of them for the rest of their lives.

It was one of her favourite photos. Toby and Tara. Taransay and Tobermory. And in their arms, their little sister. Molly.

The right thing to give to the project.

'Ah ha!' said a voice, over the sound of drilling in the main hall. 'Just the person! Tara, come and give me your opinion on something.'

Keith strode down the corridor, his yellow hard hat incongruous above his cord jacket and jeans.

Dad jeans, thought Tara. Some things never changed.

But she gave him a hug anyway.

'Can you settle an argument for me about where we should put the commemorative plaque?' he said. 'There's a debate raging and a decision needs to be made. I'm supposed to be heading off in an hour or two. This was only supposed to be a site visit, but you know what it's like . . .'

'I know what *you're* like. You want to micromanage every tiny thing. And I'm not getting involved in that,' said Tara. 'Ask Alice. It's her job.'

Boundaries were her new thing. Eric said she needed to work on making a new one every day until it was second nature. Tara wasn't sure she wanted to go that far, but saying a firm no was surprisingly thrilling.

'I've got something for you,' she said to change the subject, and handed him a gift bag.

'What's this?' Keith pulled the tissue wrapping from the parcel, and Tara was pleased to see delight illuminate his face.

'Where did you find this?' He looked up. There was a hint of a tear in his eye. No, more than a hint; a definite tear. 'This is my *favourite* photograph of you two. It used to be on the kitchen shelf, didn't it? By the window?'

It was Toby and Tara's Year 6 school photograph: they were dressed in identical green Longhampton Primary jumpers, with identical short haircuts, but while Toby was grinning wildly, Tara was gazing desperately at the camera. It was as if they'd agreed to pull opposite expressions for a dare.

'I asked your mum for this a few times,' he said. 'She never replied.'

'It was in the last storage box, I found it a few nights ago.' She paused, still trying to be fair. 'I think Mum wanted the house to be hers again once we left. But she kept everything.'

Tara and Toby had sat up until dawn going through the boxes until their childhood lay around them, like the fragments of their shipwrecked lives. Their baby teeth, and coils of black hair. Christmas decorations made from glitter and fingerprints. Tara's netball medals. Branston's puppy collar. Some still-wrapped gifts. Photos. Lots of photos. A route back into a past Tara thought had been lost for ever, and, more important to her, proof of a happiness that had definitely existed. Proof, too, that her mum hadn't thrown everything away – or wanted to.

'Thank you for making a copy of that photo album, by the way,' he said.

'No problem.' The album had been in the bottom of the last box, wrapped in Toby's football top.

'I'm glad it survived. Molly had a ball going through that. Laughing at my clothes. Laughing at my hair. My shoes. My leather jacket.' He pretended to look crushed. 'Who knew there was so much to laugh at?'

'She hasn't even *seen* the home videos yet.' Tara rolled her eyes. 'Save those for next time, eh?'

Keith smiled wryly. 'I'm glad there'll be a next time.'

'Me too.'

He sat down on the wooden benches lining the corridor of the new hall and patted the space next to him. 'Have you got a minute? There's something I've wanted to tell you for a while.'

Tara sat down. She thought about making a joke, but didn't. Keith seemed unusually serious.

He rubbed his beard. 'When I was with Sarah in the clinic, it took me back to my own rock-bottom moment. Your mum – quite rightly – spotted my drinking problem years before I did. She tried to talk me into rehab when you were about six, but I wouldn't go, because obviously I didn't have a problem. She threw me out a few times, but I managed to talk her into letting me back. And then the whole thing with Diane happened, and *that* really hit me where it hurt . . .'

Keith stopped, abruptly. 'But that's not what this is about. The point is, after we split Ruth had strict rules about you two. I can't blame her. There were a few near misses. She wouldn't let me see you if she thought I'd been drinking, and I've got to be honest, sometimes it was easier not to see you.'

'You missed weekends,' Tara pointed out. 'And birthdays.'

'Some I missed, some she wouldn't let me take you.'

'And then we didn't want to see you. Because you didn't want to see us.'

Keith bowed his head, as if riding out a punch. 'Anyway, this story has a happy ending, sort of. About eleven, twelve years ago I was in Cyprus with some friends, two of whom brought along their baby. The most adorable toddler, all smiles and tiny fingers. Reminded me of you at that age. We'd had a long lunch and I was feeling a bit sorry for myself, so I thought I'd phone you and tell you that I'd just seen a baby that looked like you.' He half-laughed, self-consciously. 'Rioja logic. But when I heard your voice, something in my heart just . . . dissolved. I missed you so much it burned inside. I was watching this tot stumbling about, and it seemed like only minutes since you'd been like that. And I'd thrown it away.'

Tara's eyes filled with tears. There was a humble honesty in his voice.

'I couldn't find the words to tell you. I was too drunk. You sounded impatient with me and for the first time, I had a clear understanding of how much I'd lost. How much more I'd lose if I didn't sort myself out. I checked into rehab the next morning. That was it.'

'That was the time you phoned me on the train?' Tara turned to look at him. 'I thought you'd misdialled.'

'It was probably the single most important phone call I ever made. And if you'd been nicer to me, I'd never have gone.'

The moment hung between them. The perspectives of Tara's memories shifted slowly like stage sets, as new information changed the landscape of her understanding, not taking pain away but moving the scenery around, showing what was hidden before. There was illness there, as well as selfishness. Addiction, and the shadows that lay behind it.

Tara knew Dad had tried to call after that. She hadn't taken his calls because of Mum. And Mum hadn't helped. The faults were on both sides.

'Dad,' said Tara simply. She took his hand and said nothing more, in case her words weren't as eloquent as her hand holding his.

'I've got a *lot* of things wrong in this life, Tara, but I want you to know that you, and Toby and Molly – you're what I'm most proud of. I wasn't the father you deserved. But at least now I know my kids have got each other. I didn't take that for granted, incidentally.' He squeezed her hand. 'Thank you, for letting Molly in.'

'I love you, Dad.' How long had she wanted to say that, and mean it, and know the words would come back to her?

'I love you, Taransay.' Keith put his arms round her and, just for a moment, Tara felt the world and all its problems and dramas stop.

Tara delivered a verdict on the plaque – opposite the entrance, so everyone would see it – and Keith walked her to her car. 'Any time you fancy a trip to London, just drop in.'

'Your place, or Sarah's?' It was a trick question, unfair. 'You're moving back in, Molly says.'

'We're giving it another try, yes.'

'Good!'

Keith nodded. 'Not just for Molly. For us. Sarah's on the right track now, and she needs me. We're a good team. Some astrologer she knows says we're the perfect match but,' he dropped his voice conspiratorially, 'I made up my birth time so . . .' He pretended to glance around nervously, and Tara laughed.

She opened her car door; the Mini had just about recovered from its ordeal after two full valets and double Magic Trees.

'So you're off to Italy next week, I hear? Tuscany?'

Not Tuscany, no. Although, to give Phil his due, he'd

taken the 'no hard feelings' text as well as a man on a self-improvement drive could.

'Venice,' said Tara. 'David and I are staying there for a week, then I've got a month's retreat in the hills. The start of my sabbatical. I'm going to be volunteering on an ancient village, helping with the archaeology, then learning how to meditate. The idea is to . . . Why are you looking at me like that?'

'I'm your father. Should I be asking questions about this young man's intentions?'

'He's looking after my cat while I'm away. That's all you need to know.'

It was funny, Tara thought, how once the dad-shaped hole in your heart was finally filled, you stopped trying to force unsuitable candidates in there. Justin, Phil . . . There was infinite space now in her heart for a real love, a proper romance, the beginning of something that might just end up being . . .

Don't jinx it, she told herself. She still saw too many disintegrating couples at the Wellness Centre to take anything for granted. Apart from which, there were already three of them in the relationship – her, David and Sybil.

'Well, happy travels if I don't see you before you leave,' said Keith, kissing her on the forehead. 'Don't forget to send me a postcard.'

'I'll be back for the big launch night,' she promised. 'I wouldn't miss this Hallowe'en party for anything.'

Tara slipped into the driver's seat, and put on her sunglasses. She turned up the radio and buzzed the windows down so she could feel the fresh air on her face. Soon, she'd be on the road trip she'd been dreaming about since she was a teenager, and she couldn't wait to get started.

This wasn't running away, she knew that now – this was *travelling*. Running away was when you had no plans to come back, no idea where you were going. Travelling was when you took your home with you, in your heart, and reached out for the world with both hands.

Tara knew where her home was, where her heart lay, who her family truly were. Compared to *that* journey, this one would be a breeze. And coming home would be the sweetest part of the trip.

Acknowledgements

It's been a strange couple of years, to say the least, and I'm even more grateful than usual for the support and enthusiasm of everyone who's helped carry *After the Rain* (and me) over the obstacle course that was 2020.

I'm endlessly grateful to my agent Lizzy Kremer for her wisdom and kindness, and to her stellar colleagues Harriet Moore, Maddalena Cavaciuti and Kaynat Begum – in fact, all the truly excellent people at David Higham Associates. Thanks too to the wonderful team at Transworld – Francesca Best, Sally Williamson, Frankie Gray, Lara Stevenson, Vicky Palmer, Hayley Barnes, Emma Burton, to name but a few – for making another beautiful book out of my Word files and scribbly sketch pads.

I've always loved a good chat, but conversation has felt particularly precious in a time when words were the only human contact we had. Thank you, Sarah Iwanszuk, for your long, enlightening conversations, and thank you, Chris Manby, for making me laugh when it was that or crying. And even bigger thanks to my locked-down family, especially my magnificent husband, Scott. Greater love hath no man than one who builds an office for his wife. Outside.

Most of all, thank you to everyone who said hello over

Acknowledgements

the last year or two – virtually, digitally or in real life. Talking about books with readers has always been the best part of being a writer, but this year each message was like a tiny beacon of light twinkling across the darkness, and it's meant more than I thought possible. Thank you – and please never stop.

Lucy Dillon grew up in Cumbria and read English at Cambridge, then read a lot of magazines as a press assistant in London, then read other people's manuscripts as a junior fiction editor. She now lives in a village outside Hereford with her husband and an Otterhound.

Lucy's books *Where the Light Gets In* and *Unexpected Lessons in Love* were both *Sunday Times* bestsellers. She has also won the Romantic Novelists' Association Contemporary Romantic Novel prize and the Romantic Novel of the Year Award for *A Hundred Pieces of Me* and *Lost Dogs and Lonely Hearts*.

You can follow her at her website www.lucydillon. com, on Twitter @lucy_dillon, on Instagram @lucydillonbooks or find her on Facebook at www.facebook.com/pages/LucyDillonBooks.

If you enjoyed *After the Rain*, keep reading for an extract of *Unexpected Lessons in Love* – a heart-warming and uplifting read

Prologue

Brooklyn Bridge, October

Jeannie was walking with Dan's hands over her eyes but she wasn't worried. Right now, here in this delicious champagne bubble of a moment, she was wrapped in a bliss that she'd never believed you could feel in real life.

So far their long weekend in New York had been one romantic surprise after another. Dan had planned it in secret, but he'd chosen everything Jeannie would have chosen herself: a morning spent browsing the vintage shops at Chelsea Market, then an afternoon crunching through copper leaves and sipping hot chocolate in Central Park. Cocktails and oysters, yellow cabs and multicoloured Times Square lights, sneaky kisses as they rode the crowded subway: every second had felt as if the two of them were starring in their own movie.

The hotel was so gorgeous Jeannie could have happily spent the whole weekend in their tiny super-chic room, with its soft rugs and even softer lighting. And of course, with Dan. Just thinking about Dan's tanned skin against the crisp white bedlinen gave her a hot rush of happiness: there were *some* highlights Jeannie wouldn't be sharing with her mum when she got home.

Today, their last day, had started with eggs and coffee

at a deli counter, then they'd joined a downtown walking tour around the haunts of Jeannie's eighties' pop heroes, where Dan had patiently taken selfies of them outside Blondie's rehearsal rooms, and Madonna's *actual flat*. Sure, it was just bricks and windows, but to Jeannie, these streets were where the soundtrack of her life had bubbled up out of nowhere, from musicians who'd once struggled just like her. Her soul had lifted when the tour guide talked about their setbacks and successes, and she'd kissed Dan with grateful love, wondering if he knew how much it meant to her that he'd obviously heard the things she *hadn't* said.

Now they were on Brooklyn Bridge, and Dan was promising her the view of a lifetime if she just kept going, one, two, three more steps.

'There,' he said, but he didn't uncover her eyes straight away. Jeannie put her own small hands, neat enough to fly across the fretboard of her ukulele, over Dan's long fingers. He had clever, strong vet's hands, hands that treated injured dogs and birthed calves. A chilly breeze was blowing off the river below, but between Dan and Jeannie, there was a rose-gold glow.

She leaned back into his body, not wanting the moment to end. The light was just fading from the sky, and Jeannie's whole soul rang with music, like euphoric birdsong surging through her veins. Her best friend Edith had assured her that happiness like this was impossible in real life. But for once, Edith Constantine was wrong. *So* wrong.

'Ready?' There was a slight tease in Dan's voice; suddenly she hoped he hadn't taken her to the edge of the bridge. Jeannie wasn't good with heights. She scrabbled to remember if she'd told Dan that – there were moments when she forgot they hadn't yet reached the boring 'user manual' stage of knowing each other. Allergies to marzipan, fear of crows, stuff you only mentioned when you'd run out of interesting things to talk about.

'Ta da!' Dan pulled his hands away and she gasped as the glittering Manhattan skyline rose in front of her, a black and silver collage of lights and towers that sparkled out of the dusk.

'Wow!' Jeannie turned within the tight circle of his arms so she was nose to nose with him. Dan was handsome from any angle. The breeze flipped his blond hair into his eyes, unusual deep denim-blue eyes, and Jeannie had to remind herself that this was actually her life. It felt too perfect, too romantic, to be real. Yet it was. This was love, at last.

'I'm so happy!' she blurted out and, to her amazement, Dan's eyes glistened just like hers. He blinked, as if he couldn't quite believe how perfect this moment was either.

And then it happened. In what seemed like slow motion, Dan unwrapped his arms from around her, stepped back and dropped to one knee. There were people walking across the bridge; some stepped around him with a tut, but others saw what was going on and stopped, indulgent smiles forming on their lips.

Jeannie blinked. No, wait. Was this . . . what she thought it was? Her heart thudded against her ribs. Was Dan going to propose? She hadn't even dared imagine this moment, and now she was in the middle of it. A proposal . . . that was a moment that only happened once. In your whole life.

Suddenly Jeannie felt dizzy, as if Dan *had* taken her to the edge of the bridge.

'Jeannie McCarthy,' Dan was saying, and now the passers-by had stopped, gathering into clumps along the sidewalk. 'I know we've only known each other for five months, but they've been the happiest five months of my life. Will you marry me?'

Manhattan rose behind Dan like a second, bigger crowd of well-wishers, smiling at the lovers, twinkling its lights like stars. Phone cameras were surreptitiously raised; breath was held. Jeannie felt as if all New York was waiting for her response.

Dan gazed up at her with those melting blue eyes. He was gorgeous, intelligent, and he'd flown her to New York to propose. Jeannie shook herself. What more could she ask for? What more did she want?

Her mouth opened before she had time to answer that in her head.

'Yes!' she said, and everyone on the bridge applauded.

UNEXPECTED LESSONS IN LOVE

Lucy Dillon

Jeannie always wanted to fall in love, and now she's finally got the whirlwind romance she dreamed of. Dan's gorgeous, he's a successful young vet, and he flew her to New York and proposed on Brooklyn Bridge. Jeannie has to remind herself this is actually her life. It seems too perfect, too magical, to be real. Yet it is.

But now she's on her way to the wedding she can't shake off the tight sensation crushing her chest. Is it just nerves . . . or is this all happening a bit too fast?

Jeannie has one last chance to shout, 'Stop!' But just as she grabs it, a bizarre twist of fate throws everything she knows into the air like confetti. What Jeannie learns about Dan, about her own heart, and about the power of love itself, will change her world for ever . . .

'Real, heart-breaking – I loved it'
Katie Fforde

WHERE THE LIGHT GETS IN

Lucy Dillon

If Lorna's learnt one thing recently, it's that courage is something you paint on like red lipstick, even when you're panicking inside. And right now, with the keys to Longhampton's gallery in her hand, Lorna feels about as courageous as Rudy, the anxious dachshund trembling beside her.

Lorna's come home to Longhampton to fulfil a long-held dream, but she knows there are ghosts she needs to lay to rest first. This is where her tight-knit family shattered into silent pieces. It's where her insecurities took root and where her own complicated love story began. It's not exactly a fresh start.

But as Lorna – and the little dog – tentatively open their cracked hearts to old friends and new ones, facing hard truths and fresh promises, something surprisingly beautiful begins to grow around the gallery, something so inspirational even Lorna couldn't have predicted the light it lets into her world . . .